For TJ. You gave me the ability to believe in magic again and made me brave enough to share my words.

CONTENTS

PART ONE

"Fierce Juno's hate, added to hostile force, shall urge thy fate." - The Aeneid

PROLOGUE

THE AFTER - TWO YEARS PRIOR

T HE NAKED BODY ATOP the ceremonial altar did not stir, much to the god's dismay. With every hour that ticked by agonizingly slowly, he found his temper growing shorter and shorter. Surely this would work. They did everything correctly, just as Prometheus instructed, even down to the blood offering of three goddesses who were now ready to exact their own vengeance upon him.

Add that to the extensive list of gods who wanted him dead.

"Why hasn't it worked yet?" His brother roared, echoing the thoughts coursing through his own mind. "The girl should be stirring right now. If this doesn't work-"

"I know." The god said to his brother. He didn't need to be reminded for the umpteenth time that if this vessel did not take, they would have no earthly chance of ever defeating *his* rule, *his* cruelty, *his* disease.

Their third brother, the youngest, was still out there and very much alive. Taunting them each day with his malice. Every move calculated to ensure the greatest amount of pain, not only on his brothers, but the very world that rejected him.

And perhaps they did deserve his wrath. He and his twin were awful to him. There's only so much someone could take before they snap, and their brother had put up with an excessive amount of torment before he became the monster he was.

It was only fitting they ended him.

However, planning their brother's demise was proving to be more challenging the longer their vessel remained inanimate on the table. The god had half a mind to find Prometheus and slit his throat out of sheer annoyance. He did not care that it would prove fruitless and childish, as long as it took some of the rage away.

"How long has it been?" His twin asked after another moment.

"It's been seven hours and if you ask me again, she will not be the only lifeless body on the altar." He snapped, earning a string of vulgar insults and a rude gesture to top it off. Despite the anger and annoyance, he smirked. It reminded him so much of their youth. The good times of their childhood - even though those memories were sparse.

As another hour came and went, both gods were growing weary. If the girl had not moved yet, no amount of curses or aimless pacing would bring her to life.

They failed.

"I think we need to admit defeat, brother." The god said to his twin, but neither one of them made the first move to collect the body. His brother's flames would dispose of it much faster than his own water.

Yet, it was the water god getting up first, silently cursing their own ineptitude, as he approached the body. "You would have saved us all, my sweets. Alas, I'm afraid I might've simply damned humanity more."

The god put his hands on the girl's body, ready to pick her up and dispose of her properly, when a surge of power went through him so fiercely it sent him flying backwards. His body hit the ground hard, but instead of feeling pain, a burst of laughter ripped through him.

"Oh Hades." Poseidon said, calling his brother, cautiously pushing himself off the floor to turn towards the altar. The body that had once been lifeless was now sitting up and staring blankly at him.

Hades met his brother's gaze, a similar expression of triumph crossed his own features as he said, "It looks like we have not failed, dear brother." Hades' expression turned predatory as he moved closer to the girl. "What should we call her, Poseidon?"

The name came easily to Poseidon. This vessel was their last chance of redemption. Their only hope to bring light back into the human world.

"Her name will be Lilith."

They stopped at the outskirts of town. Any further and their power would start to weaken; Dasos' own defense against the power-hungry gods who wreaked havoc so many years ago. From the corner of his eye, Poseidon watched as his brother assessed Lilith.

"She's not going anywhere, brother. Why is it you continue to torture yourself with worry?" Poseidon inquired, but not unkindly.

"Because if this doesn't work, you and I will have no chance of ending his tyrannical rule. She's our last hope." Hades repeated as if Poseidon hadn't been thinking the exact same thing. Like their entire existence didn't hinge on this moment.

The girl stood between them, silent and pliable, a canvas yet to be painted. She would not remember this moment or how she came to be, but they didn't need her to remember creation. They needed her to forge their future.

The moment she crossed the invisible threshold of Dasos, the fiery goddess would come to life. Words, customs, and knowledge would be ripe for the picking, taking up residence inside of her. All the little goddess had to do was step forward, and she would appear like any other seven-teen-year-old girl in Dasos.

"What if they don't trust her?" Hades asked. "If they turn her away?"

It was a risk they accounted for, and their plans would have to change if Dasos rejected her. Months of meticulous planning would be for naught.

Poseidon ignored him; he didn't possess an answer his brother yearned for. Instead, he lowered himself to eye level with the new goddess. Lilith did not acknowledge him; her gaze trained ahead, looking blankly upon the silhouetted town.

"Little Goddess, look at me." Poseidon's voice came out as a command, willing her to look at him.

She was slow to respond and jerky with her movements, but soon the girl's neck turned, and those murky, expressionless eyes bored into him.

He had her attention now.

"Your name is Lilith Serah, and you were made to find the power *he* is harboring in Dasos. Nod if you understand." Poseidon waited expectantly, hoping he understood his words.

A faint tilt of the girl's head was the only confirmation he received from her.

"Poseidon, it's time. The town is waking up. She needs to go now." Hades spoke, impatience biting his words.

"Lilith Serah." He echoed, standing tall. He nudged the girl forward and stepped aside.

Lilith stumbled but caught herself once both feet crossed into Dasonian territory. The change in her was immediate. Her movements, once choppy and awkward, held a new grace and poise not there before. Poseidon didn't need to see her to know that her vacant eyes turned doe-eyed, resembling a scared girl lost in the woods.

The brothers observed as their creation did as they could not; walk straight to the gates of Dasos, calling out for help and refuge. A chorus of shouts and orders greeted her plea as Lilith stood trembling in nothing but a thin tunic and trousers a size too big for her body.

A few moments later, Poseidon watched as the old gate slowly opened. A woman with coiled hair stood on the other side. Two men flanked her: one older who carried a sword on his hip while the other appeared around the same age as Lilith, looking upon her with curiosity.

"What is your name?" The woman spoke, her voice gentle and kind.

"Lilith Serah." The girl said automatically, just as Poseidon instructed.

"Where did you come from, Lilith Serah?"

Besides him, Poseidon heard his brother intake a deep breath. This was their moment; the moment of truth.

All eyes were on the newcomer, but Lilith didn't so much as squirm under their scrutiny. "I...I don't remember. Please, I'm tired and cold. I don't have anywhere else to go."

For a long pause, no one spoke or moved. They all waited for the woman to speak; clearly, she was the leader. A slow, warm smile spread across her face. "Welcome to Dasos, Lilith. Come."

Hades' body visibly relaxed, and Poseidon couldn't hide the grin spreading across his features. They watched wordlessly as their creation stepped inside the gates and disappeared into Dasos.

"It is done." Poseidon said.

"Now we wait." Replied his brother.

The brothers would wait for another two years until they saw their goddess again.

CHAPTER ONE

THE AFTER

L ILITH HATED FALLING.

The damp terrain made traction nearly impossible, and a particularly slippery patch of grass sent Lilith sprawling unceremoniously onto the cold, hard ground. A shot of white-hot pain erupted in her knee as the weight of her body crashed down and her breath was stolen from her gasping lips. The pain she could handle. It was the reddish flush to her already rosy cheeks and the surge of embarrassment coloring her face that proved difficult. As she expected, the laughter came only a beat later.

"Beautifully done, Lilith, darling. Perhaps next time, you'll keep your legs planted fully underneath you. In my experience, it prevents pesky falls." A deep voice came from the thicket of trees behind her, his laugh reverberating around in the dense forest. Lilith cursed the gods for their cruel sense of humor and their untimely jokes. Especially where Finian was involved.

Finian, Lilith's companion since her arrival to Dasos two years ago, the first friendly face upon a sea of distrust. He quickly became the bane of her existence ever since.

But also the man she loved.

Finian stood above her now, offering his hand, callused from long days of strenuous labor as a blacksmith's apprentice. He loved this woman, even when she stared at him in annoyance. Lilith, half tempted to slap his hand away and ignore the slight smirk curving his lips, growled at him. He was enjoying this far too much.

Insolent boy, she thought.

Despite her best efforts, Lilith could not deny his help. She reached for his outstretched hand and used the last of her energy to pick herself off the ground. Her knee already showed signs of a purplish bruise. Finian noticed too and tilted his head to the side, frowning. "Idina will have a salve for your knee. We should head back-"

"No." Lilith said, quick to interrupt. It took far too much coaxing and many promises of shoveling manure for the next week and a half for Idina to even consider letting her voyage into the forest surrounding their village. She had to promise to bring Finian along before Idina begrudgingly accepted.

"I'm going to be shoveling shit for the next ten days and I'll probably never compel Idina to let me leave Dasos again. We are going." Lilith urged, earning a wolfish grin from Finian, who seemed more inclined to let her go now he knew a bruise would not send her crying back to the village. Still, he considered taking her home regardless of her protests.

"Let's go." Lilith said again and did not wait for his protests before she traveled deeper into the forest. Only a handful of people from Dasos traveled this far in the few short years since Lilith moved to Dasos and fewer had made it back. The woods were not unusually hard to navigate unless one retained no sense of direction. True danger lay within an encounter from *them*.

The Unhallowed.

It was something she thought about often, though getting anyone in her village to speak of the chaos proved hopeless, notably when she was the one asking. The people of Dasos still did not trust her -- at least not completely. No one knew the red-headed stranger or where she came from. Despite her best efforts, she could not recall her life before Dasos, not even a glimmer of a memory. People took her memory loss as secrecy or an unwillingness to share parts of her life before Dasos. She spoke the language of the villagers

and understood their customs, but she couldn't recall how she knew these things while so much of her life remained a mystery.

When she heard the Unhallowed mentioned for the very first time by Meryle Grey, the town's only shoemaker, Lilith questioned the man about this creature he seemed so frightened of. He stared at her as if she sprouted an extra head but offered no explanation.

Lilith understood why people like Idina or her neighbor friend, Kei, did not want to discuss the Unhallowed; most people tended to avoid unsavory topics about demise. The only person who ever broached the subject was Finian, and Lilith craved to string together the ambiguous information she had gathered from the villagers since her arrival. Which, admittedly, was not much.

So perhaps her outing with him had more motive than she let on.

She noted the soft footfalls behind her, and she knew Finian was only a few paces behind, weaving the same intricate path. Close enough to step in if she needed him, but far enough back to allow her space. She knew his movements as well as she knew her own.

Soon the sound of the river invaded their senses. Though it was the same river that flowed perpendicular to Dasos, it was new to Lilith. Just like the trees were new. And the sounds of woodland creatures created a new song the further they retreated. Finian's scowl as he took in the lush greenery around them was also new and surprising. It didn't belong on his usual serene face.

"This is what you wanted to see? The same damn river we bathe in? The one where I'm subjected to watch 1,000-year-old Margery wash every fold and wrinkle on her body?" He grimaced, shuddering at the image burned into his mind of the older woman who doted on him.

"You will one day look like her, you know." Lilith reminded him playfully.

"Well, I sure hope my favorite parts don't suddenly change into those that resemble an old lady's. Where would that leave us?" A playful shove from Lilith sent Finian back a step, laughing at his own inappropriate joke.

"That favorite part of yours will have to find a way to entertain itself tonight." Lilith said coyly, earning another bark of laughter from Finian. Gods she loved the sound of his laughter. It reminded her of a melodious musical instrument, never failing to make her smile.

"You wound me, Lil." He smirked and reached for her. This time she did not try to fight him. Instead, she leaned in and embraced his comforting touch. To be held in his arms, her head fitting perfectly within the nook of his neck, easily became her favorite place. She heard other girls say they felt their hearts beat as one when they were held by their lover. Lilith didn't believe that. Not with Finian. Their hearts beat opposite one another, their breaths never quite matching up. But love was not determined by the matching of bodily functions, but rather the need to always have the person next to you -- knowing life would be less adventurous without them. Lilith did not need Finian to survive nor did Finian need her to survive, but the loss of one of them would haunt the other forever.

Which was why she needed to mentally prepare for the Unhallowing to separate them one day.

"So, are you going to tell me why you dragged me out here into the forest?" Finian inquired, breaking Lilith away from her thoughts. She untangled herself from his strong arms and crouched down on the grassy earth beneath her.

"Another sparring lesson?" He continued as he took a seat next to her, his long legs sprawled out in front of him and hands resting behind him, palms down.

For the last few months, Lilith had come to Finian and insisted he train with her. She did not have to argue long; they both knew of the horrors waiting outside the village. Knew lack of formal training, or what passed as formal training, meant instant death. Even being a warrior did not necessarily guarantee survival.

Lilith picked up Finian's lessons quickly. They practiced with swords and daggers, but she became partial to the weight and feel of the daggers. They were much easier to carry and conceal. She never left her home without *Peace Bringer*, even now. But Lilith didn't bring Finian outside the walls of Dasos to spar without an audience. No, she brought him here for knowledge.

For a story.

Too many ears were back at the village, eager to eaves-drop. Too many people were prone to becoming upset. Some would stop their conversations altogether. She could not risk the possibility of someone overhearing and the news getting back to Idina. Idina had a big heart, but Lilith often thought it overbearing. She was not a child, after all. Granted, she did not know her true age, but saw the children of Dasos and judging off of looks and body differences alone, Lilith figured she had plenty of years over them. She was still younger than people like Idina, though. To Idina, she supposed, Lilith might be seen as a child. She understood the need to protect and shield someone against the cruelties of the world.

But she survived on her own, hadn't she? She had no one with her when she ventured into Dasos for the first time. Surely that meant she had been surviving on her own. From the training with Finian, Lilith was well versed in defense and weaponry. The dagger felt like an extension of her body and her movements suggested she had been well-trained previously.

"I wanted to talk." She admitted. "And I also want you to tell me about the Unhallowed."

The mood swiftly changed as the male next to her went tense. Finian shifted awkwardly, ringing his dark hands to-gether as if he did not know what to do with them or where to place them. Lilith wanted to reach out and grab his hand, bring them into her lap and reassure him, but she did not dare move or touch him. She needed him to talk and feared any touch given by her would cause him to lose his nerve.

Instead, she let the tension build between them.

After an uncomfortable silence lingered between them, Lilith soon started to think Finian wouldn't talk, and this had all been for nothing. Before her disappointment grew, Finian finally asked, "Was this why you invited me out here? To get information out of me?"

There was a hardness in his voice Lilith never heard before, or at least never aimed at her. Perhaps she made a mistake. She felt like the only one who wanted to know the story of the Unhallowed, and yet was the only one who had mere fragments and pieces that did not quite fit together.

"No...I mean, not entirely." Lilith stammered, pausing a moment to collect herself. She had one last chance to convince him this was worth his time. "Okay, yes. I know there are a million different ways we could spend our time and I'm sorry I did not tell you sooner. But you are the only person that has never shied away from any of my questions-"

"How are you certain I know the entire history?" Finian interrupted.

"Because you are a storyteller." Lilith saw the way Finian commanded a crowd of children and adults. He spoke vividly of warriors valiantly fighting for justice. Of forgotten princesses who slayed their own dragons. Of villains on their own harrowing journey for redemption. If there was a story, Finian would tell it.

Still, he looked reluctant as he took a seat on the lush ground, patting a spot next to him. Wordlessly, Lilith filled the spot, sitting close to share his warmth. It wasn't a particularly cold afternoon, but the slight nip of winter kissed their skin, reminding them that fall's days were numbered.

"Why is this important to you? Why now? Out of the two years you've been here, we've broached this topic only a handful of times." He became curious, as he acquiesced to Lilith's curiosity.

It had never been her intention to wait so long to have this conversation. It was never too far from her mind, but when she was with Finian the two were preoccupied with dueling, chores, or...other things that reddened her cheeks to think about. Although that was fun, it left very few opportunities to have this conversation without interference.

"Is this because of Astrid?" Finian pried, abruptly pulling her away from those thoughts. Astrid had been her friend, or at least friendly around Lilith. In truth, she had very few friends, not due to lack of trying. Dasos was simply weary of her. But Astrid always had a smile for her and showed her kindness, which went a long way.

But Astrid was dead and had been for 5 days. The sickness took her rapidly and showed no signs, none that could be detected anyway. All Lilith remembered was Astrid going home to her family and the following morning, her lifeless body was carried out of her home. Her mother's wails still haunted Lilith and would forever be etched into the depths of her memory.

"It's because of all of them, Finian." She finally said, gesturing aimlessly around them. "I have been here for two years and in that time, no one has told me anything about this disease. Dasos still doesn't trust me-"

"That's hardly accurate. There are people in Dasos that do."

"You and Idina don't count. And I love you both, but neither of you have offered up much of anything in that regard." She countered.

"Lilith, you must know that my knowledge is limited. No one knows the true story. There are only fragments of reports and personal accounts passed down from other people. I've picked up a few things over the years from people I've met. Some versions have been similar, and some contradict each other. It is remarkably difficult to decipher fact from myth and I'm not sure if I have done that." He relented.

"But you have a story." It was not a question. She knew in her core he held the story, and she needed to hear it. "Please, Finian." She begged softly, her voice barely above a whisper. Lilith almost felt bad as she watched the struggling emotions play across his face, but she rapidly suppressed the feeling. This was her last-ditch effort to gain information from him.

"You're an enchantress, Li. An evil, beautiful enchantress." He said, his lips curved up into a half grin. He laid back on the grass, pulling Lilith down with him, so she rested her head on his chest. She listened to the soft thudding of his heart, treasuring every beat. The only other sound came from the current of water that lay just to the right of them. More than anything, she wished to pause this moment.

"How should I begin?" He wondered.

"You are quite fond of 'Once upon a time.'"

That earned Lilith another cocky smile. "Very well. Once upon a time there was a strong God. He was the best lover in all the lands and known to the world as Finian, Large Co-" Lilith immediately slapped his chest and pulled away from him. Finian roared with laughter and put his hands up in mock surrender. "Okay, okay. Wrong Unhallowing story."

"Finian Taren!"

"Everyone's a critic." He shook his head dismissively, as if she hurt his pride. "But for you, Enchantress, I will try again." After a show of dramatically clearing his throat, wiggling underneath her to get comfortable, and sighing, he finally began.

"As much as I like my 'Once Upon a Times,' this doesn't warrant such a wistful beginning. I also know you are seeking an elaborate story that will answer all of your questions, but I can't give you that either. What I can give you, though, are names."

"Names?" Lilith asked, confused. What could she possibly do with names? Did he expect her to have a sudden revelation upon hearing them?

Seeing the uncertainty written across her face, Finian knew he had mere seconds before she lashed out with that silver tongue of hers. The same tongue that sent shivers down his spine just thinking about it.

No, he needed to focus.

"The name of the Great Gods. I'm sure you've heard at least whisperings of them back at Dasos. Most of us have denied the Great Gods since they turned their back on us long ago. Yet some still cling to the hope that one day they will fix the wrongs of this world."

"So what are their names?" Lilith tried her best not to sound overly impatient, but the tone of her voice betrayed her once again. Even still, she hadn't the faintest idea of how mere names would be beneficial at all.

"My stories and those stories told to me by the ones who continue to worship them, have all called the brothers Poseidon, Hades, and Zeus." Finian said, revealing their names.

A wave of something near nostalgia hit Lilith. It crashed into her so intensely that she found it hard to breathe. Why did these names have this effect on her? They meant nothing, signified nothing. Yet...she could not help but feel a pang of recognition as a flash of a memory slipped away. But it had been a memory. She was fairly certain of that.

Finian caught the look on her face and furrowed his brow in concern. "Lil? Sweetheart, are you okay?" Though he felt silly for asking. Clearly her mind was elsewhere; the distress on her face told him that much. Then a thought dawned on him. Maybe those names meant more to her than either of them realized. If this was any indication of her past, it would be the first thing either one of them learned about her life before Dasos.

"Do you recognize their names?" He asked, closely watching her.

The glazed look in Lilith's eyes soon vanished and wherever her mind had been moments ago, now anchored her back into reality. Slowly she turned to Finian, and with a slight quiver to her voice she said, "I thought-for a moment..." But her words died on her lips. Those names meant nothing to her. They were faceless gods and nothing more. "Never mind, I must have heard those names around the village. I still don't understand what they have to do with the Unhallowed though."

Reluctance etched across his features as he wished he could slip inside her mind, if only to catch a glimpse of the memory the names dredged up. Lilith, however, had other plans and gently nudged him to continue. "They have everything to do with the Unhallowed, at least from what I've gathered. One of the brothers was cruel and unjust. Zeus was drunk on power, but not the favored brother. Poseidon and Hades were. Zeus was consumed with rage and held a considerable amount of power, which only leads to disaster. He cared for no one, but wanted to reign supreme, and force all gods and mankind to bow to him."

"They wouldn't accept his rule so willingly, would they?" She broke off, her mind reeling with this new material. How could she not remember ever hearing about the gods and Unhallowed?

"Of course not. He knew by killing his brothers, there would be no one to stand in his way, no one stopping him from taking the throne." Finian added, only to be interrupted once again.

"He killed his own brothers?" It seemed unbelievable that a person - no, a god - could be so cruel.

"This is where the stories diverge. Some say he killed his brothers and displayed their bodies at the palace gates, but others believe he banished Poseidon and Hades. Either way, they were gone, and he proclaimed himself the king. However, Zeus upset many of the survivors who were not willing to accept his tyrannical reign. His kingdom was built on chaos and destruction, and the few gods left behind, cursed his kingdom with a plague best fitting for a tyrant." Finian concluded.

"The Unhallowed?" She guessed.

He nodded, his face weary, as if he carried the story for too long and it had been weighing heavily on him. "Chaos and destruction -- that is our curse."

"Because of the actions of a few power-hungry gods, we get fucked over?"

A laugh void of humor escaped Finian's lips. "So eloquently put, Enchantress. But I'm a dreamer," He shrugged, breaking the silence once again. "I don't think the Unhallowing will be our penance for all time."

"How can you say that after everything you know about the Unhallowed?" Exasperated, she turned to look at his beautiful face. Finian smiled at her, his dark skin standing out against the scenery of the green and brown forest.

"Because if not, then what's the point? Of all of this?" He asked and gestured to the world around them for emphasis. "I refuse to believe this is all there is. I have to believe that one day, even if it is centuries from now, the world will change. The world will be a better and safer place. Something or someone will bring about change. If I think any other way, then...what's the point? Using your language, Enchantress, the world is one fucked up place. But this is my silver lining. I need to believe in something. Even if it sounds stupid and naïve."

More than anything, Lilith understood. "You aren't naïve, Finian. You're an optimist, and we need more people like you."

Hope. They needed hope.

CHAPTER TWO

THE BEFORE

T HE MIDWIFE HAD BEEN called upon at dusk and arrived approximately ten minutes later. Phaedra had been hand selected by the king himself, five years ago, during the queen's first pregnancy. Ecstatic that his beautiful, young wife could produce twin boys, he saw to it that Queen Rhea inherited the best midwife the Dasonian Empire could offer. Phaedra had been the obvious choice, being favored by both Queen Rhea and King Cronus. If she wasn't warming one bed, she was in the other. The midwifery duties didn't include those of the sexual nature; she just enjoyed the pastime.

Tonight, however, Phaedra sat beside her Queen, holding her hand tightly as another wave of pain consumed her, ripping through her body. A piercing scream filled her chambers as another contraction came and went. The contractions were coming more often and each more ferocious than the last.

The twins nearly killed the woman a mere five years ago when the queen was barely more than a child. Virginal and petite, the seventeen-year-old queen had been chosen for her beauty and the allure of a strong bloodline. House Gaia was well-known for producing strong men and beautiful women. Cronus became so seduced by the opportunity of having tenacious heirs that he would happily marry an old crone, if she were from House Gaia and still within childbearing years.

After all, he only needed a wife for breeding purposes.

Nevertheless, the day princess Rhea arrived in Dasos, dressed in the vibrant greens of the Dasonian empire, Cronus stiffened, at a loss for words. It was likely the first time he had been rendered silent. Although he heard many rumors and tales of the princess's beauty, none of them came close to the goddess of a woman that stood in front of him.

Like the rest of the women in her family, she was petite with a cinched waist, one that made men wonder what lay beneath the bodice. Her skin was unmarked and sun-kissed, detailing an easy and pampered life. The king thought her hobbies must be those of the frivolous nature women were fond of, like sunbathing and keeping up with the latest court gossip. However, it was her hair Cronus loved most of all: a soft and silky black mane that hung halfway down her back.

"Good afternoon, Your Majesty." And that voice, easily one belonging to a siren, ready to lure men into the deepest, darkest depths of the sea, serenaded the ruthless king. Rhea bowed low, her long hair falling around her as she rose. "My mother, Queen Gaia, sends her love. She is still in mourning over the death of her husband, my father, King Caelus, and hopes you forgive her absence."

"My condolences to you and yours. Your father was a good man." Cronus responded, pushing himself off his throne, taking long strides to fill the distance between them.

A wicked smile curled her lips. "Lying doesn't become you, Your Majesty. I believe you described my father as a 'lice-infested bastard whose balls have yet to drop.'" The room immediately quieted. Everyone was holding their collective breaths, waiting for Cronus to strike the woman for her crude and abrasive nature. Instead, he did something quite unexpected.

Cronus threw his head back and barked out a laugh that could only be described as joyous. A unified exhale erupted around the room with a few other nobles joining in on the laughter, albeit awkwardly. "My, my, princess. What a tongue you have on you. True, I was not a friend of your father's, and his death does not phase me in the least. It was only a matter of time before one of his own turned on him. There are worse ways to die than a clean dagger through the heart. What happened to his murderer anyway?"

"What happens to most murderers in my kingdom," she said, "he warmed my mother's bed before being beheaded. My mother shared the same sentiments about my father as you do, However, a queen has a role to play for her people, hence the mourning period."

The king smirked. This princess proved to be more than a pretty face. She was vastly different from the usual women he bedded at court. They were eager to please him and say what he wanted to hear. He suspected Rhea didn't bend to other's wills easily and never let anyone control her.

Did he trust princess Rhea though? No, not entirely, but the woman would be interesting to have at his side if he could win her over. Cronus always loved a challenge.

"We are to be wed, princess. How do you feel about that?" He asked, finally closing the gap between them. Cronus was at least a head or two taller than Rhea, but her short stature did little to diminish the powerful presence she possessed. Rhea would make a good queen, perhaps a great one.

"I'm pleased. My father would never approve this arrangement, but he was foolish. Our kingdoms are strong. He would rather see us at war than united. My marriage to you will ensure my kingdom is safe."

"So this is your duty?"

"Isn't it yours?" Rhea asked, meeting the king's obsidian eyes. "You will find me a suitable wife, Your Majesty. And perhaps you will come to admire me. I know you are hoping for heirs and I'm ready to bear children. My only request is I get to name them and assist in their studies. They should know their mother's kingdom just as well as they know their father's."

Cronus listened to her requests and then gestured to a servant. "Send for the Overseer and let him know we re-quire his presence and blessing for marriage. Princess Rhea is to be my Queen."

"Yes, Your Majesty, right away, Your Majesty." The meek servant said before swiftly leaving the room, happy to put some distance between himself and the King. Once Cronus finished bellowing orders at a few other servants and members of his court, he turned back to his bride to be. "Princess Rhea, I accept your terms."

One year into marriage, Queen Rhea gave birth to not one, but two strong boys. True to his earlier promise, Cronus allowed Rhea to name their sons, for he did not care much for the names. He cared about their future and raising them to be the greatest warriors Dasos had ever seen. One glance at her two boys, identical minus the tufts of hair upon their head, the names came easily. They were to be called Poseidon and Hades.

Rhea's pregnancy had not been an easy one, with numerous complications that eventually put her on bed rest. But the most deadly had been the amount of blood she lost giving birth to her two sons. Phaedra, her midwife, had been there for her first-born boys, and called for the physician to treat the dying queen. Cronus, to everyone's surprise, had fallen deeply in love with his young queen and threatened every soul in the room. If Rhea died, they would follow suit.

It had taken the physician everything he knew about healing and medicine to keep the queen alive, but after a turbulent few hours, the queen's condition stabilized. All this time, Cronus was to remain outside. There were very few things the King hated more than waiting. By the time

Phaedra came out, Cronus was ready to barrel past her to get to his children and wife. "So? My wife? The babes?"

"They are all fine, Your Majesty." Phaedra grinned, taking the hands of the King. Even though Cronus was in love with his wife, he was still a man...a King with needs. While Rhea had not been able to please him while her pregnancy progressed, Phaedra filled that role. He suspected Phaedra also slept with his wife, but never took the time to truly investigate his assumption.

"Queen Rhea fought hard and was rewarded with two, strong baby boys. She has named them Poseidon and Hades. I just finished cleaning up the room while tending to your wife and babes. You are welcome to see her." She said, bringing his hands to her lips and pressed the softest of kisses to them, while her eyes promised they would celebrate this moment later in his private chambers.

Cronus rushed in. His beautiful Rhea, despite her unkempt hair and tired face, looked as lovely as she did when he first laid eyes on her. The King's gaze soon turned down and looked at the two squirming bundles in her arms.

"Would you like to hold your sons?" Rhea smiled. And though her voice sounded faint, she still smiled and looked down at the twins with a fierce love only a mother could give.

Nervously, Cronus sat down on the edge of the bed. The babes were so small. He feared breaking their feeble bones in his iron grip; he certainly wasn't as gentle as Rhea. "Tell me which one is Hades and which is Poseidon."

Rhea did not ask him again to hold their sons. If he wanted to hold them, he'd make an effort. "The one nuzzled into my left breast in Hades. He will have dark hair; you can already see the darker strands. Poseidon's hair is lighter, resembling yours. Are you pleased?"

"Pleased? Rhea, you have made me the happiest man in Dasos. There will be a party in your honor as we celebrate the births of our sons. As soon as you are well." In a rare moment of kindness, Cronus leaned forward and kissed her tenderly. "I love you."

"Don't go soft on me, Cronus. It concerns me." Rhea smirked in a way that shared just how much she loved her husband as well, despite his faults and concubines. Rhea wasn't exactly a saint either. She could be cruel when it suited her and took lovers when her husband was away. Though she never gave her heart to anyone but him. That belonged to Cronus alone.

"Cronus," She started again, her tone changing from light to urgent. This caught his attention, and he turned to stare at his wife. "I have given you two sons at once. Few queens can say that. The pregnancy was not easy, and I fear if I'm put through that again, I will not survive. I cannot bear you anymore children. Your two sons will have to be enough. If you must have another child, you will need to father a bastard."

The thought of a bastard son repulsed the King, and he vehemently shook his head in protest. "Nonsense. I have two sons. I do not wish for a bastard to have a claim on the Dasonian throne. Even if a woman ends up pregnant, I will not accept the child."

It was as much as she could hope for and put her fears to rest. "Very well. Now, you may want to leave. The wet nurse needs to feed our boys."

With one final kiss, the King of Dasos took his leave.

For five glorious years, the castle thrived with two spirited and active young princes. True to his word, Cronus did not demand another heir, though Rhea heard whispers of bastard born children, many fleeing the kingdom out of fear of Rhea's wrath. He still shared her bed frequently, but Rhea had to get more...creative in their nightly endeavors as well as seek out the herbs that would prevent her body from holding another baby. It worked out in her favor for five years.

Until it didn't.

It was a warm summer day, even for Dasos. The queen just left her morning visit with her sons. Hades and Poseidon would soon travel alongside their father on their very first tour of their future kingdom. Cronus said they'd be gone a month, longer than Rhea had ever been away from her boys. She agreed purely because her sons needed to observe their future kingdom, and her husband promised to write often.

It was not proper for a Queen to be on the road for so long, and Rhea was needed at the castle to oversee council meetings and allocate responsibilities for the day-to-day necessities. It was merely busy work until the King returned home.

However, there was a new reason Rhea could not join her husband and sons on their voyage, one unbeknownst to her. While walking back to her chambers with her handmaiden, an intense pain in her lower abdomen had her doubling over, clutching her stomach.

"My Queen!" Her handmaiden shrieked. The woman looked around wildly, wanting to scream for assistance.

Before she could call upon the guards and started the influx of gossip that would surely follow, Rhea quickly reached out to grab the wailing girl, shutting her up at once. "Don't," Rhea gritted through her teeth. The handmaiden looked stricken, but another pointed glare from the queen had her backing down. "Just get me to my room. Please." The queen hardly ever used such polite mannerisms, so the woman knew the severity of the situation called for action.

The handmaiden...Chloe? --nodded. She was sure the woman introduced herself as such, but Rhea hadn't bothered learning the names of every maid in the castle. Chloe put her arm around the queen to lead her back into her chambers. Thankfully, her rooms were empty. Rhea's ladies in waiting had been dismissed for the day as the queen needed time alone to breathe freely. Chloe gently eased Rhea into her usual chair by the window.

"Your Majesty, you're pale." Chloe pointed out the obvious. Rhea had half the mind to throw up her morning breakfast all over the simple girl because of her brainless observations. But she knew she must be kind to the girl since she needed her help. Chloe was all she had at the moment.

"Chloe, do you remember the last time you changed my sheets due to my monthly bleeding?"

Realization finally dawned on the girl as she racked her brain to remember the last time she changed the bedding. "It's been a few months, my queen. Do you think-"

"What other explanation is there?" Rhea snapped. She remembered the pains she felt while pregnant with the twins. They felt similar to the one she was feeling now. She remembered the dizziness and sickness that plagued her day after day, but she didn't understand how. She took all the precautions necessary, save for abstaining from sex altogether. The physician mentioned her methods were not foolproof, but it had a high preventative rate.

For once, Rhea despised being the exception.

"Chloe, listen to me." Rhea said, grabbing the handmaiden by her forearm. Fortunately, Chloe grasped the severity of the situation and nodded at her to continue. "I want to keep this secret...for now. The King need not know at this moment. You are my only confidant right now. That means if anyone finds out about this pregnancy, I will personally hold you responsible."

The veiled threat was not lost on the handmaiden. If there was one thing Chloe knew how to do, it was surviving. "Yes, Your Majesty. Your secret is safe with me. But," she paused, too nervous to ask the burning questions on the tip of her tongue.

"Speak freely, Chloe. We are past pleasantries and for-malities."

"Are you going to keep the baby? I've heard of methods women use to end their pregnancy. I can learn what they are if you wish." Chloe suggests, knowing the Queen would most likely die if she carried this baby to term. She had not been here for the birth of the twins, but she heard the horrific stories. Rhea would not be able to survive another pregnancy.

Even knowing that, the queen still shook her head no. "I'm many things, Chloe, I know you've heard most of them, but I will not give up on my baby. It appears the King will have another heir."

The months that followed were a whirlwind of emo-tions. Chloe proved herself to be quite a loyal friend. Rhea soon elevated her status to one of her ladies in wait-ing. Chloe was there for every early morning sickness, every late-night craving, and when she was no longer able to hide her pregnancy, Chloe was at her side when she told Cronus.

The King had been furious. Furious at Rhea for keeping such a secret from him, furious she had not yet contacted the midwife, and furious his stubborn wife wanted to keep the baby.

"But you'll die, Rhea!" Cronus argued, every time they tried discussing her baby. *The leech.* For that was how Cronus saw the abomination growing in her belly, ready to take life from his mother.

"Only in body, husband. Not in spirit. You cannot con-vince me otherwise. Your child will be here in a few short months, and I will see to it he's taken care of." Rhea always responded in kind, effectively stopping any further discus-sion on the matter.

Each week that went by, the Queen grew bigger and bigger, while Cronus became crueler. A few weeks before Rhea was expected to give birth, she collapsed at a dinner party, almost falling on her face, but Cronus was faster. He caught his Queen and demanded the aid of his guards to get their Queen to her bed. "And call for Chloe and the midwife, Phaedra. See that they join the Queen at once."

The kingdom soon spoke about the fainting Queen, pregnant with the King's third legitimate child. Chloe was quick to dispel or shut down any talk of the Queen within the royal courts. There were whispers about Cronus selecting a new, more beautiful, and younger wife when Rhea died.

"How quickly they forget." Rhea murmured, the night she went into labor. Phaedra was doing her best to stop the intense pain of her contractions but wielding little to no results. "Chloe, I once again need to ask a favor from you."

"Anything, my Queen. Anything you wish."

"When my son is born, I want you to make sure he is protected and loved. I fear what Cronus will do to Zeus once I'm gone."

"Zeus, my Queen?"

"I have a feeling this baby is another boy." Rhea smiled sadly. "And if that is the case, his name will be Zeus. See that he is cared for properly. Even if Cronus does not love him, let him find a mother's love within you."

As if saying his name summoned him, the door to her chamber opened and Cronus strode in. "Leave us." He commanded the room. Chloe hesitated, but soon left, staying right outside the door. "You too, Phaedra."

"But, Your Majesty, I need to be in here in case-"

"Leave!" Cronus bellowed. He never raised his voice at Phaedra and the woman recoiled like she had been struck. She left without another word, though she kept her head high while trying to muster up the last bit of dignity she possessed.

Once they were alone, Cronus sat at her bedside, reaching for her hands. This was the first time the two of them had been alone in months. He stopped joining her in bed the moment he found out about her pregnancy. Rhea could detect the dark circles under his eyes and the worry that aged him before his time. "You cannot leave me, Rhea. I forbid it. Is this child so important that you throw away your life?"

Rhea reached out and ran her hand up his chest, stopping at his neck. "I'm not throwing away my life, my love. I'm creating a new life. I'm giving you another son; one I already love just as much as Poseidon and Hades."

"Your boys need a mother." Cronus replied, lips pressed into a tight line.

That gave Rhea pause. She choked back the sob that threatened to leave her lips. Thinking of her sons sent her spiraling into an endless darkness that threatened to consume her. "I know...I know. They have their nurses, and they have a father. I'm sure you will fill their heads with stories of their mother. Please be kind to me while telling them. They will have to live off their memories of me. It'll have to be enough."

"And what of me? Do I deserve to be alone?" He asked, the pain heavy in his voice. If Rhea didn't know better, she would have guessed he was on the verge of crying. Though Cronus never cried.

"No. No, my love you do not. You will find a new queen-"

"No one will ever be you!" He roared, cutting her off. The room remained silent as the tension slowly dispersed and Cronus deflated, his anger giving way to grief.

"No, they aren't me. But you will make do. I love you, my dear Cronus. I have loved you since the day you received me in your throne room and my affection has only grown since. I assure you, this is as hard on me as it is for you." She hesitated and then added. "Are the boys asleep?"

"Yes, safe in their beds."

"Good. You'll remind them their mother loved them, won't you, Cronus?"

He didn't reply, only nodded his head. He was a man defeated and Cronus was not used to accepting defeat. She wasn't sure which one of them was dying tonight, her or Cronus's heart? Though she wanted to say more, the king stood abruptly. "I will not bear witness to your death." He said, finally letting go of her hand. She could have sworn there were tears in his eyes, but he blinked them away as his expression went blank. "I will start preparing your funeral. It shall be grand, as you were in life." And with that, he left his wife for the last time.

Only when he left did she begin to weep. Phaedra and Chloe both reentered the room and held the Queen while she cried, as her body grew weaker.

"It's nearly time." Phaedra said, shortly after Rhea composed herself. She would not leave this world a crying mess. She would leave it as the Queen she was. But only after Zeus was born.

Phaedra moved between the queen's legs once more before looking up and meeting the eyes of Chloe, giving her a curt nod. It was time. Rhea's frail body was withering away quickly, and they feared the baby would be in distress. She needed to last long enough to see her son breathe his first breath.

As expected, her labor was strenuous. The pain became unbearable, but Phaedra made Chloe keep Rhea conscious. If the queen slipped away, not only would she not see her baby enter this world, but they might lose both Rhea and Zeus. All this pain would be for naught.

"I see the baby, my Queen, keep pushing! Yes, the babe is almost here." Phaedra encouraged. With a blood-curdling scream, Rhea used the last of her energy to bring her baby into this world.

"Is it a boy?" Rhea cried, her eyelids drooping. It became increasingly harder for her to stay awake. Sleeping would be easy. Sleeping would be peaceful.

Chloe looked down at the baby and smiled. "Yes, my Queen. It's a boy!"

"A healthy boy. Listen to that cry!" Phaedra gasped, concentrating on cleaning off the baby, making sure there weren't any obvious problems or deficiencies with the babe. But there was nothing marking him different from his brothers. However, instead of the dark, obsidian eyes of his father and brothers, he had his mother's soft hazel eyes.

As soon as the baby was swaddled, Phaedra handed him over to the dying Queen. Chloe helped Rhea hold her son since even that small feat proved difficult. "Zeus." Rhea whispered gently, her voice little more than a simple caress to the senses. "You will be a fighter, my strong boy. Never forget your mother loves you very much. I'm so sorry for leaving you behind. Please, Chloe, make sure he knows that." The last part she urged to her most trusted friend. "And make sure he knows how sorry I am. For the mess I left behind."

With tears in her eyes, Chloe took the boy and gave him back to Phaedra to care for. "He will never forget that his mother died to bring him into the world. He will know how much he meant to you."

But when Chloe turned around, the Queen of Dasos was dead.

CHAPTER THREE

THE AFTER

L ILITH AND FINIAN ARRIVED back at Dasos by dusk. The smell of garlic and cumin greeted them, reminding her she not eaten since the previous evening. Her stomach growled in anticipation for what awaited her at home; the thought of the delicious roast Idina would undoubtedly prepare, served with fresh vegetables, made Lilith salivate. Obtaining the vegetables cost her half a day's labor on Kei's family farm, but it was worth the tempting meal.

The town, Lilith supposed, was like any other organized town left within this world. Of course, she only heard stories, but most had a common way of living. Everyone pitched in, whether it be tending to the crops, forging weapons, or caring for the orphaned children. She was taught early on how important an active role in the Dasos community was. Each person was pivotal in keeping society running and failure undoubtedly meant loss of food, supplies, or human lives.

Most towns were said to be run similarly, by a group of the longest living occupants called the Onlookers. There was a common misconception all Onlookers were elderly, but since very few people lived long enough to sprout even a strand of gray in their hair, many Onlookers were young. Many current Onlookers accepted the job simply because it was thrust upon them after a former Onlooker succumbed to the Unhallowing. There was no formal process in becoming an Onlooker; it was passed down to the people who lived in the town the longest. They kept the peace and enforced the regulations agreed upon by the town and Onlookers before them.

That was not to say every town was ruled justly. Some Onlookers became corrupted by the modicum of power they possessed. Luckily, Dasos experienced very few power struggles amongst Onlookers. Lilith's own adopted mother, Idina, was the longest serving Onlooker and well respected by the community. She made most of her appearances in the town as a healer, caring for those who were sick. More often than she wished to talk about, Idina made sure to be present in many of the homes during a person's Unhallowing. Much to Lilith's dismay, Idina refused to give her much information about the process and Lilith never pushed her on the subject. The dark circles and somber expression convinced her otherwise.

"Do you want me to accompany you back to your house?" Finian asked, directing her attention back to the present. Just in time too, for a Watcher atop a horse nearly stampeded over her. As far as death went, that would have been the most humiliating way to go.

"You better check on Mavis. She will be undone if you neglect to report back." Mavis, Finian's headstrong and adorable six-year-old sister, demanded to be brought along with them into the forest. Their father all but held her back from escaping when Finian left this morning.

"Yeah," He winced, knowing he would receive an earful from said six-year-old. "I won't be long and then I will meet you at your home for dinner. Wait for me, I don't need you eating all the potatoes again." He smirked and kissed away her protests.

Her lips were still flushed when she entered her cottage home. It was diminutive, though Idina preferred the term "cozy." The layout matched every other cottage in town since the focus had been on hasty construction rather than style and looks. One large room served as a kitchen and family space and two small rooms served as bedrooms. The bedroom was spacious enough for a bed, but little else. Idina had a few art pieces placed upon her wall from children of the village, while Lilith preferred her walls bare. Occasionally she placed her weapons on the hooks she hammered into the walls. It wasn't the most ideal place for her dagger and swords, but she liked being close to her weapons in case the need to protect her loved ones ever arose.

Closing the door behind her, Lilith shrugged off the woolen cloak and hung it on the back of a chair. A woman, only a little more than a decade or so older, turned from her perch on the fireplace. Idina's face brightened in relief when she saw her, only serving to make Lilith feel guilty for causing unneeded stress.

Even now, well into her third decade of life, Idina was beautiful. Time had not laid her hands upon her body yet. Her deep brown skin was virtually blemish free, save for the slight shadows under her hollowed eyes. Her hair was black and coiled. Most days she pulled it back into a loose ponytail, but on the rare occasion, Idina wore it down. Lilith always thought she looked girlish and even prettier with it down, especially when she smiled. The only rough part of Idina was her hands. They weathered much abuse over the years from caring for patients, tending to the gardens, and performing daily household chores.

With all the extra activities Idina took on as an Onlooker and Healer for the town, the woman had grown to become far too thin for Lilith's liking. Oftentimes, she would catch her adopted mother giving up her own food to a hungry child or a grieving mother. Idina used her kindness as a weapon and wielded it for good. But like any warrior, she gave too much, often suffering the consequences of her sacrifices.

Despite her popularity and beauty, Idina had not taken a partner. Lilith was sure the woman enjoyed the pleasures of others in the past, but she seldom spoke of anyone in town with interest. Whether her adopted mother preferred the company of men or women eluded her completely. She often claimed she was far too busy to indulge in follies of the heart, though Lilith sensed there was more to it. However, Idina was entitled to her own secrets.

"Good evening, my dear. Did you enjoy your time away from Dasos?" Idina's voice sounded calm, but her eyes betrayed the tension lurking behind the surface. It cost her a great deal to let her daughter go into the forest and away from the safety of the village. "I'm surprised your young man is nowhere to be found. He follows you like a smitten puppy, which I presume, is quite fitting."

If Idina expected her to blush, Lilith showed no sign of embarrassment, only a glimpse of amusement.

"I'm not sure smitten puppy is the term I would use, mother," she said.

"Oh?" Idina raised a brow at that. "Then what word would you use then?"

"Pesky. Nuisance. A pesky nuisance." Both women laughed at his expense. Lilith then crossed the room and found herself engulfed in her mother's warm embrace. She smelled of sage and lavender, the fragrance of a town healer. Her scent always made Lilith feel safe and secure. At her age, (just shy of twenty-- she assumed, but didn't know for certain), it seemed funny to rely on her mother to coddle her as if she were a mere babe. Secretly she could not deny the feeling of belonging she found within her nurturing arms.

"I missed you." Idina murmured against the vibrant red of Lilith's hair.

"And you worried yourself sick."

"Yet, still you left."

"To which you agreed." Lilith said and pulled away from her embrace. Perhaps her tone came off harsher than what she intended. Idina seemed to flinch almost imperceptibly. Softening only slightly, Lilith continued, "I know you want to protect me. You are far too kind for this world, Idina." She used her adopted mother's real name intentionally. It was the only thing she had in her arsenal against her mother to indicate she was not a child but an adult, indeed capable of handling herself. After all, she took care of herself before Dasos, before Idina...even if she had no memory of that time.

"But you must remember that I do not need your constant supervision. Not even you can shield me from everything, no matter how hard you try. You raised me for the last two years to be strong, kind, and resourceful. You gave me all the tools I need."

"My dear, I will not insult you by talking down to you about life experience or a mother's love. I doubt I will ever stop worrying about you, but I understand you are a woman who does not need her mother to coddle and question her every move."

Lilith could not help the smile that formed on her face. Actually, that was *literally* what she wanted only moments ago, to be held by her mother and rocked soothingly. Even though those very arms could be smothering and overbearing at times, she knew her mother meant well.

"Still," Idina carried on. "It pains me to pass on the news I received from Warrior Adolphi today." She spoke with a nonchalance that contradicted the dread quickly consuming Lilith.

What the hell did Warrior Adolphi want with her? He didn't make house calls or seek out individuals. At least not for favorable reasons. Warrior Adolphi was not the town's most congenial resident. She supposed it would not bode well for Dasos if their lead Warrior was friendly and inviting, but it also did not fare well with her knowing she was on his radar. She had not caused trouble. Well...not too much trouble anyway.

"What did Adolphi want?"

Idina gave her a pointed stare, one only mothers could give an insubordinate child. "Warrior Adolphi wanted to know about you. Apparently, he has seen you and Finian sparring in between duties and has not seen sword play like that in quite some time. He asked me if...well, if you had ever considered joining the ranks of Warrior?"

Surely Lilith had not heard her correctly. Being sought after by the leader of Dasos Warriors was no small thing. Of course, she would have preferred Adolphi to come straight to her if he had a proposition. Though she assumed the reason why he went to Idina was due to the fact he was sweet on her.

Realizing her mother still waited for an answer, Lilith cleared her throat. "What about Finian? He must notice I'm not practicing alone. Finian is a fantastic swordsman."

"I asked about that too." She admitted, "But, Finian is also one of our only blacksmiths in town. His expertise in that field is crucial and Alphi-"

"Alphi? Since when have you called him Alphi?"

"Adolphi," Idina corrected, but it was too late. Lilith saw the slight red hue that flushed her cheeks. She needed to investigate the reason behind the blush later.

"As I was saying, my contemptuous daughter, Adolphi believes Finian's skills, though admirable and on par with your own, would be best served as a blacksmith." Her mother finished and went back to check on the delicious smelling roast currently warming over the fire.

Lilith saw and understood the logic. What were warriors without their weapons? Nothing more than a shield. And although Lilith would gladly lay down her life to save the ones she loved, she didn't particularly want to die. If she were being honest, she did not want her Finian to be a Warrior. He's the man that told the stories, not starred in them. There was power in words and Finian was the strongest at wielding them. She would not stand to see the light flushed out of him if he were exposed to more of the darker elements of this world. They already dealt with so much.

Perhaps she did not have the power to write his story, but that was not going to stop her from protecting him.

"I want to do it." Lilith said at last. "I want to train as a Warrior of Dasos. No matter how short my time may be."

Idina expected that answer, but still found herself flinching at her daughter's comment. She accepted she could not protect her beloved daughter from everything, but a piece of her yearned to shield Lilith from the inevitable, as if Idina truly had such powers. She was skilled in healing simple sickness or bloody wounds. She helped bring life into this world and held the hands of those leaving it but lacked the ability to stop the Unhallowing. Some curses could never be broken.

"I knew you'd say that, my dear. Which is why I told him you'd be interested. He asks you to meet him tomorrow, early morning by the western edge of town. He says he has an assignment for you, but the nature of it he'd not disclose with me. Adolphi said that all I needed to know was he'd have you home before sundown. Honestly, I don't want to know the specifics. I'd worry too much, but I told Alphi if you come back with a single bruise, I will unleash the wrath of whatever god of chaos still lingers and obliterate him." Idina promised, causing Lilith to laugh at her mother's fiery spirit she loved so much.

"No one will cross you, mother. Not if they value their life...or sanity." It was best for everyone if Idina was kept happy. As a town Onlooker, she had the power to enforce rules that affected everyone. Although she was not one to abuse her power, she been known to enforce a strict town curfew after major town incidents.

Lilith looked at her mother as she carefully assessed tonight's dinner. Her stomach growled in response to the hearty meat Idina lifted from the fire.

"Instead of drooling over our dinner, why don't you retrieve the bowls, hmm?" Idina said and shooed her away. "Will Finian be joining us? Maybe we can discuss your future with one another. Or would you rather I pass on before you bring me grandchildren?"

"Idina!" Lilith hissed. Not so much on the grandchildren part, but at the suggestion of her death. Perhaps Lilith was overly protective of the woman too and went into a panic when she thought of life after her mother passed. Goddess, she hoped for plenty more years with her mother before...

She refused to finish that thought. Instead, she made her way to the wooden hutch and retrieved the bowls for dinner. Idina did not apologize for her words, only stared, daring her to argue with the inevitability.

She wasn't foolish enough to delude herself in such ways, but she still would not discuss it.

"Whether you get grandchildren is not fully up to me. If Finian and I choose to marry, I'll make sure he asks for your blessings. Until then, he'll join us for dinner and bring over the half loaf of bread you asked for. Mavis almost took his head off with a doll last time he took the whole loaf."

Idina laughed, taking the bowl from her daughter's outstretched hands. "That sister of his is precious, and he's so wonderful with her-"

"Perhaps you missed the part where Mavis threw a doll. At his head."

"Really Lilith, you needn't judge him too harshly. Quite a few men have taken dolls to the head. They are men. Most, if not all, probably deserve it."

Lilith could count several times when she too wanted to fling something at Finian's head for being absolutely insufferable. Granted, she supposed he might have wanted to throw a doll at her head too when she got moody. Particularly around the time of her bleeding. She couldn't blame him for that.

Much.

"The man of yours better grace us with his presence soon before my dinner runs cold." Pouring the last of the broth, Idina balanced the three hot bowls in her arms as she carried them to the table. The table was small and often left splinters in Lilith's hands. Removing them was extremely unpleasant. Despite that, eating dinner around this table was one thing she looked forward to daily. Time stopped, just for a moment, every evening as the three of them laughed, joked, shared secrets, and admitted fears. Perhaps small for some, she cherished this time more than anything.

As if their conversation summoned him, Finian soon appeared at their threshold. He knocked, waiting approximately two seconds before letting himself in. On his person, he carried a half loaf of bread (smart man) and softened butter. "Hello, ladies."

"Why do you still knock? At this point, you should just walk in." Lilith remarked in a way of greeting.

Finian looked aghast, as if she just suggested he skip naked through town. "My lady, what if either of you are indecent? How improper of me to stumble across such a scene!"

Lilith scoffed. "What, you think Idina and I are in here naked? She's my mother!"

"What you and your mother do in your spare time is none of my concern. Perhaps you are free women who reject garments in any form for they are oppressive and restricting. As a matter of fact..."

"I really wish I had a doll right now."

"A doll?"

"Never you mind. Just stop talking." Lilith said, not sure if she should smack him or kiss him. She decided on the latter. She placed a simple, tender kiss on his lips, before taking the bread and butter from him and adding it to the table.

"Will your father and sister be joining us today?" Idina interjected, taking her normal spot at the head of the table. It was rather impressive and oftentimes a game to squeeze in three people at the table. Lack of seating would not deter her mother though. "I did not make quite enough food, but I would be happy to make something else."

"That's quite kind, Madame Idina, but no. Mavis and my father will be joining Sir Telmanz tonight. He hasn't been quite the same since his daughter succumbed to the Unhallowing." He said, his voice softening at the mention of the death of a young girl.

Idina looked solemn. Lilith was sure her mother had been in the room during the process. "That poor man. Every one of his daughters and wife have died in the past four years. He's had to witness them all. I cannot begin to fathom his pain."

Finian flinched. Besides her mother, Finian was the only one of them that knew firsthand what it meant to mourn the loss of the loved one after the Unhallowing. He had been fourteen when he watched his mother die. He never told her any details and Lilith never asked. It was not her place to know.

"Enough of this talk." Idina cut in, pulling both Lilith and Finian from the darkness plaguing them. "I've prepared your favorite meal after your adventure today and Lilith's good news-"

"You have good news?" Finian cut her off, then realized he spoke over Idina. Embarrassed, he apologized to her.

"I'll tell you later." She assured him, not wanting to discuss her new town title yet. Not when he would have questions. Finian nodded, though the ambiguity between them unsettled him.

He made a mental note to ask about Idina's comment later.

"Please, eat. Don't let it get cold," Idina encouraged. Lilith didn't need any more encouragement; she took the first bite and groaned.

Heaven.

CHAPTER FOUR

THE AFTER

WITH THEIR BELLIES FULL of Idina's delicious meal, Lilith retreated to her bedroom for the night and Finian followed close behind. There had been little discussions about sleeping arrangements for the night. All Finian had to do was look at Lilith and no disputes over their nighttime plans arose. This was fine with her, she slept better in his arms. Truthfully, Finian also needed the comforting touch when the inevitable nightmares plagued his sleep. Curse the fates for their unholy affinities to breed fear where fear should not exist.

"Idina likes you." Lilith said, as she shut the makeshift door behind her. It closed with a resounding *thud*. In truth, Idina had known Finian longer, but the pair never said more than the occasional greeting before Lilith.

Finian's lip quirked up, smirking. Once she would have loved wiping the arrogant expression off his patronizing face, but that urge changed long ago. Now, Lilith strove to make his dark features light up, to glimpse the boy she met and fallen for two years ago. "And how do you know that, Lil?"

"Because if she didn't, you wouldn't be in my room about to soil her daughter." Lilith returned the knowing smirk that earned her a bark of laughter.

"Perhaps her *daughter* will be the one to soil *me*. After all, this would not be the first time you led me into your quarters and seduced me, Enchantress. I am more than the appendage between my legs, you know. In fact, I have a personality; you wouldn't be privy to it though, considering the amount of time you spend with said appendage."

Lilith tossed the first thing she found, which happened to be a leather-bound journal on her bedside table. Finian ducked just in time, narrowly missing a shot to the head. When he recovered from the flying journal, he calmly straightened, holding his hands up in mock surrender. "My apologies, Lil. Didn't mean to offend you. My appendage and I deeply apologize."

"You are a crude man, Finian Taren. How I ever came to love you is beyond me." She scowled, turning her back to him. Then she reached behind her to undo the laces of the lambskin corset. It offered some protection against sharp objects since the hide was tough. Nowhere as protective as the armor given to the Warriors of Dasos.

Struggling to reach the top laces, rough hands pushed away her struggling ones. How easy it was for her to be this close and shed all her insecurities. She heard endless stories from people in town who spoke harshly of the deficiencies of their bodies and how they yearned to change the flaws within themselves to better please their lovers.

The need to change her body for Finian never crossed her mind. Ever. Admittedly, she remembered being shy the first time he saw her completely naked, but he had been just as nervous. Nervous. Not insecure. Finian trembled when she approached his cot and continued to tremble throughout their first time.

Not once did she think to change pieces about herself. He caressed her hips that weren't as petite as the other girls and ran his cool hands against her small breasts. She kissed his wide jaw, and crooked nose, and then gripped his scarred back. Neither cared about the other's imperfections. Their love was not defined by mere physical attributes, but rather the spiritual bond that connected two souls.

Her corset soon fell from her body, leaving her in only the blue tunic and the black riding pants. Finian's gaze racked over her body, the amusement from earlier dying away and replaced by something new...something hungry.

Lilith's entire body grew hot.

"If you only knew what you do to me, Lilith. How much you have changed my life since you've arrived. I wish-"

Lilith did not get the chance to discover what he wished. At that moment, the need to feel his lips against hers crashed around her so intensely that she could no longer deny her need. She pressed herself tightly against him and kissed away his wish. Wishes were not guaranteed, but this moment, this singular moment was, and Lilith planned to make the most of it.

She did not know who moved them towards the bed, only that she fell back against the bedding and Finian hovered over her. Finian looked down at her as if she were a goddess, one he planned to worship. It made Lilith's cheeks flush with color as she thought of all the ways Finian was skilled in worshiping her. Her body quivered with excitement.

Finding the drawstrings of his pants, Lilith took her time loosening them, making sure her finger brushed over his most sensitive spots. Finian let out a groan of pleasure that sent tingles down her spine. A whimper of protest left her lips as he pulled away, which earned her a coy smile. With a wink, he lifted his shirt over his head and threw it down next to Lilith's cast-off corset. "My Lilith...I plan on devouring you tonight."

"And how is that different from every other night, Fin?" She mused, moving her hands up to explore the chest she often appreciated. Lilith traced every muscle and scar that lined his body, memorizing each part of him.

"Because," as he spoke, Finian grabbed the bottom of her tunic and lifted it. She arched her back, and the tunic was quickly removed, leaving her naked from the waist up. With his cold hand, Finian moved them to her chest, cupping her. Her nipples pebbled in response. "Tonight, I will repay every night you left me writhing with pleasure atop my cot.

I would much rather have you be the one crying out my name."

A devious grin crossed his features as he kissed down her body. Lilith swore silently and thanked whatever god remained for sending Idina out of the house tonight. She could not face her mother's knowing smile in the morning when she discovered the two of them exiting her bedroom. The walls of their home did not block out sound well and Idina certainly did not need to hear this.

She would hear a lot if she were home.

"It's about time you stopped being so selfish." Lilith purred, running a hand through his thick hair. She loved the way it felt underneath her touch and pull. "I was beginning to think you needed the herbs to help excite you."

"Herbs? You wound me. Enchantress, all I need is one look at you and your beautiful body, and I am lost to the passion. It helps immensely that you are not an ugly toad. Then I might need the assistance of those herbs." Finian smiled, running his fingers across the waistband of her pants. It was even more agonizing when he dipped his head down and pressed soft kisses to her hips and navel. This man would be the death of her, and she would not mind it. In fact, she would meet death with open arms if it meant an eternity of love and pleasure with Finian.

Before Lilith could process what happened, Finian had her pants down, and she kicked them off the rest of the way, baring herself to him willingly. She'd never been one to shy away from his gaze, even as he took in the most intimate parts of her. There was something uniquely beautiful about trusting someone so profoundly that seeing them in their most vulnerable state created passion and devotion rather than scorn and malice.

She met him with the same look of desire when he finished stripping out of his last garment. She observed the flush of his cheeks, the same one he always got when he stood nude in front of her. He never said it aloud, but Lilith had an inkling Finian thought he was not worthy enough to warm her bed. She did not know how the preposterous thought made its way into his head.

Gently, she forced him to lower his gaze so her eyes could sweep over his body, stopping at the thick, hard length between his legs. He wanted her; maybe as much as Lilith wanted Finian. His body stood at attention, begging to be touched.

Damn, he was perfect.

"Finian, look at me." she said, reaching out to cup his face. Gradually, his anxious eyes met Lilith's hazel ones. "Don't you dare bow your head away from me when you make me yours. I want to see your face when we make love. Look at me and know that this is the love you deserve. The love we both deserve."

Finian hesitated. The earlier bravado he once held was quickly replaced with worry and timidness. Lilith knew him well enough to know he had something else on his mind, but now was not the time to bring up such worries. They had the rest of the night to talk through the serious stuff.

She much preferred putting their mouths to other uses.

"It's just you and me, Fin. Always just you and me."

This time, Finian didn't shy away from her gaze. A ghost of a smile shadowed his lips as he repeated her words back. "You and me, Lil, you and me."

With that, Lilith closed the space between them. The kiss changed. No longer soft and teasing, this kiss made her toes curl and her heart flutter from the urgency behind it. His lips did not stay on hers for long, they soon found her neck and his teeth grazed her skin, nipping occasionally. Lower and lower he went, his tongue tenderly teasing her nipples, but not nearly as long as she wanted.

Molten heat erupted in her core from his teasing. She wasn't above begging to get what she wanted, and at that moment, she wanted so much more than what he was giving her.

"Finian." Lilith groaned. It came out as a plea, but the rest of the words didn't follow. Her moan swallowed what came after, and then he finally landed between her legs. This. This is what she wanted. Needed.

He looked up at her briefly, his knowing smile sending more shivers down her body. She knew exactly what he planned to do, but she still found herself gasping when his mouth found the apex of her thighs and his tongue began to probe and search. He knew what her body craved and how to use his tongue to have her writhing for him.

He was relentless with his strokes, never letting up, even as she begged him for more. Finian groaned, finding his own body heating up and dripping with need. But not yet. Not until he had her squirming from pleasure. Not until she screamed and found her first release.

Luckily, he didn't have to wait long. His tongue, that damned magic tongue, stroked her perfectly for the last time and Lilith came undone. He continued to kiss her until she slowly came down from the intensity of her climax.

"We aren't done." She growled once Lilith found her voice again. Finian deliberately moved lazily back up her body, taking his sweet ass time.

"I didn't expect we would be, Lil. There's plenty more I want to do with you and this sinful body of yours."

"Then allow me to help."

She didn't wait for him to answer as she led him inside of her. He filled her completely, wonderfully. Her lips knew no other name but his, no other body but the one moving inside hers. His hands roamed her body, causing her to dig her heels into his back. His tongue, that wicked tongue, performed magic again. That was the only way she knew how to describe what he did to her. Through it all, she could only say one thing.

Finian.

Finian.

Finian.

Moonlight wafted through the parted curtains, providing a modicum of light. Lilith crawled off Finian and nestled her tired body against his. Looking up, she spotted the same silly grin he wore after sex. It filled her with warmth, even after all this time.

"We did good. Didn't we?" She panted.

"Good? Enchantress, that was particularly brilliant. Feel free to ride me like your stallion any day."

Lilith flushed. In the heat of the moment, words may have slipped her tongue that would later make her cringe. Hot and bothered Lilith was more vocal than calm and collected Lilith. Still, she meant every word she spoke...even if the phrasing would make the most adventurous lovers blush.

Finian turned his body to face hers, wrapping his strong, toned arms around her. Absentmindedly, he traced a single finger in circles, tracing the small birthmark on her hip.

The mark was only marginally darker than her sun-kissed coloring. Finian would have glanced over it if it weren't for the very distinct shape of the mark. It looked like a sun tattooed on her hip. Though when he asked, Lilith shrugged and said she'd never paid much attention, but he did because he noticed everything about her.

The way she bites her cheek when she's deep in thought.

The way her body quivers when his hands, fingers, or tongue finds just the right spot.

The way she loves life. Every single day.

It was why Finian wanted to marry her.

As if reading her thoughts, Lilith looked up at him, smiling. "What are you thinking about, Fin?" she asked gently, her voice getting lower as she grew tired. Her eyelids were fluttering, as she battled sleep. He should let her rest, but the selfish part of him wanted her to stay awake for just a little longer.

"You never did tell me your good news. From earlier." He said, breaking the silence.

Lilith blinked once. Twice. The news from earlier felt so long ago. A treacherous feeling of betrayal filled the pit of her stomach. Would Fin be mad? Rationally, she knew he was not the type of man to be jealous of her new placement alongside Adolphi and the few other Dasos Warriors. However, they both practiced almost every day in hopes that Adolphi would catch sight of their talents.

"Adolphi visited with Idina today." She admitted, searching his face for hurt or anger...but all she saw was curiosity. Swallowing back her anxiety, Lilith continued. "He noticed us sparring and approached Idina about whether or not I would be interested in joining his ranks. I'm to meet him tomorrow morning. Just me."

She waited, continuing to search his face for any hints of his emotions, but Fin appeared lost in his own mind. The pregnant silence was getting to her, and she quickly blurted, "I asked Idina why Adolphi was not interested in you. She said that you are the best blacksmith in our village, and he could not afford to lose your talents. I'm sorry, Fin."

"Sorry?" Finian scoffed. "Lil, were you *nervous* about telling me?" He took her silence as confirmation. "Sweetheart, I appreciate you rallying for me, but I bear no hard feelings. I'm thrilled that Adolphi pulled his head out of his ass long enough to discover your talents. Dasos will be a safer place with you protecting its borders."

Immense love and pride -- and a little relief -- swelled in her heart. The earlier tension eased tremendously at his quick acceptance. Some men would bark at having their women in a position of power, but not her Finian. "I only wish you were by my side."

"Some people were born to brandish tools while others were destined to create them." Finian said. "Besides, I don't trust anyone else to make weaponry suitable for the woman I love."

Love.

It did not matter how many times he spoke those words; Lilith doubted the butterflies in her stomach would ever cease. She did not want them to go away. They served to remind her of the excitement and hope she felt every time he was near. Hope for the future, for a better one.

Or at least one long enough to spend whatever time she had left with him.

"Lilith."

Hearing her name spoken aloud startled her. He did not often speak her full name; he preferred Lil, Enchantress, or Sweetheart. Glancing up, she studied his face, noticing the signs of his worry: the tension in his tight jaw, his lips pressed together to hold back words he couldn't quite form, and not once did his eyes meet hers.

This, more than anything, unnerved her. "What is it?"

"I want to have a serious conversation with you. About us."

Whatever Lilith thought he would say, that was certainly not at the top of her list. Hell, it had not even been on the list. Momentarily, a horrific thought of Finian leaving her weaved its way through her mind, planting seeds of doubt. What had tonight been then? A final effort to save their relationship? One last fuck before he called it quits?

These treacherous thoughts and more ran freely, so she barely registered what Finian said. It was not until he nudged her arm teasingly that she pulled herself away from the tirade of uncertainty. "Did you hear me, Li?" Finian asked, looking at her expectantly and with...fear? Panic?

"Uh, no." She admitted. "Sorry, what did you say?"

Whatever it had been clearly agonized him. He shifted in her bed, propping himself up on his elbow, so he could study her face. He reached out with his other hand to grab hers, lacing their fingers together delicately. "Do try to pay attention this time, Li. I don't like repeating myself." He teased, though fear still lingered in his eyes. Jokes were his coping mechanisms, something he did when he was troubled.

"You think being a storyteller, I would be able to express myself better, but I'm tongue-tied when I'm around you, Enchantress, so forgive my ineptitude. Do you remember that house on the east side of town, by the horse stalls? It used to belong to a single guy...Alexei, maybe? Anyway, since his passing, the house has remained empty."

Though the memory was vague, Lilith remembered passing by Alexei on her way to shovel horse shit from the stables. The memory did not strictly scream romantic, but she nodded regardless.

"Well, the house has just been sitting there, waiting for a new family to move in. We haven't gotten a new resident in Dasos since...well since you came two years ago and there are no young couples in need of a house. It seems wrong for a perfectly fine home to go to waste, so I went to the Onlookers-"

"You went to my mother?" Lilith interrupted. "Without me knowing? Why?"

"Idina was there, yes, but I didn't go to *her*. I went to see the council." Finian clarified, as if that were a big distinction. She supposed it was. "Since I'm twenty-one, it is within my rights to have my own home. In exchange for my continued labor as a Blacksmith, the council accepted my request for the house. I'm moving in tomorrow."

Lilith was impressed. Not because he managed to appeal to the council in favor of his new home, but that he kept this a secret for so long. Finian was many things, but a secret keeper he was not. "Why did you not tell me sooner? If you didn't need my help, I could have been there for moral support."

"Because I wanted to make sure I got the house before I asked you to make an honest man out of me."

Oh.

Oh.

This was the second time in the last thirty minutes he surprised her and rendered her speechless. Lilith stared blankly, blinking every so often. Honestly, it wasn't a good look for her, but Finian thought her gaping fish face was adorable.

What Finian asked was no small feat. To commit to someone in this world was both courageous and foolish. There was only one way it could end: forcing your loved one to watch you descend into madness until you were no longer yourself. The Unhallowing made a person lose all sense of purpose -- of right and wrong -- and in return became a monster.

But...love was the single most important thing and the only sense of normalcy left within a ruined world. If love was not worth the risk, not worth the hurt, pain, and tears, then existence became meaningless. Lilith needed to believe that through love, life was worth living.

"You want me to leave Idina and move into the house by the stables?" asked Lilith.

Finian flinched. He knew Idina would already be a factor against him. "I do. I know you are nervous about leaving her behind, but I've talked to her about this too. She's not opposed. In fact, she gave me her blessing to ask you to move in and...to become my wife."

"Finian Taren, are you asking me to marry you?"

"Uh, well I'm trying. How am I doing? Because I feel like an ass."

Lilith, despite her best efforts, laughed at his adorable attempt at a marriage proposal. Ignoring the slight awkwardness of the situation, her heart beat quicker at the thought of becoming his wife and starting a family together.

Would they have children? Idina mentioned wanting grandchildren earlier, and knowing that she was aware of Finian's proposal, her words from earlier took on a new reality. Was this why she broached the subject? She pictured a plump little boy with Finian's dark skin and curly hair. A sweet smile and an infectious laugh like his father.

With sudden clarity, Lilith knew, without a doubt, that whatever time she had left, whatever course her life took, her only path would be with Finian.

Then perhaps because she felt a little cruel, she replied. "Tomorrow night, under our tree on the forest edge, I'll give you my answer. Can you wait that long?"

"For you, Enchantress, I would wait a thousand lives."

CHAPTER FIVE

THE BEFORE

F IVE MONTHS PASSED SINCE the late Queen's death and
the castle still mourned her memory. Rhea was more
popular in death than she'd been during her life. Whispers
of her courage, kindness, and bravery were still talked about
in hushed corners and in dark alleyways out of fear the king
would overhear. Just as Rhea prescribed, Chloe took on the
responsibility of raising her beloved son.

Whatever pleasantries King Cronus once possessed died
the day his queen breathed her final breath. As promised,
her funeral was a grand procession and lasted days. Months
after her death, Cronus continued to receive condolences
from neighboring kingdoms and visits from Lords and
Ladies with extravagant gifts for the new widower.

The worst visit came a month after the funeral, when
Rhea's mother, Queen Gaia, came to Dasos to request an
audience with the king. True to her nature, little warning
arrived beforehand to prepare the castle for her arrival.
Naturally, it was the very first thing Queen Gaia commented
on upon her arrival.

"Your lack of a welcoming party insults me, Cronus. If I
did not know any better, I might assume you did not want
me to visit." The Northern Queen said, entering the main
gardens of the castle. She wasn't alone; she never traveled
alone. Her party encompassed her captain of the guard
and a few dozen of his soldiers, ladies-in-waiting, and her
oldest and most treasured advisor, Lord Kotas. Beside Gaia
herself, Kotas held the most power, making him a dangerous

enemy, but quite a remarkable ally. Cronus wondered if Rhea were still with him, if Lord Kotas might have eventually pledged his service to Rhea. Rumor was, he had been sweet on her.

"You gave us little time to coordinate, Gaia. My staff didn't prepare for unannounced guests." He dropped the titles since Gaia seemed inclined to do the same.

Gaia's eyes roamed the pristine throne room, looking for these busy servants. None were found. "I'm sure their preparations will be suitable."

The underlying insult to his staff did not go unnoticed. Cronus gritted his teeth together, keeping his anger in check. "So why are you here, Gaia, hmm? You are a few weeks late to the funeral."

"We arranged our own. One fitting for my daughter and it was truly spectacular. Shame you missed it." Just hearing her voice grated on Cronus's nerves. This woman was the bane of his existence. Never once had she come to visit Dasos. She always sent her cronies in her stead, which was typically Lord Kotas. The plump, balding man said little today though, which was unusual for him. He never passed up an opportunity to make his presence and opinions known.

"However, I do not wish to trade passive aggressive insults laced in backhanded compliments. I came to see him."

"Who is him?"

"Do not play me for a fool, Cronus. You know precisely who I'm talking about." Gaia snapped, her composure slipping. Cronus smirked, pleased he put a crack in her armor. One thing Gaia hated above all else was losing her patience and composure in front of others.

But yes, he knew exactly who she meant. The abomination that took the one thing he wanted more than anything else. He slept soundlessly in the nursery while his wife lay to rest within a cemented box.

She had come for Zeus.

"What do you want with him?"

"For the first time, Cronus, I believe we are on the same page. I want to see the baby so precious my daughter killed herself to bear. I also have a proposition for you."

That gave him pause. A proposition? What could Gaia want with Zeus? Better yet, what did Cronus want from Gaia? Despite Rhea's death, their kingdoms were at peace with one another and allied. Not to mention he was still in possession of his two sons, Hades and Poseidon. Cronus knew without a doubt, Gaia was fond of her grandsons.

Mostly because she recognized the potential within the boys and the power of having twin grandsons.

The silence held heavy between them, neither one of the powerful royals willing to break it. Cronus's stubbornness wouldn't allow him to yield to this witch.

"Have you not considered the possibilities of a third heir? One you want nothing to do with. No risks involved when you are dealing with his life. Think of the asset he could be to our kingdoms. What he could do for Poseidon and Hades." Gaia offered, clearly having thought long and hard over the fate of his third son, the rejected boy. She held no love for him either.

After a moment of thought, Cronus turned to his nearest guard. "Tell Lady Chloe I require her presence and make sure she brings the boy."

With a curt nod, the guard made a hasty exit. "Well, now that you've revealed the nature of your visit, let's discuss this proposition of yours over wine and food."

"For once, Cronus, we are in agreement."

Turning his back on the Northern Queen and her party, Cronus led them to the dining hall where he often entertained nobles. Chloe arrived moments later with a wiggling bundle in her arm. Upon surveying the room, her features paled, and bile began building up in her throat. The arrival of queen Gaia, who had yet set foot in Dasos, even when her daughter married Cronus, only meant one thing.

Zeus.

Since the death of her dearest friend, Chloe kept her promise to care for Zeus as her own. His father had yet to show affection for his son. Hell, Cronus did not so much as look at Zeus. From the moment of his birth, Zeus already had a target on his back. His life would not be one of comfort and ease like his brothers.

"Your Majesties." Chloe bowed low, wondering what earned her this summons. "How may I be of service?"

"Hand the boy over to his grandmother. She wishes to see him," came the order from her King.

Instinctually, Chloe wanted to take Zeus and run the other way, but by doing that, it would mean a certain death for both of them. She had no choice but to bow and hand Zeus over to Queen Gaia. To her astonishment, the Queen wasn't the one reaching out for the baby. Lord Kotas stood and took the boy. Zeus did not so much as stir as every eye in the room fixated on him for the first time in his short life.

Lord Kotas assessed the boy as if he were a newfound commodity rather than a real, breathing baby. He nodded at his queen when he finished assessing Zeus. A lion inspecting an innocent lamb. "He holds the features of House Gaia strongly. He's small, even for a babe, but the potential within him is vast. Killing him would serve us no purpose but having him alive and raised by the proper guidance would benefit both kingdoms."

Kill? They had come to kill the prince? Out of sheer desperation, Chloe spoke up without thinking of the repercussions. "I'm raising him, my lord. I will see to it that he is well taken care of."

"That is not what I mean, you wretched girl. Need I remind you not to speak unless spoken to? You may find that tongue unattached if you continue to piss me off." Kotas threatened.

The king didn't come to her rescue, but Chloe had not expected him to. He appeared bored by the exchange and waved both of their words away. "So, enlighten me, Gaia. The time for secrecy has passed."

Gaia reached for her wine and took a sip, if only to make Cronus wait a moment longer. He frowned at her from across the room, the displeasure written plainly across his face. The feeling was mutual.

"Our families have something in common, Cronus. We both strive for perfection and power, but with our quest for it, we created quite a stir. I have heard rumors about possible hostage situations, and I will not allow threats towards my true grandsons. But now we have a bargaining chip. Blood of both of our royal families. When the time is right, our dear Zeus may prove useful in placating our enemies."

"You'll allow him to live only to slaughter him later? In hopes that it might please the Southern kingdoms?" Chloe yelled and before she saw it coming, Lord Kotas was out of his seat as his hand collided with the side of her face, sending Chloe sprawling to the ground. She had never been touched in such a way before, not even by the cruel King Cronus. The pain in her cheek ached, but the shock left her dazed.

"I said not to speak, what did you not understand? Are you daft? Why you keep this woman around, is a mystery to me, King Cronus." He spat.

"You, Kotas, will do well to remember that you are a guest in my home, and I will not have you touching anymore of my people. There's plenty of prisoners you can take your anger out on. If you can't keep yourself in control of your emotions, your presence is not needed. Now sit."

Kotas shot a glare at Chloe, the anger seeping through his entire posture. If he had his way, she'd be without her head, instead of just a red cheek.

"Please, your majesty. Let me care for the boy as I have been doing. I'll leave this castle. You can tell the kingdom that he died unexpectedly. We will never bother you again."

She begged and picked herself up from the floor. Her pain in her cheek still throbbed, but she momentarily pushed it aside.

Cronus entertained that idea. His face gave little away, but he also had not immediately shut it down. That meant he was processing, at least from her experience. Not even Gaia dared to speak.

Cronus weighed the possibilities of Zeus being a token of trade. He needed a good bartering chip, especially since he once again denied King Vulcan a marriage between Vulcan's daughter and himself. He couldn't imagine sharing a castle with that old maid, let alone a bed. Cronus also refused to allow the marriage of Vulcan's two younger daughters - well into their twelfth year- to his boys, who were only five. They too would be old hags by the time his sons were of marriageable age.

With each denial, king Vulcan grew increasingly angrier and impatient. Maybe Zeus was of more use to him alive than dead.

"Very well." He said after an abnormal long wait. The tension in the room dissipated, but Chloe worried still. "Rhea entrusted Chloe to raise the insufferable boy, and for some reason she seems to enjoy that role. She will see that Zeus is brought up knowing the customs and rules of court. But he will be forbidden to join us for any gathering, any ceremony, or dinner unless I specifically request him. Then I expect him to behave as a prince should behave."

"Let me add on to that." Queen Gaia interjected. "He must also know how to play the political game. That is not something a mere peasant girl can teach him. Which is why I will be leaving Lord Kotas here to oversee his progress and education."

Kotas looked as shocked as everyone else around the table. Gaia had not warned him of that part of the plan and Chloe took some amusement out of his displeasure. It was fleeting, though, because it meant that Kotas would be closer to her than she cared for.

"Your Majesty, are you sure-"

"Do not question me, Kotas. You will stay behind and oversee the child's development. Now, Cronus," she turned her attention back to the King of Dasos and raised her glass. "Do we have a deal?"

Reaching forward, Cronus took his goblet and held it up. "For now, Gaia, our alliance holds." He said and drank. Gaia lips moved up into a knowing smile. she sipped her wine. "Now," Cronus continued, "Chloe, take the babe away. I've had enough political discourse. I'd much rather eat. You are dismissed."

Bowing her head, Chloe hurried to grab Zeus from Kotas. His cold stare bore into her, but he remained silent as he handed over the baby. "Thank you, Your Majesties. I will not fail you."

She turned and did everything in her power to keep herself from bolting, knowing eyes closely guarded her departure. Zeus started to cry the moment they were out of hearing distance from his father and grandfather. "Hush, my little prince. Never let them see you cry. One day, you will be greater than everyone in this room."

Until then, Chloe would love her late friend's son. For no one else would.

CHAPTER SIX

THE AFTER

F OR THE PAST FEW years, Finian often had vivid dreams that varied from night to night. Sometimes the nightmares debilitated Finian, wherein he felt suffocated, as the entire world crashed down around him. He awoke sweaty and breathless. Other times the dreams were simpler. He found himself in the forest outside Dasos, but never alone. A man always appeared in his dreams. His features were never clear, nor did he ever speak. The two simply sat in silence, watching the river flow.

He had never thought any further about the man once he woke, only a sense of relief that his nightmares didn't haunt his sleep.

When he fell asleep that night, Lilith curled around him as his own protective blanket, Finian found himself at the usual river, so he knew he'd escaped his nightmare for one more night. As far as dreams went, it wasn't fantastical or whimsical, but he didn't mind the monotony.

This time, the unidentified man was missing. For the first time since he could remember, he sat alone. Things were finally peaceful.

"Hello, Finian."

Finian jumped at the sound of an unfamiliar deep voice. He scrambled to his feet, lacking all the grace and poise he normally possessed. No one was around to witness his embarrassment, besides the person in his dream.

The large man standing in front of him looked amused -- at his expense, no doubt. "At ease, boy. No one is here to harm you. I just wanted to talk."

Talk? It seemed strange that after all this time, this man wanted to speak to him. Finian could not be certain, but he assumed that this man was the same one that frequented his dreams. Only now he could make out his features, and they were...intimidating.

Standing at least six feet tall, the man exuded power. He wore very little, save for the black trousers, exposing his solid, muscular chest. His arms told Finian that a single punch from him would leave a man sprawled across the floor in a bloodied mess. He doubted many men were stupid enough to challenge him in a fight. The man looked used to getting what he wanted. He held himself gracefully, sure and confident.

"Are you done ogling me boy, or should I spin around and let you take in the entire view?" Once again, amusement laced his voice. Amusement and slight curiosity. It was veiled better than Finian's gaping, but the man stared at Finian like a stranger he waited his entire life to meet.

When he found his voice, Finian asked the question playing at the tip of his tongue. "Who are you?"

The man didn't answer, which only proved to irritate him more. Instead, the man walked to the bank of the river, concentrating on the forest beyond.

"You know, all of this used to be Dasos." The man said, ignoring Finian's question and gesturing out to the endless trees before him. "In fact, Dasos was once a thriving, powerful kingdom. Its border expanded across rivers and mountains. In its day, it was considered the grandest kingdom above all others." He stopped and sighed in resignation. "It's a shame to see the kingdom now. Hollow and dying. Dasos could have been more...should be more."

"I don't understand. Dasos is a simple village. One of many. It's been that way for years, probably centuries if our records are anything to go by." Finian argued, having seen those documents himself.

"Like I said, it wasn't always a village. Still, I wanted you to be raised here. Call me sentimental, but I'm fond of Dasos. Even if she doesn't deserve that love, I cannot seem to let her go."

This man was crazy, and by far the oddest encounter he ever had. The stranger did not make any sense. What did he mean about being raised here? Finian didn't get a vote on that matter. He lived in Dasos because his family had always lived here.

Had this man lived in Dasos once? He spoke as if he had, but long ago. Finian couldn't picture the kingdom the man described, not when his home appeared slightly better than ruins.

Perhaps Finian was thinking too much about his dream.

Still, his thoughts spun awry, and he could not begin to sort out everything this stranger said. "Who are you?" He asked again.

This time, the man's gaze turned to Finian, momentarily forgetting the boy standing beside him. "A friend."

Well, that was helpful. Not.

"Okay, *friend*, can you tell me why you have never spoken to me before? I've seen you in my dreams, but this is the first time you've ever approached me. Why?"

"You ask many questions...you're very inquisitive. They call you a storyteller in the village, do they not? You must come by your curious disposition naturally."

Finian felt the man spoke in a different language for all the sense he made to Finian. His sleep deprived mind could not piece the puzzle together. Why did the man never show his face in nightmares, but enjoyed showing up to the peaceful, serene dreams of Dasos?

The stranger was different and odd in many ways, but Finian couldn't place the familiarity he felt when he looked at the man. Not only within his dream, Finian was certain he had seen him before. In Dasos? That wasn't likely; Finian knew everyone in his village. Then where had he seen this man before?

"Do...do I know you?"

Finian expected the stranger to laugh at him, or at least scoff at the absurdity of his question. But for a moment, Finian swore he saw a flash of pain cross the man's features like Finian's words wounded him. A second later the pain vanished, replaced with a newfound ferocity. He only hoped he wasn't the target for the emotion.

"You do not know me, but I know you. To answer your previous question, you can call me Thunder. I do not have much time; there is much I wish to tell you. But time, damned time, has never been a friend to me. So, I need you to listen well."

The stranger -- Thunder -- reached out, quick as a snake, and grasped Finian's wrist in a vice-like grip. Finian's own instincts took over, remembering those long days he spent outside with Lilith for hours, learning and mimicking everything he had seen from Dasos Warriors. Thunder was a bigger foe than Lilith, giving the man an advantage over him. He needed to find Thunder's weakness, and quickly.

Big, muscular, and strong Thunder.

Easier said than done.

"Don't fight me, Finian Taren. I am not the enemy here, but they are not far off. You reek of them." Thunder's grip only tightened, causing Finian to grit his teeth in pain. He felt it unfair to feel pain in a dream, but his throbbing arm said otherwise.

"Let go of me."

"Stop struggling."

"Then. Let. Go."

Thunder did not relent, even as Finian persisted. Of course he would dream up the one person with no weaknesses. He tried throwing the weight of his body against Thunder in hopes to catch him off guard, but the man was pure muscle. It was like throwing yourself against a boulder, though Finian felt he stood a better chance against a boulder.

"I need to give you something. They are coming soon, but I fear there is a player already on the field. I won't leave you unprotected."

Once again, confusion and anger surge through his body. One thing he hated above all else was not being given all the information. Thunder dangled a forbidden fruit in front of him, close enough to graze, but too far to grab. The talk of the allusive "them" only proved to confuse him further. How did Thunder expect to help him? More information would be a good start.

Could he be talking about the Unhallowed? Did Thunder mean to warn him of a possible attack? This seemed like valuable information, considering it was the most likely threat to Dasos.

The questions died on his lips when Thunder brought his hand up. His eyes were playing tricks on him because he swore Thunder's hand glowed. More frighteningly, he brought his hand closer to Finian's arm and the yellowish, blue glow only intensified.

"This might hurt."

Without further warning, Thunder gripped his forearm and Finian's entire body ignited. This was more than a brief touch to a scalding hot pot; that pain was abrupt but fleeting. Finian felt this burn in his bones. Thunder planned to kill him.

If he died in his dream, would he wake up? Or would Lilith find him unmoving and cold to the touch?

Whatever his fate, he hoped it came to fruition soon because the pain shooting through his arm made him want to beg for death--anything to stop the burning.

As quickly as it came on, the pain suddenly eased and Thunder's grip went lax, before dropping his arm altogether. Finian expected charred skin, if there was even an arm left, but where Thunder gripped him, his skin showed no sign of the inexplicable pain he had just endured.

"What the fucking hells?" Finian roared.

"I've branded you." He said, as if that explained everything. "You'll see my mark show up in a few days and when it does, you will need me more than ever. You'll be able to do things you've only dreamed about. Do not fear these changes. The more you reject what's to come, the less control you'll have."

"Gods, Thunder! Stop talking in riddles for one damn moment and tell me what the fuck just happened? What did you do to me?"

Finian wanted to grab him and force Thunder to look at him, but the man appeared content to stare past him. Thunder stared into the forest behind them, like he had spotted an unknown enemy and was unsure when they would strike. The longer he stared at Thunder, Finian noticed the image of the man started to distort and lose shape. It took another moment for him to realize that the entire world around them began to slowly lose focus.

"Alas, we are out of time, my boy. Death is coming to Dasos. Be ready and remember, do not fight it."

"Fight what, you asshole!?"

The sound of his voice echoed around him, fading swiftly. Thunder and the forest became little more than an arrangement of blurry colors. Soon, everything went dark.

Finian awoke with a gasp.

CHAPTER SEVEN

THE AFTER

A NEW DAY BROUGHT darkened clouds, looming above the village like a grim warning. The scent of rain hung heavy in the air, making the already gloomy day send a sense of foreboding through the town. The damp earth made it impossible for Lilith to move approximately three feet before her shoes were no longer visible underneath the mud.

Even so, she trudged on.

It had taken some convincing to disengage herself from Finian, mostly on her part, but the prospect of meeting with Adolphi and shadowing him for the day provided enough motivation she needed to rise before the sun. Getting dressed in the dark without the flicker of candlelight had been challenging, but she managed.

Finian woke up abruptly, scaring her while she dressed. She wondered if he had another nightmare, but upon bringing that up, Finian shook his head and dismissed it for his over imagination. His eyes held a haunted look to them, hinting he wasn't being entirely truthful. If he wanted to talk to her about it, he would in his own time; she wouldn't force him. She also really had to leave. Being late on her very first day would be a mark against her.

Before she walked out of her room, a warm hand reached out and wrapped itself around her wrist, pulling her back towards the bed.

"I'm going to be late." She chastised.

Damn him if he didn't smirk and shrug his shoulders. "You can spare a minute."

"Adolphi-"

"Please Lil, don't say another man's name when I have you in bed." He said, which earned him a smack on the arm. "Sorry." Though his voice sounded anything but sorry.

"You are an ass, Taren, you know that, right?"

"You never let me forget it." Finian said and pulled her close. Whatever weird dream he experienced, Finian quickly pushed aside, and forgot momentarily. When he spoke again, his soft lips brushed against hers in a whisper of a kiss. "Tonight, you'll give me your answer?" He hoped, his voice turning gruff.

Her answer about marriage.

Finian still looked shy, but hopeful. He was crazy if he believed she would say anything other than yes. She leaned down and pressed her lips to his, kissing him gently, letting her lips linger before pulling away. "Tonight, Fin, our lives will change." She smiled in a way of answering.

Leaving without giving him an answer wasn't ideal, but she wanted to make sure their passionate night didn't cloud her judgment. It also was only fitting she gave him her answer where they fell in love for the first time.

Clearly satisfied with her response, Finian rested back against the mattress. "I love you. Don't scare the men."

"No promises." Lilith grinned wickedly before feeling her way out of the door.

Which was how she found herself in front of the stables, just where Adolphi mentioned meeting. The Warrior Commander had yet to arrive but considering most of Dasos still slept, snuggled up in their beds. His arrival would be easy to hear when he finally approached.

The village itself appeared to sleep as well. Dasos was small, but enough residents occupied the village that the cacophony of voices and commotion could be heard throughout the day. A dozen children or so played in the streets or kicked an old rag in the grassy opening. Other voices included those of the village's merchants, bartering their supply away, or the animals roaming the terrain of their enclosures.

Sometimes though, the streets filled with wailing, the sound of pure heartbreak and pain. Lilith remembered those the most since they were forever etched into her memories. A haunting reminder of the inevitability of their own Unhallowing.

While most people attempted to do everything within their capabilities to ignore or deny the sickness, she found herself drawn to it. Perhaps that constituted her as peculiar, but she could not help the grotesque infatuation with the process. Finian's story from yesterday served to remind her she still had a lot to learn about the Unhallowed.

She hoped by joining the Warriors, she'd be privy to more secrets. After all, she could not fight against something about which she had no information. A warrior's true strength lies within the knowledge of one's opponent.

"Ah Serah, you made it." Warrior Adolphi said, coming out of the mist. His insistent need to use her last name once bothered her, but over time, it felt more like acceptance than a formality. He must have been on duty last night, judging by the dark circles under his eyes and his slouching frame, she suspected he was pulling a double shift to train her.

"Was there any doubt?"

"Your mother mentioned Finian stayed the night. I'm surprised you had enough energy to get out of bed."

Gritting her teeth, she shot the lead Warrior with a piercing glare. She made a note to verbally kick Idina's ass for letting her new commander know of her nightly activities. His knowing smirk set her blood boiling.

"Will you please tell me what you'll have me do today?" Lilith asked curtly, detouring the conversation away from - *that* topic.

Adolphi thought about teasing her more but thought better of it. What was it with Dasonian men and the insistent need to patronize? Instead, he tilted his chin, gaze fluttering past her as he gestured to a familiar house. "Before I allow you on patrols and defense, you need to look a familiar face in the eye and kill them."

If Adolphi expected her to flinch or recoil, she did not give him the satisfaction. Of course that would be a part of her job, she was not naïve to think she would never be placed in a situation where she would have to terminate a friend or family member.

Or a lover.

"Have you Silenced someone close to you?" She asked, the words pouring from her mouth before she could think better of them. It occurred to her that she never thought of the Warrior as having a family. For as long as she had known him, Adolphi lived a solitary life and only ever spent any of his free time with Idina.

A dark shadow passed the warrior's eyes briefly, reliving a traumatic experience she possessed no knowledge of. The silence continued to stretch out between them, and she began to wonder if she broke Adolphi by dredging up memories that were better off buried. "I'm sorry, I shouldn't ha-"

"Yes."

"What?"

"You asked if I have ever silenced anyone I was close to...and the answer is yes. A long time ago. I was barely any older than you and I had not yet migrated to Dasos. I lived at a similar camp, though it was smaller and did not operate nearly as efficiently as Dasos." Adolphi said softly.

Lilith was getting an opportunity few others were given, but she didn't understand why he wanted to divulge personal information to her. The warrior was extremely private and gave little of his past away. She supposed Idina had an inkling of his past, but she never shared that knowledge with her adopted daughter. Lilith should stop him from saying more and spare him from reliving the past, but her curiosity won out.

"As we so often do here in Dasos, I married young." He continued, offering up a small piece of himself with one sentence. She took it as an olive branch. "Her name was Theodora. We were married for a total of two years before she became pregnant with our first child. We were ecstatic because we tried for so long, even though I was hesitant about children. I thought it might be selfish to bring a child into a world where it could only end in sorrow.

"She did not have an easy pregnancy and was bedridden the entire time. I'm ashamed to admit, but I begged her to end the pregnancy, and she vehemently refused. I could not stand to watch her die.

"Then a month before she was expected to give birth...the disease struck. I think she felt it coming because the moment I lost her to the Unhallowing, before she was no longer my Theodora, she looked at me one last time. It was full of love and fear, though I don't think the fear was for her. I think she understood what I would have to do, and she blamed herself, even in death.

"I knew the moment she lost herself. Her eyes...for as long as I live, I'll never forget the malice and loathing I saw in her expression. She said something to me in a voice I didn't recognize. I reached for my knife, but I wasn't fast enough. She plunged the blade into her belly repeatedly, killing the child she loved so fiercely.

"Something in me snapped. I grabbed the knife before she could stab her stomach again and slit her throat. I Silenced her."

When Adolphi finished his story, neither of them spoke. Lilith slowly processed everything he shared, trying to wrap her mind around his experience and how he still faced this threat every day without reliving that horrible moment.

"Adolphi, I'm sorry. I can't-"

"Don't," Adolphi cut her off, shaking his head. "I didn't tell you to gain your sympathy or pity. You need to be aware of the reality. You claim you want to be a warrior of Dasos and I'm prepared to take you on, but you must be able to look a familiar face in the eyes and silence them. Are you willing to do that?"

Adolphi believed those who sought out a position as one of his Warriors needed to hear about the reality of what they were up against. He could not spend his time training a Warrior, only for them to quit a month later because they couldn't handle the impossible situations that came with the territory. No, it was best to be proactive now.

Was she ready? Was she capable of taking a life even for the sake of peace? What if that life belonged to Finian or Idina? Would she have enough strength to plunge the dagger into their hearts to free them from the curse?

She shuddered at the thought, not wanting to face that reality. Maybe that made her weak, but she liked to think it made her human.

"So, we are going to see an Unhallowed?" She asked, wondering where they kept a sick person without endangering the community.

"We are not certain, but the possibility is likely. Idina was called upon late last night by one of your neighbors. Their daughter has fallen deathly ill, a sign the process might soon begin. Her name is Kei. Do you know of her?"

A sudden pang of sorrow overcame her. Sweet Kei. One of her first friends at Dasos. Her family owned the farm near her home, and she often accompanied Lilith on their morning chores. They spoke about their dreams and how they envisioned the rest of their lives would be. Now Kei's life stood on a precipice.

"I know her, yeah." She said faintly.

Adolphi looked apologetic. He might not know the girl personally, but he knew the hardships that followed when a life was taken too soon. "Then this will be challenging for you. I cannot prepare you for what you are about to see or how the family reacts. At any point if this gets to be too much, you say the word and I will get you out of there. You are not oath bound to the warriors yet. You will not be viewed as a coward for being unable to handle unimaginable hells."

"Great pep talk, sir." She murmured under her breath, nervously tucking her hair behind her ear. Despite her new-found rising anxiety, she was determined to see this through to the end. If not for her, then for Kei, who had been nothing but sweet to her over the last few years. She deserved peace and familiar faces around her during her last moments.

"Thank you, sir, I understand the difficulties, but I will not turn my back on a friend."

"You say that now, but-"

"And I will continue to say it." Lilith interrupted him. "I am ready to bear witness."

Chapter Eight

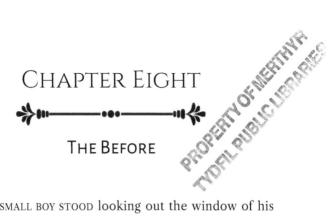

The Before

T HE SMALL BOY STOOD looking out the window of his tower. He propped himself up on the tip of his toes to see over the sill. Evening was the only time mitera Chloe allowed him to stare out at the men in armor as they fought and sharpened their swords. In fact, it was one of the few times he saw fresh faces. His circle was small, but mitera Chloe often reminded him that it was for his own safety.

Apparently, safety meant being confined to this tower in the giant castle. It never made sense to him why he couldn't leave this room and go explore. No one forbade the other children from playing outside, coming and going as they pleased. He begged mitera Chloe to allow him just five minutes to run around and play with the other kids. He swore repeatedly he'd come back inside and never ask for anything ever again.

He always got the same answer. "It is not safe for you out there, my little thunder. Here you are safe. Here we will always be together. Do you understand, Zeus?"

He didn't understand, not fully. Not when other children were allowed to wander the castle grounds. Weren't they in danger too or was the danger specific to him? He could not have angered anyone; he hadn't had the opportunity to!

Well, there was one person who did not like him. Lord Kotas. This was perfectly fine with Zeus because he did not feel overly fond of the man either. He was rude and fat, which did not seem like a good combination. His stuffed bunny was fat, but his bunny had never yelled at him like

Lord Kotas did every time he visited. He yelled at his mitera Chloe and called her horrible names he did not understand. It always made him cry, which served to make Lord Kotas angry and yell at him all over again.

Zeus often thought about taking one of the sewing needles mitera Chloe used to fix holes in his chiton and shoving it into his belly, so he exploded. He once told this to mitera Chloe, and she laughed softly before scolding him. She wasn't truly mad at him though, not if she thought his idea was funny. Still, she banned him from touching her needles, putting an abrupt end to his evil plan.

"What are they doing today, Zeus?" Chloe asked, opening the clay oven to allow their dinner to start cooling. Unable to get any meat for the soup, Chloe made sure she added all his favorite vegetables and let him pick through their small stash of spices. Even if it tasted funny, Chloe said they would love it regardless because they made it together.

"Today they are practicing with shields, and they are so big, mitera! And-"

"Mitera Chloe, sweet Zeus." Chloe swiftly corrected him, a new hardness to her voice. "Do you remember why you must call me by such a formal name?"

Zeus did, but he still thought it was dumb. "Because my real mitera died giving birth to me and I need to show her respect." He said flatly, reciting the line from memory. "But I don't care about her, you are my mitera and only you!"

"Zeus!" The sound of her voice made him jump and his eyes widened in surprise. He bit his lip, feeling the tears begin to pool. Mitera Chloe never yelled at him like that before, only Lord Kotas. He flinched away, wondering if she would strike him like Lord Kotas had done a handful of times.

The steam in Chloe slowly dissipated when she noticed the change in Zeus's demeanor. She didn't mean to scare the boy, and she hadn't planned on snapping at him. Rhea was a sensitive subject to her. She hated that she was the only one who loved her so fiercely when others rarely thought of the former Queen.

"Come here, my little thunder." Chloe said soothingly and patted her lap. Hesitantly, Zeus pulled himself away from the window and moved towards her. He crawled up into her lap and accepted her warm embrace.

"I am sorry, my sweet boy. Your mother-your real mother-meant so much to me. She loved you more than anything in this world, and she wanted me to remind you every day she is looking after you. You may not know her, but I did and out of respect, it is necessary for you to refer to me in such a formal way." Her features softened more, then she tapped him lightly on the nose. Zeus giggled. "That does not mean I do not love you. I will always be your mitera in this world and your closest family in the next."

"Yes, mitera Chloe." Zeus sniffled and nestled his chubby face against her bosom. His adolescent mind prevented him from understanding her intense love for a person who died. Dead was dead. He did not think you needed to keep promises to the dead, but he didn't mention that. He did not want her to use the mean voice again.

"Tell me about the warriors again. What were they doing?" She asked soothingly, comforting Zeus like a pair of warm arms around him. Only his mitera Chloe made him feel safe against mean people like Lord Kotas.

"They had huge shields out, as big as me. And they were hitting each other with their swords but their shields protected them. But some got hit and fell down. I bet that hurt horribly."

"I imagine it would, little one. Luckily, they have their own miteras to take care of them."

That caused Zeus to giggle as he thought of one of those giant men sitting in the laps of their tiny miteras. "That's silly. Miteras don't take care of big people."

"Why not?"

"Well...because...they are big!" He sputtered. "They can take care of themselves. Right?"

It was Chloe's turn to laugh. "In my experience, even big men always need their mother's touch. If not them, their wives. One day you'll have a pretty little wife. Won't that be nice?" She asked.

"Ew!" Zeus made a face. He would rather eat bugs off the cold stone floor than ever marry a girl. Not that he met any, but he had seen some from his window. They wore hideous dresses and played with dolls. He preferred his small tower; at least he had a few toys he'd actually want to play with up here.

"You won't always feel this way. In fact, one day-"

A hard pounding on the door made both jump. "Who is that?" Zeus whispered as his mitera Chloe gently pushed him out of her lap.

"Zeus, stay behind me and don't say a word unless I tell you too." Chloe hadn't expected a visitor either. Lord Kotas shouldn't be scheduled to come for another week. Like clockwork, Kotas checked in with them at the first of the month, every month, without fail. Zeus had memorized his schedule too and dreaded the days Lord Kotas visited. It was never pleasant, and he always ate all the food.

"By the order of the king, open up this instant!" A voice bellowed, making Zeus immediately think about the warriors outside. Did they come here for him? Had they caught him watching their practices and now want to take him away?

Chloe crossed the room in a few short strides and fumbled with the door. Her body shook, making this mundane task harder. Not a moment too late, the door swung open just as the guards prepared to enter by force. She recognized the guard as Malik, captain of the king's guard which meant...

"Your Majesty." Chloe bowed low, wondering if anyone else heard her pounding heart. King Cronus stood before her in a lavishly colored chiton and a midnight black cloak. He looked windswept, as if he had just arrived by horse. Had the King been away, and she not known? Usually, Chloe excelled at tracking the King's whereabouts, but she heard very little from her friends in the palace kitchen.

"Lady Chloe, apologies for our poor timing, but this simply could not wait." Cronus said, in a tone that suggested he was not in the least bit sorry. His sharp features turned to Malik. "Wait outside the door. No one comes in."

Malik nodded, bowing his head as a sign of utmost respect before barking orders at his men. Soon, just the three of them stood inside the small tower. With three people inside, their small home felt suffocating and much more like a lion's den.

Cronus took in the room and made a face of disgust. "You've certainly fallen far in this world, Chloe. Once you would not have even considered living in such squalor."

Chloe's cheek flushed with both shame and rage. "If I recall correctly, you decided this old tower was most suitable for raising your heir and despite my many pleas, I have yet been given better housing."

Raising his...heir? What did that mean? Zeus knew the adults were talking about something really important, but he didn't understand what that was. He didn't think he should hear any of this. Mitera Chloe was angry, and the man did not look happy either.

"Your requests have been noted. However, more pressing issues forced me to put it aside until now. I'm here to discuss the boy."

Both of their attention soon turned to the boy in the corner. Zeus wished he had magical powers to turn himself invisible, wishing to be far away from the scary newcomer in the room. He did not like how the man glared at him, his dark eyes bore into Zeus, inspecting him like a pig for a slaughter.

For Cronus, looking at the boy felt like looking at a younger version of Rhea. The ache had not completely gone away, even after five years. He doubted the sorrow would ever leave him. Zeus had his mother's dark hair and kind eyes. His chubby face held no similarities to Cronus, except the nose that was slightly too large for his small face.

The longer he stared at Zeus, the more he thought of all he lost and the woman who should be standing in front of him. Instead, her life ended far too suddenly to save a child she did not know.

"Can he speak?" The King barked, breaking the tense silence of the room.

"He can. He's not some animal-"

"I want the boy to speak for himself." Cronus snapped. "I want him to tell me his name".

Zeus glanced over at mitera Chloe. She still seemed scared, but her expression changed to a smile when their eyes met. It was enough to give him the courage to speak to the new stranger. "My name is Zeus."

"What age are you?"

Zeus held up five tiny fingers. "Five."

"Is that it? You came here to ask him for his name and age, two things you already know?" Chloe grew impatient. If Cronus thought she would be okay with his unexpected visit and vague questions, he clearly underestimated her. It was a mistake he made too often.

"Watch your tone, Chloe. I am still your King, despite your personal feelings about me. The only reason you are allowed to stay on castle grounds is because my wife loved you. You defy your King every day by loving this murderer."

Cronus then pointed at him. Zeus's eyes went wide. He wasn't a murderer! He had not been allowed to leave the tower and received no visitors other than Lord Kotas. More so than that, he was a child with the strength of a mere boy. The tears came on suddenly and Zeus could not stop them from falling freely.

"That's quite enough." Chloe said sharply and moved in front of Zeus, standing between the two. Scared, he grabbed mitera Chloe's leg and hid behind her, hiding his face in the fabrics of her simple chiton. "Are you going to tell us why you are here after all these years?"

Cronus's eyes narrowed, and he contemplated slapping the discourteous woman. No one got under his skin quite like his late wife's former Lady-in-Waiting. She knew just what to say to get a reaction out of him. Chloe was lucky that he arrived in a good mood this evening. Cronus finally received a lead on his current conquest, Ambrosia -- the long-forgotten elixir rumored to have extraordinary abilities.

Immortality and power.

Now his time was being pulled in other directions, most specifically toward King Vulcan and his increasingly malicious demands of an alliance. It was only a matter of time before the King of Caister officially declared Dasos an enemy. Typically, Cronus would not have blinked twice since his forces were far greater in numbers and strength than most of the other kingdoms. Except Caister was as sizable as Dasos with more allies. All smaller kingdoms, but their numbers combined rivaled those of Dasos.

Which is why, after five long years, Cronus had come to collect the one thing that could keep the peace for a while longer. Regardless of what happened to Zeus, Cronus knew he would win the favor of other kingdoms when he finally accepted a marriage between Vulcan's granddaughter and Zeus. If Vulcan decided he didn't like the terms and killed Zeus, well...that would also work in his favor.

"I accept your requests for more accommodating housing and in the morning, you will be moved to the west wing. It's under construction, but I'm sure you both can make do. It's bigger than-" Cronus looked around the small, damp tower, "here."

"Moreover, it is time for the boy to live up to his usefulness. I do not need to remind you why he is permitted to remain breathing, do I? Lord Kotas will oversee his education from here on out. He will also receive an education in swordsmanship, though that one is contingent upon his behavior and performances. I need Zeus to play the role of a prince."

"He *is* a prince." Chloe seethed. "What of Hades and Poseidon? You claim that Zeus is not your son, therefore not an heir to the Dasos throne, why not arrange a marriage with one of them?"

Chloe understood why even as she asked. She had known since the day Zeus was born. Zeus would be used as a pawn for both Cronus and Gaia. Cronus would never jeopardize the safety of his beloved sons, especially when he strove for absolute power.

"You should at least let him interact with his brothers, and train alongside them." Chloe relented, wanting to give her boy a small gift. "If he is to be perceived as your beloved prince, he needs to be seen by your people. He also needs to be able to interact with kids his own age to get accustomed to the court's ways. You cannot send him into the lion's den without a blade."

"You will not tell me what I can and cannot do with the boy." He snarled. "His fate will be what I see fit."

"And you aren't seeing past your nose! You have a third son that you are willing to sacrifice so easily when instead you should be using him as your own personal weapon." Even as she said the words, Chloe felt traitorous. She hated talking about Zeus as if his life did not matter, writing him off as nothing more than an object, but this was the only way she could keep him safe. If Cronus found him useful, then his chances of survival were higher.

The King seemed to be mulling over her words, so Chloe continued. "Train him with his brothers. Train him to be an assassin and teach him the ways of the court. Let people see him and trust him. He could learn to be your spy and your weapon. Your enemies would never see him coming."

Zeus glanced up at mitera Chloe, eyes wide with a mixture of fear and confusion. Why did she talk about him like he wasn't in the room? He did not want to be a spy or a weapon, he just wanted friends and a family.

"My, my, my, Chloe." The King, his smile turning sinister as he studied the woman. Most women begged him to look at them the way he was looking at her, but all Chloe felt was disgust.

"You would have made a great confidant or mistress. Shame you wanted to be the nanny. We will play the game your way for now, but my words still hold true. Lord Kotas will see to it that he is educated, and I'll allow him to train alongside my sons, if nothing else, I may enjoy seeing Hades break his nose. He's gotten quite good at that."

"But, my sweet Chloe," Cronus continued, the haughty smile replaced with one of a vicious King. "If Zeus should perform unsatisfactorily or embarrass me in any way, he will not be the only one punished for his transgressions."

With that vague threat, the king turned and took his leave. Before Malik shut the door behind him, the king called one more thing over his shoulder, "The guards will fetch you tomorrow. You have tonight to prepare the boy. His training will start at sunrise."

The door shut with a grim finality, leaving the two of them in a darkened room. Zeus's cries stopped the moment the door shut, finding himself too confused from the exchange to be sad. The man said a lot of things, but only one thing stuck out. He had brothers.

"Mitera Chloe, what is going to happen to me?" he asked, his voice small and scared. Chloe frowned. He was only a boy and already he had to deal with the harsh world he was born into. Perhaps it would have been kinder if he had died alongside his mother.

She winced at such a dark thought. Of course that would not be better. Dead was final, but alive, Zeus had a chance to decide his own fate. It was becoming dismal and more impossible by the day, but she had to have hope. If not for hope, life would be all consuming and suffocating.

Taking his hand, she guided her boy back to the spot they occupied moments ago, before Cronus waltzed in and shattered their fragile bubble. Zeus climbed back into her lap, and she held him like a babe, clutching him close to her bosom.

"There are things I have not told you yet, Zeus. Things I wanted to protect you from, but I'm afraid that time is ending. My mother always used to tell me that knowledge is our greatest power and with it we are at our strongest. To be without is to be ignorant and blind to the world around us.

"I have made you ignorant for so long and that is my deepest regret. That ends tonight. You are going to need to be both strong and smart from this day on. Do you understand, my love?"

He wanted to, but Zeus was unsure if he did. Or perhaps he was too frightened to understand. Still, he nodded. Chloe let out a deep sigh, ready to expel the heavy burden holding her down for the last five years.

"Your name is Zeus of House Gaia and House Cronus, first of your name, prince of Dasos, brother of Hades and Poseidon...and you were never supposed to be born."

Then, Chloe broke her boy's heart by telling him his tragic story of being the unwanted son. At the end of the night, they wept until sleep claimed them both.

True to his father's word, the next morning Zeus and Chloe woke up to a visit from Malik, Captain of the King's Royal Guard. Malik looked much the same as he did the previous night, though the circles under his eyes were slightly more pronounced. He no longer looked like a deadly assassin. Malik just looked...tired.

"I'm here to escort you and...*Zeus*." He said his name as if it were a vile world, never meant to be spoken. Zeus sank back deeper into the folds of mitera Chloe's simple dress, wishing he could be as brave as the men who carried the swords.

"I'm here to escort you and Zeus to the west wing of the castle. King Cronus apologizes for his delayed response regarding your housing and expresses his sorrow for your new chambers that are still under construction."

"I'm sure he is quite sorrowful and apologetic." Chloe sneered, her voice dripping with contempt and anger. "His pretty words do not work on me, Malik. You, of all people, should know by now."

For a moment, the two stared at each other, both too stubborn to back down. The tension between Chloe and Malik made Zeus wonder if they had this argument before, though he could not imagine when his mitera Chloe would have ever spoken to the guard.

"Chloe, please just give this up. You can walk away from this. The King will restore your status and you can live like you once lived. Is marrying me truly worse than your life now?" Malik asked, his gaze unwavering.

Marriage? Give up? Zeus heard the words but could not make sense of them. Mitera Chloe never mentioned marriage; she promised it would only ever be the two of them. Two was safe, two was what he knew. Now Malik was proposing to insert himself into their lives and to steal mitera Chloe away?

"You once asked me why I don't believe in a man's love. Do you remember?" Chloe inquired. "I answered that men only love their ambitions. I still believe that to be true, but I also believe if a man loved me, genuinely loved me, he would never ask me to abandon my promises and responsibilities. He wouldn't see my life as a sequence of failures or think I'm too stubborn for my own good. He would meet me where I am and not where he wants me to be."

"Chloe-"

"That's enough." Chloe held up her hand, silencing him. From the looks of it, Malik had not been one to experience rejection before. Women wanted him, not only for his physical attractiveness, but his high rank in court. He could provide them with the life women dreamed about. Chloe had never been one of those women and Malik was unable to wrap his mind around that. He was a good man, even a great one depending on who was asked, but Chloe never saw that. The woman's sheer stubbornness fueled a rage within him.

"I believe you are going to escort Zeus and I to our new chambers now, isn't that correct?" Chloe wondered, once the silence went on long enough.

With one last scornful look at Zeus, Malik inclined his head, motioning for them to follow him. Chloe grabbed the small sack of clothes and Zeus picked up his own, along with a handful of toys before leaving the tower behind, hopefully forever.

Zeus had never been allowed to see much of the palace. A few times, mitera Chloe took him to another room to meet with Lord Kotas, but they never walked far. This time, Malik escorted them to the opposite side of the castle and though Zeus was a little frightened, his childish curiosity and wonderment triumphed.

The first thing he noticed were the guards, all donning the same green and gray uniforms of House Cronus. The crest consisted of two swords engulfed in the flames that forged them, embossed on their left breast. Each guard they passed stared at Zeus, their expressions ranging from curiosity, distrust, and mild amusement. He moved faster, making sure to never stray too far from Malik and Chloe.

The interior of the castle was beautifully decorated, which surprised Zeus because he couldn't picture Cronus discussing furniture and art. The walls were decorated with exquisite tapestries full of colors Zeus had no name for. Each piece of furniture, no matter how small, had been crafted perfectly to appear as an extension of the castle. Flowers pulled the room together, filling every available surface, and smelling of springtime and sunshine. A rarity for this time of year.

As Zeus began to wonder about how much longer they would have to walk, Malik stopped abruptly. "The west wing." He announced.

The west wing left much to be desired. Cronus did not lie when he said it was under construction. The corridor was dark and damp. The tapestries, furniture, and flowers that decorated much of the castle, did not extend to this wing. There were very few windows, giving off an ominous feeling of confinement.

Malik opened the door to their new room and Zeus half expected to find shackles and a dead body, but inside stood a small table, clearly worn away by time, with two uphol-stered chairs. There was no oven or anything resembling a kitchen area, only a bed that may have once belonged to a king or queen.

"This is your room, Chloe. The boy will have the adjoin-ing room to the left. Cronus felt the need for privacy." Malik explained.

"Whatever for?" Chloe feigned confusion, putting her bag down on the new bed.

"He did not specify, but you should thank him for his generosity nonetheless." Malik replied before he walked to-wards the other door, nearly hidden by the table. He opened it and stepped aside for Zeus to look in. The room was significantly smaller than Chloe's room, but in comparison to the room back in the tower, it was massive. It even had a real bed and not the straw cot that Chloe made for him. It was a kind gesture on her part, but the bed scratched him in his sleep.

"You will have meals brought to you three times a day and taken away once you are finished. Once a week, King Cronus will send in a maid, along with a trusted guard, to clean your chambers and see to the boy's clothing. He has granted permission for you to walk the courtyards while Zeus attends his lessons with the King's rightful twin heirs and to report back as soon as his last lesson ends for the day. Tardiness will not be tolerated and will be dealt with as the King sees fit. Lastly, if anyone asks, you are the boy's nanny. Zeus is a prince in name only and when around others, you will need to address him as such. What you call one another behind locked doors is entirely up to you. Do you understand your direct orders?" Malik finished his spiel, his cold gaze focused on Chloe, not once acknowledging Zeus.

For once, Chloe held her tongue. To argue would be as successful as yelling at a locked door to open. "We understand. You have done your duty and may leave us for the night." She dismissed him without further thought. Except Malik did not leave right away. He lingered, looking as if he wanted to say more. Chloe's abrupt dismissal detoured him in the end and Malik finally took his leave, leaving the two of them alone at last.

"So," Mitera Chloe turned towards Zeus, her lips upturned in a mischievous grin. "Do you think this room has any secret passages?"

Zeus returned the mischievous smile and the two promptly gallivanted through their rooms, looking for secret passageways that did not exist and created made up stories about thieves, heroes, and treasure. They spoke occasionally about Zeus's excitement for lessons and meeting his older brothers, while Chloe listened, nodding appropriately.

Every few minutes her eyes would wander towards the door with a worried expression.

The very next day Zeus started his regal training. At five years old, Zeus did not understand the deep resentment his father had for him. The only reason Cronus allowed him to study, and train was to turn Zeus into a pawn; a human weapon he could use and sacrifice on a whim.

Zeus decided to act the part of a dutiful son -- once mitera Chloe explained what dutiful meant, of course. He went to all his classes earlier than expected of him. He listened to his tutors and memorized the history and court lessons, finding himself deeply interested in the rich politics of court.

Swordsmanship was the only area in which he was lacking, but that was partially to do with his age and size. He was much smaller than his brothers and five years younger. They had been trained with a sword since they had the strength to pick one up and neither went easy on him. In fact, Hades and Poseidon thought an appropriate greeting to their brother was a game of war.

"We are brave Dasonian warriors." Hades explained during their first practice together, eyes glinting with amusement. He exchanged knowing glances with Poseidon. "And you are our enemy to the south. Winner gets all the glory and bragging rights."

As far as prizes went, Zeus thought this one seriously lacked. What was he to do with glory? And to whom would he brag to? Still, he wanted to impress his brothers and desperately wanted them to like him. So, he agreed to their silly game.

That had been a mistake.

Before he realized the game had begun, his brothers closed in. Hades swept his wooden sword underneath his legs, causing Zeus to lose his balance and stumble backwards. Poseidon brought his sword down for the killing blow, hitting his stomach at full force and sending him sprawling to the ground.

The tears came before he could stop them. He felt pain before, but nothing compared to this. Lord Kotas's slaps hurt, but they were little more than a sting. The practice sword left him gasping in pain. Even breathing hurt. Zeus tried to stop the sobs from coming, but they erupted from his shuddering body despite his attempts.

"We win." Poseidon smiled and made no attempt to help his younger brother off the ground. "Next time we won't go easy on you."

From that day, Zeus vowed to himself he would never give his brothers the satisfaction of seeing him cry again. No matter how many times they bruised his ribs, broke his nose, or humiliated him, Zeus would stay true to his word. If he couldn't gain his brother's love, then he would strive for their respect.

CHAPTER NINE

THE AFTER

K EI HAD BEEN MANY things to Lilith over the past two years in Dasos: a familiar friendly face, a chore partner in the stables, and a constant informant of all the latest gossip in Dasos. If Lilith claimed any friends, Kei made the top of the short list. Her eager and excited demeanor never wavered, even on the grimmest of days. Her very personality made her beautiful and easily approachable.

The haggard and trembling figure on the ground was not the Kei she remembered, however. No, the girl on the ground was breathing hard and rocking back and forth. Her eyes were alert, almost beady, as she took in the commotion all around her.

Mrs. Edman stroked her daughter's hair, but Kei seemed agitated by her touch. Each stroke of her hair, a greasy, disarray mess, made her flinch. Mrs. Edman didn't care; she was too busy weeping over a daughter that wasn't yet dead.

This seemed crueler than dying. At least dying made sense. What was happening to Kei was inhuman and unnatural. It served to remind every person in the small cottage what fate waited for them at the end of their journey. No one escaped the cursed unscathed.

The Edman's cottage felt cramped with so many bodies in a small space, but they couldn't seem to get close enough to their daughter. Their only daughter. Idina waited patiently for Mrs. Edman to stop crying into her daughter's shoulder before she went back to tending to Kei. Although Idina was well versed in many areas of medicine and healing, she was powerless to do anything during the Unhallowing process. She couldn't heal Kei, but she could comfort a grieving family.

Adolphi cleared his throat and the attention of everyone in the room shifted to the two of them. Lilith caught her mother's eyes first. She offered her daughter a sad smile, the only comfort she could give to her over a dying friend. Lilith returned it, though the smile appeared forced and hollow.

Lilith was surprised to spot Kei's attention on her. Their eyes met, and she couldn't help but notice how vacant her friend's stare seemed. However, for her friend, Lilith held her stare hoping their wordless communication conveyed everything she couldn't say.

I'm here. I won't leave you. You will be remembered.

"Lilith." Mr. Edman untangled himself from his daughter. He was an older man, but the grief of losing his only child aged him ten years. He reached out and pulled her into a tight embrace. Stunned by his sudden touch, Lilith tensed before putting her arms back around him. Like his wife and daughter, Mr. Edman was skin and bones. She was afraid to squeeze him too hard out of fear of breaking him.

"Thank you for coming. Kei would want you to be here." The man said, voice cracking as he spoke of her. "She talked about you often. You were one of her dearest friends."

"I'm not dead yet, father."

The tension in the room was palpable as a wave of silence washed over everyone. The world paused as they all turned toward the voice. Kei still leaned against the wall, though the act of keeping herself up right took most of her energy.

Kei's eyes swept the room, taking in everyone's varied expressions of grief, until her eyes landed back on Lilith. They were glossy and tinged with red, Lilith suspected from crying.

Or maybe it was part of the Unhallowing process, Lilith thought in horror.

For a moment, no one spoke. Maybe, like Lilith, they simply did not know what to say. Though it seemed wrong not to say anything to Kei, especially since her time was fleeting, but what did one say to a dying friend? "All will be okay," seemed wildly inappropriate because everything was most definitely not going to be okay.

Kei's life was ending.

"Stop staring at me like that." Kei spoke, interrupting her thoughts. Lilith had the decency to look embarrassed at having been caught gawking at Kei.

"I'm sorry, Kei. I'm so sorry for-"

"For what? For staring? Or for witnessing my death? Why are you even here?" Kei spat, with a ferocity she had never used before. The Kei she befriended was sweet, sincere, and even-tempered. In fact, Lilith didn't think she ever heard the girl snap or raise her voice at anyone.

"Darling, Lilith is here to-" Mrs. Edman tried to console her daughter, but Kei lashed out again.

"I know why she is here! Why all of you are here! You've been waiting for this moment ever since she arrived. I know you want to hurt me. You are the plague they warned us about, you bitch!"

"Kei!" Mrs. Edman sobbed as she reached for her daughter. An inhuman like sound left her lips as her menacing stare turned towards her mother. Mr. Edman promptly appeared behind his daughter, taking both of her arms. Kei only struggled for a minute before her wild expression went slack.

The change was gradual, but Lilith watched Kei slowly come to the realization of what she said. Her face no longer held the hatred it once did, but replaced with true, naked fear. Her eyes, now her own, filled with horror as she looked up at Lilith.

"Lilith...I'm...I'm so sorry. That wasn't me. I swear. It's happening. I know it's happening. I'm losing myself." She cried and turned to her mother whose heart broke in front of everyone's eyes. "Mother, I don't want to hurt you. Please." She begged.

Begged to be Silenced.

"Hellena, it's time." Idina's gentle voice broke apart mother and daughter, as both heads turned to face her. "Kei's slipping faster and prolonging the Silencing will only make this harder on everyone. I fear if we wait any longer, your last memories with Kei will be tainted. I don't want that for you."

"Idina, how do I leave her? How do I let my only daughter die? There must be some other way. Please, we still have a little time!" Mrs. Edman started to fling herself at Idina, but Mr. Edman stopped her. She crumpled to the ground as her body convulsed in sobs.

The hysteria coming from Mrs. Edman was not new to Idina; she saw her fair share of grieving parents begging to save their children. It never got easier to tell them, as tenderly as one could under these circumstances, that their loved ones would be taken from them. She took the brunt of their anger and venomous words. At times, she even took their blows. Once was enough for Adolphi to insist Idina take him or another warrior with her when she made house visits.

Unfortunately, she needed to make them far too often.

"This is the last kindness you can offer her. She-"

"Kindness? Letting my daughter die is a kindness?" Mrs. Edman's eyes narrowed as her anger found an outlet within Idina. Sensing this, Adolphi shifted closer to her as Mr. Edman moved to crouch down next to his wife and daughter.

"Darling, Idina is here out of kindness and love for our family. We can't blame her for the inevitable." He said in an attempt to reason with his wife, but Lilith saw the frenzied look in her eyes. Not one of an Unhallowed, but that of a mother who could no longer protect her daughter. She lashed out with the only other weapon she had; appealing to the heart of another mother.

Lilith understood, even before Mrs. Edman's gaze snapped towards her, what she'd say. "What if this was Lilith? What if your own daughter was about to be killed before your eyes, would you stand aside and let it happen?"

Idina didn't flinch at the words, her face, still gentle and full of sorrow for the Edmans, remained unchanged. She heard this before so the shock it once might have held wore off long ago.

"If we live in the 'what ifs' we would drive ourselves mad and forget to live. One day. Lilith and I will be put in this same position and if she goes before me, my world will end. We are mothers. We want to protect our children from the horrors of this world, but even we are powerless against this faceless foe." For the briefest of moments, Idina shuddered, thinking how it could have been Lilith on the floor, moments away from losing her sense of self completely.

"This is the one thing you all can control as a family." She continued softly, reaching out to take Mrs. Edman's hand. "You can let your daughter leave this world with dignity, knowing her family loves her more than anything. That will be the last thing she remembers and the last memory you get to share with Kei while she is still Kei."

"This is what I want, Mother." Kei responded to Idina's words with certainty. Despite her tears, Lilith thought this was the bravest thing she had ever seen. Kei would be facing death on her own terms, despite the fear and anxiety that comes with the unknown. "I want to remember you and Papa."

"Please Hellena. We can't let this go on much longer. Kei's ready. We have to respect that." Mr. Edman said, though he sounded like a broken man, grasping for one last minute of composure for his daughter. One last moment where they would still be a family, before one member went missing. Losing a family member was like losing an essential part of yourself. It changed the very foundation of your life.

Seeing the Edmans cling to the fleeting moments made Lilith believe every word she heard about losing someone. Kei would be the one dying tonight, but could she really call the painful existence the Edmans were now forced to endure, *living*?

"Idina will see them out, but you and I will stay." Adolphi whispered from behind Lilith.

That caught her by surprise. "Stay? Then why are they leaving?"

"No parent should witness a Silencing. Idina leads them out and prays with the grieving family."

Lilith tried to hide her scoff but was unsuccessful. "Pray? To whom? The gods damned us long ago." The ferocity in her own voice astonished even her.

Adolphi bristled next to her; Lilith clearly struck a nerve with him. "It brings comfort and for that, we should not sneer at one seeking solace in the wake of death."

She wanted to say more about the wretched gods, but it wouldn't bring any comfort to the room. If praying to nameless gods brought comfort, who was Lilith to take it away.

Idina helped Mrs. Edman up and lead her away from Kei, while her husband stared blankly at his daughter. The reality of the moment hit Mrs. Edman full force because the older woman started to wail. This was unlike anything Lilith had heard before, a sound so melancholy and tortured. The pain and devastation of the cry jerked her husband out of his own dark thoughts. "Hellena." He murmured and brought his wife into his arms and helped Idina ease them toward the door.

"My girl! I love you; we love you! Wait for us, I swear you won't be alone for long."

With that last ominous declaration from Mrs. Edman, Idina closed the door to the little hut, leaving the two of them alone with Kei.

It was better this way, thought Lilith, the Edmans did not need to experience what happened next. But...what would happen next? Of course, she knew her friend needed to be Silenced, but did Adolphi mean for her to do it? Or was he going to show her the proper way? *Was* there even a proper way? Their fates were cruel enough, Lilith did not want to continue the suffering.

Whatever was left of Kei faded swiftly. When the door shut behind the Edman's, something changed in Kei. It was as if whatever string tethering her soul into this world snapped with the resounding thud of the door. She just...sank.

There was no other way Lilith could describe what she witnessed. If it were possible to see a soul leave the body, she would have sworn she saw Kei's depart. The girl's shoulders slumped forward, and her head lolled awkwardly to the side. A soft whimpering sound slowly filled the room and Lilith assumed Kei was crying. As the sound got louder, she realized Kei wasn't crying.

She was laughing.

"This is normal. Don't put your guard down. Did you bring Peace Bringer?" Adolphi addressed her, but his eyes stayed on Kei. The girl laughed harder still, so loud Lilith had to shout over the laughter to confirm *Peace Bringer* was already in her hand. "A thorough slash across her neck will end the poor girl's suffering."

Then, as suddenly as it came, the laughing stopped, and the room was thrown into silence once again. This unsettled Lilith because the silence allowed for no clues on Kei's progression and felt...final. It *was* final, and she could not afford to think any other way. What she had to do would not be easy, no need in making it harder than it needed to be with naïve thoughts of redemption.

"*Lilith.*" Adolphi's stern voice growled.

"What are you waiting for?" Kei asked, breaking her silence. Her voice was low and teasing, finding this to be a game where she had the upper hand. When Kei looked up, Lilith saw it instantly in her eyes. No longer were they warm brown eyes; the color changed to a muted gray, almost white. It was the only clue hinting at being an Unhallowed. If that was the only indication someone made the change, then identifying one early would prove difficult, if not impossible.

"Are you afraid? Perhaps the Great Lilith has joined a game she has no right to play." Kei said and pushed her tiny body up. Adolphi shifted, unsheathing his own sword. It seemed almost comical a large man like Adolphi was wielding a weapon against a small girl like Kei.

"Lilith, you need to do it. Don't engage, end it now." Adolphi instructed, speaking to her but never taking his eyes off Kei. She was paying little mind to the warrior. Her eyes locked in on her prey, looking every bit of a predator she had become.

"The Gods are disappointed in you. You aren't what they expected. You've done nothing of importance but bed the bloody blacksmith. He's making you weak. You'll fail. You'll fail and watch everything you love die right in front of your eyes."

Lilith cocked her head to the side, taking a step forward. That only excited the creature -- she couldn't see her as Kei anymore. Her friend was dead. "The Gods are dead, just as you will be soon."

Another laugh, this one wild and high-pitched. "Dead? No, no. Not dead. Just...waiting."

"Stop this, Lilith. Enough. Silence her." Adolphi's patience was running thin, warning her to complete the deed before he was forced to intervene.

"You're weak. Worthless dirt not fit for the body you walk in." Those were the last words the creature said to her before flinging her entire body weight at Lilith. It was a sloppy, but unexpected move and Lilith went down hard with the

Unhallowed on top of her, thrashing her arms around in a frenzy, trying to reach any part of Lilith.

"Lilith!"

"No!" She shouted at Adolphi who quickly approached. "No!" This was her one opportunity to show Adolphi and herself she was capable of this gruesome task. The Unhallowed roared the moment Lilith reached for *Peace Bringer*, letting out a blood-curdling scream.

The Unhallowed attempted diving for Lilith's arm to wrestle the knife from her grasp, but Lilith expected the move. With as much force as she could muster, she plunged the knife upwards at the same time as the creature dove. The scene played out gruesomely and lacked all the dignity Kei deserved.

The knife found its mark and lodged itself into her neck, protruding out the other side. The sound of blood filling her mouth would haunt Lilith for nights. It trickled down her lips and neck, soaking the front of her tunic. Something flickered in Kei's eyes reminded Lilith so much of Kei that for a second, she thought she made a terrible mistake.

The irrational thought momentarily clouded her mind, before rationality kicked back in. She saw the change in Kei and knew she had made no mistake. Lilith now watched her friend suffocate in her own blood, the light leaving her eyes for good before her body went limp and sunk to the floor.

"Lilith are you okay?" Kei's discarded body lifted off her and Lilith gasped, filling her lungs with the air she desperately needed. Apparently, her breath sounded labored because Adolphi was on his knees beside her, looking over her body for any wounds. He trusted her enough to complete the Silencing, only jumping in now it was over.

"I'm fine. It's okay, I'm not hurt." She wasn't hurt, but her mind still reeled from what just took place. She made her first kill. It should have felt more monumental than it did. Instead, it felt...empty. She gained nothing from the kill, no satisfaction or glory from doing what was right.

Adolphi read the different emotions across her features and his tough warrior exterior softened into something more...fatherly. "She was your friend." He said gently.

"Yes."

"And you killed her."

"I did."

Adolphi paused and searched her face. She suspected he was looking for tears or regret, but he would find none of those things in her expression. The tears would come later, but not the guilt. Silencing Kei had been extremely difficult, but also necessary. Her friend did not deserve to become the monster she feared.

She knew at that moment she would do it again.

Something in Adolphi's expression changed, and he stared at the girl he had known for the past two years. He never looked down on her, but he also never looked at her like this -- respect fit for a warrior. An equal.

"What you did tonight was noble. You never forget your first kill and I'm sorry yours had to be a friend. Any doubts I had about your placement vanished. You were meant to be a warrior, Lilith. I'll speak to Idina tonight about your new assignment." He said.

Pride swelled within her chest. Praise from Adolphi was not to be taken lightly. Though she did not envy him having that conversation with her mother, no matter how much Idina claimed to be okay with this placement. Lilith knew she would worry herself sick.

"But next time you are face to face with an Unhallowed, you will not hesitate." Adolphi reprimanded, replacing the pride she felt with shame. Hadn't she told him she wouldn't waver? When at that moment, that was exactly what she did. "Hesitation means death. You were lucky this time, but luck will only get you so far."

Adolphi finally offered her his hand, Lilith, now feeling conflicted about her actions, took it and pulled herself off the floor. Her tunic was splattered with specks of blood, not enough to stain but enough to be noticeable until she could find a clean one. "What do we do with the body?"

The body in question sprawled unceremoniously on the cool rock flooring. Kei deserved a proper resting place. "Do we call her parents?

"Absolutely not." Adolphi said quickly, shaking his head. "They just lost their child and are grieving. Seeing her like this with the knife wound through the neck would send the Edmans into a manic state. No, they've said their good-byes. It's up to us to dispose of the body."

Dasos only "disposed" of bodies one way and her stomach tightened; fire.

Adolphi seemed to have read her mind, for he said, "Fire. It's the quickest and most efficient way. Some believe fire purifies the body before sending the soul into its final resting place."

Although Lilith was skeptical about souls and eternal resting places, she agreed Kei's body needed to be put to rest. It was not a necessity for the dead as much as it was a comfort for the living. Perhaps this small act of kindness would wash the blood clean from her hands.

"We take the body into the fire and make a pyre in the woods. We stand watch as their body becomes ash. I use that time to reflect and mourn-if I had known the person." Adolphi slid his arms underneath Kei's small body and picked her off the floor. Her head lolled to the side, reminding Lilith her knife was still embedded deeply into her neck. Adolphi did not hesitate to pull it out; *Peace Bringer* made a sickening wet sound when it finally released. "You'll want to clean that." He said and handed it back.

Adolphi led Lilith out of the room. Idina must have taken the Edmans back to her home because they were not in the main room of the house. They did not have to see Adolphi load her bloody body into a wagon or watch as he covered her with a deeply stained sheet. A few people walked by, slowing down as they passed the wagon. They were both saddened and fascinated by death, especially if that dead person was just a neighbor and not a beloved family member or friend.

"We need to get going. It'll be dark in a few hours, and I don't wish to cause any more of a disturbance in town."

Disturbance.

That was what Kei had amounted to. Lilith was sure Adolphi did not mean it as such, but she suddenly felt very protective of her friend. She watched the warrior ready the horse before grabbing for the reins. "Let me take her. Alone."

Adolphi turned his head towards her, refusal lingering on his tongue, but before he could get a word out, Lilith hastily continued. "There's no need for both of us to go. I have helped light fires and burn bodies before. If her family cannot be with her, then let me. I need to do this for her." *And for me*, she thought but did not voice.

It turned out she did not need to. Adolphi's expression softened. If anyone understood how mentally draining your first Silencing was, Adolphi did. Still, he looked reluctant, and Lilith could only guess that it was because of Idina. "Please. Let me do this. I know the forest. I'll be back before sundown. Right now, Idina needs you more than I do."

Her mother's name seemed to be the final push he needed because he relented with a slow nod of his head. "By nightfall, if you are a moment late, not even I can shield you from the wrath of Idina."

Despite the situation, both Warriors smiled. "Then I will make sure I am not late." She grinned and mounted the horse. Adolphi did one last check to make sure the wagon was properly hooked up and that she had enough kindling to start the fire.

"You did well today, Serah. I wish I could tell you it gets easier, but it does not. Don't lose that heart of yours. Always lead with it." Adolphi said and gave the horse one more pack. "Off you go."

And so, Lilith then left to bury her only friend.

CHAPTER TEN

THE AFTER

F INIAN STRUGGLED TO COME to terms with last night's
dream after his bizarre encounter with Thunder. His
dreams had the tendency to feel real most nights, but this
happened to be the first time he went to work with physical
pain in the exact spot Thunder touched. He easily ignored
the ache in his arm when Lilith's impending answer still
loomed over him like a dark cloud though.

He did not want to assume she would say yes to his proposal, but would it be naïve to think otherwise? They never
explicitly talked about their future; a tough subject with
the threat of the Unhallowed, but they spoke of a singular
future. A future that intertwined together and weaved love
to create a tapestry of intricate designs. Was it perfect? Not
exactly. There were tears and broken threads from years of
uncertainty and loss, but despite the imperfections, hope
still held it firmly together.

"Finian, did you hear me, son?" A loud voice echoed
around him, successfully pulling him away from thoughts
of marriage and Thunder. He looked down at the blade he
forged for the better half of the afternoon and noticed the
steel had started to cool.

The voice — his father's voice — sounded concerned.
How long did Finian stare off when he needed to be crafting
a new weapon for Dasonian Warriors? Long enough for his
father to notice.

"Are you well?" Jarin Taren asked, a large man with arms
the size of tree trunks from years of heavy labor. Many

people often remarked on the similarities between the two, but Finian could only see the differences. His dad was fair skinned while Finian had dark, chestnut skin. His father's eyes were a plain hazel color, indistinguishable amongst the sea of brown eyes, while Finian had a rich green color with specks of brown. He supposed they were both tall and shared a rounded nose, but that's where the similarities ended.

What people actually meant was Finian looked like his mother, Nehema. She shared his dark complexion, eyes, and coiled hair. She had been beautiful, a goddess in the eyes of her family, and a well-liked citizen of Dasos...until she became an Unhallowed nearly five years ago, leaving Jarin and a sixteen-year-old Finian to raise a baby. Mavis never got to know her mother. The cruel fates even robbed her of any resemblance to Nehema. Mavis was a perfect image of her father.

"Finian, are you well?" His father asked again, this time putting down his mallet. He considered his son, his face pulled taught in concern. Jarin provided comfort, always allowing his son to confide in him.

Not wanting to further worry his father, Finian offered a warm smile he hoped reassured him. "I'm fine. Just distracted."

"Ah, yes I forgot. You asked Lilith to wed you. And what of her response? Am I gaining a fierce, red-headed daughter-in-law?" Jarin joked.

"She did not give me an answer." He admitted.

His father's jovial face turned into one of sympathy, assuming she denied him. "Don't pity me yet, father. I'm irresistible," Finian smirked playfully. "Besides, she promised me an answer this evening. I don't think I have need to worry, if these last two years are any indication." Yet he still was, a small part of him wondered if Lilith wanted more than what Finian could offer. More than what Dasos could offer.

"You are doing a lot better than me when I asked your mother to marry me." His father laughed, his face went wistful with memories of his youth and his time courting Nehema." I asked your mother to marry me the day after she told me about her pregnancy. Oh, don't give me that face, I would have asked her to marry me regardless of whether she was carrying my child or not. Your mother gave me the same expression you just did, one that told me she was skeptical about whether my intentions were out of love or duty.

"I needed to convince her that marriage had been my plan all along, so I pulled out a ring I forged a few days prior. Your mother saw that ring and cried, and at that moment, she knew my love for her remained true and unwavering. I placed the ring on her finger before she could answer, and you know what she said to me?"

"Why isn't it gold?" Finian supplied, earning a laugh from his father.

"No, she said, 'this is lovely, I will call on you tomorrow.' And then left me! On my knee." Jarin barked out a laugh, clearly finding it amusing now. "I was beside myself with worry all night. I thought she would decline my offer and I'd be out both a wife and a ring. I did not sleep at all that night. Your mother, cruel wrench, made me suffer all the next day and well into the evening.

"I almost gave up hope and was ready to drink myself into a stupor, when your mother knocked on the door. She carried a bag full of her belongings and a fresh loaf of bread, that's all. She kissed me and said she arranged for her father to marry us the following morning. Six months later, you were born."

His father did not often talk about his mother; Finian suspected it brought him too much pain. Even now, his father sounded pained from the story, though he smiled through most of it. "All this to say that I hope you and Lilith have a beautiful life together and don't take your time for granted. Do you understand, son?"

More than anything, Finian understood. He knew time was fleeting and every second spent was a second worthy of importance. "I do, and I plan on spending them with my best friend." The other half of his heart.

"Good...good, Well, I do believe that's enough of this-" Jarin gestured vaguely around the room, "-for one day. I'll finish here and you can prepare for your evening."

"Father, I don't mind-"

"Never you mind, son. It's not every day that there is an engagement in town. Best to be prepared for such matters. I'll know if you come home crying that she left and made you my responsibility."

"Lucky you." Finian snickered and gave his father a tight hug. "Thank you." He then added softer. There weren't many moments of tenderness between them, not since Nehema died. Finian had been forced to grow up and his father was keen on letting him.

"Now go." Jarin urged once more, leading Finian towards the door. It did not take any more prompting after that.

Although he knew he should, Finian did not go straight home. It would be hours yet until Lilith finished with Adolphi, and he did not want to stew in his own puzzled thoughts.

The day was leisurely coming to an end, the children who usually roamed the square had all gone home for early supper. The last of the merchants closed down their wagons, done with the day's required labor. In the west, the sun slowly set, the rustic orangey-red of the sky merging with the blacks and purples of the fresh night sky. Even the air held a bit of a chill, reminding him yet again that winter would be here soon.

It was the time of evening where the night shift Warriors relieved the daytime Warriors and updated their replacement with any news that took place during their watch.

Dasos was a relatively quiet town with few outside problems. However, the real reason the town wanted to see the
Warriors stationed around the borders of Dasos was for
security. People felt safe when someone guarded the town,
and the villagers respected the Warriors. No one was willing
to anger their protector out of fear they'd be left defenseless
within the walls of their own homes.

It was a challenging job very few people wanted, except,
of course, Lilith. Others ran away from trouble, but she ran
towards it, head held high, with curiosity and wonderment
in her eyes. She was not made for the walls of Dasos. Finian
often thought Dasos contained Lilith, rather than homed
her. She was the heroine of every story he come to love,
which was why he fell for her. She became the only story
worth telling, the only story that truly mattered.

Finian continued to walk, his feet leading without being
told to do so. They brought him to the edge of town. A
small fence composed of wood and rocks served as the
barrier between this town and whatever lay beyond. Up
close, it looked pathetic and not sturdy enough to hold
deer back, much less an Unhallowed. Without the Warriors,
there would be little defense and security when it came to
the well-being of Dasos.

Finian knew the Warrior who typically took the evening
shift: Percy. Percy was ten years his senior and born and
raised in Dasos. The Warrior saw many people come and go
and watched his own family succumb to the disease. Only
his wife and six-year-old son carried on his family name,
though his son had fallen ill a week ago and still had not
fully recovered.

Perhaps that was the reason he ran late tonight, Finian
thought as he gazed upon the empty watch tower. Watch
tower was a kind name for the molded and tarnished structure that stood only five feet high. Despite its flaws, it allowed Percy to peer out and warn the town of any upcoming
threats.

It was unusual for him to be late, and far more unusual for no one to be posted at his station. Finian felt an obligation to man the post. He always brought his dagger, never wanting to be without one should a crisis arise. Someone needed to be on watch and he was the only abled body around.

Having made up his mind, Finian took his life in his own hands climbing up the ladder. It creaked and sagged under his weight, which did not leave him feeling steady when he reached the top. Falling five feet wouldn't kill him, but it would hurt both his body and pride significantly.

From this vantage point, he was surprised at how much he could see through the thicket of trees. The sun was setting quickly; what little light they had begun to fade. Scouting at night proved to be acutely difficult, even for a trained eye.

For now, Finian took comfort in the remaining light, illuminating the forest beyond Dasos. His gaze swept to the east, and then the west, taking in the land. Up ahead, a rustling in the trees drew his attention towards a blurry outline of a large figure. At first, he passed it off as nothing more than a bear. Dasos saw their fair share of bears wandering close to town in hopes of a meal.

Then the figure moved forward, out of the grove of trees and into view...on two legs. His massive size and height made it easy for anyone to mistake him as a forest creature. The figure stood with the height of a bear, but the closer he came, the more Finian could make out his features: very human and extremely familiar.

Except this time, the man wasn't naked from the waist up. He wore a solid brown tunic with the same black trousers from Finian's dream. His wavy hair was pulled back, tied loosely at the nape of his neck. And his eyes...those familiar green eyes, stared right back at him.

Thunder.

Surely his eyes were deceiving him because the man that stood nestled between trees could not be the man who frequented his dreams for as long as he could remember.

Thunder was not real, only a figment of his overly active imagination. He did not exist.

And yet...

Instinctively, Finian reached for the arm Thunder gripped in his dream and traced his fingers along the skin. It surprised him to find it tender to the touch, making him glance down. What once had been perfectly smooth unmarred skin, was now marked. Instead of finding random scars, the mark held more of an intricate design. The bottom looked like a star his sister might have drawn, all lines and no points. The top of the star had a longer line that ended in an upwards arrow.

"Death is coming to Dasos. Be ready and remember, do not fight it."

Those were the last words Thunder spoke to him before Finian woke up, and now he was here in Dasos. He peered up again, as if expecting him to disappear and also hoping for the mark to have a plausible explanation.

But no, he had not been mistaken. Thunder was here, still staring intently at Finian. For a moment, neither man stirred, both waiting for the other to make the first move. Thunder stood tall and regal, a man used to being obeyed, but completely out of place amongst the trees boarding Dasos.

A slow smile spread across Thunder's peach-colored lips. He spoke and despite being far away, too far away, the words carried to him as if Thunder spoke directly into his ear.

"They are coming. Get out now, boy. It won't be long. I can't protect you once they're here."

So many questions bubbled to the surface, making Finian want to jump Dasos's fence and demand Thunder answer each question without speaking in riddles. He wanted to shout - to scream - and demand answers. Also, he wanted to be certain his mind was not completely going mad. Wasn't that a sign of the unhallowing process, seeing things that weren't real?

A new panic filled him, one far grimmer than the vague omen Thunder gave him. Adrenaline surged through him, fueling his actions as he reached down, grabbing for his knife. It was at that moment a hand reached out and grabbed his forearm.

Whirling around with a fierce cry, Finian brought his dagger down swiftly, aiming for any part of his attacker. His move had been sloppy, and the man blocked the blow that would have only slashed his arm.

"Whoa-at ease, Fin!" A familiar voice said. It only took Finian a moment to place it. Percy finally arrived and managed to get all the way up to the watchtower without Finian hearing him approach. If it had been an enemy, like Thunder, he would be standing in a pool of his own blood.

"Where have you been?" His voice came out more accusatory than Finian meant.

Percy cocked his brow, giving him a pointed look, assessing him as all Warriors did. "By the north wall. Strangest thing, a few yards of the wall had been scorched. We couldn't find any footprints or the source of the fire. Adolphi thinks a few stray embers caused the destruction." He said before adding, "What are you doing up here? And why do you look as if you've seen a ghost?"

"There was a man-" Finian gestured behind him to where Thunder stood, or where he should have been standing. By the time both men turned to look in his direction, Thunder was gone. Disappeared.

The movement was slow, so as not to draw attention to his hand placement, but Finian caught Percy's hand moving to his sword, sheathed at his hip. "What man, Finian? There is no man."

There is no man.

But there had been...hadn't there? Thunder, the Thunder from his dreams, had stood within viewing distance of Dasos. If he merely left, Finian would have seen his retreating body.

"Are you okay? Perhaps you should-"

"I'm fine." Finian barked, cutting off Percy who appeared vexed by Finian's abrasive manner. Yet he did not have time for apologies, and he definitely did not want to answer any questions that Percy might have.

He started his descent from the tower. Percy peaked his head over the side. "Thank you for staying at my post. Adolphi may need you and your father's assistance on the fence. It's not-"

Whatever Percy meant to say, Finian would never know. The man stumbled once and Finian thought he got light-headed, until he saw a long, slender arrow protruding from the back of his skull, only to have gone straight through and come out of his eye.

Blood pooled down his face, so dark, it appeared black. Percy's face slowly drained of color as he swayed back and forth.

For a moment, the world seemed to stop. The surrounding noises faded, and it was just the two of them. Their gazes meant briefly; Finian's full of horror and Percy's vacant of any emotion, before he toppled backwards and fell from the tower, dead before he even hit the ground.

Then the screams came, loud and sudden.

Finian didn't think. He just climbed back up the ladder and stumbled to the top of the watchtower to see the scene play out before him. Dasos was bleeding. Unknown faces he never encountered surged forward, taking down mothers with their children, fathers defending their families, and children protecting their grandparents.

"Death is coming to Dasos."

The Unhallowed were here.

CHAPTER ELEVEN

THE BEFORE

Z EUS ONCE LOOKED FORWARD to his evening lessons, but that felt like a lifetime ago. Now they served to defend himself against his brothers' cruelty. He foolishly hoped the years in the tower were a test all princes went through before being lavished with gifts, silks, and riches. Now, five years later, Zeus understood the truth.

"My thunder, will you not join your old mitera Chloe for dinner?" Chloe asked him one evening right before he left for practice.

"You are not old, mitera Chloe." He replied, stopping at the door for a brief moment. Chloe had aged but insinuating she was old was a far stretch. She still held her beauty, even though new faint wrinkles appeared underneath her eyes and her hair lost its luster long ago. Chloe was far from the youngest, unwed maiden in the castle, but she still turned heads with her beauty.

"I cannot miss training with Sir Ilys. Father would think I'm neglecting my duties."

"You are not the one neglecting your duties, Thunder, - *he* is." Chloe said bitterly, the same tone she always used when talking about his father. Zeus couldn't blame her. He wasn't overly fond of his father either. He was a stern, unforgiving man and made up his mind long ago that Zeus committed a great crime against him, holding him personally responsible for the death of his beloved Rhea.

Zeus would never tell mitera Chloe this out of fear of breaking her heart, but he hated Rhea, more than he hated his father. The mother he had never known left him an unfair and unjust life...and for what? Rhea gained nothing from Zeus's birth. Nothing but her own death.

"Tomorrow I will have dinner with you. I promise." He said, smiling at her.

"Don't break a woman's heart with false promises, my boy." She said, though returned the smile that always made him feel comforted. "Off you go. I'll fetch you after your hour is done."

Zeus did not tell Chloe he didn't need her to pick him up from training when he could get there himself. It was her chance to leave the damp wing, one Cronus, unsurprisingly, never finished remodeling. Far be it for him to deny her a walk in the fresh air and peace of mind for his well-being.

As usual, Zeus arrived at his lesson earlier than necessary. Sir Ilys was already on the training ground, taking out not one, but three swords from the weaponry. Two years ago, Sir Ilys made the decision to switch from wooden swords to real blades, albeit dull, that would not cause significant injury for a skilled fighter. Contact with one still hurt and oftentimes left a bruise.

"Ah, Zeus. Perfect timing, son. Your brothers will be joining us tonight." Sir Ilys said, and Zeus did his best not to outwardly groan or grimace at the news. He trained alongside his brothers before, he just preferred the days when it was only Sir Ilys and him.

They did not wait long, for once, his brothers showed up a few minutes later, looking alert and sober. The twins were fifteen now, considered men by the court and treated as the adult princes they were.

"Hello brother." Hades smiled, though there was nothing friendly about it.

Poseidon, for his part, appeared mildly annoyed. "Let's skip the pleasantries, shall we?" He ignored the looks from both of his brothers and Poseidon took the sword Ilys offered him, giving it a few practice swings to test the weight. "Remind me again as to why we are not using real swords?"

Sir Ilys answered this question many times, but his patience continued as he explained again. "It is to prevent injury. You and Hades may be considered men, but Zeus is still a boy. We also have no need to practice with real swords and I would much rather you three not kill one another over trivial boyhood dramatics."

That was not the real reason and Zeus took a small amount of satisfaction in knowing the truth. Last month Sir Ilys had been in a rare state of anger after his visit with King Cronus. The King claimed Sir Ilys lacked in his ability to teach his sons how to become valiant warriors and insinuated he might be too old for the job he currently held.

"Valiant warriors?" He had scoffed, watching Zeus practice basic defense maneuvers, "Some bloody warriors. If a sword were a woman, then they may know how to grip it properly. Remember Zeus, never be distracted by the allure of sex or companionship. You are a true warrior, and you must never lose sight of your true purpose."

King Cronus had gotten the valiant warrior son he always hoped for, just not in the son he wanted.

Sir Ilys tossed the two remaining swords to the unarmed boys. "Let's get to it then, shall we?" He asked and took them through a series of warm ups before he allowed them to spar against him.

Hades went first. He matched Sir Ilys in strength, but brute force alone would not make a warrior. Hades was an open book; his opponent could easily read his next move and block the blows effectively. He managed to last a total of three minutes before Sir Ilys dealt what would normally be a killing blow if the blade had been sharp. Hades still hissed in pain and wordlessly took his place next to Zeus.

Poseidon came up next. He was not as strong as Hades, but he was quicker on his feet. He did not fight with the same arrogance of his brother and with more training, Poseidon could become an unbeatable force. Perhaps even better than Sir Ilys. Though he lasted longer than his brother, Poseidon was struck down in the end, grunting as the dull sword connected with his chest.

"We have a lot of work to do." Sir Ilys said like a disappointed father. "Zeus, are you ready, boy?"

Both brothers turned to stare down at him, with a look of contempt. They wrote him off as an unworthy opponent. Sir Ilys stated numerous times to never underestimate your enemy or risk losing a fight.

Perhaps that notion alone spurred Zeus to say his next words.

"I wish to challenge my brothers, Sir Ilys. If they'll duel me."

Momentarily everyone seemed to be at a loss for words. Then suddenly and without warning, Hades began to laugh cruelly. "Do you enjoy pain and humiliation, baby brother?"

Before Zeus could defend himself, Sir Ilys came to his rescue. "Watch your tone boy. Your brother shows up to every practice and excels in his training. That is much more than you can say."

Hades scowled at the Swords Master, and Zeus began to wonder if he knew how to make any other expression. "Very well then. We shall duel as the young princeling requested. Unfortunately, the numbers are not in his favor. Two against one. That hardly seems fair."

"In war, we may fight hundreds of men." Zeus said. "So, thank the stars I only have two brothers."

That earned him a smirk from Hades and a laugh from Poseidon. "You are many things, Zeus, but shy and meek are not among them."

It was one of the only compliments his brother had given him. If this were an inkling of respect given, Zeus would accept it. Dueling his brothers, both at the same time, was a monumental task he was unsure would end in his victory. Working together, they had always been a strong and deadly pair, but Zeus could be strong too. There was no shame in losing, especially to opponents bigger, stronger, and older than him.

Sir Ilys looked displeased but relented. "Anything below the neck is fair game. I will not render aid should you be bested." The swords master then took a step backwards, away from striking distance and nodded his head, signaling them to begin.

Zeus sprang into action, using his small stature and quick movements to his advantage. He went for Hades first, simply because this brother angered him the most, and used his swords to swipe his feet from under them. With a loud curse, Hades went down hard, landing ineptly on his back. It was not a killing blow, so he had not taken down his opponent, but he did buy himself some time.

Poseidon was harder; he was not blinded by his own arrogance like Hades. His moves were more practiced and calculated. Zeus thrust his sword out, but Poseidon predicted his move and their swords clashed in an echoing roar. Again and again, they struck, two predators keen on getting the killing blow. Hades did not rejoin the fight, he seemed more interested in seeing the events play out.

Zeus's shoulders sagged, the sword becoming heavier as he tired. Dodging, ducking, and lunging, following Poseidon's intricate dance, proved more difficult than he thought. Zeus lacked stamina -- he didn't even realize he lacked stamina -- but somehow Poseidon knew and continued to play it safe until his opponent tired.

Zeus's movements were sluggish, and his muscles protested with each swipe of his blade. Poseidon, who had paced himself, struck hard and fast, swung his sword high.

Poseidon aimed for his neck.

Sir Ilys screamed out a reprimand, but it was too late. The sword came faster and all of Zeus's training urged him to pick up the sword and strike back, but his brother was fast, and Zeus only had enough time to lift his sword and absorb the impact. The force alone sent Zeus to his knees, his entire body ringing.

"That's enough!" Sir Ilys yelled, stepping in between the brothers, and forcefully pushing Poseidon back. Still on an adrenaline high, Poseidon lifted his sword against the swords master, but Sir Ilys lunged forward, grabbing his man's sword arm. "You challenge me and I'll have you down on your back in seconds. My blade isn't dull, prince."

"Well, this has all been quite entertaining."

All four of their heads snapped back to see who the voice belonged to. The twin princes straightened up, face hardening. Sir Ilys bowed his head respectfully and Zeus knew who stood behind before he even turned around. How much had he seen?

Getting up slowly, the youngest son of Cronus turned to face his father, the King. Cronus smiled, an unpleasant and disorienting sight, Zeus thought. He had a spark in his eye that almost looked gleeful. He noticed his father wore his riding attire, meaning he had just arrived home from a hunt. Cronus was not the type of man to stroll leisurely through his kingdom, not without a motive.

"Your Grace," Sir Ilys greeted. "I was unaware you would be joining us for this evening's lesson."

"As was I." Cronus mused, surveying each of his sons and paying little regard to the swords master. His eyes then landed on Zeus, and he could not help the slight tremble coursing through him. "You fought well, boy."

You fought well, boy.

If Zeus's entire body did not ache, he would have imagined himself dreaming. His father never acknowledged him, much less given him a compliment before. Expectant eyes were upon him, urging him to say something. His tongue lay heavy in his mouth, unable to produce even the smallest of sounds. Cronus, unbeknownst to his problem, turned away from him to address his twins.

"As for you two," Cronus started. "I hoped I would see more of an improvement from my last visit. Instead, what do I see? Hades being sent to his knees by a ten-year-old boy and Poseidon unable to end the duel swiftly. You both bring shame to me today."

Hades and Poseidon dared a glance at Zeus, mirroring the same expressions of loathing. "We will see to it we practice harder, father. Our deepest apologies." Hades graveled, bowing his head in a sign of respect in what he hoped came across as remorse.

"So you shall. If you wish to join me as I pave the way into a new era of Kings, I expect my heirs to be fierce warriors who earned the respect of their kingdom. Perhaps you could learn something from Zeus after all." Cronus reprimand held none of the sharpness typically reserved for Zeus or anyone else he considered unworthy of his attention. Still, it was more firmness than Zeus ever heard directed at his brothers. "Now off you go. I need you well-rested for tomorrow."

Without another word, Poseidon and Hades pushed past Zeus and retreated into the castle, making the youngest brother wonder about tomorrow. Zeus was only privy to the castle's gossip because he caught glimpses of conversations from his father's staff. Not one of the maids or seamstresses mentioned anything of importance happening tomorrow. That unsettled Zeus, not knowing what Cronus planned.

"Before you go, boy. I would like a word." Cronus said, turning Zeus's blood to ice. He couldn't tell the King no and walk away with his life. However, a small, traitorous part of him wanted to hear what his father had to say. Cronus rarely asked to speak to him. For a moment, Zeus did not know how to answer. What were the proper protocols for speaking with a king? Yes, his tutors taught him how to formally address a ruler, but did the same principles apply when one was speaking to their father?

Thankfully, Cronus did not seem bothered by Zeus's lack of...well, everything, and took his silence as resignation. "I have seen you practice with Sir Ilys for the past month. You have impressed me with your strength and tenacity, those are things I can appreciate, things that make a good soldier."

"Th...Thank you, fa-Your Grace." Zeus stuttered, opting for his title, rather than acknowledging their relations.

"I'm increasing your training time. You will spend less time with your tutors, for I've also been made aware you've far surpassed their expectations as well. You must take after your mo-" Cronus stopped himself, having spoken carelessly. He had not mentioned her since she died in childbirth. All to produce the third heir he never wanted.

Zeus saw the change in his father. His jovial disposition from moments ago hardened and his eyes lost some of the teasing shine from earlier. It was a talent really, that Zeus managed to piss off Cronus by simply existing.

"I have use for you boy. Tomorrow night, visitors from the south will arrive. You may have heard me speaking of Vulcan, King of Caister. You may also recall we are not on the friendliest terms." He said.

Vulcan and Cronus had a rocky history with a teetering semblance of peace. Mitera Chloe mentioned Vulcan had been promised to Rhea before she was born. Rhea had been expected to marry the King when she came of age. Instead, his mother saw value in marrying Cronus and convinced her mother to break the alliance. Vulcan never quite got over the blow to his ego and loss of power that came with marrying Gaia's only daughter.

"I do Your Grace. Do you wish me to stay in my room?" He asked since Cronus liked Zeus out of the public's eyes when visitors arrived in the palace.

"Oh no, boy, quite the contrary. It has come to my attention Vulcan may be in possession of a rare elixir I desire. At the very least, I have reason to believe he knows the whereabouts of the elixir. He has come under the guise of a truce between us because he believes I've finally agreed to a marriage."

At the mention of marriage, Zeus grew pale, and bile rose in his throat. Mitera Chloe mentioned that one day, Zeus may be used as a marriage pawn, but he had not expected that day to come so soon.

The look on his face made Cronus bark out laughter. "Afraid of a woman, boy? Don't tell me you enjoy the company of men."

Zeus wanted to scream that he was only ten! He enjoyed the company of his wooden soldiers. Girls were becoming slightly more interesting to him, but not enough to warrant marriage. From what he remembered, Vulcan's daughters were old now, far older than even Cronus would think it appropriate to marry his ten-year-old son to. He was certain the daughters had children his age-

Oh.

"I have agreed to the marriage alliance between his youngest granddaughter Metis and you. Metis is only eight and once she hits womanhood, we will arrange a marriage. At least this is what Vulcan believes. What I want from you, boy, is to play the part of a prince, my dutiful heir. You will befriend Metis, gain her trust. Perhaps she will even love you, but I care very little about such trivial emotions. You will be my spy. You will get Metis to tell you everything she knows about her grandfather." Zeus said, his tone full of command.

Zeus did not hesitate. Perhaps it was pathetic, but he took a certain amount of pride in doing something he knew his brothers could not. "I will. But...Your Grace-"

"Father, boy," Cronus interrupted. "We both better get used to it now."

"Father," he continued. "I do have one question. What would an eight-year-old girl know of a King's secrets?"

At the question, Cronus's lip quirked up into a smile resembling a hungry lion who spotted dinner. There was wicked delight behind his features and Zeus wondered what this elixir would be capable of if Cronus was willing to take extreme measures to obtain information from a little girl.

"That is a great question, boy. Metis happens to be a favorite of Vulcan's, thus making her his biggest weakness. He has been known to cut grown men down for looking at her wrong or upsetting her. If he plans to use the elixir, it will extend to her as well."

"You expect this to take years then? I am to make her fall in love with me and then deceive her? Is that what you want?" Zeus asked, his child's brain slowly wrapping around the idea that his first assignment given to him by his father was to deceive the only other person who might ever come to love him.

"I expect you two will marry before I get my hands on it. I'm not known for my patience, this I know. However, I will make an exception for this. It will allow me time to prepare, and I shall need it to mold Hades and Poseidon into the men they are destined to be." He said.

It always came back to his brothers. Zeus would be doing all the work but only his brothers would bask in the glory. Whatever that glory may be, Zeus still did not know what the elixir was and why Cronus was willing to wait years for it. "May I ask what this elixir is? Why do you wish to possess it, father?"

Zeus half expected Cronus to dismiss him. It would be well within his right to deny Zeus an explanation. He was only the means to an end. His usefulness did not equate to his father's trust.

Yet, Cronus did not dismiss him or scold him for his insolence. He did something far more terrifying. He smiled, directly at him. Not through him, not at his expense, but to Zeus as if they were equals. The words he spoke would haunt Zeus for years to come.

"Why, Ambrosia, son. I will live out my immortality as the God King and my reign shall know no limit."

The last time Zeus sat at the dining hall table his feet hovered over the ground. Mitera Chloe had been at his side like a mother hen, fussing over him. It was not typical for her to give him that much attention at dinner, but Zeus knew she tried to overcompensate for everyone else's evasive manner.

As he was led into the dining hall this time, Cronus paraded him in front of his royal guests as if he were a prize to be won. It left Zeus missing the times of being ignored and overlooked. Being on display felt...intimate, and he did not have Chloe with him. She provided a buffer, but without his mitera near he felt more exposed than usual.

If Cronus noticed his son's discomfort, he said nothing. Far be it for the King of Dasos to show any type of sympathy for others' discomfort. Cronus's face remained calm and unreadable. He looked as foreign as the group of strangers occupying the dining hall.

Well, mostly strangers.

Gaia, his grandmother, sat perched at one head of the table, looking on with bored curiosity. He had not known she would be here, making him question her visit. Zeus's interactions with his grandmother were minimal. She was an old Queen now, well into her fifth or sixth decade. Gaia was an impressive woman, even at her age. She commanded a room with a single look or hand gesture. People did not only respect her, but they also worshiped her. In a world dominated by men, Queen Gaia reigned supreme.

With Gaia here, it meant Lord Kotas was also present. His round, red face held a permanent frown. His eyes narrowed when he saw Zeus, silently threatening him. Do not embarrass me, boy, his expression seemed to say. Zeus did not ask to be paraded around the room like cattle, but very few people ever asked him what he wanted. They demanded and expected him to play along.

He was a pawn for the crown to use at whim and Cronus was about to make his first move.

"King Vulcan," Cronus addressed the man donned in southern regalia and flanked by guards who wore the sigil of House Vulcan. "It has been years, my old friend."

Vulcan gave a derisive snort. "Friend? Now I know the years have not been kind to your memory. Reluctant acquaintances, perhaps."

"All the same." Cronus dismissed him and gestured to his former mother-in-law. "You are acquainted with my departed wife's mother, Queen Gaia of Vodena."

It was not a question, but Vulcan answered anyway. "I do, it's nice to see you again, Gaia."

"It seems Cronus is not the only one here who knows how to tell such pretty lies. Please, take a seat." Gaia gestured to a spot already set up for Vulcan. "I must say, I'm surprised you showed up without Metis. Is she not the reason we are all here? Her, and our darling prince Zeus, of course."

All eyes moved towards Zeus, who wished the earth would open up and swallow him whole. He practiced the ways of courts many times and could perfectly explain how a prince should act and behave in any situation. Putting his teaching into practice was an entirely different beast. He lacked the confidence and entitlement his brothers possessed in abundance. What he did possess was the ability to act. He studied his family and other royals extensively and knew their mannerisms well. Perhaps acting the part would get him through this evening unscathed.

"Of course, of course." Vulcan said, unabashedly taking a large drink of wine. Zeus noticed neither his grandmother nor father touched theirs. This was not unnatural for them. His father only drank on special occasions and around his most devoted friends and his grandmother...well Zeus could not recall a time she indulged in such folly.

"My granddaughter did accompany me. She's awaiting my word in the carriage. I wanted to put my old heart at ease before I allowed my beloved granddaughter to enter. You understand the need to protect our heirs." Vulcan said pointedly as he looked at Cronus. It was clear he suspected a different outcome upon their arrival. He didn't think the bastard would be foolish enough to slaughter his grand-daughter in plain view, but he underestimated Cronus in the past. Vulcan swore to never do it again.

Cronus smiled at Vulcan: a lion easing his prey into a false sense of security. Zeus suspected Cronus also enjoyed the song and dance but held a different opinion about who was prey and predator.

"Heirs are quite precious, aren't they? Our greatest trea-sures. They bring us many joys, but with joys plenty of woes too. Isn't that right Zeus?" Cronus directed the last part to him.

"You would know, wouldn't you, Cronus? How many bas-tards have you got running around now? I've heard recently of a daughter by the name of De-"

"That's quite enough." Cronus hissed, interrupting King Vulcan. The southern King smirked, knowing his comment irritated Cronus. "I claim no bastard. Right, boy?" All eyes on the room swiveled back to Zeus.

"Erm, yes father." He coughed nervously and felt the in-stant disapproval radiating from Cronus and Lord Kotas. Childishly, Zeus wanted to remind his father he had no time to prepare for this meeting, since he sprung it on him at the last minute. That would only prove to piss them off more.

"Please excuse my son. He lacks the poise of my eldest two, but it is to be expected when one is coddled one's whole life." Cronus said in a way of explanation. Zeus's cheeks grew hot. Coddled? He called growing up in a small, unfinished room and beaten if he so much as looked at someone the wrong way, coddled? The bastard.

"It's quite alright. I was much the same when I first met my betrothed. The boy will turn into a man soon. All it takes is one fine pair of t-"

"That's quite enough." Gaia cut off Vulcan before he could finish his sentence. "As you can see, your granddaughter is quite safe, as are you and your men. If you would be so kind to allow her in, so we can continue this meeting, I would greatly appreciate it."

Vulcan frowned, unhappy about the interruption. "Very well." He motioned for a guard and whispered inaudibly. Nodding, the guard left only to return with an array of more guards and in the center -- a girl.

Metis.

The girl was little more than eight years old, her heart-shaped face, boarding on chubby. Every other part of her was tiny and delicate. She shared her family's dark features, a startling contrast to the white interior of the castle. Zeus found himself staring at the girl, wondering who spent the time braiding small strands of her hair. He would never be able to sit still for so long as someone pulled and tugged on his hair and weaved it intricately together.

The way Vulcan stared at Metis, as if she were the sun around which his whole life orbited, sent pangs of jealousy through Zeus. It was not fair, but a small part of him immediately hated Metis for eliciting that much love and admiration from her family. Vulcan didn't try to hide or keep her a secret. No, he wanted everyone to know Metis was his granddaughter.

"King Cronus, Queen Gaia. I would like to formally introduce my most favorite granddaughter, princess Metis of House Vulcan."

Metis curtsied, bowing her head low out of respect for the rulers before her. She held that position before straightening herself up and turning towards Zeus. She stopped and surveyed, inspecting him as he had done to her a few minutes ago. "And prince Zeus. I'm very excited to meet you."

He doubted that, but Metis followed the expected script. No child wanted to meet their betrothed and talk policy. Vulcan thought he was doing her a great favor by arranging a political marriage between their lands. If he knew the true reason Cronus paired them together, he'd declare war. With his numbers, Vulcan stood a good chance at defeating Cronus too.

Since everyone looked at him expectantly, Zeus put on a smile he had seen his brothers give girls numerous times. He inclined his head, not quite a bow, but enough to show respect. "Princess Metis. Your hair is lovely." He had been admiring it earlier and it felt natural for him to say. Judging by the reddening of her cheeks, he had been successful in his attempt at flattery.

"Well, now that is out of the way, let us eat. I do hate cold lamb." Gaia said, and so they sat.

Dinner was not as agonizing as Zeus anticipated. He found himself laughing along with Vulcan's stories of wild hog hunting expeditions and late nights with copious numbers of women. Okay, that part Zeus could have done without, even if he did not understand all the parts and where said parts were going. Cronus also seemed to be amused by Vulcan's story. Gaia was the only person at the table unimpressed with the man's tales. To be fair, Gaia had never been impressed with anything a man said or did before. Men were means to an end.

She did take a particular liking to Metis. During dinner, Gaia asked Metis to join her for a quick stroll through the gardens while they waited for dessert. Metis was not the only one hesitant; Vulcan insisted Metis be accompanied by her guards. Gaia nodded but didn't indulge him further. Metis left with the Queen, arriving back twenty-minutes later with a pleasant smile on their faces.

By the time dinner ended, several hours had passed. Mitera Chloe would be worried about Zeus's whereabouts. Or maybe someone sent word to her that Zeus was in attendance with King Cronus, King Vulcan, and Queen Gaia. He suspected that would only worry her more. Best to let her think practice was running later than usual.

"Shall we discuss the reason we are all here? The joining of two houses." Cronus spoke once the last of the dessert was taken away. A creamy tart with honey. Zeus almost licked the plate clean.

"It's quite simple, Cronus. I offer the hand of my favorite granddaughter to your youngest son Zeus. When she comes of age, Metis will be pronounced Queen and Zeus will be her prince consort." Vulcan explained, speaking as if Zeus or Metis were not in present company.

"And what shall I receive in return? Your granddaughter will be a mighty force and Zeus will exist in portraits." Cronus challenged.

"You will get an army."

"I have an army."

"Mine's bigger."

The two rival kings stared at one another in contempt. The energy in the room palpable, both opponents awaiting the other to make their next move.

Unexpectedly, Gaia broke the tense silence. "There is something else we desire. Something I hear you may possess."

Cronus jerked his head towards Gaia, narrowing his eyes. They entered this meeting as a united front, but clearly had not discussed this conversation. Zeus felt his father's anger coming in waves and for once not directed at him.

"And what is it you think I have, Queen Gaia?" Vulcan asked, like a cat dangling cheese in front of his mouse.

But Gaia was no mouse and played games with Kings for the better part of her life. She had seen Kings fall and others rise to power, while she remained constant. "We are in search of Ambrosia. I have been told by many respected sources you know the whereabouts of the elixir."

"I see. Grant me this, Gaia, what is it you want with Ambrosia?" Vulcan asked.

"The healing properties, of course. Is there more I should know about it?"

"Of course not." Vulcan lied. Zeus knew how to spot a liar. It only took a slight twitch in the lips or roaming eyes. Each person had a small gesture that gave them away, and Vulcan's happened to be his posture. He sat up straighter, holding more tension in his shoulders than before.

This was the reason Cronus and Gaia arranged this marriage. Zeus would need to become a spy to learn more about Ambrosia. He needed to learn if it really turned men immortal.

"I appreciate your...interest in Ambrosia, but this is hardly a time to discuss such matters. We are here to celebrate the union of two-" he paused and smiled at Gaia, "Forgive me, three, powerful houses. Today, we toast the union of princess Metis and her betrothed, prince Zeus."

Cronus frowned, but Gaia was unphased by Vulcan's response. "We will speak more about this soon, but now we drink." Cronus agreed and motioned for the servants to refill their wine glasses. Two small glasses of wine were placed in front of both Metis and Zeus.

"To the children." Vulcan smiled, raising his glass. He smiled fondly at his granddaughter, nothing but love on his face for Metis. Zeus could not help but hate her. Just a little.

"May they bring us riches beyond our wildest dreams." Cronus proclaimed, raising his glass in toast. "Drink, boy." He whispered harshly when Zeus did not grab his drink.

So, Zeus drank.

CHAPTER TWELVE

THE AFTER

K EI'S SOUL WAS LAID to rest as the sun set. It seemed like the perfect moment, if one existed in death, to depart with the sun. Her body burnt until her ashes lifted into the air by the breeze and scattered along the forest floor, rejoining the earth where life once began. The only solace Lilith found in her friend's death was that Kei never had the chance to hurt her loved ones. She did not completely lose herself and died with the last bit of dignity she held.

Adolphi had been right to not allow her parents here for her final send off. Seeing Kei's flesh burn and melt off her body had been horrendous, the accompanying smell enough to make her gag. If it had been Finian or Idina on the pyre, she would not have possessed the mental or emotional capacity to handle their burning.

When the last ember flickered away and nothing remained of Kei, Lilith bowed her head in respect and murmured a final goodbye, hoping wherever Kei was now, she would be able to hear her. "May your soul find peace and your presence never be forgotten."

Her duty fulfilled, Lilith saddled her horse, Stormy, giving his mane an appreciative stroke. The ride back would take a good thirty minutes and the last of the sunlight slowly slipped into darkness. Stormy made this trek countless times, so he'd just have to be her eyes in the dark. "Let's go back home, boy." And as if understanding her, the horse took off towards Dasos.

Her mind drifted, thinking about the answer she would give Finian. He asked to move in together. More so than that, he wanted her hand in marriage. There was no doubt in her mind that she loved him, and no other person she would rather spend the rest of her days with. Still, she hesitated.

What did she know of wifely duties? Did Finian expect her to have children right away? Lilith didn't think she wanted to have kids any time soon. The selfish part of her wanted to continue to advance as a Warrior, and a child would make that dream nearly impossible. She'd be out for the better half of a year and even then, there was no guarantee she'd be able to resume her position.

No, this was Finian. Her Finian and they always faced problems together. He never pressured her into anything she felt uncomfortable with and allowed her to make her own choices, she'd end up making a few mistakes. Those were *her* mistakes to make and learn from, and Finian would be there to support her.

There only seemed to be one answer that made sense. One that both her heart and her mind agreed upon.

Lilith smiled at her own little secret, giddy in anticipation about giving him her answer. With her mind preoccupied with thoughts of their upcoming encounter, she hardly noticed their approach into Dasos territory. Stormy stopped abruptly, nearly bucking her off in his haste to retreat. The horse forced her to dismount before attempting to grab the reins. As soon as she freed Stormy though, he took off, back the way they came.

Something was wrong.

The sounds of the forest no longer comforted her. She could not hear the lulling melody of the insects that comforted her at night. The sound replacing the music sounded...inhuman. In fact, she doubted the sounds came from the forest as all. And...did she see smoke? Lilith made a point of traveling deep into the woods before giving Kei a proper send off, so she knew the smoke originated closer to Dasos.

Then the screaming began.

The sound of anguish and fear poured its way through her bones, rendering her motionless, as if frozen in time.

It didn't stop. The wail continued until it met an abrupt end, only to be picked up by another and then another. A thicket of trees blocked the view into the village and Lilith only saw blurs of movement, not recognizable through the foliage. The air suddenly became thick with a metallic smell.

Blood.

Keep moving, keep moving. Her mind chanted in attempts to get her legs moving. You're a warrior, dammit, get your ass to Dasos!

Lilith could not think of a worse time for her body not to comply with her request. She'd fallen under a spell, fighting the invisible tethers holding her in place. The more she struggled, the more her body screamed in protest.

A flash of faces went through her mind, starting with Idina's, her sweet protective mother. The woman who took her in two years ago without a second thought and loved her like her own daughter. Then to a round-faced little girl, Mavis, who sat and listened to nighttime stories, as Lilith stroked her hair. Lastly to Finian, the boy who accepted her immediately upon her arrival, who taught her how to fight and how to love.

She needed to force her body to move.

She started running, her legs carrying her as fast as she could push herself. She did not stop, not even when the branches slashed into her arms or when her legs began to cramp. The closer she got, the louder the screams became.

Breaking through the last groups of trees felt like a small triumph, though she stumbled a time or two in her haste for Dasos. When she finally cleared the forest, Lilith stopped dead in her tracks at the sight before her.

Slaughter.

Dasos painted in blood.

"No." She croaked, her voice breaking on the single sylla-ble. She could no longer tell what was louder, the screams of the dying and wounded or her own heartbeat.

Dasos stood as the beacon of light in the darkness. Except this light held no security or comfort. The flames danced atop roofs and carts, gaining momentum despite the linger-ing of last night's rainfall.

At first the chaotic scene was a mixture of rapidly moving colors and shapes. Lilith's mind desperately tried to make sense of it all. Though when her vision cleared, and she could see her home for the war zone that it was, nothing prepared for the onslaught of bloodshed and destruction.

The ground was soaked in blood, coloring the earth red.

Bodies -- people she saw every day over the last two years -- lay in ruins on the ground. Their bodies shredded as if they had been mauled to death by wild animals. She may have been inclined to believe that, except--

Heads.

On spikes.

Her stomach lurched as the nausea hit her full force. She clutched her stomach, dry heaving. *Get yourself together. Get moving before you die too!* Her inner voice screamed, having the sense and clarity she lacked. It was a coward's move, but Lilith could not bring herself to look at the heads on spikes. She said a silent plea to anyone listening that her loved ones were not among the dead. If she could find Idina or Finian then-

"Unhallowed!" Someone screamed, confirming what Lilith already suspected but hoped against.

Dasos was meant to be a stronghold, standing as a safe place in this world for the past few decades. Adolphi or-chestrated vigilant safety and protective rituals and made the town participate in practice drills once a month.

Apparently, the drills had all been for nothing. No careful or methodical plan proved foolproof; Dasos' current state testified to that. Even the mighty, in the end, would fall.

Suddenly, a blade of a sword swung recklessly in her direction, missing Lilith by mere centimeters. She rounded on her attacker only to see a woman, or what she supposed was once a woman, snarl in frustration. The Unhallowed was dirty from head to toe and had a deep gash on the side of her thigh. She would die of that soon, but Unhallowed did not feel pain in the same sense that normal people did. They would continue to fight until their last, dying breath.

Judging by her haggard and gray complexion, it would not be much longer.

"You Dasos bitch!" The woman roared and lurched forward with her sword again. Her movements were wild but sloppy, opening herself up to an easy kill. A kill that would have to come from Lilith's blade.

At the last moment, Lilith unsheathed *Peace Bringer* and buried the knife deep within the woman's chest. The woman gasped and struggled weakly, before going limp in her arms.

The second person she killed today.

There would be time to dwell over this later, or so she hoped, but right now nothing was more important than finding Finian and Idina.

Letting the dead woman fall to the ground in a crumpled heap, Lilith pushed forward. "Finian! Idina! Mavis!" She screamed, but her voice was but a whisper in an otherwise cacophonous sea of sound.

A feral cry sounded again, just as a group of three Unhallowed leaped onto the backs of Walt Havard, a guard in Adolphi's army. He had been trying to escort four children -- orphaned children? -- out to safety.

Walt was a big man drawing in all the Unhallowed's attention. He went down hard, only deflecting the crudely made daggers long enough to give the group of children time to escape. "Run! Don't look back, no matter what you hear!" He shouted.

The oldest child, eleven or twelve, stared at the fallen warrior in abject horror. The younger kids stood paralyzed too, unsure where to go or who to listen to, needing direction and guidance from someone who could get them to safety.

Without thinking, Lilith rushed ahead, running at full speed. "Come! This way!" She yelled, scooping up the youngest who looked no older than four. Lilith tugged on the oldest girl, urging her forward. "Don't look back. Keep running and don't stop."

Survival instincts kicked in for the girl. She trusted Lilith enough to lead them to safety.

She only hoped that the children's trust was warranted.

"Keep straight. Don't look behind!" She urged again, cradling the small child closer to her chest as she ran. The extra weight she carried slowed her down, allowing the others to keep up with her.

Even as they pushed ahead, they couldn't escape the sound of Walt's scream as the mob of Unhallowed gutted him on the floor. Two of the kids began to scream while the other two almost stopped.

"Keep running!" She ordered frantically, unable to hide her own rising panic and the bile that threatened to leave her stomach.

Lilith needed to decide now before the attackers ambushed them next. She wouldn't be able to defend the children and herself. If she knew where Finian was, he would be able to watch her back. But where the hell was he?

"There!" She gestured to the stables, untouched by the flames and void of any horses that once occupied them. The rancid stench of feces hit strong as she horded the children into one of the stalls, passing off the youngest to a girl just shy of her teen years.

"What's your name?" Lilith asked, trying to keep the panic out of her voice.

The young girl's lip quivered, her body visibly shaking now that the adrenaline wore off. "Amelia." She whispered.

"Amelia," Lilith said gently and placed a hand on the girl's shoulder. "I know you are scared. So am I."

Those words shocked Amelia. Children often assumed adults could not experience fear, but age did little to diminish the building panic that plagued the senses when the unexpected happened. "You are?" She whimpered.

"I am." Lilith confirmed, nodding her head. "But even scared people can be brave and I'm going to need you to be brave. Okay? Stay here and keep quiet. I'm making you the leader, okay? Don't move from this spot unless someone you don't know finds you. Can you do that, Amelia?"

It was not fair to ask so much from such a young girl, but Lilith needed to be back out amid Dasos. She couldn't stay here with them when Idina and Finian were missing.

Amelia looked like she'd rather Lilith not leave as fresh tears poured down her dirty cheeks. To her credit though, she sucked in her bottom lip and nodded her head imperceptibly. "Okay, but you'll be back?"

"I promise." Lilith didn't know how she'd keep this promise, but once safe, she'd make sure they were cared for and looked after. "You are very brave, Amelia. You'll make a fine Warrior one day."

With that, Lilith gave Amelia a swift salute before running out of the barn. Although her thighs burned from extortion, the need to find her loved ones outweighed any discomfort. The grisly sight of heads on spikes came into view once again and a sickening feeling struck her as a familiar face stared blankly back at her. Mrs. Edman, Kei's mother, who had been sobbing over the death of her only daughter not just hours ago, was now dead. Her body lost amongst the chaos.

Mr. Edman's head was next to hers, though it took Lilith a moment longer to recognize him. His face was bruised and puffy, showing signs of a struggle. He clearly tried fighting, but the Edmans were farmers. They had little to no fighting expertise. She imagined Mr. Edman tried to fight Unhallowed away to give his wife time to flee. Mrs. Edman had either been too slow or unwilling to leave her husband.

The only solace Lilith took now was that she hoped the Edmans were together, in whatever lay beyond this life.

There was no time for mourning. No time to pay her respects to the dead and give them the proper burial they deserved. Not when Dasos burned, and her people lay dying. The flames now stretched towards the fields, consuming their food supply. The Unhallowed were coherent enough to know their food supply was crucial to Dasonian existence. By burning down their crops, they damned the entire town, regardless of whether they lived through this massacre.

A hand reached out and grabbed her, pulling her out of her dire thoughts. Lilith screamed before whirling with *Peace Bringer*, ready to plunge the dagger into her attacker's throat.

"Whoa, whoa, whoa!" The familiar voice said, immediately letting her go and taking a step back with his hands in the air. "Lil, it's me. It's me! Don't stab me!"

It took Lilith a moment to register Finian's face, but as soon as she did, a heavy weight lifted off her chest, and she nearly fell to the ground and wept. Instead, she threw herself into his arms, kissing him roughly but ended the moment all too quickly. "I thought you were dead." She panted, clinging to him as she frantically assessed his body for wounds.

"I'm fine." He said gruffly, indicating he was anything but fine. Blood stains soaked into his tunic, and he looked exhausted. He also favored his left side, putting very little weight on his right.

Finian noticed her wandering gaze and tried to straighten up, but a low hiss of pain escaped him, betraying his promise of being "fine."

"I was tackled from behind by an Unhallowed. She knocked me down and I rolled my foot, but I promise that is the extent of my injuries." He said, satisfying her curiosity.

"Have you seen my mother? Is she with Adolphi? What happened? How did our walls get breached?" A million other questions came to her, but they still stood in the middle of mayhem, easy targets for their enemies. Now was not an opportune time to go over the attack.

Finian had the same thoughts and gestured for Lilith to follow him. They headed towards her home, but surely Idina couldn't still be in their house, could she? No, her mother would have fled. Unless...

"I was with Idina for a while until Adolphi showed up. I knew she'd be safe with him, but he told me you were still out in the woods and had no idea about the attack. I needed to find you." He met her eyes for a moment, before picking up his pace to a jog.

Not until she heard the screams did Lilith realize they were running into the massacre. While she had been pre-occupied with finding her mother, Finian thought like a Warrior and brought her into the fight.

"The Unhallowed overtook our borders. We anticipate an attack of a few, maybe a dozen or so at a time, but there were at least thirty of them. Our warriors were spread thin across our walls and weren't prepared for an ambush attack on one section. Percy and I were the only two on the watchtower and..." Finian shook his head, unable to retell what he witnessed." By the time they alerted the town, it was too late. The Unhallowed were already here." Finian said, stopping short of the battle raging before them.

Right outside his shop.

"I don't imagine you took the sword I made with you?" He asked, knowing her answer. True, she only left with *Peace Bringer*, the small dagger Finian gifted her, because it was easier to carry and fit perfectly on her hip. The realization of her stupidity in leaving with minimal protection dawned on her. She had been so foolish.

Cursing softly as he fumbled with the lock, Finian continued to struggle with the door. The tension grew palpable between them before the door swung open at last. "For fuck's sake, remind me to never lock this damn door again."

She doubted there would be a next time since Dasos was burning to the ground, but she kept that thought to herself.

"Here. You'll need a sword. *Peace Bringer* won't give you the ability to quickly dispose of the enemy. No matter how good you are with that dagger, it won't be enough now." He said.

"You continue to save my ass. I guess that's why I keep you around."

Finian barked out a laugh, which sounded so out of place in their current environment. "Well, I happen to really like that ass and if that's why you keep me around Enchantress, then so be it."

The mood sobered quickly once Lilith had the sword in her hand. "No matter what happens, Fin, you better wait for me."

Looking determined and more of a warrior than she had ever seen him before, Finian nodded. "We fight. We live. There's no alternative."

And she hoped that there wasn't.

"I need to find Idina. I need to make sure I can get her out of here safely, if Adolphi hasn't already. Go after your father and sister, Fin. Don't argue with me, we don't have time for this." Lilith added hastily, seeing him about to protest. Each second ticking by equated to another precious moment lost, and she couldn't afford to gamble with Idina's life.

She wanted to tell him many things, but they had a duty to Dasos. More importantly, they had a duty to their family. Finian was not happy leaving her, the struggle playing out across his face. Reluctantly, he nodded, taking a step backwards. "Go. We'll find each other. I swear, Serah, if you end up dead, I'll never forgive you."

"If I end up dead, I won't ever forgive myself either." Was the last thing she said to him before running towards her home. The only home she had ever known burned around her. More bodies slumped to the ground, either dead, dying, or sobbing over their murdered family members.

The ball of dread forming in the pit of Lilith's stomach since returning to a burning Dasos threatened to consume her. She blindly passed faces and bodies she recognized...all dead. Hot, angry tears stung her eyes and whether the tears were for the fallen or her own self-pity, she did not know. Her mind tortured her with images of Idina, and the images of the worst possible outcome threatened to overwhelm her.

An arrow flew by, missing her head by mere centimeters, and landing in the grass in front of her. "Dasos bitch!" A loud, male voice boomed behind her, bringing her to a sudden halt.

"Your friend already used that insult. Is it common for Un-hallowed to share a brain or are you just particularly dense?" Lilith shot back, rounding on the large figure approaching her. Insults she could do. Insults did not require thinking about her loved ones being alive or dead.

The large Unhallowed man laughed, showing off his rotten teeth. He had not been attractive in his previous life and becoming an Unhallowed only enhanced his ugly appearance. "Wicked little tongue, girlie. What else can it do?" He smirked and loaded another arrow into his bow.

"Many things. Unfortunately, you'll not live long enough to know." She sprung, raising the sword that Finian gifted her and brought it down hard on the man's hand. The cut wasn't deep enough but served its purpose.

"You little whore!" The Unhallowed yelled, his nearly severed hand dangling uselessly, dropping the bow and arrow he once held.

"That's what you get for bringing a bow to a sword fight. Be glad I did not sever another appendage."

Both looked down, despite Lilith's best efforts. The Unhallowed drew his legs together, but angled towards her once more, ready to strangle her with his bare hands -- well hand. The Unhallowed was clumsy and Lilith was angry, which did not bode well for the man lunging for her. It was almost comical the way he landed on her sword as if it were a skewer, and he the meat meant to dangle over the open fire.

"Rot in hell and when you get there, tell them that Lilith Serah sent you." She spat and twisted her knife, forcing the Unhallowed to make a wet, gurgle sound. She saw the light go out of his eyes as he slumped forward, giving her just enough time to pull her sword out before he landed face first in the dirt.

It was a fitting death for such a nasty man. She could not dwell on the fact that he had not always been like this, bloodthirsty and spiteful; it was easier for her to see him as wholly evil rather than something more complicated. If she started to think that way, she would go insane before she made it to her house.

Which was only a few yards away. In the distance, the house sat ominously, taunting her with the secrets that awaited her within. The light from the flames had not yet reached this part of town and neither had the Unhallowed. Honestly, she doubted her mother would be home, but since this was the last place Idina mentioned going, it would be the first place Lilith checked.

The street was quiet, no laughter of little children or bartering from shopkeepers ran throughout the small area, making Lilith realize how much comfort she took from the normalcy of everyday life in Dasos. Approaching the front of her house felt like standing at the top of the highest peak, looking down in preparation to jump, and hoping water awaited her at the bottom.

With her last bit of mental strength, Lilith pushed open the door to her home of two years. It was surreal to step into the house; she could almost pretend that everything was normal and the Unhallowed were not within the walls of Dasos slaughtering her people. She did not know what she expected; Idina at the table drinking a glass of hot tea? Adolphi sitting across from her, giving her that rare smile he seemed to reserve for her exclusively.

What she found instead was much different. The table had been pushed against the wall, blocking the door, but moved to make a hasty exit. Household items were thrown to the ground, some shattered beyond recognition, making it harder for Lilith to navigate through the house without stepping on glass. She checked Idina's room first. Before she checked, she already knew her mother would not be hiding in there. Nor was she in Lilith's,

Did this mean they escaped? Was Adolphi with her like Lilith believed him to be? She knew her mom well enough to know she would never leave without her. Her stubbornness knew no bounds when it came to her daughter and not even Adolphi would be able to stop her. So that meant she had to be in Dasos...but where?

Lilith turned and exited her room, making her way through the broken glass and disarray to leave the house. She stood outside her door, momentarily at a loss for where to go. Finian would surely have found his family by now and be getting them to safety before he returned for her. He was brave, but not foolish; he would trust Lilith enough to survive on her own. She needed to do the same for him.

There was only one other place she had not searched yet: the training ground. If Idina was with Adolphi, the Warrior likely took her to meet up with other Warriors, so he could give out orders and find Idina a suitable weapon. Lilith took off in a sprint, following the path she knew well.

The closer she got to the training grounds, the muddier and wetter the ground became. A sinking suspicion told her the ground was not only slick with water. Judging by the coppery smell in the air, the grass had its fair share of blood. The few Unhallowed who spotted her attempted to swing their daggers violently in her direction, but were cut down, adding to the growing pile of bodies.

Piles and piles of bodies. Men she guessed to be warriors laid dead on the training grounds. Their blood soaking into the earth, laid out like an offering. The fighting started here, and the Warriors had tried their best to create a shield between Dasos and the Unhallowed, but the Unhallowed had come from all directions, overpowering Dasos small force. The Warriors must have known they'd be slain but knowing the sacrifice would buy everyone else a few more moments to escape, they did so willingly.

Tears flowed freely down her cheeks as more bodies came into view. She did not know all of them, which meant they had been the Unhallowed, but the rest were her people. She felt as if she were in a trance, walking aimlessly and without thought or purpose. An invisible rope tied itself around her torso, pulling her forward to what she was meant to see.

What, deep in her subconscious, she already knew.

Her feet carried her to the edge of the vast field where Warriors, villagers, and children would practice and learn how to defend themselves. Instead of jovial laughter and playful banter, all she heard was her own heartbeat and distant screaming, because Lilith was the only living person amongst a sea of the dead.

With vacant eyes, she took in her surroundings feeling numb. She was forced to bear witness to the death of one friend today, now she would be forced to do the same for the entirety of Dasos. New screams erupted around her and it took her awhile to realize that the sound came from her. The yell of anguish ripped through her entire core was brought on from the image she had been staring at the entire time. Her brain simply refused to believe it.

In the center of the field, as if they had been one of the first to fall, lay a woman with her head tilted at an odd angle. There was blood on her, but Lilith did not think it belonged to her. Another body, a burly man, was sprawled out next to her. There were several puncture wounds on his body, but the darkest wound came from his chest.

The woman had been killed first, by the looks of it, and he had tried to put up a fight to avenge her death. It must have taken a whole pack of Unhallowed to bring him down, and in his last moments he had reached for the last person he wanted to see before his death.

Idina.

"No!" A raw scream sounding like a wounded animal erupted from Lilith's lips as she sank to her knees, losing the last bit of hope she harbored. Her legs no longer worked, but she had to see, she needed to hold her mother one last time. So, Lilith crawled, dignity be damned. She couldn't get a hold of her emotions. The sobs shook her entire body. Her throat hurt from screaming, but she couldn't stop. The practical side of her mind knew she just gave out her location to any Unhallowed in the area, but that no longer seemed important.

Let them come.

Lilith finished closing the gap between her and her fallen mother. Gingerly, as if made of glass, she pulled Idina into her lap, taking extra care of her broken neck. Not that it mattered; Idina could no longer feel anything, and she would not ever feel anything again. Neither would Adolphi.

"I'm sorry, Idina. I'm so sorry." They should have had more time. She should have been helping Lilith prepare for her wedding ceremony and eventually help her through her first pregnancy. She had wanted to be a grandmother more than anything and now she never would. Lilith would trade anything to see her mother's beautiful brown eyes again and her friendly smile. She wanted her mother's arms around her, rubbing her back and promising that everything would be okay.

Lilith had wanted so much for her mother. She had hoped Adolphi would find the courage to ask Idina to marry him and watch them become grandparents together. She hoped now, wherever they were, Adolphi was with her, and she told him to not blame himself for her death. Her dying was never his fault; he just had the misfortune of living through it.

"I need you. Please mother, I still need you." But of course, Idina did not respond. Her eyes were forever closed, and she would never speak again. Lilith pulled her close, cradling her mother's body against her own and sobbing into her hair that still smelled faintly like flowers.

"Well, isn't this touching?" Sneered a voice from behind her. A voice that belonged to an Unhallowed. She turned ever so slightly to detect a woman carrying a Dasos sword-one probably made by Finian. Seemed fitting that his weapon would be the end of her and yet so cruel. Lilith looked down at her hip, only now realizing she had dropped her sword when she fell to the ground earlier.

Resigned to her fate and at peace with the fact she would soon see Idina again, Lilith dropped her head into the crook of her mother's broken neck and waited for the sword to pierce straight through her. She vaguely wondered if she'd feel the pain, but right now Lilith felt nothing. She would welcome death if it meant she'd wake up seeing Idina again.

Her final thought went to Finian. He would be terribly upset when he found her body. She did not want to hurt him, but she'd wait for him. He would want that. When his time came, Lilith would be the one to greet him on the other side, she knew their souls would find each other.

"I'm sorry Fin. I love you." She whispered, bracing herself for the end. Then she would find peace.

But the pain never came. Instead, she heard a blade fly through the air and hit its target with a sickening crunch.

"You think you are going to leave me, Lil? I'm not giving up on you."

Finian.

Despite everything, he found her. She had been prepared to die, but now faced with the prospect of living, she felt incredibly terrified and unprepared. Damn him.

"She's gone, Fin. She's gone and so is Adolphi."

Strong arms wrapped around her from behind and gently tried pulling her away. Lilith struggled, but Finian held her tighter. "Stop, Lilith. Stop! She's gone and you can't bring her back."

Those words hit her full force, knocking the air right out of her lungs. Finian was lying. How could he be so cruel? Idina was fine! She....no. No, Idina was not fine, but she was no longer in pain. The body on the ground served as a shell for the woman who once occupied it.

"We have to go, Lil. Are you hurt? Can you walk?" He asked, looking over her body for wounds. He wouldn't find any, her only wounds were within, and she doubted those would ever heal.

She took his outstretched hand, and he helped her to her feet. Her legs were heavy and foreign weights to her. It took a moment to steady herself and to calm her breathing. "Wait," she said, a thought suddenly coming to her. "Your father? Mavis? Did you get them out?"

Finian tensed, his jaw set, keeping whatever he was not telling her inside. He would not meet her gaze. "Finian. Dammit, tell me! Did they make it out or not?"

"It doesn't matter. We need to go. Now."

"*Doesn't matter?* Doesn't matter?!" Lilith knew she was near hysterics, but there was no stopping the panic. How could he be so calm in the wake of all this? "Finian, my family is dead. I need to hear some good news. Please tell me that your father and Mavis made it out alive, that they are waiting for us in the forest."

"I can't say that Lilith. I'm sorry-"

"Why can't you?!"

"Because they are dead!" Finian turned around so abruptly that he practically ran into her. He did not step back either but continued to look at her with an expression she had never seen before, and it scared her. "They are dead. Neither of them had the chance to make it out of the house. Mavis was slaughtered in her own bed and my father-" His voice cracked a little, the emotion becoming overbearing. "He was in two, Lilith."

"Finian, I'm-"

"Don't you dare say sorry." He hissed.

"I wasn't going to." She said softly, teetering on the edge of unadulterated sadness herself. But focusing on his pain made her forget hers and that was a small reprieve. "I was going to say "I'm here. I'll always be here. Just like you'll always be here for me. Right?"

This time, Finian was the one to choke back a sob. Dead was dead but having to see his little sister and father slain like animals...that was a whole other level that Lilith was not prepared for. Her heart hurt for him and for everything they lost tonight.

Finian let out an anguished scream, something inside him finally snapping. Saying it aloud made their death real and every emotion he held back erupted out of him like a rushing river. She watched the man she loved grow hard and guarded. She feared she would never be able to see his goofy smile again, at least not for an awfully long time. Hell, she was unsure if she would ever find the courage to smile at him like before either.

Lilith took his hand, giving it a gentle squeeze to reassure him that she was still here. Even though they lost everyone they loved in a single night, they still had each other. Gently, she dropped his hand, turning once more to look back at the destruction still unfolding in front of them, no less than half a mile away.

"If we exit through the south side of the wall, we should be able to bypass much of the Unhallowed left within the city. Most have migrated into-"

A pause. A second passed.

Then another.

And another.

"Migrated where?" Lilith asked, turning around. For a second, she wondered why Finian stopped mid-sentence, his mouth still agape with unspoken words. "Finian?" She said again, with a hint of panic in her eyes.

That was when her brain registered the arrow protruding out of his chest. It had been a clean shot from behind, the bloodied tip going straight through the intended target. He swayed slightly, his eyes taking on a new sheen they had not possessed before.

"No." Lilith choked on her words. This was not happening, she was not watching Finian, her last surviving loved one, die in front of her. She lost enough for one night; Finian couldn't leave her. She wouldn't allow it.

"Lilith, I-" Was all he managed to sputter out before dropping to his knees.

"Fin!" She cried, diving for him before he face planted and caused more damage by the arrow. "Look at me Fin, everything is going to be okay. You must trust me. We just need to move. Once we are in the forest, we can rest, and I'll take the arrow out. You just have to be strong for another few minutes. You can do that, can't you?"

It took every ounce of strength left to lift his head and stare into Lilith's eyes. Her vision was obstructed by tears, but she could have sworn he smiled at her. "It's not so bad, Lil. I think you'd like it here." He murmured.

"Like it where, Finian? Baby, stay with me. I'll...I'll carry you. Just stay with me." She pleaded, even knowing she would not have the strength to carry him, but she would try until her legs gave out.

"Here." He said again, looking beyond her. He was delusional with blood loss because there was nothing "not so bad" about Dasos currently. "I'll wait for you, Enchantress. I'll wait for you for a thousand years."

"Dammit Fin!" She wailed, wanting to shake him but fearing she would only hurt him more. "You aren't going anywhere. You are staying right here. With me. Okay? We are going to get married."

"You say yes?"

"Of course I do, you foolish boy! But you must live, Fin. I can't be in this world without you. Please, don't leave me." Her pleading fell on deaf ears. She realized his breathing stilled and his chest no longer rose and fell normally. His eyes drooped until they finally closed.

"NO!" She shrieked, this time shaking him. He did not so much as grunt. "You bastard! You promised you wouldn't die. You fucking promised me!"

But he did. He left her alone. She had arrived in Dasos alone and now she would be forced to leave Dasos alone. Idina was lost to her and now Finian had left her behind, lost with no direction.

"I can't do this, Fin, I can't do this." The world closed in around her. No matter how deep a breath she took, she still felt suffocated. Her body shook, and she didn't know how to gain back control. Her vision began to go dark around the edges, and she desperately tried fighting the darkness off. She did not know exactly what she tried to fight but knew she could not win against an unseen force.

The last thing she saw was a tall man in a black tunic, perhaps death welcoming her home, before everything went dark.

CHAPTER THIRTEEN

THE AFTER

T HE MAN MOVED SILENTLY in the night, camouflaged in shadows. He watched the destruction play out in morbid fascination. Death hovered over the town, gently caressing it with his touch and pulled people into the darkness. Many times, Death looked him in the face, but they kept a fragile peace and so Death never took his soul.

The slaughter of Dasos took place over the span of one hour. Or was it two? Time became irrelevant to him a long time ago. He was cursed to walk this world as an immortal. Perhaps his morbid fascination was also laced with jealousy. How often had he wished for Death, only for it to never come? Of course, this moment was not about him. A particular reason led him here, and he would not be distracted.

He had seen the girl before, but never this close. Never in her home, or...what remained of her home. Being back in Dasos did little to quench the unease boiling in the pit of his stomach. Dasos changed over the centuries, but few things transcended time and weather. Only the rivers and lush forest. If he closed his eyes, he could almost pretend he was back home, when Dasos was his home.

He was unsure if nostalgia or trepidation made him wait in the shadows, well after the battle ended. The few survivors, all Unhallowed, turned on one another and attacked until only one remained. A boy, no more than fifteen, surveyed his surroundings with a devious grin and howled in delight. His job now completed; he was free to walk aimlessly until his next kill.

When the boy finally took his leave, the man came into the light. There was no fear in anyone seeing him now since he was completely alone with the dead. The man stood six feet tall. He was well-built, but little remained of his youthfulness. Streaks of gray colored his neatly brushed hair, giving him an appearance of a man in his fourth decade. What little remained of his former beauty passed as a warm, friendly image.

The man trudged through the mud and blood, his eyes occasionally wandering from body to body. He felt no kinship with any of the departed and mustering up sorrow proved incredibly difficult. He had seen many dead bodies, so what were a few more? Time turned his heart crueler, but time remained to repent and fix his actions from the past. He just needed the girl.

Lilith.

He continued to walk, gliding through the bodies like a lost shadow, glowing bright under the moonlight. It did not take long to reach the spot on which she fell. Tonight proved too difficult for her and that weakness would cost them. The boy, Finian, proved a greater distraction than both Hades and Poseidon bargained for. After all this time, they continued to underestimate key players on the board, but he knew better. That mistake cost him heavily in the past and it was one mistake he would never make again.

Love was a despicable thing and made foolish people do deplorable things. However, in this case, it worked in his favor. He needed Lilith, but he also knew the girl would not come with him willingly or alone. By taking away the people she loved all in one night, he successfully isolated her and then willed her to sleep. He blessed her really, for sleeping took away the pain of reality. When she awoke, she would be thankful for this small reprieve.

Which would be soon. He needed to move fast so Lilith could recover without the reminder of her fallen town. She lay in a crumpled heap on the floor, easily mistaken for one of the dead. Her body once covered her lover's, but Finian's body vanished. That concerned him, it meant he was running out of time. If he had known Finian belonged to *him*, he would have made sure nothing remained of the boy. Another foolish mistake.

With a deep sigh, he leaned down and took Lilith into his arms. She was surprisingly light but carrying another person would make his travels slower. He was strong but used the modicum of power he still controlled to keep her in a deep state of sleep. The rest went towards the exertion it would take to carry and shield her presence for a couple of hours until they reached his camp.

"Before long Lilith, you will have the revenge you seek. It's time, little goddess." He whispered into her deep, auburn hair.

Then, for the second time in his life, he turned away from Dasos and retreated. The next time he returned, he hoped he could restore the wrong he created centuries ago.

PART TWO

"'I thought: I cannot bear this world a moment longer.' '
Then, child, make another.'" - Madeline Miller

CHAPTER FOURTEEN

THE BEFORE

My Dearest Zeus,

I thoroughly enjoyed our summer together. The castle is a lot less interesting without another person my age here. The closest I have are my cousins, but the oldest is 5 and the youngest is but a babe. I fear I may lose my mind with little else to do but walk to our favorite lake. It is not the same traveling without you. I have no one to share my secrets with or swim in the lake my grandfather forbade us from. My grandfather has noticed a change in me and says I suffer from love sickness, but I'm not sure if he's right. I know we are to be married, but we've promised each other we will always be friends. Married people just seem so unhappy and I don't want to be unhappy with you, Zeus. I want to have fun always and explore the world. You want that too, right? Anyway, my sweet Zeus, grandfather says we will be traveling to Dasos in a fortnight to celebrate the wedding ceremony of Poseidon and Lady Amphitrite. I've heard she's really beautiful and her father has more money than even my grandfather!

Until we meet again, sweet Zeus.

Yours entirely,

Metis

Zeus finished reading the letter and smiled. He pictured Metis sitting at her white oak desk, writing in her beautiful script, and putting emphasis on each letter that crossed or dotted. It had only been eight days since Zeus left the southern kingdom from his two month stay. At first, he dreaded the two-month departure because he had never been away from mitera Chloe for so long. She reminded him that two months away also meant two months away from his father and twin brothers. The prospect of going to the southern kingdom became more enticing.

Zeus had been promised to princess Metis for two years and in that time, they had only visited each other a handful of times. Their interactions were always supervised by Cronus, Vulcan, or Gaia. Still, Zeus had a job to perform. One that Cronus and Gaia never let him forget. Getting any information about Ambrosia proved difficult with the lack of alone time with Metis. Vulcan still did not trust him alone with his granddaughter.

Which is why it came as quite a surprise when Vulcan requested Zeus visit his kingdom to partake in the summer festival. "Two months is a long time, boy. A person can learn many things in two months." Cronus had said after receiving the request.

"You will leave at morning's light escorted by a few of my guards. They will ensure your safe travel. I have made arrangements for them to stay with you while you are away, to which Vulcan agreed." Cronus continued.

Zeus doubted the southern King was particularly excited about the editions to his kingdom. Though to him, it likely appeared as an overprotective and loving father wanting to assure his son's safety. If Vulcan truly knew Cronus though, he would see the King held no love in his black heart for Zeus.

"Malik will be one of the guards accompanying you. Every week you will report to him with any information you learn while in the southern kingdom. This is your first time to prove your usefulness to me, boy. You will not like what happens if you fail me."

"Yes, father." Ever the obedient son, Zeus replied. Cronus never explained the repercussions, but Zeus knew better than to ask too many questions and provoke his father's wrath.

Zeus fully intended to uphold his end of the deal. The first few days spent at Vulcan's kingdom, he talked very little and listened to Metis. He learned of her love for books and fantastical adventures. She loved dancing with her family, even if she was not the best at it. She despised embroidery because she always poked herself with a needle, and her mom would grow angry when she spotted the tiny blood droplets all over the linen. Metis also hated most vegetables but ate them so her mother and grandfather would allow her dessert.

The more time he spent with Metis, the more he wanted to learn about her. Her favorite colors, foods, and plays. Zeus seldom spoke about himself and only ever asked her questions. At the end of week one, he understood Metis better than his own brothers. Yet, he neglected to obtain the most vital information about Ambrosia; the entire reason he was allowed to go.

After the first week, Zeus reported to Malik and gave an unsatisfactory report -- according to his father. Zeus received a scathing letter with promises of consequences to come. A beating ensued afterwards. Not from Cronus, of course, since his father was home at Dasos. No, he allowed Malik to deliver the punishment.

A small part of him still loved Chloe and Zeus benefited from that, but only barely. He allowed his men to rough him up, but they couldn't leave any visible marks because of the questions that would follow. A slight limp the next day didn't raise any suspicions or second glances though. The only person who noticed a change in Zeus had been Metis.

"Are you certain you are okay, Zeus? You look stiff and are walking funny." Metis eyed him, not believing his feeble explanations.

"I'm fine, princess, really. I twisted my foot last night on my way to the privy."

"Well why didn't you tell me that before?" She giggled.

Zeus smiled at her laugh. It was high-pitched and inviting, making others want to join in when they heard it. "I feared you'd laugh at me."

A sudden flush to the girl's cheeks stopped her laughter. "Oh Zeus, I'm sorry. I should not laugh. This castle is full of sharp corners, and it is easy to stumble if you do not know your way."

He hadn't liked seeing her embarrassed and spent the rest of the day making it up to her. He listened to her favorite books and allowed himself to be swayed into dancing. Metis was a breath of fresh air and Zeus found himself enjoying each second spent with her.

Still, every week he reported back to Malik. He only broached the subject of Ambrosia a few times but never pushed the matter. Some weeks he could not give enough information to satisfy his father and thus the beatings ensued. Each one a little worse than the last, as if they took out all their frustrations and anger on him. Fortunately, years of intense sword practice and endurance training taught him to limit the impact of the blows.

That did not stop the pain from coming though.

It had been worth it, every fist or boot. For once in his life, he was not under the watchful eyes of his father or grandmother. There were also no signs of Lord Kotas, for he stayed back in Dasos. Zeus was thoroughly grateful for that. Although he missed mitera Chloe, they exchanged letters frequently enough that missing her became a lingering side effect.

Zeus and Metis filled most of their days at the lake, swimming even though her grandfather warned them against it numerous times. They would wait until their clothes were mostly dry before returning home, usually dodging the watchful eyes of the castle. On the rare occurrence they were caught, no real punishment was given. Metis held the hearts of all her family members, so they did little but fuss over them before sending both back to their rooms.

The day he was to return home, Metis cried. She tried to hide her tears by wiping them away before they could fall or covering up her sobs with little coughs. She had gone to wipe another tear away when she thought Zeus was not looking, but he had grabbed her hand and kissed it gently. "Until next time, princess Metis."

Standing only a breath away from each other, he looked down at her and had the sudden, foreign urge to kiss her. He never had the urge before, but now the need was a strong pull he could not deny.

He leaned down gingerly, giving her time to pull away. The same look crossed her face, and he half expected her to back away, but Metis tilted her chin up and closed her eyes. Then their lips met, and they kissed. Just like that. Softly and a little awkwardly, but Zeus thought it perfect. He pulled back and smiled at her blushing cheeks. "Goodbye, Metis."

The entire ride home he thought of her lips, her smile, and the look she gave him when he left. A look of a friend who loved him. If he was honest with himself, he thought about that kiss many days after arriving home. Mitera Chloe caught him smiling at random times and eventually got the story from him. He was unsure who had been more excited about the kiss: him or Chloe.

"Is that a note from a certain princess?" Chloe asked, grounding him back into the present and away from his memories of summer vacation.

"You've not read it?"

"Of course not, Thunder. I hoped you would tell me about this letter that has left you smiling like a court fool."

One of the many reasons mitera Chloe was wonderful was she allowed Zeus privacy. She allowed him to share what he wished and because of that, he found himself wanting to share everything without fear of judgment. She'd offer advice and only insert herself into a situation as a last resort.

"It's from Metis. She is bored at the castle without me but excited to be here soon for Poseidon's wedding. I did not realize father invited them. Does that mean we're invited too?" He asked.

"We are." Chloe said slowly, calculating her next words, "but as an act of appearance only." Meaning they weren't wanted there, but to keep up the charade, Cronus had to invite his youngest son to attend.

"I didn't realize Poseidon was ready to marry. He and Hades enjoy going through the ladies of court." Zeus said.

"Yes, it came as quite a shock to everyone. I think Cronus had his hand at play. Though Poseidon seems smitten with Lady Amphitrite. She comes from money and a strong family. She is also beautiful, which never hurts. I think your father is eager to seek an alliance within his court."

"Why within? I thought his goal was Caister, the southern kingdom?"

"True," Chloe nodded in agreement. "But good rulers understand that kingdoms can fall within. It's best to keep those in your inner circle happy."

"So, Poseidon is not in love? This is a political marriage?" Zeus asked.

Chloe dusted the flour off her hands. Today served as her cooking day, and she spent it making bread for the week. It always made the small quarters smell of yeast. "Royal marriages are rarely for love. There is always a political agenda behind each pairing. But," she paused, thinking. "I do think this pairing is blossoming into something more."

It was odd to think of Poseidon in love. He could not picture the tall, fierce man enthralled with something delicate and beautiful. Was Poseidon capable of kindness and love? Hades most certainly wasn't, but perhaps Poseidon possessed a sliver of compassion.

"Do you think Metis and I will fall in love?" Zeus asked before he thought better of it.

Chloe gave him a look of sadness and heartbreak. It made him flush with embarrassment and anger because he knew the answer before she spoke. "I want that for you, my Thunder. You deserve a woman's love, but I do not think it is wise to get attached. Your marriage to Metis goes beyond politics. You are there for a purpose and will ultimately steal from her family. Love cannot be built on a foundation of lies."

"But maybe I won't have to betray her. Maybe she will freely give me information and share the elixir. Maybe they are not in possession of Ambrosia. It wouldn't need to end-"

Before he finished his sentence, Chloe put her hand up to stop his childish ramblings. "I know you enjoyed your time in Caister, and you may even see Metis as a friend. But I warn you, dear boy, do not invest too much hope in those fantasies. I fear they will only leave you heartbroken and bitter."

The last part came from experience. Zeus remembered Chloe had once been madly in love with Malik, but the two drifted apart when Chloe took full responsibility for raising Zeus.

Another thing he ruined.

The note in his hand now felt hollow and empty. A note for someone else because Metis did not really want to befriend or love Zeus. Metis thought of him as a different person because she could never learn of the real him.

Chloe wanted nothing more than to reach out and pull Zeus into his arms. He was becoming a young man now and that felt like coddling. She doubted he would appreciate her arms around him.

A loud, sudden knock startled them both. "My, what is it this time?" Chloe mumbled and turned to open the door. As if knowing Zeus was just thinking about him, Malik stood outside, looking grim and haggard. He had seen the captain look tired or worn out, but this was different.

Malik did not acknowledge Zeus, not at first. His attention solely focused on Chloe. He conveyed so many unspoken words in the look he gave her, but Zeus could not decipher any of it. Whatever it was, he sensed it to be bad.

"Chloe," he started, checking his surroundings before stepping closer and talking in an urgent whisper. "You stubborn woman, I beg of you to listen to me. Leave this palace at once. Leave *him*." Malik spat out the last words, staring at Zeus with a newfound hatred he never saw from the captain before. One that rivaled the way his father stared at him.

"Zeus is my boy. I made a promise-"

"To a dead Queen! And look at where that has gotten you! Living in rags, barely more than a peasant."

The slap came so suddenly that the world around them paused for a second. Chloe's hand stung, but she hardly noticed it. Her eyes widened in both surprise and fear. She hit a guard. Not just any guard either. She hit Malik, the captain of the King's guard.

Fury rendered Malik speechless for another few seconds before he slowly turned back to face Chloe. If he were any other man, he might return the slap and dealt his own retaliation. But what love he still held for Chloe kept his twitching fist closely at his side. "I cannot protect you from him forever. This is my final warning, Chloe. Leave now. I will give you anything you desire. Just leave the boy."

Chloe stared at her former lover. She once pictured a life with him. Part of her still wanted that and his offer, despite her best efforts, tempted her. Hadn't she always believed she would marry Malik? Queen Rhea had blessed their union, and they were to be wed the following season. But then Rhea died, and Chloe was left to care for her child; the boy she considered hers now.

Which was why Malik was ready for verbal confirmation; her words would forever cement the lost future he had been holding on to for years. "I will not leave. I will never leave. Zeus will always come first for me."

Malik hung his head, but only for a moment. When he raised it again, the last bit of compassion died away, and he now wore a mask of indifference. "Very well. Then King Cronus summons both you and Zeus to his study at once. I will escort you now."

Malik left no room for argument; he turned his back with the expectation that Chloe and Zeus would follow behind. He met mitera Chloe's eyes briefly, all but begging for her to stay behind. If she did not back down with the captain of the guard, she would most certainly not relent for her adopted son either. "Come, my love."

Malik led them through the eerily quiet palace. The dinner feast ended nearly an hour ago and the palace servants had cleared off the table, making it appear unused. Only a few guards lingered, taking up their posts for the night. Malik recognized the guards, and each greeted him with a respectful nod that their captain reciprocated.

Before long, the three of them stood outside the King's office. Malik did not knock. He opened the door and stepped aside. His expression gave no hint as to what Zeus and Chloe were walking into. Ordinarily Zeus would not worry, many meetings with his father desensitized him to Cronus's antics. Yet, he found himself unnerved because the King never called for Chloe to join. Up until this point, Cronus only ever allowed Chloe to wait outside.

Cronus sat behind his desk, looking burdened upon their arrival. It was not as if Zeus begged Malik to arrange an audience with Cronus; he would have been perfectly fine to avoid his father until Poseidon's wedding.

"Thank you, Malik. You can wait outside. This won't take long." Cronus dismissed him. Malik hesitated momentarily; his gaze flicking over to Chloe. She did not meet his stare, which was enough for him to take his leave.

The door closed with a resounding thud, leaving them alone with the King. Well, alone was not entirely accurate. He had two personal guards flanking him. Zeus recognized both as Kael and Hephstes, the guards who escorted him on his trip to the southern kingdom. Their presence cast an ominous feeling in the pit of his stomach. Kael and Hephstes were not normally assigned to the King, both too rough around the edges for such a prestigious position.

There could only be one reason they were here. Zeus felt sick.

"I have not had a conversation with you since you've returned. I've been preoccupied with wedding planning. Admittedly I thought you would seek me out, Zeus. As my personal spy in Caister, any information you gain must be reported back. Had I not made myself clear before?" Cronus asked calmly, which made Zeus feel more on edge. His father's calm demeanor was extremely deceiving.

"King Cronus, how was Zeus to know to come to you? You've never allowed him to hold counsel with you before." Chloe argued, seemingly unaware of the tense situation.

"I did not ask you to speak, Chloe. This is a conversation between me and my son. Please try to refrain from speaking." He discarded her as easily as one would a petulant child. Chloe's face reddened, but she kept her mouth shut.

"So, I ask you again boy, is there anything you wish to tell me about what you learned during your time with princess Metis?"

Zeus furiously searched his brain for any new pieces of information he might have left out, anything to satisfy the king's curiosity. In truth, his reason for being there changed once he had gotten to know Metis better. Ambrosia never left his mind, not with the King's guard looming over his head at all times, but it no longer seemed important to him.

"I've reported everything I learned, father. Princess Metis did not know much about Ambrosia." Zeus said, which was not technically a lie. Metis did not know much about the elixir on the few occasions he brought it up. He just did not press her on the issue.

Cronus seemed to read his thoughts because he did not look convinced by his pathetic excuse. Judging by the look on Chloe's face, neither did she.

"Did you talk to other people? Search the castle? Make alliances with people in Vulcan's inner circle. Don't underestimate the servants, they are a breeding ground for gossip." Cronus questioned.

"Alliances?" He wavered. Zeus had been focused on getting acquainted Metis; perhaps a little too much. Hearing it said aloud made him feel foolish. He wanted to prove himself to Cronus, even though the man did not deserve his loyalty.

"Yes, Zeus, alliances. You were gone for two months and the information I received from you proved all but useless. What do you have to say for yourself?"

Nothing. He had no excuses. For the very first time in his life, he had felt a sense of freedom while he was away. He did not have to hide in a half-finished part of a castle. No one despised him, and he was welcomed at the table for every meal. They treated him like a prince, and he started to believe he truly was one and not a poor imitation of a royal.

Zeus's silence only made Cronus angrier. He brought his fist down hard on the desk, scattering loose papers to the floor. "Your incompetence has pushed back my plans yet again. I'm nowhere closer to getting my hands on Ambrosia than I was two years ago. Two fucking months, boy! You were at the southern kingdom for two fucking months and could not even acquire a few alliances! I hoped the punishments I put into place would remind you of the importance of your job-'

"Punishments? What punishments?" Chloe interrupted, looking between the King and his son.

"Interrupt me again, Chloe, and I will cut your tongue out of your damn mouth." It was not the first time he threatened to dismember her, but it lacked its usual teasing. Zeus knew his mitera Chloe well enough that she would be willing to test his threat. Before she had the chance to speak, Zeus grabbed her hand and squeezed it. It was a small gesture, but it said, *"It's okay. We're okay."*

"This past week has allowed me time to think. Kael and Hephstes carried out the punishment as instructed, but it did little to encourage the obedience I expect from those that work for me. I figured we should try other means." At that, Cronus turned to Chloe with a smile that sent chills down Zeus's spine. Suddenly, he understood why his father wanted Chloe there.

Something in him snapped.

"No! I will do as you ask. Please do not touch her!" Zeus bellowed, trying to push her behind him, but his father grabbed his arm and yanked him away. He was surprisingly strong, though he should have expected his father's strength from years of hunting trips.

"Restrain him and seize her." Cronus ordered and before Zeus could do any more to stop what was about to happen, two strong hands grabbed him from behind and pulled his arms behind his back roughly. He struggled but that only made Hephstes agitated. Hephstes forced Zeus down on his knees, pinning him under his weight.

Kael had Chloe and led her to the edge of Cronus's desk, forcing her to bend over. He bound her hands together, kneeing her in the stomach when she tried to fight him.

"It is best if you don't struggle, Chloe dear. This will be over soon, I assure you. The more either of you struggle, the longer this unfortunate punishment will go on. No one wants to see you hurt less than I, my sweet Chloe. Regrettably, my son does not share the same sentiments." He said.

Kael produced a long, black whip from behind the King's desk. Zeus's eyes went wide; he did not register the tears rolling down his own cheeks. He wanted to look away, but Hephstes kept his head in place. It should be him being whipped. Chloe was innocent. Her only crime was loving him. He hated himself at that moment. He hated Cronus with a fiery passion. Never had he wanted to kill a person, not even his horrible brothers. If he were given a sword, Zeus would not hesitate running it through the King's evil, black heart.

"Since she's a woman, five will suffice. Make it quick, I have someone awaiting my company in bed." Cronus gave the order as if she were nothing more than a small nuisance and not the only mother Zeus had ever known.

Mitera Chloe met Zeus' eyes. She was shaking and could not hide the fear etched across her features. She managed the faintest of smiles for Zeus, once again putting him first. The whip came down so fast that at first Zeus thought he imagined it. Then Chloe's screams filled the room as Kael brought the whip down for a second time. He heard the cowhide slash into Chloe's back.

The screams grew louder, and Zeus could no longer tell the difference between his screams and hers. Each crack came harder than the last. By the time Kael dealt the fifth blow, Chloe no longer possessed the energy to stand. She fell to the ground, crying and curling in on herself. When she landed, her entire back became exposed to Zeus. Angry purple bruises were already forming. That was the least of her injuries. The blood and opened flesh ignited a fire within him. One day he would avenge Chloe for what they did to her.

Cronus ordered Hephstes and Kael to leave after untying Chloe's wrist. She did not so much as move or acknowledge them when Kael tossed a cloak her way to cover up. "I hope you learned an important lesson here, Zeus." Cronus said once they were alone. "If you displease me again, I assure you that your next punishment will be much worse."

Cronus moved to leave. Before he walked out of his study, he turned to Chloe, who had gone still on the floor. For a moment, Zeus thought he saw regret on his father's face, but it was gone before he could be certain and replaced with contempt. "Unfortunately, your only crime is loving an unwanted son. Was it worth it? Is *he* worth it?"

Cronus did not wait for an answer. He walked out without another word. Zeus slowly crawled over to her. She seemed so far away in her fragile body. "Mitera Chloe..." He croaked but did not receive an answer. She did not look at him. Her eyes were open, but they looked vacant.

Then another person appeared in the room. He slipped in so soundlessly that Zeus realized he could have slit his throat and Zeus would have never seen it coming. Malik crouched down next to Chloe and draped the cloak around her exposed back. She did not flinch away from him, even as he picked her up, careful of her wounded back.

"You knew." Zeus whispered. His tongue felt heavy in his mouth. "You knew and didn't do anything!"

"I tried!" Malik hissed. Chloe whimpered. He coddled her like a baby until she settled down again before speaking. He was still angry, but his voice was softer. "I tried getting her out. I knew something bad would happen, but I did not expect this. The King made no mention of what he planned to do with her. Don't direct your anger at me. Not when you are the one who put her in this situation. I will never understand her love for you, not when she should have so much more."

Chloe deserved to have a family of her own. She could be the wife of the captain of the King's guard. Their life would be one filled with ease, political dinners, and balls. Instead, Chloe laid broken in the arms of the man who loved her but could not have her.

"Word of advice, give your father what he wants. Don't gamble with the lives of those around you. Today was a mercy, but next time neither of us will be so lucky."

Zeus watched Malik carry Chloe away, neither of them saying more. As much as he wanted to hate Cronus, his guards, or Malik, none of them were to blame. Not really.

Chloe was beaten because of him. The anger, hatred, and disgust he was feeling belonged to him and him alone.

It was another hour before Zeus picked himself up off the floor and made his way back to his quarters. Malik was gone, but Chloe lay in bed. She was on her side, facing the door. Zeus saw the white of her eyes, and he knew she was awake.

"Mitera Chloe?" He murmured softly, approaching the bed. She did not answer him, but she looked at him this time. "I'm sorry. I'm so sorry. I swear to you this will never happen again. I will never let anyone harm you or lay a hand to you. I swear on my life."

Still, Chloe did not respond. Zeus knew she needed time and did not push it. He leaned forward and gently kissed the top of her head. "I love you." He spoke tenderly and left to retire to his room for the night. Once alone, he wept for his adopted mother and the pain he brought upon the one person that meant more to him than his own life.

It would be some time before he would be able to look at her and not want to cry.

CHAPTER FIFTEEN

THE AFTER

L ILITH DID NOT REMEMBER the last time she dreamed. The very idea of dreams was odd to her. Finian often spoke of them and retold fantastical tales. It was odd to think when a person went to sleep, their brain did not shut off; instead, it created a whimsical land of make believe for their napping spirit to play in until daybreak. Darkness always held its claim over her while she slept, but this time she dreamed vividly of beautiful men and women, adorned with lavish silks and colorful jewels.

They all felt so familiar to her, though she wondered where she would have ever encountered such people. The people of her dreams appeared otherworldly. Through their grace and poise, unimaginable power radiated from them, making her feel like a fleeting thought in comparison, unworthy of occupying the same space.

Soon the dream blurred until only two faces were left amongst the sea of beautiful people. They were nearly identical, except where one had hair as golden as the sun, the other's hair was as dark as a starless sky. Lilith wondered if they were going to speak to her, but soon they faded into oblivion as she slowly began to wake up.

The ache in her body was the first thing she felt when her eyes flickered open. Her muscles were sore and protested violently when she stretched. She reached for Finian, but the space next to her was vacant.

"Fin?" Her voice carried in the dark, but she did not receive an answer back. Perhaps he left to relieve himself and would be back any minute. Or he-

Dasos.

The thought came abruptly and without warning. Dasos had burned and blood soaked the grass, coating everything in red. She had been burying a friend when her home went up in flames. Death had walked among them, taking friends she had known since her arrival. Amongst the dead had been Idina, her mother, along with Adolphi. They had died together, but that held little comfort for her. Her chest swelled with emotion and fresh tears fell.

And then Finian, her Fin. Her heart shattered when she saw Idina lying dead on the ground, amongst the fallen soldiers and Unhallowed. Finian had been there to pick her back up and give her the strength she needed. She had been prepared to leave, but the Unhallowed took him from her too.

She remembered holding Fin as he took his last breath. He had promised to wait for her, even as she begged him to stay. The arrow had hit its target and Finian took his last breath in her arms. It was the last thing she remembered before her mind went dark. Before she awoke in a strange cot on the floor inside a...tent?

Lilith's eyes finally adjusted to the dark. The cloth of the tent was thick, patched in a few places. The top of the tent hung only a foot or so above her, allowing little room to stand. Next to her cot, lay another, neatly made but empty of a body. Many questions ran through her mind, but the most pressing were how had she arrived in this tent and who brought her here?

The pain of losing her entire family all in one evening threatened to take hold of her. Lilith needed to put her focus on something other than the gray cloud looming over her. Summoning up a bit of energy, she pushed herself up into a sitting position.

She noticed she wore a clean tunic and breeches. It disturbed her that someone, hopefully female, had seen her naked. Though the idea of sleeping caked in blood seemed less appealing, so she supposed this was a better alternative.

Opening the flap of the tent, Lilith walked out, expecting to see the sun. Instead, she was met with a dark sky, the light not yet making an appearance. Another tent stood adjacent, a fire between the two. Lilith was certain she smelled food and her stomach rumbled. She could not remember the last time she ate, and she was utterly ravenous.

By the fire, two people huddled together and talked in hushed whispers. The male was older, even older than Idina had been. He had salt and pepper hair with a matching beard trimmed close to his chin. He spoke to a girl who looked as if she could be his daughter. Neither of them noticed Lilith until she stood only a few paces behind them, trying to overhear their conversation.

Before she could make out what she said, the girl turned and looked surprised to see her. "Oh, you are up." She said simply. The man turned to Lilith, eyes running up and down her body. Not in a creepy way that some older men looked at younger women as they contemplated what lay beneath their clothes, but rather with friendly curiosity and a hint of pity.

"You must be hungry. You've been out a long time. Sit down and I'll get you some food." The girl said, not waiting for Lilith to answer. She turned towards the fire and began to dish out breakfast into a clay bowl. Lilith did not look away from either of them, still uncertain about these people and whether she should trust them. However, at that moment, her stomach growled in protest, leaving her with little choice but to take a seat on a well-placed log.

The silence stretched between them and soon Lilith's curiosity got the better of her. Finian had once mentioned she could never let a question go unasked and now she was about to prove his point. "Who are you?" She demanded as the girl handed her the bowl full of an unknown soup. Even the spices were unfamiliar to her. None of that mattered, however, as she gave in to her hunger.

"Friends, we hope." The girl smiled and took a seat next to her. "My name is Demi. And this is my father, Basil, but you can call him Bas."

Basil -- Bas -- smiled at her reassuringly, a gesture she did not return. Lilith did not know these people, and she did not have the energy to smile or take part in pleasantries. Fortunately, Bas sensed her reluctance and did not push her to speak. He kept his gaze trained on her; afraid she would disappear at any moment.

She could not escape her emotions; the heavy burden of losing everything she loved pressed tightly down upon her. Misplaced anger roared within Lilith at Demi and Bas, who were very much alive, when countless others perished. They weren't Dasonians, she would have remembered them from home, but they had been close enough to hear the slaughter.

"How did I get here?" She finally asked through a mouthful of food.

"I can answer that." Bas said and gave his daughter a look. A silent exchange went between the two. Suspicion crept over Lilith, and she wondered if her new companions were deciding on what she needed to know.

"So answer it. Staring at your daughter does little to ease the tension. All I remember is finding my mother dead and watching my lover die in my arms. Tell me what happened." Despite her best efforts, Lilith could not keep the anguish out of her voice. She blinked rapidly to keep the tears from falling, but a few stubborn ones fell anyway.

"I know you just experienced a great loss." Bas said softly, shrugging off the shawl he wore and placed it around Lilith. It was a cool morning and the clothes Demi put her in were threadbare.

"Demi and I are nomadic. We have traveled these lands for...quite some time, claiming no home other than one another. Demi stayed back at the campsite while I went in search of tonight's meal. I suppose I wandered further than I bargained for because I soon stumbled across a burning town.

"I'm but one person, but I had hoped to help in any way I could. By the time I arrived, your home -- Dasos, I believe -- was little more than ash." He said as the events from that night played on loop in her mind. So much blood and senseless death.

A sudden thought came over Lilith. Children. At one point, she had led a group of children into a barn and promised to come back and escort them safely out of chaos. The oldest had not yet reached teen hood and the youngest one she had to carry to get to safety. "Did you see a barn? You would have had to come across it if you walked through town. It was where we housed most of our livestock."

The silence that followed provided the answer she hoped against. "I'm sorry." Bas said and he truly did sound sorry. "But there was nothing left standing. The flames had come on so swiftly. If anyone was inside, I hope they perished quickly. They are with the gods now."

Lilith snorted. "There are no gods." Gods would not allow children to burn to death or for so many other innocent people to be slaughtered. They would not have allowed the world to have Unhallowed unless each god was cruel and ruthless. In which case, she hoped that no Dasonian souls ended up with them.

Both Demi and Bas shared another knowing glance and Lilith supposed she offended them. She had known a few people back at Dasos who worshiped and prayed to gods, but it was not popular amongst many from her village. The polite thing would be to apologize, but she held no sympathy for those who believed in mythical beings.

"I eventually found you," Bas stated, ignoring the awkward tension passing between them. "In truth Lilith, I felt drawn to you. Your soul called out for help, and I answered the call."

Of course her rescuers would be delusional worshipers.

Lilith furrowed her brows and gently placed her empty bowl in front of her. She silently calculated how long it would take for her to make a run for it. Bas looked to be in decent shape, but she was certain she could outrun him. Demi, on the other hand, was not injured and well rested. She would gain on Lilith before she made it out of the camp site.

"Wait, how do you know my name?" Lilith questioned suddenly, having just occurred to her that Bas addressed her by her first name. She had not introduced herself to the strangers and had been unconscious when they first met.

Bas shifted awkwardly in his seat, looking uncomfortable. "You mentioned it when I carried you back here."

Lie. A weak one at that. Instinctively she reached for the dagger at her hip but remembered she no longer wore her clothes from the previous night. Whoever changed her, which she hoped had been Demi, must have taken her weapons. It was something she would do but pissed her off all the same.

"How far away are we from Dasos?" Lilith continued to question. "I know my town and I don't recognize where we are. You happened to stumble across my home and carry me all the way back here? Forgive me, Bas, but you don't come across as a man that could carry the dead weight of a woman for more than ten minutes."

Silence.

She was beginning to realize when Demi and Bas did not want to answer a question, they stayed silent. Lilith wondered again who these people were and why Bas had conveniently found her when he did.

"Talk or I'm leaving." She threatened.

"And where would you go, Lilith?" Bas asked, cocking a brow. The friendly man she had met first when exiting the tent was no longer there. Like a chameleon, he shed his skin and showed his true colors, taking up a defensive stance. "You have no home, no family. You may be able to survive on your own for a month, possibly two, but there is only one way this ends if you leave."

"Who are you?" She gritted through her teeth, punctuating every word. A surge of energy ran through her. Her muscles no longer ached, instead her body buzzed with unused energy.

"Enough." Demi said, dropping the sweet, timid girl act. She glared at Bas, lip curling in frustration. "We promised when we found her, we wouldn't lie. Frankly, Bas," She spat his name, making it sound like a sickness rather than a name. "We are running out of time. He is only getting stronger and is now in possession of another that shares his blood. We've waited long enough."

Demi ignored Bas's refusals and stood up. "It was not by chance we found you at Dasos. We have been following you since your creation and monitoring your progress. You are a skilled fighter, though there is much you still need to learn."

"You're confusing the girl." Bas sighed, relenting to Demi. "Hades and Poseidon did not bother giving her any memories other than the ones from Dasos. If you are going to speak to her, we start at the beginning."

They spoke of her as if she were not sitting in front of them. Nothing they said made sense. Hades and Poseidon? Those names meant nothing to her and yet, she could not help but feel a certain kinship when she thought of them. She had often been put into conversations she knew little about, since her memory only consisted of her arrival at Dasos. Everything before was nonexistent. She did not, however, appreciate others dictating what she should or should not know.

"I'm going to pretend you did not just say you've been watching me since...creation? Whatever the hell that means. I've had a really shitty night so excuse me if I'm not processing things as quickly as I should. Whenever either of you are ready to make sense, I am ready to listen." Lilith would listen, but it did not mean that she would believe them. They hadn't made themselves the most trustworthy of companions, and she hadn't even been around them long.

Bas pushed himself off the ground and contemplated his answer before looking at Demi for confirmation. "Is Bas really your father?" Lilith asked since their dynamics shifted slightly. They did not share many of the same physical features except for their almond-colored eyes.

Demi found the comment funny and laughed. "Unfortunately. Bastard daughter if you want to get technical. He had no interest in me before, but Bas is lacking in family. Suddenly, he decided I was worthy of his time."

"A decision I regret every day." Bas mused and answered with a taunting smirk from his daughter. Lilith did not quite know what to make of their dysfunctional relationship, but she suspected they didn't either.

"Wonderful. So happy for you both." She spat, growing impatient with their bickering and secrets. More of her sanity chipped away and the dam she built within to hold back emotions threatened to burst. The darkness pushed in, tempting Lilith to let it consume her. When did living become such a burden that the promise of eternal oblivion seemed more comforting?

But no. Giving up would mean Idina and Finian died for nothing. That there would be no one alive to carry their memory and didn't they deserve to live on, even in name alone? She would bear the burden of living if it meant that the two people she loved most would continue to live on through her.

"Please." She spoke again with no traces of her earlier cynicism. "I don't have the energy for games and half veiled truths. You have come for me and now here I am. You said it yourself, Bas. I don't have anything. No family, no home. I've nothing else to lose. I ask you again, tell me why I'm here."

"I think it might be easier to show you." Demi said and motioned for Lilith to follow her. "Bas, you should remain here. Give us a moment without you breathing down our necks. It's not becoming of you."

"I wouldn't have to supervise you if you would do as you're told."

"Maybe we should evaluate where my stubborn nature comes from? Or are we not ready for that conversation yet?" Demi laughed before looping her arm through Lilith as if they'd been friends for years rather than strangers who just met. "My father tends to bring out the worst in people, I apologize in advance."

Demi left Bas grumbling to himself about shameless women and their inability to relent. "Ignore him. I find it makes the day more pleasant."

"Why are you with him then?" Lilith asked, as they got further away from Bas. Soon he was only a blurry shadow in the distance. "I understand that he is your father, but you don't seem particularly fond of him."

"Oh Lilith, if you have lived as long as I, you'll find that even a bad companion is better than being alone with one's thoughts."

Lilith stared at Demi in disbelief. The woman looked to be around her age, give or take a few years. She was beautiful and captivating in a way Lilith had never seen before. Not a single scar or imperfection touched her body. Her sun kissed skin held a youthful innocence. Old would not be a term Lilith would use when describing Demi.

Once they traveled a safe distance away from camp and her father, Demi came to an abrupt halt. "Let me just look at you." She said, her eyes trailing over every inch of her body. The assessment seemed more intimate than it should have been. "I see my brothers' handiwork at play. A touch of Aphrodite and splash of Athena. They were always fond of those two."

Demi was completely delusional; Lilith was sure of it now. She played into their crazy antics for too long. "Well, what a lovely chat, but I do believe I should be on my way. You and your father have been...interesting to say the least but-"

"You think we are crazy." Demi cut in and although Lilith agreed with that statement, she thought it best not to respond. Luckily, Demi did not seem offended, only amused. "I cannot speak for Bas, but I'm perfectly sane. So are many others like us."

"Us?"

"You. Me. Bas. *Us*." Demi said rather unhelpfully. "The Divine."

"I don't understand." Lilith said, racking her brain. It was not a phrase she heard before. "Who are the Divine?"

"Us, do pay attention Lilith." Demi said and had the audacity to be frustrated with her. "Let me show you."

Lilith waited and watched. What was it she was supposed to be waiting for? Demi stood there, looking at her. The moment was anticlimactic, but Lilith should not have expected a different outcome. She had nothing but a series of weird encounters since she had awoken.

Then something in Demi changed. Subtle at first, just a flicker of color in her eyes. The warm brown hue lightened and now held flecks of green. Her lush golden hair shone and glistened as if made from the sun itself. Her lovely features changed from beautiful to an image of perfection. Lilith nearly dropped to her knees, wanting to worship the woman before her.

Instead, she stood in awe, forgetting words and movement.

"Don't gape, Lilith." Demi said. Her voice changed too, sounding melodic and serene. "I told you earlier I have so much we need to tell you. We are the same in many ways, though you happen to be the most valuable player in this game.

"You said earlier that you did not believe in gods or goddesses." Demi continued. "Which is fair, we haven't had control over this world since our creation. We want to fix that, which is why Hades and Poseidon created you."

With every spoken word, more questions surfaced. There were those names again, Hades and Poseidon. Each time she heard their names, a familiar feeling came over her. along with inklings from a long-ago memory.

Demi, in all her new unearthly beauty, moved forward until she was only a breath away from Lilith. The smell of fresh grass filled the surrounding air. "The Divine, or more commonly known as gods and goddesses, are very much real. And you, young Lilith, are the last of us. The last goddess of The Divine."

Chapter Sixteen

The After

H<small>E WAS INFINITE.</small>
The world was vast, but he was bigger. Every cell, down to the last atom of his being was alive, truly alive, for the first time in his life. He had no body, no face, not even a name. It all seemed so trivial now. Those things had been tethers, keeping him restrained to mediocrity. The ropes that once bound him were no more and in death he was irrevocably freed.

Though there was sadness, albeit a small seed planted deep within. In his previous life, for he was now awoken and living anew, there had been…something he cared deeply for. A place? A person? He could not remember, each time he thought a memory surfaced, it vanished before fully taking shape. Leaving him with pangs of longing and sadness, which were at odds with his new reality.

Since death, he grew beyond mortal feelings and reasoning. In many ways he was enlightened and found matters of the heart a terrible nuisance humans seemed so very fond of. It was a shame that most of life was spent in heartbreak or melancholy when there were far better things to experience. Death was the true start of life, everything before was a place of limbo. Somewhere people stayed until they were chosen for greatness.

Just as he was.

The soft kiss of oblivion tempted to lure him deeper into her black abyss. Relaxing, he no longer wanted to fight the uncertainty awaiting him at the end of his journey. He expected eternal peace.

What he got was pain.

White hot pain seared through the body he was brought back into. It hurt...a lot. Being trampled by a dozen horses would have been the kinder alternative. What cruelty was this? To bring him back to this state where all he felt was pain.

"Finian?" A voice murmured. It sounded miles away and unfamiliar. It occurred to him that the voice was speaking to him. He *was* Finian, and someone wanted him to respond.

Unfortunately, Finian's tongue felt like lead in his mouth. Could the voice not register the pain he was currently feeling? Even breathing hurt, making him pant in shallow breaths.

A hand moved to his chest and sent a powerful jolt through him. Finian screamed loudly, the pain becoming all consuming. At any minute his body would catch on fire; surely this is what it felt like to be burning alive. Just when he thought the pain would overtake him entirely, the hand on his chest pulled away and with it, the pain.

"I'm sorry about that." The voice spoke, sounding familiar though he could not place it. "It was essential to save your life. I'm sure you'll find a way to forgive me."

Finian finally recognized the speaker. This was the second time he heard the voice outside his dreams. He was still unable to open his eyes, let alone move, to see if the man's face was as arrogant as Finian suspected it to be.

"The pain will go away, though you will be sore for a few days. All things considered, you were lucky I got to you in time before my brother could take your soul. I would not have gotten you back if he laid his hands on you." The man said, rummaging around near where Finian lay.

He heard the clinking sound of a glass being filled and then placed upon a surface near him. "You'll want to drink that when you decide to open your eyes. Foul liquid, but it does wonders for injuries such as yours."

Injuries such as his? Oh, right, he had been shot. Through the heart. With an arrow. It had happened so suddenly that at first, Finian hadn't registered the pain. He smelled the blood, and that had caused him to look down at the crimson stain forming on his chest. Still, he had not felt any pain, only a dull ache. He remembered screaming, though the screams had not belonged to him, and then remembered falling onto the ground.

Lilith had been there to catch him. His Enchantress. She held him as he bled, crying and cursing his name. She begged him not to leave her, since he promised no matter where she went, he would never be far behind. He also remembered Lilith had agreed to marry him and then...

Then he died. On the ground, in the midst of a bloody battle against the Unhallowed.

Dread formed within his stomach at the thought of Lilith. Was she here with him? Did she escape? His mind would not let him think of the alternative, he would know if Lilith died. She was out there, he sensed her. They were soulmates, two parts of a whole. If something happened to her, he would most certainly know.

With immense effort, Finian blinked. His vision blurred and then slowly came back into focus. He lay in a bed, one that could easily fit an entire family. The room was elegantly furnished and Finian felt like a protagonist in one of his stories about far off kingdoms with princes chasing after maidens. The surrounding room was suited for a king.

"Hello, Finian."

Finian jumped and instantly regretted the move. He hissed in pain and clamped his hand over the spot the arrow struck him. He half expected his hand to come away damp with blood, but his wound had been neatly bandaged. There was a slight pink hue to the dressing, though nothing to cause alarm. Other than the fact he shouldn't be alive.

"Drink." The man said again, holding out the milky substance. Now Finian knew for sure his eyes played tricks on him because the man before him was the same man plaguing his dreams. The same man who visited just before the attack on Dasos.

Thunder.

"I'm dead." He croaked and accepted the medicine. Thunder was right, the liquid tasted like complete shit, and it took everything in his power to keep the foul medicine down. Thunder did not speak, though he watched him intently, making sure Finian drank every last drop.

Satisfied when he did, Thunder took the glass from him and set it on the bedside table. "You were, yes, but you are no longer dead. Like I said earlier, I was able to obtain your soul before my brother laid claim to you."

Just like his dreams, Thunder made no sense and only proved to make Finian irritated. Still, he did not want to show Thunder he was getting the best of him. "Let's pretend I have no idea what you are saying." Which he didn't. "In a way I will understand, explain to me what the hell you just said."

That earned him a laugh from Thunder. Good. He would rather see him amused than angry. At least this way he might get some answers out of him. "Do you remember the night I visited you in your dream?" Thunder asked, surprising Finian. He had not expected him to bring up any of their interactions in the dream. "The one where I spoke to you for the first time?"

Finian remembered. He had spoken in riddles and branded him. The pain felt identical to the pain Thunder caused him moments ago. "Yes. You told me you were a friend, and I would need you. You said I have powers and to not fight them. Regrettably, I died so that pretty much puts a damper on your plans."

"Finian, we've been over this. You are no longer dead. This conversation is getting tiresome, accept the fact you are very much alive." Thunder sighed. He was agitated with Finian's inability to look past that simple fact. The mortals had raised the boy; he understood he needed to be mindful of his upbringing. "And your powers did manifest, though not in a way I suspected. We wouldn't be having this conversation if they didn't."

"Are you going to start giving me answers or are we going to continue this little song and dance? Frankly, I'm a lousy dancer and my patience has all but left me."

"Very well," Thunder said with a bemused grin. Finian hated this man held so many answers and provided few of them. "I warn you though, you may not like what you hear. I can't force you to believe me, but I have no reason to lie to you. Not anymore."

"Not anymore?"

"Don't interrupt. This will be a longer story if you do." Thunder said, effectively shutting Finian up for now. He would bombard the man with questions after, but now he was too desperate for any pieces of information.

Zeus's game of deception needed to end. No matter that his intentions had been pure, those same intentions led Finian to believe a lie since birth. It amazed Thunder how easy deceiving became, but after a life of being hated, ignored, and lied to, he did what he needed to survive.

"In order for you to understand, I need to start at the beginning. You are a storyteller, are you not? I think you'll appreciate this one." Thunder smiled, waiting for a reaction. Finian did not give him any, so he went on. "My biggest crime to date was my birth. You see, I was never supposed to be here. Through my mother's stubbornness is why I stand before you now.

"My father lost his beloved queen that day and gained a son who murdered her. My existence mocked him every day and reminded him of what he lost. My life served as a reminder to his two sons, my brothers, that their youngest brother stole their mother from them. You can see why they wouldn't be happy with me."

"Actually I can't." Finian said, unable to remain silent. He was not very fond of Thunder, but it was unfair for his family to blame him for the death of his mother. His birth had been her choice. If anything, his father and brothers should have loved him fiercely because he was the last link they had to her. "You did nothing wrong."

The look Thunder gave him was one of wonder and pride. He stared at Finian like a prized possession, though not in a way of ownership, but something else. Thunder stared at him like kin.

"My birth family would think differently, but the woman who raised me would agree with you. I think you would have liked her and her you." Thunder's voice grew soft and sorrowful as he looked out the small window near Finian's bed. His thoughts were elsewhere, remembering the woman who shaped him.

Remembering what he had been forced to do to her.

"Eventually my life only had one purpose: to serve the whims of my father, the King. I became his weapon and spy. I did horrible things to please him. As easy as it would be to blame my father for betraying the only two people I loved, my actions and my choices alone are what I must atone for. I will forever live with regret, but I will never be used as a sword or shield for any King again.

"So I became King." Thunder went on, but no smugness resonated in his tone. He sounded lonely. "I suppose the correct term is god. No King is immortal, only gods carry that burden."

A god? The word sent tendrils of anger through him as he thought of what gods had done for his people. Nothing. They let the chaos and death run rampant and did nothing to stop it. If Thunder claimed to be an all-powerful being, then why had he let their pleas for help go unanswered?

Thunder saw the anger in the boy's eyes and held up his hands in surrender. "I am one god, Finian. You must understand that. I'm powerful, but I have limitations. I can do little to help mortals, not in any way that matters."

"But you could protect us!" Finian shot back.

"I would save a few, but what of the others that also need my help and call for me at that moment? Are you suggesting I let their cries go unanswered? Should I choose who is worthy of my help and let others suffer like you have suffered in Dasos?" Thunder asked, staring pointedly at Finian.

Admittedly, he had a point, but it felt like Thunder wasn't trying at all to protect anyone. Finian heard of evil spirits before, and they were often depicted as handsome and alluring, attractive both in body and personality. Thunder possessed both qualities, and yet he hesitated to call the man before him evil.

Intimidating, perhaps, but not evil.

"Even if I could help everyone, the endless fighting would drain my powers. My time is better suited figuring out who cursed the mortals rather than fighting an endless fight. Wouldn't you agree?" Thunder asked.

Finian ignored his question. "If not you, then who?" Finian inquired, wondering just how long this god had been alive and if he made any progress during his time.

"That is the question, isn't it?" Thunder grinned, finally stopping his pacing to lean against the wall. "I guess it depends on whom you ask. My brothers would like to think I started this curse. Their foolish friends are also keen on making me the villain, so it's the role I play."

"I'm not asking them." Finian said. "I'm asking you."

Thunder laughed, his eyes gleaming with amusement. "You are exactly as I have pictured you to be, young Finian. You give me hope for what is to come." He said, making Finian wonder what he meant by that comment. Though true to form, he supplied no further explanations. "I'm not certain who started this curse. Though I suspect there is a new player on the board we have not accounted for."

All the information proved to be a lot for him to wrap his mind around, starting from the fact he died but Thunder saved him. Why would this god, who Finian assumed held some sort of power or ability, want to save him, a mortal? He had nothing to offer Thunder other than companionship, healing practice, and a good story or two.

The silence between them grew uncomfortable. Finian felt like Thunder waited for him to ask a specific question, though he knew not which. Expectation hung heavy between them, but Finian didn't know where to start.

Thunder's sigh of resignation told Finian he was going to break the silence. What he did not expect was for Thunder to approach him and lean over the bed. The man reached for the wrap on Finian's chest and began to undo the expertly packed bandage. He started to protest, but his curiosity got the better of him. He wondered what the wound looked like underneath, since the arrow had gone through his chest and protruded from the other side.

He did not see a horrid puncture wound like he expected. Finian brought his hand up to graze his chest. No gaping hole or bloodied wound met his touch. Only skin that miraculously threaded back together, though still tender to the touch.

"How long have I been asleep?" He wondered, since it was the only rational question he could think of. In order for his skin to appear as it did, he must have been asleep for weeks.

"One day." Thunder replied, taking the very breath from Finian's lungs.

"That's impossible." He sputtered foolishly. Many impossible things were happening right in front of him, including Thunder himself. Still, it didn't feel real until this moment with undeniable proof.

"And yet, it is so." Thunder said, smiling. "I promised you I would not lie to you, but I'm afraid I have two more confessions since we are having such a wonderful time bonding." He mused and perched at the end of the bed.

"You know me as Thunder. Although that technically is not a lie, it is not my true name. Thunder was given to me by a person I loved. My name is Zeus, a forgotten god of Dasos."

The name Zeus meant nothing to Finian, though he never knew the gods to have names. The few people who still clung to a hope of saviors worshiped unnamed gods and goddesses. From what he gathered, there were many gods, each with their own affinity. Thunder, now Zeus, did not mention having any special affinity. Granted, Finian had not bothered asking.

"So, your name is Zeus, a powerful god of...something." Finian started. "And you saved me from your brother because you did not want him to take my soul? I also wear your mark because I'm important to you for some reason. You need me."

The thought was slow at forming, but when it came, Finian could not stop the idea from taking form. Some things about Zeus had been familiar, not only because he saw the man in his dreams, but because he saw Zeus's same features everyday reflected back at him.

One of Finian's biggest insecurities was he never quite belonged to his family. Sure, his father and sister loved him, but he had been closer to his mother. Mavis took after their father, but he did not share any of those traits. There was always an invisible wall between them, neither tried penetrating. If they ignored their differences, they could pretend they were really father and son.

Though he had been as real of a father as any. Even if Jarin didn't share the same blood as Finian, he had still been his father. Mavis had still been his sister and now both were gone. Slaughtered before Finian could get to them. The pain lashed through his heart, and he doubted he'd ever be able to think of his family without feeling like he failed them.

"What is your next confession, Zeus?" He asked, needing his dismal thoughts to leave. All the evidence from the last few years reared its ugly head, demanding to be heard. Which was why Finian couldn't muster any shock when Zeus spoke the truth at last.

"You are my son, Finian. The Divine. It is time you live up to your full potential."

CHAPTER SEVENTEEN

THE BEFORE

T WO WEEKS WENT BY since the night in his father's study and Chloe had not spoken more than a few words to her son since. She was never outright rude to him, but Zeus knew she was hurting. Even though her back healed, leaving behind the scars of her torture, she was still haunted by the memory. Every time there was a knock on the door, which mercifully was infrequent, Chloe jumped and nervously wrung her hands together.

Seeing such a strong woman broken down into a ghost of her former self, pained Zeus. His mitera Chloe had always been a fierce, strong woman who wouldn't be silenced. She was one of the few people who had never been afraid to stand up against Cronus. People admired that about her, even if they did not say it directly to her. Zeus saw admiration in their expressions; it mirrored his own.

It was the day before Poseidon and Amphitrite's wedding and King Vulcan was set to arrive by the end of the day. Metis wrote to Zeus several days ago expressing her excitement about the wedding and for seeing him again, but he didn't send a reply. Hephstes read the letters addressed to Zeus, which he only found out about when the guard delivered an open letter and recited some of Metis's words back to him.

She had a new dress she believed he would like. Did he have a lake they could swim in or a garden they could walk through? Could she meet any of his friends? She would only be there a few days, but she wanted to see what Dasos had to offer.

As if Zeus had the privilege of knowing Dasos as intimately as other royals.

He did not have the energy to respond with false pleasantries, nor did he know what words would be misconstrued by his father. He would not put another person in jeopardy because he wished to have a friend. One he would end up betraying in the end anyway.

On the eve of his brother's wedding, Zeus got ready to welcome King Vulcan and princess Metis. Half an hour ago, Malik stopped by to drop off clothes. They weren't new, but the clothes were nicer than anything else he owned. He assumed they once belonged to one of his brothers. He was playing the role of a prince and needed to look the part. Except royal clothing was far more intricate than his normal tunic, and he did not have maids to help him dress.

"You look like you could use some help."

Startled, Zeus jumped back. His knees hit the back of his bed, and he caught himself before he toppled over. Chloe giggled and he never heard such a sweeter sound. "Yes, I think you could. I made you herbal tea for your nerves."

"I'm not nervous."

Neither of them believed him. Chloe always caught him in a lie, and he was always quick to expose his wrong doings. "Take the tea, Thunder. It's a big day for you. You haven't seen Metis in a little over three weeks."

It was the most she said to him since that night. He tried to broach the subject a few times, but she claimed she was too tired, so Zeus never pushed her. The more he did, the more she pulled away.

The tension between them still weighed heavily on him. The guilt was not something he could dismiss and move on from, even if she did. Mitera Chloe did not owe him anything, especially not Zeus's attempt to explain himself, but his stubbornness wouldn't let him forget it.

"Mitera Chloe, you don't have to do this. You don't need to pretend to want to be around me or pretend things are normal. I have failed you. Malik was right. I don't want you to get hurt again. You can leave and-"

"Leave?"

"-forget about me. I don't deserve your love."

"That's quite enough!" Chloe raised her voice, putting the cup of tea down a little too forcefully that half of it sloshed over the side. Her volume shocked even her, and she offered an apologetic smile. "Sit down, Thunder. I think it's time we talked about what happened."

With his chiton only half off, Zeus forgot about fixing his clothes. Chloe moved to take a seat next to him, placing her hand on his knee. "Many do not understand why I stay, and I know you are questioning it yourself." She paused and hesitated, wondering if she should voice her next thoughts.

After a pregnant pause where Zeus thought she changed her mind, she continued. "I won't lie to you, Zeus. I questioned leaving too. I wondered why I was still here when I could be somewhere safe with family outside of Dasos."

Hearing those words spoken aloud brought more pain than Zeus anticipated. He feared she would finally realize he was not worth the pain and heartache that came with being his guardian. Chloe wasn't a young maiden anymore, but she could still find a husband. Someone would want to marry her. Hell, Malik still would if she walked up to him now and offered herself.

"But," Chloe smiled, the familiar motherly one she reserved solely for him. "Raising you has become less of a promise to your mother and more because I wanted to. I have never loved anyone the way I love you. You will always be Rhea's son, but I think she would be okay with sharing you. You deserve a mother and I deserve a son. No matter what, my Thunder, I will always be by your side. We are each other's chosen family. I choose you; do you choose me?"

"Of course I do, but mitera Chloe-"

"Mitera, will do. I've always told you to call me mitera Chloe to honor your mother. However, we honor her every day and I believe she would want this."

Mitera. Chloe was his mitera. His mother. He had always seen this woman as such but respected her wishes. The title was too formal and served to remind him he wasn't truly hers. They played house, and he had the role of a son, but it was only a role. Something they could play out in front of people but shattered once the curtain closed.

He had a mother. A real mother.

"Mitera." He tested out the word and both smiled. He was fairly certain he had tears in his eyes, but Chloe was polite enough not to comment. "I love you and I choose you. But it was because of me you were whipped. It's my fault."

"No, it's not. None of that was your fault, baby. Your father is a cruel man. He alone made the decision to punish me. You took many beatings and did not tell me. I took five lashes. He made his point and it's over now."

"But what if-"

"We can't live in what ifs Zeus." Chloe said gently. "We would drive ourselves crazy. As of now, Cronus is showing little interest in us. He is far too preoccupied with your brother's wedding. Use these next three days to learn all you can about Ambrosia. Any new information will please him and make him feel like his lesson worked."

"Mitera, Metis is my friend. This feels wrong."

Chloe smiled sadly at him. She reached for his hand and clasped it. "I know." She said softly. She sounded apologetic, especially knowing Zeus had never had friends before her. "She seems like a lovely girl. It's unfortunate she is mixed up in this, and you are in this position."

They both knew he had a job to complete. One he could not turn down again. As much as he liked Metis and valued her friendship, his marriage to her would only serve his father's purpose. She would figure that out soon enough and hate him like most people did. Until then, he would act as the doting prince his father wanted him to be.

"Now enough of this. We have guests to prepare for. Let me help you get ready. Tell me the last time you bathed? Judging by your stench, far too long. Strip, boy and fill the water bucket. I'll wash your hair."

"Mitera....I can wash my own hair." He groaned.

"Oh, can you? I'm uncertain you remember how. Strip. Stop being shy, I've changed far too many of your soiled clothes for you to blush like a lovesick girl."

His mitera would hear no more of his complaining as she ushered him into the water despite his protest. She scrubbed his head, lathering every inch of his thick hair. He stayed in the bath until it went cold and then Chloe finally released him from the murky water. He hated to admit it, but she had been right. How one person accumulated so much dirt, he did not know.

Chloe then helped Zeus into his clothing, saving his hair for last. She ran her fingers through his hair, doing her best to undo all the tangles. He really needed a haircut, but they did not have time for it now. His hair reached his shoulders and now started to become a nuisance at practice.

"I'll cut it tomorrow, before the wedding." Chloe answered, reading his expression. "For tonight, it looks fine. How do you feel?"

"Nervous." He admitted.

"It's okay to be nervous. Just don't let the nerves take over. Metis already likes you, so the difficult part is done." She beamed and kissed his temple. "Let me change, and we will head to the throne room together."

Twenty minutes later, Zeus stood beside his older brother in the King's throne room. Hades sneered as he approached, making him wonder if his brother knew any other greeting or if he was particularly fond of that one. Poseidon paid him little mind. Amphitrite was at his side, and he whispered something into her ear, making the woman giggle. The only one that said anything was Cronus.

"Nice of you to finally join us." He commented, gaze flickering over to Chloe. She stood still as a statue, never once wavering under his scrutinizing gaze. Cronus got the best of her once, but her tears would not be freely given a second time. There were many things to admire about his mitera, but her tenacity scored the highest on the list.

"Apologies father. It took a little longer than I hoped. I wanted to make sure I looked the part." A simple lie, but he need not know Chloe made him scrub every inch of his body to clean the grime off.

Cronus made a *"hmph"* sound, dismissing the conversation. Which was fine by him, the less his father interacted with him, the better. If only he could force Hades to do the same. His brother had not taken his eyes off him since he arrived. Zeus was unsure why his brother hated him so passionately, save for the fact Zeus dared to exist. Not that Poseidon was much better, but in comparison Hades made Poseidon look like his best friend.

"Is there something I can help you with, brother?"

"I'm not your brother." Hades sneered.

"Funny, I was certain we were." Zeus smirked at him. "May I ask why you hate me today?"

"Do I need a reason other than you're here and our mother isn't?"

Zeus sighed. He wanted to remind his brother he had nothing to do with that accident twelve years ago. Rhea gave birth to him, despite knowing the risk. Oftentimes, Zeus believed there was a deeper meaning for Hades' hate, he just had not figured it out yet. His brother was blinded by anger each time they were around each other. Which, thankfully, was not often.

"Are you ladies finished bickering?" Cronus snapped, just as the doors to the room opened, spilling out four guards. These guards did not wear the colors of Dasos, but the vibrant purples of Caister. Two more guards entered ahead of their king, stopping shy of the steps. Next to enter was king Vulcan himself. It had not been a month since they saw each other last, but Vulcan appeared older somehow. His skin was gaunt, and he had faint dark circles under his eyes. Fortunately, the King had not lost his kind smile.

The smile was deceiving. Vulcan could be cruel if the situation called for it. He had seen the older King order servants whipped if they stole extra food from the kitchen or slacked on their duties. He never lifted a hand against Metis; his love for his granddaughter was pure and strong.

Metis had not yet made an appearance. Zeus looked past the southern King and watched as another pair of guards walked in, each flanking the princess. Seeing her in Dasos unnerved him. In Caister, it was easier to pretend he was an important member of the royal family. No one really knew him, only his title and that carried a lot of weight.

Dasos was different though. Here, everyone within the walls of the castle knew he was the unwanted son. He had not been off castle grounds, except to travel, so he did not know what the commoners thought of him. He was certain rumors spread; royal gossip would always be the main topic of conversation.

Metis wore a lavender chiton, tied tightly around her waist, but flowed freely down her petite body. The pastel colors complimented her dark skin, making her look almost ethereal. When she spotted him, a small blush crept across her cheeks before she beamed at him. Despite the tension from earlier, Zeus returned the smile.

"Are all the guards necessary, Vulcan? This is a wedding, not a slaughter." Cronus said, finally addressing the other King. He pushed himself off his throne and closed the distance between them.

"You would be amazed at how quickly the tides change. I like knowing those I love are protected. I'm sure you can understand." Vulcan said and clasped the other King's hand in a formal greeting. Two of the most powerful men together in a room put everyone on edge.

When Gaia arrived tomorrow, many more would keep their distance out of fear of losing a vital body part.

"Let's move past such pleasantries, yes? Your boy is getting married!" Vulcan slapped Cronus on the shoulder in a friendly gesture and the whole room held their breath. Vulcan did not seem to notice or simply did not care as he moved to shake hands with Poseidon. "Congratulations, young prince. May you find glory in battle and in bed." He winked.

Poseidon smirked. No one needed to wish him glory in bed. He found that on his own; his numerous bastards were proof of that. "Thank you, my lord. Dasos welcomes you. Please, let me introduce you to my fiancé Amphitrite, daughter of Gaetan and Anastasia Andos."

Amphitrite curtsied low to the floor, showing utmost respect in the presence of royalty. She was a high-born girl, but not yet a princess. That title would be bestowed upon her tomorrow. "King Vulcan, your reputation precedes you. It is truly an honor."

"Ah, she's a good one, prince. Very good indeed." He laughed boisterously. "And where's the other-ah, Hades! Another strapping young prince. Your ugly father was blessed with handsome sons, he should consider himself lucky! Only thing worse than ugly children is ugly grandchildren."

"Lucky for you, you ugly bastard, your granddaughter received all the good genes in your family." Cronus jabbed, a slight edge to his voice that Vulcan missed. "Zeus, come greet your betrothed, son."

Metis looked so small next to his father's large presence. All eyes looked upon him as he approached the princess, his smile never once wavering despite the audience. "Princess Metis, good to see you again." He said.

Metis took him by surprise by flinging herself into his arms and hugging him firmly. Heat rushed to his cheeks, coloring them red. "Zeus! I've missed you. It has felt so much longer than a few weeks. Did you receive my last letter?"

Zeus laughed at her enthusiasm, aware his father watched him. "I did. I apologize for not writing, I did not think you would receive it in time."

"Isn't it precious? They exchange letters frequently. Didn't think we were creating true love, did you?" Vulcan asked, earning a few laughs.

"Grandfather! Please, Zeus is my friend. We don't want to be a married couple who end up hating each other. Oh...my apologies prince Poseidon. I'm sure you and Lady Amphitrite will be quite happy together." Metis said, earning a tight smile from Poseidon.

Soon, drinks and appetizers were brought out and the room lit up as they partook in drinks and celebrated the prince and his lady. After an hour, festivities began to wind down and Zeus escorted Metis to her chambers. Vulcan had left earlier with one of Lady Amphitrite's friends who was notorious for warming the bed of any royal, no matter her age.

"Does Hades have a betrothed?" Metis asked as Zeus led her towards the north wing, the one reserved for royal visitors. She had not stopped asking him questions since they left the throne room, her inquisitive nature unable to take a break.

"No, Hades enjoys his freedom too much. I think eventually my father will make him marry, but for now he is focused on Poseidon."

"And us."

"Hmm?"

"He's focused on us too. We will be wed as soon as I become a woman. Many of the girls my age already had their first bleeding. It's only a matter of time now until I'm ready for marriage." She explained.

Oh. Zeus forgot their marriage hinged on her first bleeding. He knew very well what she meant since he lived with his mitera. The first time he saw the bloody sheets, he believed she had been stabbed. Chloe calmly sat him down and explained to him the wonders of the female body. It did not sound so wonderful to him, but she smacked his head when he voiced that opinion openly.

"Grandfather says it will still be some time before he makes me Queen, even after we are wed. He's not ready to give up the throne and that is fine by me. Being Queen is something I prepared my entire life for, but I'm not quite ready to take on that responsibility yet." She continued.

"I will be your prince consort." Zeus added, since his father had not bargained for anything more. There was no need, he would not be around long enough to be anything to Metis. That thought alone made his stomach tighten with guilt.

Soon they stood outside her room and suddenly he no longer knew what to say. He felt like a bashful little boy, standing next to a pretty girl. Well, that was exactly what he was.

"Are you nervous, Zeus?" Metis asked, a small smile creeping up her lips.

"Erm, no. I just, uhm...we have made it to your room."

"We have."

"I am supposed to see you safe."

"You are."

"So, I should probably leave."

"You should."

Another long silence between them, but Zeus had the sneaking suspicion he was the only one who felt awkward, and tongue-tied. Metis hid her giggles. How could one girl unnerve him so much?

"So, I'll see you tomorrow at the wedding. Goodnight, princess Metis." Zeus leaned down and kissed the top of her forehead. This time, the princess did giggle and pulled him into a hug.

"Tomorrow then. We will dance the night away and you can show me more of Dasos. Goodnight, sweet Zeus." Metis finally released him, giving him a final smile before disappearing behind the door.

Walking back to his room, Zeus felt lighter on his feet.

The entire kingdom came to celebrate the wedding of Poseidon and Amphitrite. Only the most prestigious guests were allowed within the castle to view the momentous occasion. Each pew was filled with guests, some nearly sitting on top of the person next to them. Those who arrived late had the unfortunate privilege of lining the walls. Every square inch of the room was filled to the brim with people, most unrecognizable. It hardly mattered if you knew the royal family personally, if Cronus invited you, the whole family was expected to show up. Refusing so would be viewed as an act of insubordination.

Cronus did not need to worry about his kingdom ignoring a direct order, since the rest of the commoners lined up outside in hopes of catching a glimpse of the new couple. The last royal wedding to take place in Dasos was Cronus's own wedding to Rhea.

After her death, the kingdom had little to celebrate. Rhea had been the one for lavish parties and events, Cronus indulged his wife because he loved her. With her gone, he no longer felt the need to put on such trivial things. His son's wedding was different.

It was the first time his brothers smiled for an extended period. Even Hades could not form a scowl at his twin's wedding. The other favored prince invited a companion to the wedding. The girl was slender, with long black hair. She was pretty in a way roses were; eye catching, but not afraid to show off her thorns if anyone dared get too close. Definitely a girl Hades would go after. She eyed Amphitrite and Poseidon with more than the customary kindness expected at a wedding. Zeus detected hints of jealousy in her stare, though many of the young maidens in the audience held similar expressions of varied degrees of envy.

Except for Metis. She appeared to be genuinely happy for the almost newlyweds. She looked upon the ceremony with a whimsical expression, reaching for Zeus's hand every so often to squeeze it during her favorite parts. When something was said about love, she would give the most darling of girlish giggles. Naturally, she received many stares, but judging eyes did not deter her.

The room erupted in a roar of applause once Poseidon and his new wife were pronounced married in the eyes of the Holy Spirits and all of Dasos. Cronus, unsurprisingly, bellowed the loudest, his pride for his son showing in waves. Seeing him like this, proud with love in his eyes, Zeus could see the man he might have been with his mother. He mourned for that man.

The wedding ceremony was grand, but it paled in comparison to the reception that followed. The festivities to honor the new couple were open to the entirety of Dasos and expanded well into the city. It did not matter that neither Poseidon nor Amphitrite would not set foot into the city tonight, the people had reason to celebrate. Although Zeus never attended a wedding, he heard the parties that followed could last days.

Once the sun set and the moon took up residence in the sky, Zeus began to grow tired. Chloe had long ago retreated, claiming she was not as young as she once was and needed to sleep. Zeus could tell her back was bothering her, but she did not want to concern him. After several refusals of help, Chloe finally retired.

Metis, despite her endless, exuberant energy, slowly tired too. She had been offered glasses of wine to celebrate and was now starting to feel the effects of the drink. Zeus, on the other hand, had not touched the wine. After seeing what fools it made of people, he felt it better to stay away from. Not that Metis was a fool, however. She only had a drink and a half, but that had been quite enough for her tiny body.

"Perhaps we should stop," Zeus laughed, catching Metis before she bumped into the servant for the second time that night. She was still coherent, which Zeus took as a good sign, but her center of gravity was off.

"I don't want to go back to my room." Metis pouted like a child, crossing her arms over her chest. It only made her appear cuter. No wonder she was a favorite of her kingdom.

"You don't have to go back to your room, princess. Why don't I give you a tour of the gardens? We don't have nearly as many flowers as your garden has, but I think you will still like it." He assured her, offering his arm.

That pleased the girl, for she looped her arm through his and happily walked with him. Before they left, Metis said she needed to clear it with her grandfather. Vulcan wasn't hard to find, his voice carried in the hall. He spoke loudly with a group of men; the same girl from the night before was draped over his arm.

"Ah, my granddaughter! Look at how lovely she is. Isn't she lovely?" There was a murmur of affirmations while everyone agreed with Vulcan's assessment.

"Oh, grandfather." She blushed. "Zeus is going to give me a tour of the gardens. May I leave?"

Vulcan eyed Zeus with no real malice, only drunken bravado. "You best keep her safe. If there's so much as a scratch, I will personally hurt you."

"Grandfather!"

Another roar of laughter as Vulcan slapped Zeus on the back a little too hard. He tried not to grimace. "I'm only joking...mostly. Of course, but not too late Metis. We will be heading back tomorrow."

"What? I thought we were staying another two days." Metis said, confused.

"Change of plans, darling. I'll share more later. Nothing to concern your pretty little head over now. It is just your mother being overprotective, as normal. Now go, run along, and have fun with your betrothed. Though, not too much fun."

With that ominous warning looming over their head, Zeus led Metis towards the gardens in the back of the castle. There was a slight chill to the air, the last of the winter's night before summer claimed the lands. Not much grew in the winter, so the garden appeared more like a flower graveyard than a blooming paradise. This did not seem to faze Metis any; she still saw beauty in the dying and left behind. It was a quality he wished he possessed.

"This is beautiful. I would spend my entire day out here, reading or writing. Though, I suppose if I were here, I wouldn't need to write you any letters." She smiled.

"You can always write me letters, even if we live together."

"When."

"Hmm?"

"When. Even when we live together." She grinned at him. "Most people who are married live in the same place. Did no one tell you? I'm sure this is coming as quite a shock." Metis giggled.

The feeling of guilt lay heavy in his stomach again. The reality is he would never have the chance to live with her, at least not forever. Once he got the information his father needed, his usefulness will have played out. Then where would Zeus be? Would Cronus let him live his life in the southern kingdom? Doubtful. Would he do what he wanted to do since Zeus's birth and finally kill his youngest? That seemed more likely.

"Zeus, are you okay? Did I...say something wrong? Is living with me so terrible?" Metis asked, her normally cheerful voice now unsure. He felt guilty again, but this time for a whole new reason. He would never be able to give her what she wanted.

"Of course not. It will be an honor and I know we will have a lovely life together. I think I just have a lot on my mind right now."

"Do you want to talk about it?"

No, he did not want to talk about how he was only pretending to be the prince she thought him to be. Nor did he want to mention the only reason Cronus agreed to the marriage was because he made Zeus his spy.

Now Zeus was running out of time.

He thought back to his mitera, the night she lay on the ground like a broken doll. Cronus had done more than wound her body; he managed to break her soul a little that day too. But now he had the perfect opportunity to talk to Metis and give Cronus new information that would hopefully tide him over. At least for a little while longer.

"I'm just thinking about a conversation I overheard today. Between my father and your grandfather." He lied smoothly, having grown accustomed to it.

Metis chewed her bottom lip nervously. Any discussion between the two Kings was never a good sign. "What did you hear?"

"That's the thing, I have not been able to figure that out. My father seemed agitated with your grandfather. He mentioned Vulcan had information on something he wanted. Something they agreed to find together."

At that, her worry was replaced with confusion. "I'm not sure what you mean. To be honest, Zeus, they fight over many things. Do you know the reason?"

"It is unfamiliar to me; I've never heard the word spoken before. The word was...Ambrosia."

Lying felt wrong, especially lying to Metis. She appeared stunned and Zeus watched her erect walls. If she was guarded that meant she knew something. He needed to know just how much.

"I...no, I'm not sure what that is." Zeus was not the only one lying tonight. Ironically, it made it easier to deceive knowing she kept her own secrets. He needed to push her a little more and since she had been drinking tonight, he did not think that would be all that difficult.

"My father called it an elixir. It's extremely rare and tremendously hard to find. Few people think it exists, but my father seems to believe it does. Vulcan seemed defensive." Zeus pried, digging for more information.

"It seems like this conversation was never meant for us to hear. My grandfather doesn't tell me everything. I only know what he thinks I need to know."

"This seemed important. If you are to be the next Queen, wouldn't King Vulcan keep you informed on such a rare elixir?"

"Well...he...I mean-" Metis tripped over her words, struggling to produce a suitable lie. Zeus took pity on her and reached for her hand like a comforting friend. Not one that was attempting to manipulate his way into her confidant. Except...that was exactly what he was doing.

"I think I made you uncomfortable. I'm sorry. You do not need to tell me anything. I suppose I just worry. You know how fragile their alliance is and I worry this disagreement will be the one that finally breaks out courtship. Perhaps I'm overreacting."

"No, no, of course not." Metis assured. She moved closer to Zeus, looking around for nosey ears. "I'm sorry, it's just...well, you see my whole life my grandfather has only made me swear once to him. He's never been harsh or cruel to me, but when he made me promise to never discuss...Ambrosia, I was scared. I've never feared him before, but I think Ambrosia is the one thing he finds more important than me."

"More important than you? How can an elixir possess more importance than his own flesh and blood?" He asked, though he really should be asking his father that question. He would never admit it, but Cronus and Vulcan were alike in many ways. Both Kings held hefty ambitions only achievable by exploiting their younger kin.

"Because of what he says it can do. He told me some Kings wish to be powerful, and some Kings wish to rule forever. Only the strongest and most worthy Kings strive for both. Ambrosia is said to make a mortal man a god, but few believe the elixir exists." She explained.

"Except for my father and your grandfather."

"Except for those two feuding Kings." She agreed. "My grandfather has devoted much of his life to locating Ambrosia and has come out unsuccessful each voyage. He swears he is getting closer though. That is probably the rumor your father heard. My mother believes your father has spies in our court."

Metis's mother sounded wise and had every right to be weary, especially since her daughter would marry a man who told all her secrets to his father. It would be kinder to stab her through the back because the pain would eventually fade. Emotional manipulation left scars that time could not heal.

"Do you believe in his endeavors? Admittedly, I would find it hard to believe my father if I thought he was chasing a dream. I would need proof."

"I once thought the same thing. I worried about my grandfather's mental state. My mother and her sisters always begged him to let go of this magical fairy tale. He would grow angry and refuse to listen to their pleas. I think it encouraged him more. He hates being told not to do something. He's stubborn in that way.

"But do I believe him? I didn't at first, but then, after a long journey through uncharted lands, he told me he stumbled upon a cave and heard the song of sirens. He claimed some of his men went into the cave but never came out. Something important was in the cave, he's sure of it. He sent dozens of his best men in but not even one returned."

Both prince and princess were silent after Metis's story. The wine made her tongue loose and her cheeks flush. More than what she anticipated sharing flowed freely from her lips, giving Zeus more information than he bargained for. He did not know the location of the cave or what lay within, but it was a start.

As if just realizing she said more than she should, Metis stood abruptly. "It's getting late, and the wine is making me sleepy. I'll have a guard escort me to bed. Before we leave tomorrow, I will find you." She offered him a smile, already backing up towards the castle. "Goodnight, Zeus." With that, she scurried off, finding one of her grandfather's guards. He stood far enough away he could not have overheard their discussion to report back to his King.

Buzzing with the latest information he received, Zeus went to seek out his father. He knew Cronus saw him leave with Metis and would be expecting an update. He would not be foolish enough to wait to be called on again.

Winding his way back through the castle, Zeus watched the last remains of the party slowly start to wind down. Drunken men groped women twice their junior. Others were slowly speaking their final goodbyes. Poseidon and Amphitrite were missing from the last few stragglers. Zeus presumed they slipped off to their marriage bed but refused to think beyond that. Hades was missing too, along with his lady companion. He did not hear Vulcan's boisterous laughter, so he knew the older King had escaped to bed for the night.

Cronus was also not in the main hall, but he did not expect to find him there.

When Zeus arrived outside the doors of his father's study, Hephstes and Kael opened the door immediately. They took one look at the prince and opened the door to the study. It was clear they had been ordered to let him in as soon as he arrived.

Malik stood by the King's desk and behind it sat Cronus. The King looked impressed. Maybe he thought he would need to drag his son out of bed and reenact the last time they were in this room together. Zeus had learned from that mistake.

"I have information about Ambrosia." He spoke, his voice unwavering as he kept his father's stare.

"I assumed. Now share boy, I have matters to attend to." Cronus said impatiently. Zeus was sure those matters included the large chested blonde he saw his father with earlier.

Zeus spoke, outlining every detail he remembered from his conversation with Metis just moments ago. The longer he spoke, sharing the secrets she trusted him with, the more the guilt flooded. He continued to push it down, blocking it out. It lingered, threatening to explode inside him.

Once he finished, Cronus smiled. A real, genuine smile. "You showed your usefulness tonight. Keep it up. If Gaia asks, tell her Metis told you nothing. No need to concern her with this yet. Now, off with you. Celebrate your achievements tonight with mead or a girl. I was your age when I laid with a woman for the first time. The older ones may not be pretty, but they are experienced."

Cronus laughed as he pushed past Zeus, leading both out of the study. The thought of sleeping with an older woman, or any woman, terrified and unnerved him. He did not take his father's advice. He continued down the same corridor and headed towards his wing of the castle, alone with his betrayal for the first time.

A few short weeks after Poseidon's wedding, Malik arrived at their door and told Chloe and Zeus to pack their bags. Mother and son stared at one another, wondering what brought this unexpected and immediate departure. Malik did not seem to be in the talking mood, though he typically never was. They stayed quiet, going through their rooms to pack a few of their prized possessions.

Once finished, Malik led them out of the castle. Zeus half expected to be ambushed by a group of Dasos guards or set ablaze simply because his father was bored. Perhaps Malik wanted to strut them around the castle guards like a group of unchoreographed dancers. He would laugh at the image of Malik dancing ungracefully, but he feared that would cause the man to snap.

Eventually, a small cottage just shy from the forest's edge came into view. It was old and weathered, but otherwise appeared livable. Zeus explored the castle grounds numerous times but never walked out this far. His mitera always warned him not to stray too far from the castle. She wanted to be able to look out her window and spot him easily.

"King Cronus thought this home would better suit you than your current quarters." Malik said, surprising both Chloe and Zeus.

"I assume he did not do this out of the kindness of his heart?" Chloe asked, but she looked over her new home with excitement. It wasn't much, but it was private and an actual house. Something she wanted for a while but given up hope for.

"Contrary to popular belief, Cronus does possess a sliver of a heart. Zeus gave him information he had been searching for and thought to reward him for his efforts."

Reward was a strong word for what they were given, but he would not push his luck. Chloe did not have to ask what Malik meant because after the night he betrayed Metis, Zeus spilled his heavy heart out to Chloe. She had not judged him, nor did she lecture him. She let her son talk and cry until he fell asleep.

"If you are needed, guards will be sent. Otherwise, your time will be spent here." Malik said. The home felt less like a prison cell and more of a new start. For two glorious years, Chloe and Zeus pretended that they led a normal life as commoners and not as unwanted guests of the King.

CHAPTER EIGHTEEN

THE AFTER

T HE ARROW MISSED ITS mark by inches, sparing the deer's life. The frightened doe escaped deeper into her surroundings, protected by the overgrown trees. This was the second deer today Lilith missed and although Demi feigned patience, she caught the disappointed sigh when another perfectly good meal escaped.

"So maybe archery is not your forte." Demi shrugged, giving her a comforting pat on her back. "Clearly Artemis was not part of your creation."

Creation.

That was still so weird to her. Humans, which she apparently was not, were born from their mother's womb, crying as they entered a strange new world. Passionate lovers did not conceive Lilith. No, she was puzzled together from the powers of gods and goddesses who possessed no love for her. They saw Lilith as a means to an end.

As insistent as Demi was in convincing Lilith that creation did not equate to pawn, the goddess supplied very little information. Demi simply repeated that two gods named Poseidon and Hades oversaw her creation. Before their assistance and the powers of the goddesses they convinced to help them, Lilith had been nothing more than mud, sticks, and leaves. As if she did not have enough of an identity crisis, now she learned she did not always *have* an identity.

"Stop thinking." Demi's voice cut through the fog clouding her mind.

"How do you know what I'm thinking?"

"I don't. I just know you are thinking. You have that far-away look on your face, and your pacing has become slower." Demi smiled, running her fingers along the barks of trees. Where they touched, small white flowers the size of her pinkie finger sprung to life. These moments, though small, served to remind Lilith she walked in the presence of a goddess. She was still unsure whether she should be pleased or pissed.

The whole divinity thing still came as a shock to her. She had grilled Demi a few nights ago and the goddess answered most of her questions. Her divinity was intrinsic, a part of her just as breathing was part of Lilith. She could change her features slightly to appear human, but otherwise could not alter her appearance. Demi said some gods and goddesses could, but only those with the divinity to do so. After that, the conversation petered out and Lilith hadn't been able to obtain another Divine 101 lesson.

"We've been so stagnant." Lilith sighed, tracing the flower petals Demi created. "We've been in the same camp for two months now, going through the same routines and I hoped something would come from it all. I need-"

"A purpose." Demi finished for her. "Listen, Lilith these last couple of months have been...challenging to say the least. However, we are getting closer to harnessing your divinity. I sense it's close."

There it was again: her divinity. Both Demi and Bas seemed convinced she possessed untapped powers within, but Lilith was most certain nothing but blood and bones rested within. If she was Divine, as her companions believed, wouldn't she have manifested those powers long ago? Wouldn't they have appeared during the battle of Dasos when she needed them the most?

"Not necessarily." Bas had said when she first asked him about it. "You are the first of your kind, Lilith. A new generation of the Divine. Your powers will manifest in time. You are still a mere babe. You were brought into this life as a young woman, but you have only been alive for a handful of years. Think of this as your infant stage."

Naturally thinking of herself as an infant was disturbing on many levels, but she could not deny the semblance of truth Bas's words held.

"Anyway," Demi went on, unfazed that her companion was only half listening. "Bas says not to take you to Hades and Poseidon until you've mastered your gift."

"What if they can help me?" Lilith countered. If they were her makers, surely, they would have some knowledge on how to tap into her divinity. At the very least, the two gods held answers to questions that plagued her thoughts daily.

Demi considered this, pursing her lips together as she thought. She wrapped her arms around her petite frame, making the goddess appear even smaller. "I've considered that." She admitted, capturing Lilith's attention. "I've often brought it up to Bas, but he feels as if more harm than good would come from meeting with Hades and Poseidon, and he does not want to risk that."

The pair approached the edges of camp. The smell of roasted meat greeted them. Bas was not as incompetent at obtaining food as Lilith had been. If the deer was capable of dueling with a sword, her efforts would have been successful. She was not suited for bows and arrows. She believed it was due to her impatience and her inability to stay still long enough to get the perfect shot.

"How'd it go?" Bas asked as the women approached the fire. He prodded at the dead creature, once a wild pig, and slowly turned the skewer. He never once glanced up.

"Best if we do not rely on Lilith to hunt for our dinner. We will starve." Demi said, earning her a swift elbow to the ribs by Lilith. "What was that for? It's true, isn't it? If we relied on you, we would fade away into obscurity."

"Although you have a point, can we at least mention that I did in fact shoot the damn arrow this time? That should be a cause to celebrate." She retorted back to the goddess.

Demi only laughed. "Sure, but one cannot be Goddess of Inadequate Archery, wouldn't you agree?"

"Enough. Leave the girl alone. She has not had enough time to come into her divinity yet, but she is close...I can sense it." Bas said, without offering any more of an explanation. He pushed himself up from his kneeling position, dusting off his hands on his breeches.

Bas seemed so sure she would be coming into her powers soon, but Lilith did not have the same mindset. For weeks on end, Demi had awoken her early so they could spend the sunlight hours training. At first, Bas instructed Demi to work on swordsmanship. It was the only time Lilith excelled. She attributed that to the grueling days spent training alongside Finian.

It still hurt to think about him, even months later. The pain of losing everyone she loved in a single night was debilitating. If she allowed those memories to consume her thoughts, there would be no stopping the wall around her heart from crumbling, leaving her with nothing but loneliness and deep sorrow.

"You are an extremely skilled fighter, Li. I don't think we should be spending the majority of our time going through different attacks when you clearly know them better than I do." Demi had said and promptly moved on to the next item on her ever-growing list.

Which was a shame, because at least through sword fighting, something that came as natural as breathing to her, provided Lilith with a connection to her past. Her body knew what to do, how to act, and where to move, but only because her brain played through all scenarios her opponent could use against her. Demi proved to be strong, but even the goddess fell to her blade. As long as Demi fought fairly and did not use her ability to manipulate the earth for her advantage, that is.

After sword training, Demi and Bas changed tactics to see if her divinity lay within elemental powers. Demi taught

Lilith how she controlled parts of the earth, growing flowers, making rocks topple off mountains, and touching a tree to age it in a matter of seconds. Needless to say, Lilith was left feeling foolish and frustrated.

Bas attempted other elements, such as fire and water, but neither of those proved successful. Bas' own powers remained somewhat of a mystery to her though. He skillfully dodged each question Lilith threw his way about his divinity.

Which was...ominous.

Demi's latest attempt had been archery, and Lilith was sure even the woodland creatures were laughing at her attempts.

None of these lessons went on long. Demi and Bas always grew tired quickly and wanted to make their way back to camp for the night. She suspected it had to do with how much they used their divinity in order to awaken hers.

"We will discover your power, Lilith. I give you my word." Bas said for the umpteenth time. She had not noticed that Demi left without saying a word, wandering off to find them drinking water.

She did that often now; walking away without saying a word.

Lilith bristled under Bas's stare once alone. He didn't make her uncomfortable, Bas showed her nothing but kindness. Still, she didn't trust him, not completely. Though she suspected the feeling was reciprocated; Bas and Demi didn't seem to trust her either.

"You keep saying that, Bas. I want to believe you, but every day that goes by we waste time. These lessons aren't accomplishing anything other than making you and Demi tired. If I'm able to meet Poseidon and Hades-"

"Oh, not this again," He groaned, shaking his head in annoyance. "I've already told you, it's not-"

"Time. I know! You say that all the time." This time it was her turn to be angry. If Bas did not understand her need to meet the men who created her, then was he really an ally? "But when is the time? Every day I come back a failure. I'm nowhere closer to figuring out who, or what I am, if you keep me away from the only two people capable of giving me answers."

"It's not that simple, Lilith! They are powerful gods, but their patience and threshold for anything other than their own personal interest is minimal."

"I would think they'd want to meet the person they created."

"If that is true, then why did they abandon you?" Bas asked, silencing the rest of her protests.

She wondered about this also, but never gave it a voice. Hearing it now brought a sting she did not expect. Perhaps it was because everything else in her world was gone and this was the only thing she could hold on to.

Bas's expression softened, his gray eyes full of sorrow and pity. "Lilith," he said, his tone far gentler than the one he used before. "I know how hard this is for you. I know-"

"You don't."

"What?"

"I said, you don't." Lilith repeated, this time louder. Her eyes stung with unshed tears. She refused to cry in front of him, not anymore. "You don't know what it is like to lose the people you love. To have your world so devastatingly shattered there isn't anything left to hold on to. You don't know what it's like to feel like me nor will you ever. You have your daughter. You have each other. I have nothing."

"Lilith..."

"Don't fucking *Lilith* me, Bas!" She screamed, no longer able to hold the fury at bay. Weeks of pent-up anger finally boiled over the surface, and she couldn't stop the argument from leaving her lips. "I refuse to have lost Idina and Finian in vain! Their deaths can't mean nothing. If I have the power to help, then I'm damn well going to seize it. I won't let you or Demi stand in my way. If I must find Hades and Poseidon myself, then so be it!"

She didn't care if she sounded like a petulant child, she needed him to understand how serious she was.

Bas looked haunted. He opened his mouth, hesitated, and then closed it again. He stayed silent for a long time, attempting to collect his thoughts. It was always what he did when he did not want to answer one of her questions. He knew it infuriated her.

The prolonged pause lasted long enough for Lilith to think Bas would not say anything at all. Then he finally spoke, forcing patience into his tone. "I know you think what Demi and I are doing here isn't helping. I know you doubt yourself but running off to find Poseidon and Hades isn't the answer. They aren't as patient as we are. I don't want you to get hurt."

Lilith blinked, taking a step back. She almost believed the sincerity in his voice, but something inside of her said Bas wasn't being entirely truthful. He reminded her of a viper, strong and poised, but the moment one turned their back on him, he'd strike without warning.

"You lie." She hissed through her teeth, feeling more certain when she saw a flash of anger flicker across his face.

"Lilith, I-"

"Who is hungry? Oh, did I interrupt something?" Neither one of them noticed Demi's return. The woman stopped short, just a few feet away. Lilith could only imagine what she had seen. Her looking as if she wanted to strangle Bas. Bas most definitely looked as if he also wouldn't mind a fight. "We can't do this every night, you two. Neither of you are budging, so what is it you wish to accomplish?"

Lilith made it known exactly what she wished to accomplish, only to be met by constant rejection. As much as Demi tried to play the neutral middleman, she often defended her father's actions without giving any reasoning.

Having lost all appetite for the cooked boar, Lilith shook her head. "I'm going to bed. Today's activities made me tired. I'll skip dinner tonight." She turned then, no longer interested in anything either one of them had to say. She ignored Demi calling her name, and continued to walk to her tent; the only privacy she possessed here. Luckily, both Demi and Bas were sensible enough not to follow her.

Once in the tent, Lilith sat upon her cot, and immediately undid the laces of her boots -- hand-me-downs from Bas. They fit a little large, but immensely preferred over forcing her foot into Demi's small boots. Her tunic came off next, in exchange for her last clean one. In the morning, she would need to go to the lake for a bath and to wash her soiled clothing. A task she put off because her days were occupied by whatever new trial Bas and Demi planned.

"Perhaps I'm the goddess of soiled laundry." She muttered sarcastically to herself, falling back into her cot once she stripped herself of her pants. The silence that followed usually unnerved her. Silence gave way to free thought, and free thought always drifted to Idina and Finian.

The attack on her family happened months ago. The days started to blur together, feeling like one long continuous day. She fell into a routine so easily and without questions. Wake up, train with Demi or Bas, come back to camp right before the sun sets. Eat dinner. Go to bed and do it all over the next day.

It was not until she no longer had it that Lilith realized how much she missed her mother's food. Idina could cook up anything with any ingredients readily at her disposal. It was her superpower.

Finian had thoroughly enjoyed Idina's cooking too. It was common for him to show up unannounced with his silly grin in place, asking when dinner would be ready. Idina would always pretend to be put out, but she had always been prepared for him to join. He was part of the family just as much as Lilith had been.

More and more memories flooded back of her mother and her lover. She was only given two years with them before the world decided to take them away. It was cruel, but in those two years she learned what it meant to love. What it meant to trust someone so completely that it formed an everlasting bond. She also learned that in fear, courage and strength blossomed. She learned these lessons from her family. The things she would take from this world to the next.

Allowing herself to think of Finian and Idina freely for the first time in a long time, Lilith closed her eyes and let the memories turn into dreams.

Lilith awoke to the sound of crickets chirping. Her tent was engulfed in a blanket of darkness with only a sliver of moonlight peeping through the flaps. The need to relieve herself brought her out of the sleep-like coma she had been blissfully under a moment ago.

Lilith groaned and swung her legs over the cot, planting them firmly on the ground. She blindly searched the tent for her pants and boots, fumbling to put them on once located. As much as she would rather not wear these items, she did not want to take a chance of being seen indecent or attacked by a bear. Then again, if a bear attacked, then no pants would be the least of her worries.

Exiting the tent, the slight chill in the air hit her senses. She wanted to get back into her cot and under her blankets as soon as possible, so she hurried into the woods. She made sure to get far enough away for privacy, but still close enough to see the camp and call for help if the bear did decide to show up.

Lilith went behind a tree and did her business, a rather humbling experience. Once finished, she pulled her pants up, fixed the strings around the waistband, and headed back to camp. However, she did not get far when she heard someone speaking.

Bas.

He wasn't alone. Lilith saw the faint outlines of a feminine body. Demi. Both still in their clothes from the previous day. She crept forward, careful to watch her footing, so she would not be discovered. It felt wrong to spy, but equally wrong to hold a secret meeting without her. Any lingering doubt she had about their breach of privacy left when she heard Demi speak her name.

"Your hold on Lilith is breaking. She trusts us less every day and I've about exhausted my arsenal of excuses."

"We haven't discovered what she is capable of yet. I'm not handing her over to them without knowing what I'm handing over. If she is as powerful as I believe her to be, we could be signing our own death certificate." Bas replied, venom in his voice when he referred to "them." By them, Lilith assumed he referred to Hades and Poseidon. The tone in his voice indicated Bas held a firm disdain for the gods.

"What if she's capable of nothing? Why are we assuming she is special when the past few months showed quite the opposite?" Lilith winced at Demi's words. Out of them both, she had started considering Demi a friend. The woman had been nothing but kind to her. Yet her words were laced with hatred. "She is a skilled fighter; I'll give her that, but her skills are that of a mortal. Against the Divine, she won't stand a chance."

"She was made to be wielded as a weapon against Zeus and his abominations. You know the Unhallowed pose as much of a threat to us as it does to the mortals."

"I'm aware." Demi said with practiced patience, as if she were talking to an insistent child. "But Lilith is also the first made Divine-"

"I was made."

"Not in the way!" Demi snarled, her brown eyes flashing with specs of red. It was not an expression the goddess usually wore. In fact, Lilith could not remember anytime Demi lost her cool. "You know this. No one has been made like her. When do we acknowledge the fact that Lilith serves no use to us?"

"You are willing to bet your life on that, Demi? Willing to lose the only leverage we have against Zeus?" Bas asked, his voice getting softer, making him sound deadly. Lilith silently moved closer, her whole body shaking with deadly rage.

How could she have been so blind? She had been taught to listen to her instinct, which told her not to trust Demi or Bas when she first met them. She had been overwhelmed with her own grief and did not want to be alone. Lilith had been all too eager to find companionship with them and ignore all the signs.

They never let her wander off alone. Not even to bathe. She was only given a weapon upon training and then it was swiftly taken from her for "safe-keeping." She was also constantly denied meeting Hades and Poseidon. She figured that Bas was just being stubborn or overprotective. She believed they had wanted to help her, but they played her for a fool. Again and again.

A fool she would no longer be.

"I'm willing to find other alternatives to save our people. To save us. I refuse to continue in the fruitless effort when Lilith has made us nothing but tired. I'm drained, Bas, and I know you are too. We are putting our strength and power into an empty vessel."

Empty vessel.

The blood coursing through her veins began to boil, flushing her pale cheeks. She wanted to scream. Wanted to wrap her hands around Demi's throat and squeeze until no light remained in those pretty eyes. She wanted-

A twig snapped underneath her foot and both heads turned in her direction. "Shit." She hissed, meeting the wide eyes of Bas and the narrowing of Demi.

"Hasn't anyone told you it's not polite to spy, Lilith dear?" Demi purred as flecks of green glimmered in her eyes. The petite goddess called upon her Divinity. The earth under her began to shake and vines grew from the ground, threatening to wrap around her legs.

"Demi, stop this!" Bas yelled for his daughter's attention. It did little to stop the onslaught of the vines and the shaking of the earth.

The woman struggled against something, not her father's words but something familiar. A sound of pure frustration left her lips as the ground stopped moving. "Dasonian bitch." She sneered and lunged. Nothing Bas could do would stop his daughter, not when she was this inexplicably angry.

Bas yelled again, but Lilith did not linger around to hear. She had no weapons or anything else to defend herself against an angry goddess. She did not even understand why Demi was so angry. She wanted a friend and Demi had filled a void. Albeit small, she had provided comfort to Lilith and made her believe she was not entirely alone in this world. She had been so careless.

Lilith pumped her legs harder, ignoring the burning in her thighs. She weaved through trees, making sure not to run in a straight line. Finian once told her the best way to flee an enemy is running diagonally. Demi was fast and she wasn't easily fooled. The soft sounds of her feet crept closer, though she remained a few places behind. She did not know where Bas went, if he were following his daughter or off somewhere else completely.

The deeper into the forest she got, the more trees began to cloud her view. The faint light from the stars shone between the branches but made seeing difficult. Lilith knew she couldn't keep running. Not only was she running blindly, but she would not be able to keep up this pace. She needed to get ground on them, and only one thing came to mind.

She needed to climb.

Lilith only ever climbed a tree once in her life and that had been to help one of the children from the village get down. He climbed too high and had been petrified to come down. Without thinking, Lilith had scaled the tree a little clumsily, but had managed to reach the boy. These trees were much taller, and she did not have the gift of sunlight on her side. Just the need to escape.

Seeing no other option, Lilith came to a stop in front of a large tree. The branches were plentiful, which would allow her something to step on and pull herself up. She needed to do so quickly. Although she did not hear Demi, she knew the goddess was not far behind, and it would be mere minutes before she caught up.

Using her upper arm strength, Lilith pulled herself up the first branch, digging her feet into the bark for traction. The pounding of her heart hammered loudly, both from exertion and fear of being caught. Still, she persisted, using her leg and arm muscles to continue her upward trajectory. A few branches sagged under her weight, and she hoped it would not snap in two under her.

The branches held, and she climbed until she reached the highest point. Looking down, all she saw was darkness. She did not know how far up she climbed, but she hoped if she could not see the ground, they would not be able to find her. She flattened herself against the tree, melting her body against the bark as Lilith desperately tried to calm her breathing.

Then she waited and listened.

A minute went by. Then another. Perhaps she lost Demi and Bas further back than she thought? Maybe they took a wrong turn or-

"Demi wait!" A harsh voice broke the silence, coming directly under her. Bas had finally caught up to her.

"We must find her." Came Demi's voice from the darkness below.

"Listen, girl. She is not over here. I don't sense her. If you wish to continue to run into oblivion, go ahead, but you aren't going to find her."

"You're the soul searcher. *Search*." Demi spat and Lilith felt the venom in her words. She did not need to see the goddess to know she was after blood. She just did not understand why.

"I'm trying, but I'm not picking up her trail. She can't get far. Let's head back and try again in the morning. We need the rest, neither one of us is in top form."

"You want to leave her out in the forest all night? Think of how far she can get!" Demi argued.

"There is nowhere for her to go!" Bas shot back. "We will find her, but not until the morning. She has nothing, nor does she know where she is going. We will find her."

Silence. Demi, Lilith assumed, contemplated his words. She must have seen reason for she reluctantly said, "We come back at first light, and we don't leave until we find her."

"Until we find her." Bas's agreement came.

Lilith waited from her perch, straining her ears. She heard the soft crunch of grass and twigs as they departed. Still, she did not trust coming down. Not yet, not until she was sure they had left. She decided to wait until the world around her maintained its quiet.

An hour passed before she felt safe enough to leave her hiding place. In the morning they would look for her again, so she needed to continue to put distance between her and the camp. Bas was right, she did not know where to go, and she had nothing on her person. This could very well be a suicide mission, but so was the risk of staying in one place.

When her feet hit the ground, Lilith took a deep breath and closed her eyes. She should head south; for she heard rumors of a neighboring town in the north. If she found the town, it would give her shelter and time to regroup. It was not much of a plan, but it was all she had.

Lilith opened her eyes and looked up to the stars to determine north.

"Hello, Lilith." Came an unfamiliar voice from behind. She whirled around, but before she could see who snuck up on her, she began to fall. Falling so fast and deep into the darkness that she no longer knew where she ended and where the darkness began. Fear consumed her, and she tried to open her mouth to scream, but black tendrils twisted around her. She became powerless to fight them off, the sheer number of black wisps overtook her instantly.

The last thing she saw before the darkness obstructed her vision was an unfamiliar dark-haired man, eyeing her curiously. Then the darkness consumed her body entirely.

CHAPTER NINETEEN

THE AFTER

TIME PASSED DIFFERENTLY IN Olympus than it did back in the mortal realm. According to his father, he created Olympus out of sheer desperation for solitude. When he was younger, to distract himself from his awful reality, he often thought of a beautiful world, set high up in the mountains and close to the clouds. The imaginary world provided a safe place full of beautiful scenery, temples, and a castle suitable for a god.

Zeus never even lifted a finger. When he needed Olympus after the day his mortality ended, the realm answered his call.

Months ago, Finian did not know different worlds existed, but he also did not know about the Divine. His divinity. A newfound power coursed through his veins, hungry and untethered as it searched for release.

At first, Finian felt like a stranger in his own body. The power Zeus bestowed upon him felt intrusive. A constant battle of dominance between him and the divinity he harbored threatened to consume him entirely. Zeus warned Finian he needed to not fight against the divinity, nor force it.

"It should come as natural as breathing. It is not a separate entity. It is a continuation of you. Just as your body is the vessel to your soul, you are the vessel to divinity. One cannot exist without the other." Zeus explained on their very first day of training, shortly after Finian healed from his near-death experience.

His father's training started with a dagger straight to the face. Finian had seconds to react before the blade would contact flesh. He dove to the right, feeling the wind from the dagger as it zoomed past. "What the hell was that for?"

"I wanted to see how quick you are on your feet. It could use some work. We will start with the basics." Came Zeus's reply.

Finian wanted to yell and inform his father there were easier ways to test agility, but he knew it would be wasted breath. "I'm a trained warrior and blacksmith. We don't need to start at the basics."

Zeus gave him a pointed look. "Your training came from mortals to be a mortal warrior. Now I will train you like the god you are. So yes, we start at the basics."

That was precisely what Zeus had him do over the course of the next few weeks. Every morning, after a protein-packed breakfast, Zeus would take him to his temple's courtyard and run him through twenty minutes of stretches to get his body ready for whatever his father planned that day.

Zeus started him on flexibility routines which were deceptively challenging. Finian once believed himself to have good control over his body and his movements, but next to Zeus he looked like an untrained toddler. Many nights he lay awake nursing his sore muscles. Zeus expressed very little sympathy for him, only amused glances and the occasional herbal tea that burned his throat going down.

They had spent two weeks on flexibility before moving on to endurance. "There's a war ahead of us, son. When you fight for hours and days on end, it is no longer about how good you are with a weapon, but rather how long you can push your body to the brink of exhaustion."

Finian imagined spending most of his time running, and that thought made him happy. Unlike many, he enjoyed running. He used that time to clear his thoughts and think of nothing but pushing his body to its limits. It provided a good distraction; although he did everything in his power not to think of her, Lilith always crept back into his mind. Being here, in this realm Zeus created, made his ache for her lessen. Knowing -- at least believing -- she was alive made life without her possible.

He had brought Lilith up once to his father, but the man had stiffened, and his tone quickly became brisk. "Let's not dwell on things we cannot control." He said and moved on without another word. So Finian stopped bringing her up.

Between endurance and flexibility training, Zeus attempted to show Finian how to use his greatest weapon: his divinity. To do this, his father had to show Finian what he was capable of. He should have been scared or hesitant, but he was curious for he had not seen Zeus's ability with his own eyes.

"There are a great many things bestowed upon me." Zeus had said to him. He had not spoken with arrogance, but as a man who carried a great burden. A pang of sympathy rang through Finian, and he found himself wanting to alleviate some of the weight on his father's shoulders. He could not fathom why he accumulated so many enemies, especially when he spoke of breaking the curse upon humans and restoring balance back into the world.

If anything, Zeus was the hero. So why was his son the only one who believed that?

The day Zeus chose to show Finian a fraction of his power, it had been sunny outside. They walked in pleasant silence, through a garden blossoming with beds of roses, chrysanthemums, and tulips. Shrubbery lined their pathway, leading to the temple. Instead of making a left like they did every morning, Zeus turned right at the fork in the garden.

"Are we not going to train in the temple?" He asked.

"Not today. I'm not in the mood to rebuild."

Not knowing what he meant by that, Finian obediently followed, more so out of curiosity rather than loyalty.

Where the garden ended, a new area began; sand and discarded weapons filled the space. There were footsteps in the sand, making him wonder if they weren't alone. Finian had not seen any other people besides his father, but perhaps his father did house more people. The scattered weapons supported the idea of others.

Zeus walked to the nearest sword protruding from the sand and picked it up. Testing his grip, he then pointed up. "Watch the sky."

An odd request, but Finian obliged. It was a clear blue day with a few puffy white clouds in the sky. The temperature almost bordered on uncomfortable warmth, but despite that it was still a lovely day.

And then the first dark cloud appeared. He blinked, unsure if his eyes were playing tricks on him, but when he looked back up, more angry gray clouds lingered above him. The wind, which had not been there a moment ago, began to pick up and the first drop of rain fell upon his head. In a matter of seconds, the few droplets of rain became a torrential downpour.

The rain became blinding and the wind deafening, sending sand in every direction. The worst was still to come. Deep roars of thunder sounded right before a blinding light shot from the sky, striking only feet in front of him. Finian cursed and lost his balance. He fell on his ass, legs sprawled in front of him. More lightning touched down, scorching the sand, but he was rooted to the spot. Each time he attempted to get up, a surge of strong wind hit him full force, knocking the air from his lungs and pinning him to the ground.

"Enough!" He screamed, though his voice got lost in the storm. He didn't see Zeus, and part of him wondered if the man abandoned him.

No sooner did that thought begin to form, the raging storm stilled. The wind slowed before vanishing completely. The roar of thunder dissipated, and the lightning followed suit. Rain and clouds were the last to depart, leaving the sky blue and sunny once again, as if nothing changed in the first place.

Standing where he had been before the storm, Zeus's eyes were a shade of blue Finian had never seen before. Yet, that was not the strangest thing about him. The sword he picked up before the storm now crackled with small bolts of lightning along the blade.

"Don't gape, boy, it's not becoming of you."

Was he gaping? If he was, Finian had every right to gape after what he just experienced. "The storm." Like an idiot, he sputtered.

"Yes."

"That was you?"

"Yes."

"And your sword?"

"Yes."

"Shit."

"Finian." Zeus chastised, though the edges of his lips quivered, failing to hide his smile. "We must work on that vocabulary of yours, son."

Son.

Those words were still so new. At times, it was easy to accept Zeus as his father, but other times he was still a stranger. A mighty stranger who held the keys to this realm. A prison? A lavishly furnished one, but a prison nonetheless. Though Finian wasn't entirely sure if this realm was a prison for him or Zeus.

"I would much rather work on my divinity." Finian admitted, pushing himself up off the ground. His drenched clothes were plastered to his body, with sand wedged into every crevice. As appealing as a warm bath sounded, he did not think he could pass up the opportunity to learn more about the power inside him. If he learned to do half of what Thunder just did...

He would have been able to save his family. To save Dasos. To save Lilith.

"Stop." A booming voice said, interrupting his thoughts. "I know what you are thinking. Believe it or not, I also know how you are feeling. Don't let the darkness consume you. It will take and ravage until nothing is left; until you are an empty vessel."

"Like the Unhallowed." Finian whispered, thinking of the soulless creatures who had once been loved ones. Fathers, mothers, sons, and daughters.

"Similar, but the Unhallowed aren't gods. They just lack a soul. Their damage is great, but nothing compared to an Unhallowing of a god or goddess." Zeus explained gravely.

Frowning, Finian said, "So we aren't safe from the curse either?"

"As far as I know the curse has not touched any of the Divine. We can be consumed by darkness though, which is why I expressed the importance of not lingering in the past. There is nothing you can change; all we can do is learn from it." Zeus said.

The conversation soon ended abruptly as the god tossed his sword to the side. "Arm." He beckoned before taking Finian's offered arm into his hand, rolling it over to expose the mark he placed upon his son.

With delicate fingers, Zeus traced the outlines of the mark before stopping in the center. For a full minute, they stood like that, not speaking, but both consumed with their inner thoughts. After another moment, a smile spread across Zeus's lips. "I feel it. Your divinity. It's... strong. Powerful. Deadly."

Finian blinked. "Deadly? Is it like your divinity?"

"Deadly doesn't necessarily mean bad. Often, death means rebirth. A fresh start." Zeus said, "and no. Not a storm, not thunder, not lightning."

"Then what?"

"Fire."

The room was dark. The smell of rosemary and thyme permeated the air, causing his stomach to tighten and growl with hunger. Even now, the fire pumping through Finian's veins, begged to be let loose. Simply wishing it to fruition was not enough, he needed to use the divinity and command the element. He had been at it for weeks, attempting to call upon the fire and was only successful a handful of times.

The first time Finian manifested fire, he burnt his clothes off. Zeus doubled over in laughter when Finian finally extinguished the flames, standing naked and wide-eyed. The second and third time, the fire circled him, licking his bare skin before flickering out. It had not been much, but Zeus said it was progress. Summoning his divinity was only half the battle, control was another.

Which led Finian to his current situation; before they indulged in the savory feast in front of them, he needed to light the candles on the table. A simple task in theory, but the intense concentration it took to bend his fire to his will left him breathless.

"Don't force it, Fin. You are the master of your fire. Stop treating it as a separate entity, but rather an extension of you." Zeus said from the opposite side of the table. At least Finian assumed his father sat at the table, it was too dark to make out a silhouette. It had been Zeus's idea of training his divinity with the incentive of food.

With his gaze still fixed on the candle directly in front of him, Finian closed his eyes, trying to calm his breathing and center himself. He imagined striking a match and watching the flame slowly spark to life. The match would then hover over a candle, pressed close to the wick until it caught flame. He then imagined striking more matches to light more candles, as the flames danced upon the wick.

Slowly, he opened his eyes and a smiling Zeus greeted him. All down the table, candles lit up the once darkened dining hall because of him. The fire glowing brightly atop the candles had been his doing, not with a match, but his divinity. The flames dancing inside his veins also become sated, thankful for a moment of release.

"Whoa." Was all he could think to say.

"Whoa, indeed." The pride evident in Zeus's face, sending a swell of pleasure through Finian's chest. "You've accomplished much in your time here. We'll make a true warrior out of you yet."

With no more reason to wait, Finian began to pile his plate with seasoned vegetables, two chicken wings, and bread. Since he burned calories at a faster rate now, most meals provided were rich in nutrients and high in protein, giving him the much needed energy to complete any training Zeus conjured up.

Shockingly enough, Finian found himself excited to train both his body and mind. He already saw the effects of those training sessions. Though he had been in good shape before, his body filled out with new muscles. He found himself able to last longer before becoming winded and his reflexes improved tremendously.

Training alongside Zeus gave Finian the opportunity to learn more about his past. From each story his father told, Finian grew angrier at the men in his father's life. Cronus, a sorry excuse for a father, forced Zeus to do his bidding, not caring whether his son lived or died. His brothers, Hades and Poseidon, were no better. They tormented their younger brother every chance they got.

The only good person in his life had been a woman by the name of Chloe. When Finian asked what became of her, his father had gone quiet. He did not push the subject further.

There was, however, one question he had yet to ask.

Finian looked up from his plate after inhaling half of the food, to stare at Zeus. The man sensed his gaze and looked up, raising a brow as if saying *yes?* By now, Zeus knew the look on his son's face when he had something on his mind.

"You've never talked about her." Finian finally said. "My mother."

For a long moment, Zeus did not respond. His face remained passive and unresponsive, but Finian was not going to relent, not about this. He kept his father's gaze, never wavering.

After what felt like minutes, Zeus sighed and finally spoke. "Nehema. I have not talked about her in years. She was a remarkable woman. I did not hear about her passing until later. By then, Hades already claimed her soul."

Although Finian had been young, he remembered the night his mother succumbed to the sickness, leaving behind a young boy and a newborn. His father, or more accurately stepfather, had been the only one in the room with her when she passed. "Why did you choose her?"

"She reminded me of a woman I used to love. She was a princess from the neighboring kingdom. My father set up the marriage, not out of the kindness of his heart, but for personal gain." He said, his words laced with venom each time he spoke of Cronus. "Nehema had the same face and spitfire attitude. Even though she was not the woman I once loved, I was still infatuated with her."

"But she was a promised woman. You slept with another man's lover." Finian argued. He could not imagine being married to one and sleeping with another. He knew it happened, but he didn't understand why.

"Not at the time." Zeus said, startling Finian. He had always assumed his father and mother courted for a couple of years before Finian had even been a thought. "Jarin was fond of your mother, yes, but he had not gotten the nerve to act upon his feelings. When your mother ended up pregnant and alone, Jarin stepped up and offered his help. He loved your mother so fiercely that he was willing to take in a baby that wasn't his.

"I can't say that I am proud of my reasons for wanting to produce an heir, for many of them are selfish. My brothers were growing restless. Their powers, like mine, grew stronger every day. I know how deep their hatred ran for me and I wanted an ally. I needed an heir to pick up the pieces if I were to fall."

Finian listened to his father's words with complete attention. No judgment lined his face; he understood why Zeus would want an heir, and he did not fault his father for that.

"I am familiar with Dasos, as I stated in one of our dreams. It used to be my home. I knew it was risky to linger in the human realm for so long, so my visits with Nehema were always short. After the fourth visit she took me back to her home and-"

"I don't need details." Finian shuddered, not wanting to hear about that particular part of the story.

Zeus only smirked as he said, "I'll spare you the details of our passion." He winked before continuing. "I knew you were conceived, but I outstayed my welcome in your realm. I could not have my brothers knowing of your existence. Not simply because you were part of me, but also they'd fear what you would become."

Finian rolled his eyes at the last bit. "That I light a few candles? Ye be warned, I guess."

Now it was Zeus's turn to roll his eyes. "You've only just begun your ascent into divinity. When your abilities fully form, you will understand why my brothers have reason to fear you.

"I veiled your presence from my brothers for as long as possible." Zeus went on, not allowing Finian to digest his previous words. "I watched over you the only way I knew how. I could not visit you in human form, for I did not want to draw any more attention to you, so I found a way to visit you in your dreams. Out of fear, I never got too close. I wanted to see you, but I was not prepared for the questions you would eventually ask. I wanted to give you a human life for as long as possible with parents that loved you."

"You still did not reach out when my mother died. Why?" Finian clenched his fists, holding back the bark of anger threatening to erupt. The first few years after his mother's death had been the hardest. Jarin was left to care for Mavis and even though Finian did not believe Jarin intentionally ignored him, the man was constantly busy raising a newborn while still completing his share of work in Dasos.

Finian had been so lonely for so long. He carried that void into manhood, filling it with welding, stories, and the occasional hook up, though the available women in Dasos was minimal. Once Lilith came into his life, a missing part of his soul was unlocked.

"I mourned Nehema's death. Dasos lost another light in the ever-growing darkness." Zeus cut in, remorsefully. Another reminder of what he lost. "I felt if I reached out to you, if you really got to know me, you'd leave too."

Raw vulnerability cut Finian like a knife. It suddenly made perfect sense. There were few people in his father's life that he loved, and they were all dead or gone. He had given each of them a piece of his heart and each time a piece of him died. Zeus was only trying to protect himself and Finian could not blame the man for his caution. He saw himself as a walking curse, destined to destroy anything in his wake.

A life of isolation and self-loathing was no life at all.

The silence continued to linger between them, unsaid words hanging heavily on their tongues. Nothing seemed adequate. Sometimes the best comfort was having a presence to accompany one's struggles. He could be Zeus's torch in the night.

"I hope I'm not interrupting a heartfelt father and son moment."

The voice, so unexpected, made Finian jump. Naturally, Zeus did not so much as bat an eye as he turned towards the new voice. A slow smile spread across his lips. "Your timing has always been impeccable, Zarek. Unfortunately, you have missed the bonding session."

"Wonderful. There's nothing I despise more than heart-felt moments." The stranger said, amused and at ease in his father's presence.

Finian had been under the impression no one came in or out of Olympus, at least not without Zeus's approval. In the weeks he had been here, Finian had not seen another person come or go. Not a single maid or a cook. Even though every night when he went back to his room, it had been cleaned and the bed always had new linens.

"So, you are the son." The man said, as he leaned against the wall, arms crossing over his muscled chest. Zarek, as his father called him, looked every bit as fierce as Finian imagined anyone ballsy enough to stroll into his father's home unannounced. He was tall and built like a Dasonian warrior. Although he appeared relaxed, Finian could not help but notice his hazel eyes accessing the room for any threats.

"And you are?" His voice came out gruff, laced with suspicion.

"A friend." Zeus answered for him. "From before."

"A friend is a stretch, eh?"

"I'm your only friend and you know it." Zeus smirked, earning a laugh from Zarek. The interaction between them was one of familiarity and complete trust that came from years of friendship.

"I did not expect you back this month. Did you come with news?" Zeus asked, their dinner momentarily forgotten.

Zarek pushed himself off the wall and moved closer to the dining table, taking an available seat. "I have many things you will be interested in hearing. But first," he paused as a goblet full of red liquid appeared before him. "We drink ourselves stupid."

CHAPTER TWENTY

THE BEFORE

TWO MORE SUMMERS CAME and went, and unfortunately, Zeus still hadn't learned anything new about Ambrosia. Partly because he only saw his betrothed a handful of times since the wedding two years ago. Most of their correspondence happened through letters. He learned that her grandfather stayed away often, on various hunting trips and visits to neighboring cities. Metis spent her busy days with tutors, learning arithmetic, philosophy, and different languages to better communicate with foreign royals. Her afternoons were spent in meetings and a multitude of other boring tedious activities that would prepare her for the throne.

Although she never said it, Zeus was certain her grandfather left on his many "hunting" trips in search of the elusive Ambrosia. Metis mentioned as soon as her grandfather left, he suddenly no longer remembered how to locate the cave, as if his mind erased the memory, leaving only fragments behind. At first, Metis passed it off as his old mind playing tricks on him, until Vulcan questioned his group of soldiers extensively. Their memories were obscured and disoriented as well.

"The cave erased his memory?" Cronus asked skeptically when Zeus relayed the information. "Vulcan is an old King; he was bound to forget his way back."

"Not just him, father. Everyone who accompanied him suffered from the same memory loss. That can't be a coincidence." Zeus prompted.

Cronus paused and considered his words. "My sources mentioned his frequent travel patterns. I blindly assumed he left for recreational purposes. I should have known."

"You've had a lot on your mind, father."

Cronus snorted. For the first time, Zeus saw the dark circles under his eyes. He furrowed his brow, and more strands of gray colored his dark hair. The search for Ambrosia had come to a halt due to recent events. Shortly after their marriage, Amphitrite was with child. Poseidon and Cronus were ready to welcome a new prince into Dasos and not one of the many bastards his twin sons produced. However, the day Amphitrite was to give birth, she woke up in a pool of her own blood. The midwife and Chloe had been called to render aid.

Two long hours later, Chloe returned home with red rimmed eyes. Zeus knew Amphitrite lost the baby before she confirmed it. The young princess had been inconsolable as the midwife took the stillborn child away, prying the infant away from his mother's arms. Poseidon took one look at his dead son and sank into a chair, not speaking.

It took months for Amphitrite to fully recover and another year before she had agreed to try for another baby. Last month, Poseidon told his father she was with child again. Naturally, they were excited but extremely cautious.

As for Hades, his brother had yet to find a wife, but warmed the bed of many high-born ladies. Inevitably, he broke their hearts and Cronus was on the receiving end of their father's wrath, claiming their daughters were forever soiled. More times than not, the women saw Hades as a way to raise their statuses in court, eager for a place alongside him. Cronus paid off more noblemen than he cared to account for.

Ironically, Zeus was the only child who was not giving him a headache.

Remembering Zeus was still in the room, Cronus rose. "We've been sitting idly for too long. Write to Metis and inform her you will be coming to Caister and are eager to spend your days with her."

"What is it you want me to look for this time, father?" Zeus wondered. He should not be feeling excitement over the prospect of seeing Metis, but he found himself buzzing with anticipation. He missed her. Did she miss him just as much? How much had she changed? She was a woman now and although they could marry, neither Vulcan nor Cronus placed their union high on their priority list.

"Vulcan is interested in topography. You will find he has an assortment of maps detailing his travels and even more of his kingdom. I want you to study them. Learn them. Find something they may have missed. You have two months. Bring home good news. I don't think I need to remind you what happens if you fail." Cronus threatened.

Zeus needed no reminders. The day Chloe was whipped never strayed far from his mind. He would not allow that mistake to happen a second time. "Yes, sir. When do I leave?"

"Two days' time."

In a few days he would be reunited with Metis and pretend to be in love with her. That was the easiest thing he knew how to do.

The Southern Kingdom had not changed much from the first time he visited many years ago. Dasos was beautiful, but Caister was unearthly. Beautiful, vast oceans stretched out for as far as the eye could see. Their ships were impressive, but Zeus had yet to be on one. He hoped to change that soon.

What the ocean did not touch, greenery and infrastructure filled. The kingdom was smaller than Dasos, but just as lively and spirited. People loitered in the streets, eager to bargain with merchants. Zeus saw children and families in the square, enjoying their day out. He envied the ease of the commoners.

They arrived at the castle as the sun began to set. Kael and a new recruit named Zarek accompanied him on the trip. Zarek once lived in Caister and knew the territory well. Cronus said he would be an asset to Zeus while they looked over the maps.

A small crowd formed outside the castle, all watching him approach. He glanced over the unfamiliar faces until he landed on the one person he recognized. She changed greatly in the last two years, but her beauty only continued to magnify. Metis was taller, though Zeus still towered over her small frame. Her body outgrew adolescence and into womanhood. The soft curves of her hips made Zeus wonder how she would feel against his rough hands. The bodice of her dress was also fuller, displaying a tease of what awaited underneath.

Zeus had changed too. He shed the scrawny body of a prepubescent boy and grew into a young man. He had solid muscles from his countless hours training to become a master swordsman. He started to grow hair in places that never sprouted hair before, including his jawline. Some days he debated shaving it off but liked how it made him appear older. Suddenly, he felt self-conscious about it. What if Metis preferred him shaven? Would she even remember what he looked like after their time apart?

All his doubts died away the moment their eyes met. Metis's smile was one of pure joy, making her even more beautiful. Did she always look like this? A goddess on earth, blessing her subjects with pure love and beauty.

Zeus barely set one foot outside the carriage before Metis threw herself into his arms, nearly knocking him over. "Zeus!" She cried. "You're here. After all this time, you are more than just an exchange of letters. I was beginning to think you only existed in my dreams."

Two years was a long time for two people to go without seeing one another. Their brief visits consisted of dinners and small functions. Neither activity provided privacy or allowed time for deep conversations. Eventually, only the exchange of letters kept the two linked.

"I'm real and you are a lot stronger than you look." Metis wound her arms tightly around him. Zeus was sure she would suffocate him. As far as dying went, he couldn't think of a better way to go than in the embrace of someone who cared for him.

"I'm sorry, I'm just excited." Metis giggled and reluctantly released him. She moved back just enough to look him over. He couldn't help but grin at the appreciation written across her face. "You have facial hair now."

Zeus reached up and scratched his chin. The only downside to having facial hair was the slight itchy feeling that came along with it. Typically, his scruff was easy to ignore but anytime someone mentioned it, his skin always began to prickle. "Do you like it, princess?"

"I do. You look more like a man than the chubby-faced boy you used to be."

Zeus roared with laughter. It felt good to laugh with genuine happiness. "Chubby face? My apologies, princess, I did not know how much my face used to bother you. I hope it is to your liking now."

"On the contrary, my sweet Zeus, I've always loved your face, boyish and now manly." She punctuated her words with a soft kiss to his cheek, making him hyper aware of the audience gathered around. Metis showed no shame as she pulled away. "I know the journey from Dasos has been long. Let's visit over dinner; a growing man like yourself must have quite the appetite."

His stomach growled at the mention of food and drinks, especially of the sweet nectar native to this kingdom. If one could drink the sun, Caister wine would be exactly that.

Soon, they were seated at a large dinner table, their plates filled with lamb, seasoned vegetables, a meaty soup he never tasted before but found himself on his second bowl, and a cinnamon custard he would save for later.

"You weren't joking when you said you were hungry. I forgot how much men eat." Metis commented as Zeus stuffed more food into his mouth. It was hard not to inhale the delicious meal and pace himself, but he managed to at least take a few bites before inhaling it.

"So, tell me everything. What has been happening in Dasos. Anything new with you? How have you been spending your time? Your brothers, how are they? And your father, is he well? Have you made any new friends? Any new girls-"

"Metis," Zeus smiled wickedly, putting a hand up to stop the onslaught of questions, ones he already answered in his letters to her. Still, he wanted to hear everything Metis had been up to since they were last together.

"Dasos has sobered much since the last time you visited. My brother's wife lost their child. The kingdom had been excited at the prospect of the baby prince but has been in mourning ever since."

"I heard about the stillbirth. I cannot imagine a mother's loss, particularly one who never met the babe they carried in their belly for nine long months. Is she well?" Metis asked, her concern for others never dimming even after all these years.

"She's with child again. Only about four months into her pregnancy, but so far, the baby is healthy according to the midwife. Poseidon has not yet made a public announcement but there are rumors of Amphitrite's pregnancy, so I believe he will address the kingdom soon."

Zeus then told Metis all about Hades and the countless women he cycled through. Metis noticed his relationship with Hades was strained, and she wanted to see if it had gotten better. It hadn't, but it also not worsened. In truth, Hades generally made himself scarce.

He then spoke of Chloe and how well his mitera had been doing since moving into their own home. He wrote to Metis the day after they moved in and excitedly described the new home, in lavish and grandiose detail. He made it seem like a second palace and not a small cottage at the edge of the castle grounds.

"No new friends to report, just the same few noble sons that join me in training. They have taken interest in the young maidens of court, specifically Amphitrite's ladies in waiting. They are oblivious to their disinterest." Zeus mused. Amphitrite's ladies would be waiting for some nobleman with money to court them. Only one of the guards got lucky enough to win the heart of one of her ladies.

"Are they beautiful?" Metis asked, trying to sound nonchalant. The question held a deeper meaning, and it made Zeus smile. He felt the same jealousy each time they passed a handsome young man who smiled at Metis. They would be blind not to notice her ethereal beauty. Most of them looked upon her with desire in their eyes, and he wondered the extent of their relationship.

Of course, he had no right to question it when he was far from the faithful and devoted betrothed she assumed him to be.

"They are beautiful, I suppose." He said, seeing her face fall slightly. "Though it is hard to gauge beauty when my betrothed is the brightest star in the sky. They pale in comparison to you, Met. Always will."

It was easy to believe in the fairy tale world they built with Zeus's lies. His feelings for her grew stronger with each passing year, so at least he could say his feelings were real. It was the one thing he did not need to lie about.

Metis's smile was dazzling, reminding him of her girlish years when it was a rarity to see her without. "There's been no other boys here that have caught my attention. It is no secret of my betrothal to a Dasonian man."

Man. Not boy.

The rest of dinner was spent chatting about anything that popped into their brains, though he let Metis lead most of the conversation. She spoke of how taxing her studies for queendom were and how little time she had to do anything for herself. By the end of the night, they shared a single lingering kiss before going off into their respective rooms.

Zeus was in the midst of changing out of his traveling clothes and into something more suitable when a brief knock sounded on the door, opening seconds after. Zarek entered. "It's late, Zarek. What news do you have for me?" He demanded.

"King Vulcan is not here."

"Yeah, I'm aware." He said, getting irritated with the new guard. He was from Caister and had not yet adopted the mannerisms of Dasonians. Time, for instance, did not matter when reporting useless information. "We were prepared for the likelihood of Vulcan away on one of his hunting trips."

"Yes, but he was scheduled to return today. Kael spoke with a few off-duty guards. Caister men speak freely when under the influence of alcohol."

"As do many people, Zarek. This is not new information. Vulcan's late return is also no reason to notify me. The day has not ended yet, though I'm working on it." Zeus stared at him pointedly, hoping the guard would get the hint.

Zarek didn't. Instead, he leaned against the wall far too casually for a guard in the presence of royalty. Granted, Zeus supposed he wasn't really a prince. "Do you have more, or do you simply wish to watch me change?"

"It wouldn't bother me." He shrugged. "I've seen my fair share of naked men."

Zeus raised an eyebrow, deciding it was too late to ask what he meant by that comment. He turned his back to the guard and continued to strip himself of his clothing. "Do you have anything useful to tell me?"

"Of course I do. Most everything I say is useful if you would listen." He said. Zeus pulled on a fresh tunic before turning around. He crossed his arms over his chest and relented, giving Zarek his undivided attention.

"King Vulcan went on a hunting escapade not even a half day's ride from here. He claimed to be coming home this morning, but he never showed. This is rare for the King, so a few guards went out to where Vulcan was staying and-"

"I assume he wasn't there."

Zarek deflated some, as if Zeus landed the punchline Zarek had been building up to. "No, they weren't there. In fact, there had been no evidence of anyone ever being there."

"So, they lied. Typical of Kings. Still am not seeing cause for alarm." Zeus said.

"The guards spoke of Vulcan's obsession with a cave he claimed he found years ago. The same cave he had not been able to find. A few guards overheard him speaking of Ambrosia again and believed him to be on another wild goose chase for the elixir." Zarek finished, satisfied with the information they gathered within a few short hours.

Zeus was impressed. The information did not help him discover the location, which would be too much to ask for on their very first night here, but it did mean they were on the right path. "We get the names of the soldiers who accompanied him on his journey. We need to befriend them and obtain as much information as we can. Even if we can't find his maps, which I'm sure he has on his person, we possess the knowledge from those who joined the King."

"Now you are thinking like a strategist." Zarek smirked, his tone far too casual once again. Admittedly, Zeus welcomed it and even enjoyed the praise. He was not used to being spoken to as an equal or a friend.

"Well forgive me, I've had minimal sleep and sat through your useless banter until you gave me something I could actually work with." Zeus said and then gestured to the door.

"Now if you would be so kind to leave, I will gladly take my rest."

Zarek offered him a mocking bow. "Goodnight, princeling." He purred before leaving, shutting the door behind him.

Perhaps Zarek would not be as horrible as Zeus believed. With that final thought, he laid down. As soon as his head hit the pillow, Zeus was fast asleep.

Vulcan did not return for another four days. By the end of day three, he had to convince Metis of why it would be a bad idea if she left in search of her grandfather. She knew how to ride a horse, but not for great distances. Nor did she know how to live outside of the castle. As calmly as he could, he explained that the only thing she would end up accomplishing was her own death.

It was their first fight, if one counted this as a fight at all. Metis was worried and scared. That anxiety manifested itself through lashing out at the people around her. Zeus did not take offense to it. He held her through the attacks and rubbed her back when her emotions overwhelmed her.

Two days passed and still no King.

Then Three.

When Vulcan returned on the fourth day, the castle let out a collective sigh of relief. The King was home and well. Haggard and dirty, but well nonetheless. Metis managed to wait until her grandfather changed out of his soiled clothes and bathed. Once he emerged from his quarters, she unleashed her fury.

"Grandfather, you had us all worried sick! You cannot leave and waltz up days later as if nothing happened. We thought the worst. It is time to stay home. You've done your traveling, now rest." Metis urged, speaking as a mother would to a disobedient child, with love and disappointment.

Instead of renouncing her for speaking to him in such a manner, Vulcan laughed and patted the top of her head. "Women, they will worry themselves to death. They do not understand men were made for long journeys. Don't let the wiles of women deter you from a goal, son, no matter how pretty or how good in bed she may be." Vulcan said, addressing Zeus.

He kept his mouth shut, especially after the dirty look Metis threw in their direction. He never understood why so many men viewed women as their inferiors but spent their whole life answering to one; whether it be a mother, wife, or sister. In truth, men were very little without the love and support from the women in his life.

"Will you at least tell us what kept you for so long and why you were not where you said you'd be?" Metis interrogated him, not in the least bit discouraged from being belittled by her grandfather.

"Can't an old man rest?" Vulcan sighed, slipping into a seat at the table. A small feast had been prepared for his return, complete with three different dishes for dessert.

"You can rest tonight. I want to know what kept my grand-father, *the King*, away for so long." She said. Zeus admired her stubbornness when it came to getting what she wanted.

"You've always been a little hellion, haven't you?" Vulcan cooed, no malice behind his words. Only pride and love for his treasured Metis. "This conversation would best be held in private. You'll forgive me of course, Zeus, but you are still the son of my most powerful competitor. You may be mar-rying my granddaughter, but your blood is still Dasonian."

"Grandfa-"

"Enough, Metis. I was in search of something, and I came back empty-handed. That is all you need to know tonight. Enough questions, girl. Let me drink my wine and eat in peace. I have little patience and a hunger that would rival the appetites of ten men." With that, the conversation end-ed.

Vulcan did not want to say where he had been while in the presence of Zeus, but that alone was the confirmation Zeus needed to know Vulcan had been in search of Ambrosia. Kael and Zarek would need to start making friends with the guards who returned with the King, and Zeus would need to use Metis for answers once again.

"Are you ill, Zeus? You haven't touched your meal." Metis frowned, gaining the attention of not only himself but Vulcan too.

"Aye, son. Do you need a healer?" The King asked.

"No, my lord. My mind is elsewhere. Forgive me." He said, winking at Metis as he took a bite of his food. Metis's eyes lingered on him for a little longer before she nodded, convinced he had not suddenly fallen ill.

All through dinner, Vulcan chatted about the different sights and the game he killed to eat during his voyage. Zeus was only half listening because the stories began to repeat after the fourth glass of wine. By the sixth, Vulcan nearly fell asleep at the table. It took two guards to escort the King to his room for the night, leaving Metis and Zeus alone.

"Do you feel better knowing he is home safe?" He questioned once Vulcan left.

"A little, but I fear he won't stay long. He never does anymore. He's consumed with locating..." She paused, looking around once to make sure they were far away from listening ears. They weren't. The kitchen staff moved in and out freely, clearing the table of food and guards were posted at every entrance. "Well, it doesn't matter. I want him to stay home this time."

"That might be difficult. I haven't had many conversations with your grandfather, but I know he loves exploring. He doesn't seem the type to stay in like a caged bird."

"A caged bird within a castle. Forgive me if I lack sympathy." She tutted, and Zeus agreed she had a point. "I don't want to think about that now. He's home and that's what matters."

Despite his return, Metis was still on edge. Something bothered her, and Zeus wondered if there was more to her concern than she let on. Her worried demeanor suggested there was.

Normally at this hour, Zeus would excuse himself for the night to go find Kael and Zarek, but the last few encounters with the guards proved useless. With more guards back from Vulcan's trip, it would take longer to befriend and extract new information from them.

So tonight, he could simply be.

"Let's go for a walk. I think we both could use some fresh air." Zeus suggested and did not wait for an answer. He took her hand and led her to her favorite part of the castle: her garden.

Caister was at the end of their winter season. A light breeze held a lingering chill, and he wished he thought to bring something warm. Metis seemed unbothered by the slight chill in the air and continued to pull Zeus along until they reached a fountain.

The fountain was stationed in the center of the garden, made specially for Metis on her thirteenth birthday. The statue in the middle was that of a twelve-foot horse, based on Metis' beloved mare that passed away a few weeks before construction began. It was still her favorite part of the garden. A place where she often visited to escape the bustle of everyday life.

For a while, neither of them spoke. The silence between them was a comfortable one, not one that needed to be filled with empty small talk. It was an intimacy Zeus felt comfortable with.

"Zeus?" Metis whispered, her voice breaking through the silence. He turned towards her, watching the indecisiveness play out on her features before her bravery won out. "Zeus, I need to tell you something."

"Anything."

"I love you."

I love you.

The words rang through his ears as his mind slowly processed what was said. Love? The only other person who ever said those words to him was Chloe, but that love was different. It was the love of a mother to her son. He never had to earn her affection; it was given without constraints. Metis *chose* to love him. She saw his flaws and imperfections but chose to love him anyway.

Metis loved him.

"Please say something." The panic in her eyes made Zeus wonder how long he had been sitting there, staring off like a fool. He could not get his damn mouth to form words. She rendered him speechless.

After a moment of opening and closing his mouth like a damn fish out of water, Metis pulled away with a fierce blush and tears in her eyes. "I'm sorry. I shouldn't assume. I know our marriage is arranged and you've been kind to me. We agreed that we would only be friends. I shouldn't-"

He kissed her.

Not the soft, goodnight kiss he would sometimes give her before she left him for the night. No, this kiss was unfiltered and passionate. He had never kissed anyone like this and was not sure if he was doing it right. He pulled her by the waist, pressing their bodies together. Metis let out a sigh of pleasure and he melted.

Gods, he loved her.

Despite everything, he loved her. He knew this couldn't be real, and he would be forced to break her heart. He was not worthy of the kindest, most caring princess because she deserved a man who was not controlled by his father. She shouldn't love him.

But she did.

Zeus finally broke the kiss, panting and flushed. Metis leaned against him, her lips puffy and wet from the kiss. It was nearly enough for him to do it again. He desperately -

wanted to do it again, and so much more. "I love you too." He said huskily.

Then they were kissing again. Somehow, they moved to the ground. Metis on top of him, and his body responded in ways it never did before. It did not help that she straddled him and moved her hips in ways he was sure was too sinful to be allowed.

Zeus wanted her, needed her. Judging by the kiss and the soft purrs coming from her, Metis felt the same way. However, they were in the gardens, and it wasn't exactly a private place, but maybe-

"Well, hello princess, prince."

Metis yelped and jumped off Zeus so fast it was as if his touch burned her skin. Zeus sat up hastily, doing his best to straighten his clothes. He didn't need the interrupter to see just how much Zeus was enjoying what they had been doing.

"I hope I am not interrupting anything." Zarek smirked, eyes traveling between the two. He knew what he had walked in on, and it delighted him.

Smug bastard.

"I came to speak to prince Zeus, but if this is an inconvenient time, I can come back later." He mused, but the moment was ruined. Whatever spell they were under broke, and Metis looked as if she wanted to be anywhere but here.

"No! No." She said a little too quickly and a little too loud. "Zeus and I were just...uh..."

"Reuniting?" Zarek supplied, loving this far too much.

"Yeah, reuniting...yeah." She nodded, and slowly began to back up. "But I was just leaving. It's nice to see you-"

"No, it wasn't." Zeus growled, earning a laugh from his guard.

"-and Zeus, I'll see you for breakfast tomorrow. Goodnight." Metis said before turning her back and walking swiftly away. Zeus watched her until she disappeared into the castle, before whirling on Zarek.

It did not have the desired effect he hoped for, since Zeus was on the floor and spun on his butt to face Zarek. He pushed himself up, still to the amusement of the guard. "You're fired." He barked.

"You can't fire me."

"I just did."

"Fine, fine. I apologize. I should not walk into a public place with no doors or walls without asking for permission. I should have assumed two lovebirds would be about to make passionate love. Forgive me." Zarek said, mocking him by bowing.

"I really hate you." Zeus said, but with no real malice behind his words. As much as he wanted to see where that moment would have taken him with Metis, he knew it would have been stupid to do that in the middle of a garden. He supposed it was best that Zarek found them.

"You don't, especially after I tell you what I just figured out." He said.

"Wait, you already figured something out? Did you question the returning soldiers?" He wondered.

Annoyingly, Zarek only grinned wolfishly, a wicked gleam in his eyes. "I have my ways, young prince. As I said, I can be quite the asset." What those ways were, Zeus did not understand. Judging by what he knew about Zarek, which wasn't much, he assumed he could get anyone to talk.

"While you were doing inappropriate things to the Caister princess, I was being useful. Apparently, King Vulcan has been quite busy during his travels, but the mind is a finicky thing. Especially for older men. They rarely remember what they do from day to day." Zarek spoke.

"Can you get to the point please? I know you have more to tell me than Vulcan's forgetful mind." Zeus replied dully, waiting for more information.

"My point," Zarek continued. "Is that King Vulcan's map, is actually a prideful soldier with an affinity for navigation. He goes by the name Hermes."

A person was better than having a map, but far less practical to stuff in one's pocket. Not to mention the convincing they would now need to do to get this man, Hermes, to talk. If he was loyal to the King, he would not be bought. He could, however, be taken. Willingly or forcefully, it would be his call.

"We have some time. Can we get him to agree to come with us before we head back to Dasos?" Zeus could write to his father and ask for more time, but his response would arrive too late. Knowing his father, he would be displeased with the delay. His patience was running thin and failure to comply would result in another punishment.

"I don't need time. He agreed and I gave him something in return." Zarek said.

Well...that news was surprising and unexpected. Zeus blinked, unsure if he heard him correctly. "How?"

"I've told you, I'm incredibly good at what I do. I'm also from here and know Hermes personally. He has a deep hatred for Dasonian soldiers, and we happen to have a spare." He spoke the words so nonchalantly that Zeus almost missed it.

"Kael...he is...?"

"Dead, young prince. Kael is dead. An unfortunate accident. You've heard about those pesky Caister bears. Always eager for a drunken man to stumble blindly into the woods when taking a piss."

"Caister has bears?"

Zarek rolled his eyes and groaned. "No, you bumbling idiot, but that is what we will tell your father if he asks. Perhaps we shouldn't tell him we gave his guard over to be slaughtered. Just a thought. And before you ask, no I do not know why Hermes wanted him dead. The less we know, the better."

"Fine." He sneered, ignoring the bumbling idiot comment. If it had been Poseidon or Hades, Zarek would not be so quick to dish out insults. Probably. "So how do we sneak

Hermes out? King Vulcan may be losing his mind, but I think he'll notice his topographer has gone missing."

"Which is why we leave now." Zarek said. "Tonight. Hermes is gathering the horses. If we don't leave now, I don't think we will have another opportunity."

Leave now? Leave without telling Metis goodbye. Leave and have her wonder where he went or if he would ever be back. Vulcan leaving was hard enough, but what would she do when she realized he left in the middle of the night and without a trace?

This day always loomed over his head, knowing he would have to abandon the fantasy. He had not expected it to come so soon and right after the moment they shared. When he was...they were...

"There'll be more girls, prince." Zarek spoke, interrupting his inner struggle. The young prince wore his heart on his sleeve when it came to Metis. "You give this one up and you are free from your father's mission."

"I don't want more girls." No one would compare to Metis. He loved her and he could not picture loving another. But Zarek was right, he needed to finish his father's seemingly endless mission. Finding Ambrosia would be his key to freedom. Chloe would be free from punishment. Metis would be free of him.

Both women he loved and cared for in different ways would be safe. He knew what he must do, but the choice left him feeling empty.

"Very well. When do we go?" He asked.

"Now."

A new voice spoke from behind him, and Zeus turned. He saw a man, older than both him and Zarek, but younger than the King. He had blonde hair, pulled back into a neat bun. What unnerved Zeus the most about the man was his eyes. They were cold and black. He knew immediately he would not be able to trust him.

"Hermes?" He presumed.

"In the flesh." He laughed as if he told a joke. "You aren't as impressive as Zarek made you out to be. I'm supposed to trust you with the most precious elixir of all time?"

"That shouldn't matter, the elixir doesn't belong to you."

"Aye, and neither to you." Hermes said. "But I think we can both benefit from it, yes?"

"I may have promised Hermes a quick drink of the elixir. A taste really. You'll never know some of it's gone." Zarek said and Zeus wanted to kill him. If he thought Zarek played out his usefulness, he would not have hesitated. The only thing saving him from a quick death was the fact Zeus did not want to be alone with Hermes.

"I suppose you want to drink Ambrosia too." Zeus said to Zarek.

To his surprise, Zarek laughed and shook his head. "No, absolutely not. At least not right now. I don't know what Ambrosia will do to us and I rather enjoy living. I'll let the power-hungry Kings take it first before I make my decision."

"Don't celebrate too soon, we may have Hermes, but we have yet to locate this cave." Zeus reminded.

"Wrong again. How about you stop stalling and allow us to leave, hmm? Or should we wait an hour, so you can fuck the princess before we depart?" Hermes grunted, pulling on the reins of the horses, implying he was ready to leave now.

All Zeus saw was red. His hand twitched at his side, reaching for his sword without thought until Zarek grabbed him by the wrist. "We need him to find the cave. Kill him and think of the outcome. Think of Chloe."

Chloe. His mitera.

Slowly, the tension eased within, though the anger lingered. He no longer wanted to kill Hermes, at least not as much. "Fine. Take us. Though one wrong move, Hermes, and I will not hesitate to sever your head from your body. Don't test my patience."

"For fucks sake, you are Cronus's son." Hermes put his hands up in mock surrender before throwing the horse's reins at him. "I won't steer you wrong. You can trust me."

Zeus did not trust him, but he mounted his horse anyway. After one more glance back at the castle, before their horses charged ahead, he thought of everything he was leaving behind. Away from Caister. Away from the King.

Away from Metis.

CHAPTER TWENTY-ONE

THE AFTER

L ILITH CAME AWAKE WITH a jolt, her breathing ragged and labored from the sudden loss of consciousness. Her mind reeled, frantically trying to piece together the events of last night. She remembered overhearing a conversation between Bas and Demi and running to escape their clutches. Then...nothing.

Panic began to build in her chest at the uncertainty of the situation. "Think!" She pleaded over the fear in her mind. "Use your training. Assess your situation. You aren't useless. You. Aren't. Useless!"

She was a warrior and a damn good one at that and didn't need her sword or *Peace Bringer* to feel powerful. She *was* powerful. Even without her equipment, Lilith was a weapon, and she could be deadly. Especially since her opponents always underestimated her.

Lilith glanced around the familiar room and swore. She was back in her old tent. The room was bare except for a pile of rumpled clothes in the corner. The cot took up most of the space, leaving little room for anything else but a small wooden chest, roughly the size of her hands. It once held *Peace Bringer*, but Bas and Demi stripped it from her, claiming to worry she would use it to take her own life. Now she knew better.

Not useless.

They had their divinity, but Lilith escaped once before. She moved quickly on her feet and threw punches that stunned her opponents. Additionally, she had something they did not possess. Anger. Raw and unadulterated anger. For everything lost, taken away, and withheld.

She had nothing left to lose.

She donned the warrior persona, pushing herself up and preparing for battle. Whether this be her last day, Lilith would not make this easy on her enemies. *Not useless.* She would yield to no one. Death would need to claim her instead because every moment she stood breathing would be a fight and if death took her...well, at least she would be reunited with her family.

Stepping outside the tent felt like a declaration of war. She expected to be met by blades or arrows but was met with nothing at all. Her earlier bravado began to slip away, replaced with confusion. Although she did not know what to expect, it never once crossed her mind that she'd be alone.

Well, not quite alone. She missed the figure sitting by the fire. His back faced her, but he didn't resemble Bas. This man was larger, both in height and size. She could tell he possessed brute strength and did not imagine those who sparred against him would live to tell the tale.

Even more shocking than his impressive physique was his clothing. He wore freshly polished leather boots without a hint of mud on them. His tunic appeared to be made specifically for his body; no luxury spared. He wore no armor except for the cuirass around his chest. Though she did not see his weapons, she assumed he was armed.

Lilith didn't realize she had walked towards him until she was a foot away. Something about this man was familiar to her, though she didn't believe she'd ever seen him before.

"You're awake." The stranger said, his voice deep and accented. "I was beginning to wonder if I needed to travel to the River Styx to retrieve you."

She did not understand what that meant. The man beckoned for her, gesturing to the vacant log directly in front of him. Instead of hesitating, Lilith closed the distance and sat down. Her curiosity always got the best of her, and she hungered for information about his identity.

Sitting across from him, Lilith could make out his features better. He was handsome, in a rugged warrior sort of way. He appeared young, a decade or so older than her, but his gray eyes held wisdom beyond his years. Everything about him screamed god. She could not describe the feeling, but she felt power lingering on him. A sense of darkness surrounded him, staying in the shadows but never too far away.

"Who are you?" She recognized him, but he was a blurry memory. Something she suppressed for far too long.

"You know who I am."

And she did. At that moment, clarity washed over her and nearly drowned her in truth.

"You are Hades. A god."

At his title, Hades smiled.

"Ah, there you go, little Lilith. I feared the distance might have made you forget your makers."

Makers.

The word sounded vile. Wrong. Makers implied he held a claim over her. A master who constructed his prize for the sole purpose of obedience. Hades and Poseidon might have made her, but they didn't shape her.

Her family at Dasos did. Strength and love from Finian. Compassion and intelligence from Idina. They never sought to possess her, never once looked at her like anything other than Lilith, the woman they both loved.

The man in front of her, Hades, wasn't her friend. He had not made himself an enemy but also not given her a reason to trust him. She met his gaze and forced herself to hold it. It was a challenge, and she was sure as hell not going to show fear or submission to him.

Whatever Hades saw in her expression made him smirk, a soft laugh escaping his lips. "You are a tough one. I should have expected that, considering what it took to make you."

"Why are you here?" So many questions ran through her mind. Where were Bas and Demi? If Hades was around, did that mean Poseidon was as well? Why did they create her only to discard her in Dasos with no memory of them? Why was he here now?

Voicing all these questions at once would give Hades leverage to use against her. Information came at a price; she wasn't so naive to think the man had shown up and saved her out of the goodness of his heart. No, Hades needed her for something, and he came to collect.

"Because I finally found you after months of someone hiding your presence."

That was...not the answer she expected, and Lilith couldn't hide the confusion etched into her face. Had the men not been the one to place her in Dasos? Was she drawn there for other reasons? But then how-

"You have questions and by the look of it, you have many." Hades said, reading her thoughts. "I'm feeling particularly generous, and we have time. Speak freely, little Lilith."

Okay, that nickname needed to go, but she would deal with that later. "What do you mean you just found me? Did you not know I lived in Dasos this entire time?"

"No, Poseidon and I were very aware you were in Dasos. We took you there and watched you walk in. You were newly made and adjusting, so we did not expect you to remember any of it. Remembering us was not important because there was a valuable player hidden in Dasos. We were not privy of who that was, but we suspected a meddling hand at play."

"So, you wanted your own pawn at Dasos."

"Smart girl." Hades said with another predatory smile. He made no attempt to correct her usage of the word pawn, which deeply unsettled Lilith.

"Neither Poseidon nor I can step foot into Dasos. That reason revolves around a rather lengthy story, but in short, we have been cast out. Stepping into Dasos might not kill us, but it would weaken us or strip us of our powers. You can see why we did not want to risk it."

They were more than willing to risk her though. As much as she wanted to be angry with them, she couldn't. Not when Dasos had provided her with love. She found a mother and met the boy who should have been her husband. They might have expected her to play the willing pawn, but Lilith established a life of her own. It had been hers, and she wouldn't let Hades soil her memories.

"Your plan was flawed. Hardly a plan at all. Set me loose in Dasos and for what? You gave me no memories or purpose." No matter how she looked at it, she could not find a scenario benefiting the two gods. Lilith was finally face to face with one of the men who created her, a moment she thought about a lot, and it lacked the clarity she hoped it would bring.

Hades was unbothered by her persistence and maintained a calm composure. If anything, he found her questions humorous. Even though he sat upon a rock, he could have been seated upon a throne with how much his presence demanded attention.

"Was it flawed?" He questioned; his brow cocked. Lilith wanted nothing more than to wipe the smug look off his expression, but she refrained. "It was not perfect, I'll admit, but our end goal had always been the same, to draw him out. We hoped that your presence would be enough of a lure to bring him back to Dasos. We were prepared to take as long as needed. In the end, he showed himself. I just regret it took the Unhallowed and slaughter of Dasos to do it."

He didn't sound regretful. Lilith lost everything and Hades viewed it as an unfortunate circumstance.

"You got what you wanted. My part is over."

A flash of anger flicked across his expression, but she did not think it was aimed towards her. Physically, Hades sat right in front of her, but he couldn't seem further away. His mind rooted deeply in the past. Whatever happened then had to be extremely awful if it made a man like Hades upset. Scared, even.

"It is far from over. You served us well, even without realizing it. Because of you, we know who the key player he placed in Dasos."

"I don't suspect you will make me privy to that information."

"I said I would answer your questions, didn't I?" Hades replied, a hint of amusement for her thirst for knowledge. "And I meant it. I would not send you into the lion's den without armor."

Except that was exactly what he did, Lilith had just been ignorant of the fact. "Who is this man you speak of?"

"My brother."

"Poseidon?" Now her head hurt, trying to keep the story straight in her mind. That proved difficult with the modicum of information Hades supplied to her. Each new piece only furthered the tangled web in her brain.

"No, little Lilith. Our youngest brother, Zeus. It has been centuries since we've sensed his presence. It appears that our baby brother sired himself a bastard son and placed him in the one place neither Poseidon nor I could breach. If I did not despise him, I might commend him on his poetic endeavors."

A third brother? It made sense, considering how much Hades seemed to despise the entity working against him. The hatred seemed personal, and the man's words only confirmed it. Idina had always said hate and love were interweaving threads knit together. Lilith did not grasp the lesson until now.

"If you knew about Zeus's son, why didn't you strike?" Lilith wondered before adding. "I suppose it doesn't matter now, though, does it? There weren't any survivors after the attack on Dasos."

The same emptiness settled over her like a familiar companion. Each time she thought back to that night a pang pierced her chest before a hollow emptiness took its place.

Hades did not answer immediately. Enough time went by before Lilith picked her gaze off the floor, only to be met by the piercing black abyss of Hades' eyes. It was intimidating, like looking into death itself, but she refused to flinch away. She was well acquainted with death after all.

The man before her almost looked uncomfortable, which made the long pause more unbearable. Right before Lilith asked her question again, Hades spoke. "I did not know the identity of his son until he reclaimed his soul from the River Styx, right before he reached his final resting place. I no longer feel the boy's soul, which means Zeus took him back to whatever place he's been hiding in all this time."

The world around her froze at Hades' words. "You can...you can bring a soul back before they enter this river? Any soul?" Could Idina still be saved? Adolphi? Finian? She could rescue their souls and then-

And then what? What was a soul without a body? How long did it take a soul to complete their journey to their final resting place? Days? Weeks? There was no guarantee that her family would still be in the river, but shouldn't she at least try?

"Stop."

The sound of Hades' voice grounded her. Judging by his expression, he knew what she had been thinking. "Once a soul enters the River Styx, they are lost to the mortal world. Your loved ones cannot be brought back."

"But you just said-"

"I know." The words came out as a hiss, making Lilith flinch from the intensity of his bite. "There should have been no way for my brother to intrude on my territory without my knowledge and take the soul of his son. He should have been pulled in and dragged to Tartarus, a place I keep my enemies, but he bypassed all my defenses. Do you

understand how much power he must possess to pull off a stunt like this?"

Lilith didn't, but she imagined a great deal if Hades was this worked up over it. Had there never been another soul that evaded death like Zeus's son? Did it change a person? It must. Souls were not meant to leave the body, only to be pulled back after one's death.

This made her wonder what could have happened if she had been informed about the plan from the beginning. How many people would be alive now? She would never know.

Finally, the question she should have asked at the very beginning surfaced, and she looked straight into the god's eyes. "Who is Zeus's son?"

"Little Lilith, I don't think you are ready for that answer."

Lilith felt lightheaded. Fear crept over her, filling her with dread. She did not want to hear the answer, but she needed to know. Needed it to be confirmed. The answer was on the tip of her tongue, but it couldn't be him.

"Tell me." Her voice came out steadier than she felt.

Hades watched her as he spoke the name and shoved the metaphorical dagger deep into her heart.

"Finian Taren."

Hope was a dangerous thing. It allowed glimmers of light to break through the darkest crevices of one's mind, placing desire where desire should not be. Once the flame ignited, there was no stopping the burning blaze as it set its course on its unwilling victim. Hope could only be satisfied once it consumed everything in sight.

Which was why Lilith could not afford to believe that Finian, her Finian, was alive. She had been there when he died and saw the arrow pierce through his chest. There had been so much blood. On her hands, all over Finian, and soaking into the hard ground. She had held him during his final moments and watched the light go out forever.

And yet...

Hope. If she let her guard down now; she would be forced to relive the pain of losing Finian. Losing Idina had wounded her but losing Idina *and* Finian broke her.

Hades goaded her, trying to give her false hope, so she'd be willing to do his bidding. There was little Lilith would not do for the chance to see him again and Hades knew that; perhaps even expected that.

"I don't believe you." Lilith said. Hades only smiled and made himself comfortable on the log. His bulky frame leaned back to rest upon the rock behind him. In his hands was the meal he had been cooking since Lilith woke up. Venison, she believed.

When Hades offered her a bowl, Lilith stubbornly refused and now regretted that decision. The deer meat smelled delicious, and her mouth salivated at the thought of a hot meal. She did not know where Hades found the time to hunt and cook a deer, but she also didn't know how long she had been unconscious for.

"I'm not surprised." Hades said, wiping his mouth with the back of his hand. "Doesn't change the fact that it's the truth though. Now, are you done being stubborn or will you let a perfectly good meal go to waste?"

Lilith's stomach growled angrily, betraying her,

Hades smirked and once again held out the meal like a peace offering. Reluctantly, because she was not so stubborn as to starve to make a point, she accepted the venison. "Thanks."

Hades watched as she dug into the meat with wild abandon. She might have felt embarrassed if she could think of anything other than the hot meal he served. It was enough to let her guard down, if only for a minute.

And then she heard screaming.

A single scream and not one of fear. No, this scream contained pure fury and vitriol.

Raw.

Hades sighed, as if the person's pain was nothing more than an inconvenience. "I suppose we should address your captors, shall we?"

Her captors?

Then it hit her. Bas and Demi. She had not thought about them since she woke up, nor did she question their disappearance in the face of Hades. This whole time they had been stowed away, and she doubted they were being restrained with a simple rope. The restraint needed to be strong enough to hold two divine entities. Two pissed off divine entities.

"Unfortunately, dear Lilith, we need to table this conversation. Other matters call to us." Hades pushed himself off the log, discarding his empty bowl on the ground. Without another word, he began his descent towards Bas and Demi.

"I guess we're going." Lilith mumbled under her breath, picking herself off the ground and jogging to catch up. The closer they got to the tent, where she assumed Hades kept them, the more her stomach churned, creating a tightening sensation in her stomach.

Although they had not known each other for long, over the last few weeks Lilith had come to consider Demi a friend and Bas a mentor, but they played her for a fool. Had it killed Demi to play nice, letting Lilith cry all over her when the nightmares and pain of losing her family had been too much to endure? Was anything Bas told her true?

Was she making a similar mistake by blindly following Hades' lead now?

So many questions ran through her mind that she did not notice Hades stopped walking. She almost plowed right into him, but the god swiftly turned around and grabbed her by the shoulders, effectively stopping her before she slammed into his chest. He lowered himself down to eye level with her. This proximity made her uncomfortable but looking away would make her appear weak.

She did not need Hades exploiting anymore of her weaknesses.

"The man in there is a liar." Hades started, grip tightening around Lilith's shoulders. "He's charming and can spin a good tale, but you must see through his lies. He seeks to use you for his own personal gain. Demi serves him and will not hesitate to double-cross you if he gives the order. He doesn't have your best interest at heart."

"But you do." Lilith spoke, her voice flat. Distrust continued to brew between them. There was a time when she might have believed his words, but the world had shown her cruelty and burned her one too many times.

"You may not believe it, but I do. Both my brother and I have your best interests at heart. We will not let any harm come to you." Hades' words sounded so sincere she almost wanted to believe him. It would be so much easier to give in to trust and not question every motive.

She would not be a prize so easily won.

Instead of answering Hades, Lilith broke free of his grip. "Let's go inside. I want to see them."

Lilith parted the flap of the tent and stepped inside. She ducked when entering, but the top was tall enough that she did not need to crouch. Still, it was cramped, especially when she felt a fourth body enter behind her.

In opposite corners of the tent were Bas and Demi. Both bound with black rope. At least she assumed it was until she noticed movement.

"Shadows from the underworld. I control them." Hades answered her unasked questions. Those shadows were the same ones to seize Lilith when Hades found her in the forest.

Unlike Demi, who looked fine but murderous, Bas suffered during his altercation with Hades. She did not know gods could bruise, but Bas's eye was rimmed with an angry purplish black bruise. It appeared a couple of days old, meaning he was healing swiftly. Still, it looked painful. To his credit, Bas did not look at either Lilith or Hades with contempt or fury in his eyes. He looked...resigned.

"Come to finish us off?" Demi sneered. Lilith couldn't believe she once thought the woman demure and timid. She looked like a vengeful goddess, ready to destroy her enemies.

"Always the one for dramatics, little sister." Hades crooned.

"Fu-" Demi started, but Lilith quickly interrupted.

"Little sister? You two are related?" Looking between the two, she saw shared similarities. Both had sharp cheekbones and the same facial structure. Where Demi clearly had more feminine features, they echoed those of Hades. The similarities were there, but if Demi was his sister, did that mean that Bas was...

"Yes, little Lilith. Demi would be my bastard sister, another spawn of our father's. You see, he cannot do his own bidding, so he beds innocent women until one produces an heir. He manipulates and molds until he creates his perfect little warrior. Isn't that right, Cronus?"

Bas -Cronus?- tensed, his mouth set in a thin line.

"Why did you just call him Cronus?" Another lie? She had been fooled into believing a wrong name. Adolphi would be pissed she trusted so readily instead of attempting to learn more about the duo who abducted her.

"Because that is his name. The mighty King Cronus, befallen into nothing more than a leech. Isn't that right, father?" Hades spat the last word out as if it were poison.

Remorse crossed Bas's face. He looked like a man who suffered greatly and regretted his choices. Still, a hint of pride echoed in his voice when he addressed his son. "I go by Bas now."

"You don't get to change your name!" Hades roared furiously, breaking his normally calm composure. "You don't get to wash away the sins of your past by calling yourself Bas. You are the greedy tyrant Cronus, who lusted after power at the expense of his kingdom. Because of you, Zeus is the most powerful being in existence and will stop at nothing from destroying mortals and gods alike.

"So, father, was it worth it? All the lies, death, and deceit? Was divinity worth this?" Hades gestured around the cramped tent, his final question looming over them like heavy rain clouds, threatening to burst any moment.

Bas, though Lilith needed to address him as Cronus now, maintained eye contact with his son, locked in their own silent battle. "If you are asking if I regret taking Ambrosia and creating the divinity, which you yourself benefited from, my answer would be no. I don't regret it. My only regret is not killing Zeus when I had the chance."

"Bullshit! You've always been a power-hungry dick, never satisfied with what stands right before you. It must kill you to know you are the weakest amongst gods. The only weapon in your arsenal is keeping things hidden, but you've done that all your life."

"As much as I love having this wonderful family moment, I would very much appreciate it if you unbound your shadows from around me, you prick."

Both men's gazes angled to meet a scowling Demi in the opposite corner, looking ready to smite them both where they stood. Though the situation was tense, Lilith suppressed an inappropriate giggle threatening to escape her lips. This family squabble seemed too mundane for gods.

Squabble was not the correct term, considering actual lives were on the line.

Hades stepped away from Cronus, disregarding the man. "No, sister, I don't think I will. You took what is mine and then chased her through the woods. I don't take kindly to people threatening what is mine."

Lilith's eyes blazed in anger. Now it was her turn to whirl on Hades, her hand once again reaching for the missing dagger at her side. "I am not yours. I will never be your weapon to wield, nor will I submit to a life of servitude."

Hades and Poseidon created her, but everything she became was due to Idina. She had instilled morals in her. Encouraged her when she announced her ambition to become a Warrior of Dasos. Lilith never had to worry about her mother manipulating or using her. Idina encouraged and gave advice when asked. Otherwise, she had the autonomy to make her own choices.

The anger in the air was almost palpable, rolling off her in waves of fury. Hades sensed her rising tension and stiffened. He paled slightly. "Lilith, you need to calm down. Now." He said and then took a step back. Away. From her. If the situation wasn't dire, Lilith would have found it comical that the god of death was afraid of her.

"Lilith." Hades hissed, this time moving all the way out of the tent. "Calm down. Your powers are too strong."

Those words were enough to shock her right out of the anger trance. Did she hear him correctly? She had not been using any powers. She did not have powers to use, if these last three months were any indication. Cronus and Demi tried numerous activities to bring forth her divinity, but to no avail.

"What are you saying? How can I use divinity on you when I have none?" Lilith asked quizzically. "Ba-erm, Cronus and Demi tried, but I don't have an affinity for anything. I'm skilled with a sword and dagger, but that is due to my training in Dasos."

Hades frowned, a puzzled expression on his face. He did not back up anymore, nor was he as pale as he had been moments ago. Lilith took that as a good sign. Hades stared at Cronus again, instead of addressing her as she hoped. "You don't know what she is?"

"No." He admitted. "I sensed her power; it spoke to me like kin. Unfortunately, I was unable to discover her divinity. I knew she had to be special if you and Poseidon decided to use the last of Ambrosia on her."

"Your little experiment did not go as planned, brother. You created a dud, a mere mortal with the blood of gods running through her veins but no actual divinity." Demi spoke unkindly. Lilith wanted to be angry, but Demi's words rang true. For wasn't that exactly what she believed too?

Hades' handsome face turned amused, his smile playing on his lips. It only made him look more beautiful and utterly terrifying at the same time. She was starting to think that was his specialty.

"The fact that you cannot sense her goddess affinity further proves that Poseidon and I succeeded in our task." He said but did not offer to elaborate. That grated on her nerves; his inability to ever give a complete answer.

"How about a demonstration, yes?" Hades asked, smirking. He then lifted his hand, waving in the air before making a fist. Nothing happened...or so Lilith thought.

Hearing rustling behind her, she spun around only to see Demi free of her binds. Cronus had not been so fortunate; his dark wisps of rope stayed firmly around his body. Demi jerked her head down, assessing her body in a moment of disbelief before her face turned into one of fury again. Redness creeped up her neck and into her cheeks; a fire igniting in her body.

"Go ahead sister. Fight her. Fight Lilith. She's unarmed and you are a goddess. I won't interfere." Hades spoke.

Lilith gaped. "Fuck you." She spat, which only earned a low chuckle from Hades.

She might stand a chance if the woman were mortal, but Demi was a strong goddess with the element of earth to aid her. Lilith had nothing but her fists. Hades had just damned her to death at the hands of his bastard sister.

But for what reason?

She did not get to ponder that long, for something wrapped around her foot and tugged her forward. Lilith lost balance as she went down hard on her knee. Grunting in pain, she managed to get up seconds before a large rock sailed past, directly where her head had been moments ago.

Demi did not just want to hurt her; she was out for blood. Panic seized Lilith momentarily as she struggled to free herself from the vines. "Worthless mortal." Demi snarled, forgoing her divinity as she lunged for Lilith, tackling the woman to the ground.

It was as if a switch went off in Demi. Her eyes, now completely black, showed no hints of the girl she had befriended and trusted. She looked almost...rabid.

Like an Unhallowed.

Realization hit her, knocking the wind right out of her lungs. Her unchecked cruelty. The crazed look in her eyes, and the frenzy movements.

Demi was going through the Unhallowing, but she was a goddess. Lilith thought the disease did not affect the gods, but no other explanation fit. Demi's fist came down in a devastating blow, too fast for Lilith to stop it. The side of her mouth exploded into white-hot pain and the metallic taste of blood filled her mouth.

"Stupid whore." The goddess spat, raising her arm again for another punch, but this time Lilith expected it. At the last possible second, she turned her head to the side, the rush of wind kissing her face. Demi screamed in pain as her fist connected to the hard ground underneath her.

Lilith rolled to the side and kicked out her legs, connecting to the goddess's stomach. Demi grunted as she stumbled back, gasping for the breath Lilith kicked out of her.

This was all too familiar. The angry, demeaning words of an Unhallowed. Fighting for her life. She had been here before, and it did not end well. Too much had been taken from her that night, people she could never replace. Rage and sorrow filled her as a primal shout left her lips.

"Come get me, little goddess. I'm ready to play."

Even to her own ears, the voice sounded foreign, belonging to someone else. A culmination of anger, sorrow, and regret filled this new need blossoming in the pits of her stomach. She did not think she could control this, and honestly, Lilith did not want to. Demi would take the bait; the goddess couldn't turn down a fight in her current state of mind.

As expected, Demi rushed her. The small goddess was quick, striking with deadly precision. If she had a sword, Demi might have the upper hand. As it was now though, the goddess relied on her brute strength, either forgetting about her divinity or saving her strength for a grander attack.

Passion and fury drove each of Demi's punches and kicks, but Lilith was fast too. The last few years had been nothing but long hours of training and her body was accustomed to taking hits and pushing past straining muscles to endure battle. She was in her element, welcoming the fatigue and adrenaline like an old friend.

A scream of pain pierced the night air as Lilith's fist made contact with Demi's face. The goddess's head snapped around with a sickening crunch, but it barely deterred the woman. Adrenaline pumped through Lilith's veins and the feeling brewing inside of her finally engulfed her, consuming Lilith's body.

One moment she remembered being angry, fury and resentment coursing through her veins, and the next moment she saw light.

White light poured out of every crevice and pore of her body. Power and creation. Death and destruction. The light burned her and left her empty. Lilith heard screaming, but she could not tell if it came from her or Demi. Nothing else existed besides the divinity using her body as its puppet.

Just as quickly as it came, the agony of the white light left her so suddenly she fell to her knees, no longer able to hold herself up. Strength deserted her, making her limbs too heavy and sluggish.

When her eyes adjusted, Lilith saw Demi sprawled on the ground at an odd angle. Dread consumed her, as she continued to stare at the body. *Move.* She silently pleaded. There had been other kills, but Lilith had been in control of each situation. This was different. The power consumed her and used Lilith's body of its own accord. She had been at the will of her own divinity.

"I...I killed her." Lilith said, voice trembling.

As soon as she spoke, Demi's chest rose. It had been ever so slight, but then it happened again. The goddess was still alive, but something was wrong.

"What happened?"

Lilith met Hades' stare who looked upon her like a dehydrated man would stare at water amid barren land.

Instead of answering, because Hades seemed to make it his life's mission to never directly answer one of her questions, he walked over to Demi and crouched down. Hades lifted two fingers to Demi's neck and waited. His nod further reassured Lilith the goddess was still alive.

"Her eyes...they matched the Unhallowed. They were so cold and distant. I thought you said the Divine can't be affected by this curse." Lilith said, still on her knees without strength.

"I didn't say that. I said we are not affected as mortals are. The disease has progressed. It started out slow at first, an intrusive thought. Blind rage. But I can see now that it is morphing rapidly. She had not gone through the change completely, but the disease did have its hold on her momentarily." Hades explained.

This provided Lilith with a modicum of hope. Hope that Demi did not truly hate her as much as she had appeared to minutes ago. She hoped most of her rage had been because the disease made her yearn for violence and destruction.

"That...that light that came out of me. Did I cure her?" She asked, which seemed like a logical conclusion.

Still, Hades laughed. "No, you did not cure her. It is my belief that the Unhallowing cannot be cured until we discover who placed the plague on this world." Hades said and straightened up.

He took a step closer to her. Then another. Soon he stood right in front of her, making Lilith tilt her head up slightly to meet his eyes.

"Do you think a mortal can escape the imprisonment of gods?" Hades asked. Before Lilith could answer, he continued. "Can a mortal hide from avenging gods? Did Cronus and Demi ever seem tired around you? The Divine don't tire easily, not unless we have seen great battles."

"What are you saying?" Lilith asked, unable to comprehend what Hades implied. How could she have been using her powers all this time and not known?

"What I am saying, little Lilith, is that your power has nothing to do with the Unhallowed, but it will be our ticket to victory. Poseidon was certain your powers would be extraordinary, but we never suspected your ability to be as powerful as it is. You, little goddess, hold the power of Divinity."

No one spoke for a minute. Not even Demi, who slowly picked herself off the ground. Though pale, she looked more coherent than she did a moment ago, resolved to her fate.

"My power is...power?" Lilith frowned.

"Yes. When we created you, my brother and I used our last drops of Ambrosia. You are the first and last of your kind. Because of that, you inherited the power to give and take divinity. Lilith darling, you can take away godhood with a snap of your fingers and give powers to the worthy." Hades said, a wicked glint in his eyes as he spoke.

"Impossible. What you are saying is impossible." Another voice piped in. Everyone turned their attention to Cronus, still ensnared by Hades' shadows. "That kind of power would be a threat to our kind, our very existence."

"If she fell into the wrong hands." Hades sneered. "Zeus does not have her nor is he aware of her ability. Lilith is our best secret and chance at fixing this. All of this." He said and gestured all around. "You were selfish and power hungry once before. The world is suffering for it now. You created Zeus, shaped him into the monster he is today. Lilith will clean up your mess because you are too weak to accomplish that on your own."

The silence hung heavy between father and son. Neither of them spoke. They were locked in a silent battle of wills. Cronus did not look like the King Hades claimed he had been. No, he looked like a man who lost everything he held dear. It almost made Lilith feel sorry for him.

Almost.

"I admit in the past I was not a good man, but I was a great King." Cronus said, breaking the silence. "Great Kings do not become that way by being good men. I raised you and your brother to follow in my footsteps and you became so much more than I could ever imagine. But let me make one thing very clear. I am not the only one who contributed to Zeus's tumultuous childhood. You did your fair share in that department yourself, boy."

Faster than Lilith could see, a resounding crack filled the evening air. Hades' fist connected to Cronus's jaw, whipping his head violently to the side. If Cronus had been human, Lilith doubted he'd be conscious now. The former King simply spit out dark blood and glared up into his son's cold stare. "If you hate me this much, why don't you kill me?"

"Death is too good for you, father." He spat the words like venom. "I want you to watch as Poseidon and I accomplish everything you never could. When we reclaim Dasos, you will forever rot in the cells below, for death is not a mercy I will ever give you."

"Presumptuous of you, seeing as how I am the one with the power to restore balance back into this world." Both men tore their gazes away from each other to see Lilith walking forward. Perhaps her eyes were playing tricks on her, but she swore both men flinched as she approached.

Good.

"I don't have the full story, but I have enough. You need me to right the wrongs you both created. Take Zeus's powers so you and Poseidon can end him and the Unhallowing. Restore Dasos to its former glory with improvements. Am I correct?" She asked.

"More or less."

"She also needs to restore my divinity!" Demi yelled from behind her.

Lilith nearly forgot she was there. She had even forgotten the blast of power hadn't cured the Unhallowed disease inside of her but took away her divinity. It was amazing how much anger one small body could hold, but Demi seemed to be made entirely of wrath. She would have been more frightening with powers. If only looks could kill, Lilith would be floating through the river Styx by now.

Even if she wanted to give Demi back her powers, Lilith didn't know how. She was not sure how she took them in the first place, only that the anger blinded her, and the divinity acted on its own volition.

Thankfully, Hades spoke before she had a chance. "Demi, it will do you good to be without your powers for a while. Perhaps you will learn humility. Once you do, I'm sure dear Lilith will happily restore you to your former glory and you can sing with the trees."

"I don't sing with tr-"

"Besides," Hades continues, interrupting Demi. "You weren't yourself moments ago. If the Unhallowing found its way to curse the gods, it would be best if you did not have your power until we are certain you will remain fully intact."

He had a point and though Demi wanted to argue, the woman had enough sense to keep her mouth shut.

"Back to our conversation, Lilith, I would like to take you to my brother. He is dealing with a few important matters, but he knows people who can help you harness your divinity. Before we can go against Zeus, we need to make you stronger, faster, and smarter than he is." Hades smiled.

"If I do this, then I want something in return."

"Anything. Name your price."

Lilith took a deep breath and met his gaze. "Finian. If he is alive like you claim him to be, then you will promise me he will not be harmed. We will find him, and he will remain at my side."

The request made Hades pause, sending a bolt of anxiety through her stomach. If he didn't agree...

"Very well."

Shocked, Lilith's eyes widened. "You agree?" She asked incredulously.

"I agree, but I cannot promise he will be the same boy you fell in love with. He has gone through a great deal and spent the last few weeks with Zeus. He may not be the man you once loved."

"I don't care. If anyone so much as lays a finger on him, there will not be a rock or crevice to hide where I will not find you. Don't. Hurt. Fin." She punctuated each word, looking between Cronus, Demi, and Hades. She lost the man she loved once, and the universe had given her a second chance.

She would not lose him again.

"Well, now that this is all settled and the fun ended, we should rest for the night. We have a long journey ahead of us tomorrow, and we can all use the rest." Hades peered at Demi and gestured to Cronus's tent. "Little sister, I will be requiring your tent tonight. You can room with Cronus for the night. My shadows will keep you both safe and secure."

Black tendrils wrapped around Demi's arms and legs, securing them just enough that escape would be near impossible. She flashed him murderous eyes. "When this is all over and I have my divinity back, I will personally make your life a living hell."

"Darling, I'm the King of the underworld. Living hell is sort of my thing." He winked, all charm and smiles.

Growling, Demi stalked off to the tent without another word. No one made any movement to help Cronus off the ground, so the god awkwardly rolled to his knees and picked himself up. The two of them watched him enter the tent after Demi and as a final safeguard, Hades sent the last of his shadows to secure the tent flap. No one would be leaving without his approval.

"Get some rest tonight, little goddess." Hades whispered. "Tomorrow, your real test begins. I want you ready." With a final look, Hades turned back and went to the unoccupied tent. Even gods needed rest.

Alone, Lilith looked up at the night sky. Her mind was a commotion of fleeting thoughts. She allowed herself to believe, for a single moment, that Finian was out there somewhere, thinking of her. Did he miss her as much as she missed him? His absence hung heavy with her, everywhere she went she carried the grief.

Idina, her mother in all but blood, came to mind next. Hades said she moved on, and she hoped that wherever her soul was, she was happy. She hoped Adolphi was with her because even in death, she believed their love to be strong. She wondered if she would have treated Lilith any differently if she knew she wasn't human.

But she knew Idina would not have. Idina loved fiercely and without barriers. She would have traveled the world to find Lilith help for harnessing her divinity. The thought brought a smile to her face. "I will make you proud." She murmured under breath. "And one day, when my body fails me and my soul departs, I shall tell you all about the adventures I went on."

She would tell her mother of the temperamental gods she had met along the way. The story of how she became tangled up in a century old family feud. How she was not born but created.

How she became Lilith the Last.

With tears of love and loss streaming down her face, Lilith walked back to her tent for the evening knowing that tomorrow, the next chapter of her life began.

CHAPTER TWENTY-TWO

THE BEFORE

Z EUS NEVER SLEPT FOR long. He grew accustomed to the lavish bed back at Caister. He even missed his bed back at home with his mitera. No matter how hard he tried to smooth the ground under him, he still woke up with small rocks digging into his skin and his clothes damp with morning dew.

It also did not help that he had been traveling for a little over two weeks with two men he did not trust. Zarek, at least, was tolerable. Zeus no longer felt disdain for the guard, and he could hold a conversation with him without wanting to strangle Zarek. He was also a skilled hunter and taught Zeus how to track down large animals for dinner.

Hermes, however, was the most intolerable person he ever had the displeasure of knowing. Every word that came out of the man's mouth grated on his nerves and made him want to slit his throat. He had the feeling Hermes would also like to make the prince bleed. To make matters worse, the esteemed topographer had a challenging time finding the cave.

The days went by in a sluggish blur, and Zeus began to lose hope. Each morning started the same, they would set out on their horses and Hermes would lead them through intricate paths mapped out in his head. Though he never seemed lost, Zeus wondered if Hermes truly knew the direction they traveled. The forests never changed, and he noticed they were going in circles. Even Zarek grew suspicious of their arrogant companion.

Their traveling came to an unsuccessful halt when the light barely peaked through the darkening sky. Hermes dismounted first, cursing blindly into the wind. "I know we're close. We've traveled into the heart of the damn forest. The cave is here, the bloody thing doesn't want to be found."

"You speak of the cave as if it were a living creature." Zeus said, dismounting his horse. He tried to ignore the strain in his thighs from countless nights of riding, but he started to feel the ache throughout his entire being. The only one of them that did not complain about discomfort was Zarek. The man was an anomaly, silent as a ghost and deadly as a wolf.

"Aye, it is. A fickle bastard." Hermes grunted. "Let's camp here for the night. I've got to shit." He announced.

"Don't let the bears get you." Zarek dead-panned.

"Fuck off." With that lovely sentiment, Hermes left.

Once the man was far enough away so they wouldn't be overheard, Zeus said, "We've been circling these damn woods for weeks, and we aren't any closer to finding the cave."

Zarek, for the first time since they met, was at a loss for words. The constant traveling with no end in sight wore heavily on him too. Unlike Zeus, Zarek could leave. Hermes stayed because Ambrosia became an obsession for him, but Zarek had no use for the elixir. "You can leave, you know. Nothing is keeping you here." He reminded him. The fact that Zarek could walk a free man filled Zeus with inexplicable anger.

"It's getting dark. I should gather wood for a fire." Zarek ignored him and walked in the opposite direction of Hermes, leaving Zeus alone at camp.

Fine, if his two companions wanted to be useless and secretive, he would do without them for a few hours. Besides, he needed to stretch his legs. No one would stop him from leaving the camp, so he headed south. He was no Hermes, but his sense of direction improved these past few weeks, and something in him told him to go south.

As he walked, his mind drifted too. First to Chloe and whether she was safe. She was likely sick with worry and questioning if her son was alive. Had Malik finally convinced her to leave? Knowing his mitera, that did not seem likely.

Then to Metis, never escaping her even miles apart from each other. It was an odd thing to think of someone you loved, but instead of happiness accompanied by fond memories, she left only pain. He would carry that pain with him always until he found a way to lift that burden.

Zeus was not sure how long he walked until he heard running water. A river? That was odd, days passed since they came across anything other than a small pond. Missing an entire river seemed unlikely, though they had grown lethargic as the days went by. His senses dulled and he became less observant because his mind was preoccupied with what they left behind.

Dropping to his knees by the bank of the river, he cupped his hands and submerged them in water. He had been warned of the negative side effects of drinking dirty water, but he was parched, and his mouth was dry. As soon as the water hit his throat, he felt like a blind man who gained the ability to see once again. No matter how much he took, he couldn't quench his thirst.

He leaned forward, getting closer. The need for water soon became a searing pain, and he abandoned his hands to lean his body over the bank of the river, drinking straight from the source. He could drink the entirety of the river, but it would not be enough.

A moment later the water pulled him under.

At first his mind did not register what was happening. Then his lungs began to burn, and reality sunk in. He had fallen into the river. He didn't remember leaning over or losing his balance. Desperately, he tried to swim against the flow, but the current steadily picked up and carried him further away. The distance did not bother him as much as the rocks and attempting to stay above water did.

He was going to drown. His muscles screamed in protest and his vision became hazy around the edges. Water filled his ears, blocking out the noise around him and leaving a soothing hum, sounding almost melodic. He stopped fighting and let his body relax. He couldn't remember a time when he experienced so much peace; a time when everything in his life was completely perfect. If an afterlife existed, it paled in comparison to what he felt now.

Letting himself go and slipping into sweet oblivion would be so easy, but he did not get the chance because arms reached for him. They grasped him until they were able to hurl his body onto the hard, firm ground. He gasped, choking on the water before throwing up. Whatever spell he was under, shattered the moment he was released.

Finally, he filled his lungs with one glorious burst of air. Zeus panted and scanned his surroundings to thank his mysterious savior, expecting to find either Hermes or Zarek, but no one else was around. Only him, and he was in a....well, he did not exactly know where the river took him.

Where soft grass should be, hard stone took its place. Instead of a fresh and earthy smell associated with the forest, all around him smelled damp and stale. It took Zeus longer than he cared to admit, which he blamed on almost drowning, to realize he landed in an enclosed space. Very much like a....

Cave.

Impossible, but no explanation sufficed for how he wound up here. He couldn't locate any visible entrances or figure out where the water came from.

If it was the cave they searched for, then he just successfully imprisoned himself within.

Zeus pushed himself off the ground. He cursed as his muscles tightened, begging for reprieve. He was alone and in the dark. Fear crept its way in, obscuring his rational thoughts. He was alone with no way out. He was alone and he would die alone. He was alone and-

"Hello, blood of Rhea."

The voice was everywhere and nowhere. Zeus jumped, reaching for the sword no longer on his waist, lost to the water. Just like the invisible hands that pulled him out, he could not find the person behind the voice. It was the cave, toying with him. Hermes said the cave was alive and now he believed him. He was but a lamb in the den of lions.

Fucking invisible lions.

"To see us you must look down." The voice came again, sounding neither male nor female, but like a chorus of people speaking at once. So, Zeus looked down. Four curious eyes stared back at him.

Not human eyes.

A woman and a man peered up out of the water, both naked from the chest up. Their skin was the color of the murky water with flecks of gold. The woman had long, flowing hair that appeared to drift around her face as if submerged in water. The man's slicked back hair stopped at his shoulders.

If it weren't for the slight glean to their skin and strange way their hair moved, they could almost pass as human, but their necks had gills like a fish. The woman rested her hand on the stone ground, and he noticed the webbing on her fingers.

They were sirens.

Zeus had been told tales of the people of the sea and rivers, but he thought they were just that, tales. Fantastical creatures that were part of the many mysteries of the sea. Even looking at the two sirens, he stood in disbelief.

The sirens continued to stare at him curiously, as if he were the creature of stories and not the other way around. The male tilted his head to the side, studying Zeus and then spoke. "Blood of Rhea. We've been expecting you. Travel through the cave and into the light. From here, find what thou art searching for."

"Expecting me? What do you mean expecting me? What will I find?" Zeus's mind reeled, trying to make sense of the bizarre encounter.

This time the woman spoke to him. Both their voices were melodic and inviting. If they wanted him dead, they would only have to sing. Was it their voice he heard before as the water overtook him? He thought the hum came from the water, but perhaps it had been something else. "No mortal has come this far. The water will hurt you no longer. Go forward, Blood of Rhea. Time is of the essence."

As one, both man and woman slowly disappeared under the water. Zeus peered over and saw their faces, looking up at him. Their features changed, and he could not believe he confused them as humans before. Nothing human remained in their features. Their golden eyes bore into him, wondering if he would continue his travels into the cave.

What other choice did he have?

Zeus took his first step forward. The cave stretched ahead, the walls getting closer together until they resembled a stone hallway. There was no entrance and no other passages visible. While he walked, he couldn't help but wonder how many sirens lay beneath the murky waters and if they were all watching him expectantly. Whatever lay at the end of the tunnel interested the creatures.

The flow of the river ended, and Zeus traveled deeper into the cave. No one walked or swam alongside him and the deeper he traveled, the more his mind told him this was a bad idea. He was quick to trust the creatures after a short conversation that ended abruptly and without warning. He didn't have his sword for protection. His fighting skills would be useless in the dark, and he didn't like the idea of being vulnerable.

Ten minutes of walking and groping the sides so he wouldn't stumble, Zeus finally caught sight of light in the distance, though faint and far off. He did not know why, but he felt like something important awaited him ahead. Something only for him. He couldn't describe the feeling, only the need to be there. Or was this more temptation from the sirens?

Zeus was a man with little to lose, but everything to gain. He continued forward, further into the tunnel until he reached the source of light. It took his eyes a moment to adjust, and longer still to process the small, enclosed space. The tunnel ended here, with no foreseeable exits besides the one he came from. A large boulder lay in the center, the top corroded away after years of weathering. A small stream of water flowed down, damping the ground with each droplet.

He approached the boulder, wondering what he was supposed to see. His fingers danced lightly over the water building up within the stone, creating a tiny puddle. It occurred to him then that he had never asked what Ambrosia looked like. Ambrosia was always described as an elixir, but never a color. His father had been certain that when Zeus saw it, he would know. The power Ambrosia held could not be replicated or mimicked. The feeling would be indescribable, which proved to only complicate his search. He chased a dream that grew bleaker by the moment.

He failed again and this time Cronus would not be there to punish him. The cave would swallow him whole soon enough. His chest began to tighten, and his breathing turned ragged. Any moment, anxiety, helplessness, and dread would take over and Zeus did not think he had the strength to fight it off.

He wanted to flee, but where would he go? The sirens spared him once, he doubted they would a second time. A blissful death served as his best option for escape. It would be painless, and he could think of her, Metis, in his final moments. He just needed to find a spot to lay down.

Ready to leave, Zeus turned...and nearly ran into a woman. "What the hell!" He yelled, falling backwards, though he caught himself on the stone behind him. He blinked once, making sure his mind was not playing tricks on him. The room was small, providing no place for the woman to hide. If she followed him, he was certain he would have heard footsteps.

This woman simply appeared. Just like the cave.

"Who are you? Where did you come from?"

The woman didn't answer his questions, only smiled softly. It didn't appear menacing, but he was not put at ease either. "Zeus. They said you were here. Let me look at you."

Figures she would know his name. Every odd creature in this bloody cave knew him, while he knew nothing of them. Maybe he was losing his mind or maybe he was already dead.

The woman did not answer him immediately. She smiled, but her eyes told a tale of great sadness and regret. Her reaction made him want to reach out and hug this mysterious woman, but he kept his arms firmly planted at his sides.

Hugging her wouldn't have worked anyway because she wasn't completely solid.

What he took as poor lighting or a trick of the eye, was in fact true. The woman looked unearthly; not even the world knew how to convey her image properly. He saw her, but she appeared to him as a beacon of light and not a solid person.

There was also something eerily familiar about her too, a memory he could not resurface. It was her eyes, those melancholy but kind eyes. He knew her, but she was also a stranger to him.

Yet he knew, though he could not say how, who this mysterious spirit was. "Your name is Rhea."

The woman laughed softly...or was she weeping? Like her eyes, the noise sounded joyous and painful. "That was my name once, yes. Though to you, I am your mitera."

"You were never my mitera." The words poured out of him before he could stop them. He couldn't hide his anger, not when she was the root of all his problems. "Chloe has and will always be my mother. My only mother. You left."

"I died."

"YOU LEFT!" He roared, his voice echoing around them, reminding Rhea repeatedly she left Zeus to be the most hated son. She thought the same thing and flinched at his accusation.

"How are you here? Are you real? I don't understand. Am I dreaming? This feels like a dream." So many questions ran through his head, and he wanted to demand that she answer every single one of them. She owed him that much.

"You have every right to hate me, Zeus." Rhea said gently, her ghostly image moving forward. When she saw him flinch, she stopped and took a step back again. "I promise, we will make this right. I have so much I need to tell you and we don't have much time."

"We have time. I have nothing but time. I'm in this cave with no way out. I'm not certain how I came here."

"That," Rhea said. "Is something I can explain. At least try to. This cave holds many wonders and many secrets. A few have stumbled here, much like yourself, but they have not been so lucky."

"You mean they died?"

"Yes, they died." She nodded. "But they were never supposed to be here. They held greed in their heart and that is what attracts the people of the water. The sirens and tritons need these people to survive. They are what help protect the secrets of the cave."

Zeus's mind spun. He did not comprehend everything she said. Today was a day filled with impossible things; Zeus had no choice but to go along with the improbable. "So why am I here?"

"You were always meant to come here. One way or another, you would have found your way here. It's in your blood. *Our* blood. We are part of the cave's many wonders." She said. Rhea saw the confusion in his mind, and carried on, slower this time.

"A long time ago, a bride was on her way to marry a King. She knew nothing of him, only that he lived far away and needed a Queen. The journey was long, and their party made many stops. On one of these stops, the bride wandered off to bathe in the lake. That is where she met a triton-"

"A what?"

"I suppose you could say a male version of a siren." She answered, unfazed by her son's interruption. "After just a few hours together, they fell in love. He took her back to his home, which was in this cave. As people in love often do, they had-"

"I understand." Zeus replied quickly, cheeks tinted in red. "After only a few hours? They fell in love?"

"Stranger things have happened, dear Zeus. For instance, you are talking to your dead mother." Rhea smiled, and Zeus relented. He gestured for her to continue. "When the bride woke up the following morning, she was back at camp, no traces of the triton she met the previous day. She wept for the love she lost, but they had to continue on their journey. She married the King and became the Queen. Early in the marriage she found out she was pregnant, and she knew, without a doubt, the baby was the triton's.

"Who was this bride?" He asked, which earned him a genuine smile from the woman.

"Why, it was your grandmother, Gaia."

Gaia. Queen Gaia. A woman as cold as ice with no heart. He could not imagine his grandmother young or in love, but if that were true, Rhea was... "You are a siren?"

"Only half." She assured him. "But half is enough for this cave. My spirit is tied here, though this is the first time I have ever manifested. I believe I am to give you what you seek."

Ambrosia, she was going to give him Ambrosia. Zeus hesitated, something he did a lot these past few days, but caution played in his favor so far. He didn't think it would be this easy. There had to be something he missed.

"I'm in search of Ambrosia. King Cronus has been in search of the elixir for years. He says it will make him a great immortal King. He plans to share it with Hades and Poseidon." Zeus said.

Again, Rhea looked ready to cry, though he suspected the dead had no tears left to shed. "I suspected his cruelty would grow alongside his need for power. I'm sure my mother is in search of Ambrosia too."

Rhea stared past him, searching for something he could not see. She frowned and turned her attention back towards Zeus. "I'm running out of time. Listen, Zeus. One day you will get the entire story, but for now you are going to have to trust me. I know that I ask for a lot, but so much hinges on what you must do.

"It is only a matter of time before the search for Ambrosia will be uncontrollable for the sirens and tritons. The elixir will fall into the hands of a person with greed in their heart and the world will descend into complete darkness. Chaos and destruction will be the only thing the world knows. But, if given to a person with a heart as big as yours, we can keep balance between your world and the spirit worlds."

"Can you not destroy it? Wouldn't that solve the problem? If Ambrosia holds this much power, then it should not exist." He said.

"And yet, it still does. This power cannot be destroyed, only distributed. The burden of immortality and power should be shared, not dominated." Rhea said and moved swiftly to the boulder behind Zeus.

He followed her with his gaze and turned around to see the water that once flowed from the top of the boulder no longer running clear. Instead, a deep crimson red swirled in its place. Zeus felt the power emanating from the Ambrosia. It was seductive and irresistible. Life and immortality sat before him and all he needed to do was reach out, cup it in the palms of his hand and drink.

"Zeus." Rhea hissed. She called his name, but he hadn't been paying attention. "Fight the temptation. If you are not careful, it will consume you. Don't let that happen. It will be your downfall."

Zeus took a step back, hoping the distance would break through the temptation. However, there was no need, for when he looked down again, the crimson liquid changed back to water. "Where did it go?" He asked, looking around but found no traces of Ambrosia.

"It's back at Dasos, where it's always been. But I warn you, you will not like what I'm about to tell you. Because you will have to do something terrible and after, you will fight with a broken heart. I never wanted this for you, my boy, and if you survive this, like I think you will, I will tell you who I really was and who you truly are."

Back at Dasos? He had traveled all this way, spent years of his life lying and spying for his father, only for Ambrosia to be back at Dasos. Always in Dasos. His jaw set, anger radiating from him. He would do whatever horrible deed was expected of him, since his entire existence has been one horrible deed after the other. He could spare losing a little more of his soul. "What do I need to do?" He asked, his voice coming out low and harsh. A stranger's voice.

"After I tell you, I will take you back to Dasos, and we may not meet again for some time, but we will meet again. Then, if you still wish to speak to me, I will tell you everything. Just know, this was never supposed to be you." Despite herself, Rhea reached out and caressed the side of his face. He grimaced, but did not actually feel her touch, just a coolness to where her hand should have been on his cheek.

"Tell me now. Don't stall any longer. I'm not concerned about your feelings; you're dead. You did not give me the same mercy. Speak, Rhea. There is nothing else for me to lose."

Rhea explained what he must do, and the last bit of his heart burned to ash because there was still one more thing he had to lose. Angry tears fell down his cheeks and his body shook with resentment. Not only for Rhea, but for himself.

When she finished talking, Zeus did not care that she already died. He would kill her all over again. He lunged, but instead of colliding with the stone behind her, his body fell into lush grass. A familiar smell scented the air around him, of rosemary and ginger. Gone was the musty cave. Rhea said she would take him to Dasos, and she did. So, he looked up.

At a cottage. The home he shared with Chloe.

CHAPTER TWENTY-THREE

THE AFTER

I N A SINGLE DRUNKEN night, Finian learned about Zeus's one and only friend Zarek, though it took glass after glass of mead to obtain any information about their past. That was a sore subject for both men. Frustratingly enough, gods did not get drunk as quickly as mortals did.

"We don't get drunk?" Finian questioned.

"Another bloody curse, isn't it?" Zarek murmured under his breath, polishing off his sixth glass of mead.

"We can." Zeus supplied, though Finian noticed he had yet to touch his second glass. "However, the amount of alcohol consumption it would take is almost tedious. Plus, the effects don't last long enough to truly go numb."

"So, we pretend." Zarek sighed, raising another glass to toast an invisible audience.

Finian stared at the man before him, unable to help himself. Since Zarek walked in, he couldn't tear his gaze away from the new male. Besides his father, Finian had seen no other person, much less another god. Zarek had an aura around him that both intrigued and frightened Finian. He was not a man one wanted as an enemy, that much he was certain of.

His father spoke of Zarek as a friend he had known since before becoming Divine. The god had to be centuries old, even though he appeared little older than Finian. He wondered if Zarek had been by his father's side the entire time, despite the villainous facade Zeus carried with him. If the new god knew anything about those rumors, which Finian suspected he did, Zarek didn't react to them.

"What news have you brought back to us? You never cease to disappoint with the tales you return with." Zeus finally asked once his friend had his fill of mead. Despite how much they drank, the barrel never ran dry.

"The boy?" Came the reply.

Finian took a moment to realize that the boy was in reference to him. His cheeks flushed, and he bit back his crude insults.

"The boy, as you have so elegantly put, is my son. My only heir. He's far from boyhood. We can trust him. Speak freely in front of him."

Zarek frowned, unsure about trusting him. Doubt etched into his expression, but he did not argue, only nodded. "Cronus found the girl. After the bloody mess in Dasos, he slipped in-"

"Impossible. He would have been without his divinity."

Zarek shrugged. "He did not need his power. He had enough strength to carry the girl out and did not stay within the walls of Dasos long enough for any lasting damage to occur."

Zeus accepted this answer with a grunt and nodded for him to continue.

"He carried the girl back to camp. I lingered close by for a few weeks as Cronus and his charming daughter Demi attempted to train her, but to no avail. I didn't sense her divinity, but her aura isn't that of a mortal either. She is a strong, a good fighter, and-"

"You said she was taken from Dasos?" Finian interjected, unable to remain silent. He did not dare to hope for the impossible, for he remembered his final night in Dasos. He remembered the blood and the screams of the dying. The slaughter had been horrific, permanently ingraining itself into his memory.

Yet Zarek suggested a survivor remained. A girl who could fight and Finian only knew of one Dasonian female Warrior.

Zarek and Zeus exchanged a look with one another, silently communicating. He refused to be kept in the dark any longer. "Don't." He hissed. "Don't keep information from me. What are you not telling me?"

"Fin-"

He cut his father off. "Don't bullshit me. You claim I can trust you, but you have been incredibly secretive. You deal in half-truths, and I will have no more of it."

He held the attention of both gods now, and this moment was a precipice. Tilting too far one way would push him over, so he needed to tread lightly. "Thunder," Finian started, using the name Zeus introduced himself as. He saw the slightest inhale of breath and Finian knew he shocked the man.

"I am not them. Your father or brothers. Secrets and deceit fueled your boyhood, but not anymore. If this is to work, we must trust each other."

Silence befell the room. Finian watched as his father's muscles unclenched, giving Zarek a small nod of approval, spurring the man to answer.

"The girl was taken from Dasos, yes." Zarek answered after gaining Zeus's approval.

"Do you know her name?"

"I do."

Doing his best to hide his agitation, Finian gritted out. "Tell me."

"Lilith Serah."

A gush of air left him as if Zarek punched his stomach. "She survived?" He croaked out, not recognizing his own voice.

"She did. Your Lilith fought valiantly, but when she watched you die, she broke. I could not get to her in time, not when we had to rescue your soul before it floated too far into the River Styx."

Lilith was alive. His Enchantress was out there now, and he was no longer in the same realm as her. He once promised Lilith he would never leave her. She had been furious and so scared while he lay dying because he was breaking that promise to her. He left her alone in a world of soulless creatures.

Was she angry with him?

More importantly, could he find a way back to her? Though he knew of no way of escaping Zeus's realm, there had to be a way. Naturally his father kept to Olympus for his personal safety, but Zarek came and went as he pleased. Finian was not tied to Olympus like his father; he assumed he was free to leave as well.

"Where is she now?" He demanded, tension coursing through his body.

Zarek shifted uncomfortably, looking troubled. "The last I saw, she was leaving with Hades. They were going to find Poseidon."

"Your brothers?" Finian turned his icy glare towards his father. The candle on the table flickered, sending a burst of fire from the wick before sputtering back to normal. "The ones who want you dead."

There was no question in his son's statement, but Zeus answered it anyway. "Yes. I'm not surprised. She was always theirs to claim. My brothers are many things, but they are not murderers." He paused and then laughed bitterly. "Well, unless it is me. They aren't going to harm her. In fact, she is probably safest with them."

"Be that as it may, we have to consider her the opposi-tion." Zarek announced, startling Finian.

"She is not our enemy!"

"You do not know that."

"I do." Finian snarled, clutching the arms of his chair. He had never been so happy for a table dividing two people. He doubted he could hold himself back otherwise. "You don't know her like I do. She's fair and just. Lilith would never harm an innocent man. She would never align herself with the enemy."

"Depending on the narrative." Zarek shrugged. "A tale can be spun in many directions and the truth is flexible at best. In their eyes, Zeus is the enemy, regardless of the circumstances putting him in that position. That is their truth, and they have a pretty damn convincing case. Lilith would not be the first who followed their lead. As long as she is with Hades and Poseidon, the girl will remain our enemy."

No matter what Finian said or how hard he tried to convince these gods of Lilith's loyalty, he wouldn't sway either man's opinion. He saw the logic behind their words; he just didn't like it. Lilith trampling through the forests with his father's enemies did not bode well for her. Then again, the same case could be made for him.

"What do we do now?" Finian questioned the gods before him.

"Prepare." Zeus declared, never once did his face betray his emotion. "You still have much to learn about your divinity. In the meantime, we will play offense and wait for my brothers to make the next move."

"So, we are hiding?" He had not meant for the words to come out as harsh as they did, but Finian could not hide his displeasure.

If Zeus were a lesser man, he might have reprimanded his son for his scorn. Yet he understood Finian's frustrations, especially when the boy thought with his heart. "We are waiting for a more opportune time. Confronting my brothers now would cause more harm than good. They would not believe me if I told them I did not start the Unhallowing curse. That is why Zarek is my eyes and ears in their realms. He can come and go unnoticed."

Finian suspected it had something to do with the god's divinity. Though one man, no matter how perceptive and inconspicuous he may be, could easily overlook vital information. If he was able to accompany Zarek...

"When do you leave next?" Finian asked, addressing him.

"The day after next, and before you ask, I'm not taking you along. Your inexperience would only get you killed."

"You give me little credit, Zarek." Finian seethed. He wasn't an ancient god, nor fooling himself into believing he matched Zarek's divinity, but he wasn't useless.

"You've been with my father since the beginning, correct?" Finian prompted. Zarek gave a curt nod and then Finian proceeded. "In that time, you have been particularly useful to him, I'm sure. However, that does not change the fact you are a single person attempting to find information about a curse no one knows who started."

Zarek looked amused, a small smirk playing on his handsome features. "And somehow you, young Finian, will be just the person I need to discover who is behind the Unhallowed?"

"I'm saying it wouldn't hurt."

Before either Zarek or Finian said more, Zeus pushed his chair back and stood. His solemn expression flickered in the dim candlelight, casting shadows across his face. "Enough. You two bicker like an old married couple."

"He wishes he were married to me." Zarek grinned at Finian's blush and incoherent sputtering.

A shadow of a smile crossed Zeus's features but was gone a moment later. "We can discuss this further in the morning. It's been a long day and I'm ready to call it a night. Finian, my boy, we will speak at breakfast." His father said, giving him one last glance before departing.

Zarek was next to leave, not once looking back or offering a parting word. Finian was left alone, but exhaustion from today's events wore him thin. He would retire for the night. When morning came, he would be ready to argue his point once again

Sleep nearly claimed Finian when the door opened, illuminating a small portion of his lavish bedroom. It took a moment for his eyes to adjust to the shadowed figure. Zarek, much to Finian's surprise, strolled into his room, dressed in the same attire from dinner. He stood perfectly poised and collected, looking as if he already had a good night's rest.

"You are still up." He said, walking forward, lighting his path with a single candle.

"Do you make a habit of sneaking in on people while they are sleeping?

Zarek smirked softly. "I would hardly count this as sneaking since you've been aware of my presence the entire time." He mused. "But if you would prefer to roleplay that scenario out-"

"No, I most definitely do not." Finian said, a little too quickly as blood flushed into his cheeks. He pushed himself up with his hands until he was propped up in a sitting position. Zarek stopped only a few feet away from him.

It was unnerving to have the god inspect him with those intense brown eyes. Even though Zeus trusted this man, Finian was not sure how to feel about Zarek. Their dinner introduction did not go well considering how many times Finian thought of strangling the god. What he hated most was the seed of doubt Zarek planted about Lilith's loyalties.

"I thought about what you said." Zarek spoke.

"I said a lot of things. You are going to have to be more specific."

That earned him another smile. Zarek's smile was as deadly as his glare. "At dinner, you mentioned the possibility of coming with me the next time I leave. Correct?"

Finian sat up straighter as he processed what Zarek said. Anticipation began to grow, but he squashed it before it bloomed. "Yes. I wish to be of use."

"You mean, you wish to see that girl. Lilith."

He didn't phrase it as a question, so Finian did not bother answering. The prospect of finding Lilith again and letting her know he was alive made leaving Olympus a tempting offer. Another part of him wanted to prove to his father he no longer had to hide away and allow everyone to assume he played the villain. Finian owed it to his father to try to get his name cleared.

Zeus rescued his soul, bringing him back from Death's doorstep. He stayed by Finian's side while he healed and told him stories of his life as a boy. Then once his body was capable, Zeus taught Finian how to use his divinity. His father wasn't perfect, but Finian saw firsthand the kindness he bestowed upon others. He would stand by his father's side in attempts to correct the injustices against him.

"Listen, as much as I do not want to admit this, you were right when you said I need an extra pair of eyes." Zarek said, moving from his rigid stance and over to the small chair by the fireplace. "The numbers against Zeus are stacking up rapidly. One wrong move, and he will be left with no one. Not that I believe any of them will ever defeat me, but on the minuscule chance that might happen, I could use a second."

Zarek's joke fell flat. The growing number of enemies against his father were raising alarms in Zarek. At the end of the day, no matter how strong the man claimed to be, he was but one god against many.

"If I agree, will you tell me what your divinity is?" Finian bartered.

"Absolutely not."

"Fine." Finian huffed but made a mental note to ask again later. "When do we leave?"

"Tonight."

Finian started to move out of his bed, but Zarek's words momentarily stopped him in his tracks. He didn't expect such a sudden departure but would not argue. If Zarek was ready to leave, then so was he.

"I'm picking up a disturbance in one of my usual spots in the human realm. It could be nothing, but I'm not willing to take that chance. Unfortunately, this means I have not had the opportunity to speak with your father about you joining me. It won't take him long to figure out we left. Are you willing to risk his wrath?"

"The question should be, are *you* willing to risk his wrath? I'm his son, I get a pass. You're just-"

"The man who stood by his side for centuries as his most trusted advisor and friend?" Zarek smirked.

"Yeah, fair enough. I suppose you get a pass too." Finian rolled his eyes, searching in the dimly lit room for his tunic.

"Finish getting ready and pack a small bag. Meet me outside the practice temple in ten minutes." Zarek said, meeting Finian's gaze. "I hope you know how to wield a weapon. If not, you'll need to learn fast."

Finian did not have any time to tell Zarek that he did, in fact, know how to wield and make weapons before the god left as suddenly as he came. A part of Finian found it odd that Zarek would change his mind so swiftly about accompanying him on his mission. The more rationalized part of his brain told him to not question him and pack his things.

He pulled on his worn black boots, lacing them tightly. In a small knapsack, he packed a spare set of clothes. As far as weapons went, he had none but figured Zarek would supply what they needed.

Ten minutes later, Finian arrived outside the temple to see Zarek already waiting for him. "Ah, just in time. I appreciate punctuality. A lost art nowadays."

Finian only shrugged. "I suppose so. Oh, did you bring weapons?"

"We are weapons, Fin. At least some of us are, but for the baby god here, I brought a dagger. It's small enough to keep on your person without detection and light enough to carry on long trips." Zarek produced a shiny, silver dagger from somewhere near his hip. Without warning, he tossed it towards Finian, causing the man to frantically fumble until the dagger was safely in his hands. He shot Zarek a scowl.

He laughed. "Very graceful, Fin."

"How was I to know you'd throw a bloody dagger at me?" He grumbled.

"Always expect the unexpected."

Before Finian could tell him where to shove his unexpected bullshit propaganda, the air around them began to change. A surge of power wafted through him, but it wasn't his own. This power radiated from Zarek. A shimmering light began to gather, slowly at first, but then rapidly picking up speed until a veil of light appeared before them.

"The moment you walk through the veil and leave Olympus, Zeus will know. Are you sure about this?" Zarek turned towards Finian, waiting for his reply.

Zeus had been nothing but kind to him throughout the duration of his stay, but he did not want this place to feel like a prison. He wanted to be useful and recruiting allies for his father was exactly that.

And then there was Lilith.

He would be lying if he said finding her was not on the top of his priority list. With a nod of his head, he responded, "Let's go."

That was all Zarek needed to hear before he reached out and took hold of Finian. "What the hell is this?" Finian grunted but Zarek pushed him through the shimmery mist, large enough for two men to walk through side-by-side.

Going through the veil was the least enjoyable experience of his life, and Finian had been shot through the heart. His entire body felt as if he were being ripped and shredded then lit on fire. He wasn't sure how much time passed, a second or a century, but as soon as the agonizing pain ended, he landed on his butt, colliding with the hard, damp earth.

Not one of his finer landings.

Zarek, that bastard, stood over him with an amused glint in his eyes. "Yeah, your first time is rough. Did I forget to mention that?"

Finian shot him a death glare, spouting out lines of profanity as he picked himself up off the ground. It didn't make Zarek stop laughing but made Finian feel better.

After taking a moment to gather himself, straightening his tunic and patting his side for the dagger, Finian assessed their surroundings. He expected Zarek to transport them to some sort of village or an abandoned cottage. Instead, they stood in the middle of an unknown forest. It was early morning and the sun still had not made an appearance, so the only light came from the glow of the moon. He heard water, but couldn't see a lake, not through the dense thicket of trees.

"Where are we?" He asked.

"At least fifty miles west of Dasos, but I can't be certain what land this is. Our destination is a cave a few yards up." Zarek said, watching the god tense.

"Why did you take us here?" He doubted their location was accidental, Zarek seemed like a guy who never did anything randomly.

"I've been coming here for years. I have a history with this cave, as does your father, but each time I come, something always prevents me from entering inside. I felt a shift the last time I came here. The cave let me get closer than ever before, but I still could not breach its walls."

Finian looked over towards Zarek. The god had his eyes trained ahead, as if visualizing something only he could see. "You speak of the cave as if it were alive." Finian laughed awkwardly.

There was no humor in Zarek's answer, however. "It is. Very much so, and I think it finally wants us to see what she's hiding."

Part of Finian wanted to tell Zarek how crazy he sounded, but the god spoke with so much conviction that it gave Finian pause. How long had Zarek been attempting to enter? There was a history with this place, but Zarek was reluctant to share and Finian would not pry...yet.

"Lead the way, oh mighty god of secrets. Let's check out your living cave. Hey, maybe you can even get it to join our side in this upcoming war. The others will never see that coming." The sarcasm oozed from his lips.

"Or perhaps, I will let you talk our enemies to death. Better yet, why don't you tell them one of your useless stories until they die of sheer boredom." Zarek quipped back.

"That was rude."

"But witty." He winked, closing the shimmering veil behind him with a flick of his wrist. "Follow me."

Not seeing another alternative, Finian followed. His eyes only made out the immediate vicinity, but when he attempted to look past Zarek, everything was shadowed in darkness. None of this bothered Zarek, for he walked ahead as if he had retraced this path many times over.

With each passing moment, Finian's anticipation began to spike. Each footfall was a step closer to their desired destination and the closer they got to this cave a feeling of foreboding washed over him.

A great power awaited ahead of him. Ancient and immeasurable. It was neither friendly nor unwelcoming. It simply existed and warranted respect. Finian now understood what Zarek meant when he said the cave was alive.

One moment, the cave seemed miles away and the next, the two men were standing right outside. The opening only fit one person at a time, and the roof stood about five feet tall. They would both have to duck in order not to bump their heads. A steady stream of water, no more than four of five inches deep, disappeared inside.

"This is as far as I have gotten in the past." Zarek's voice pierced through the surrounding silence. "I've never been able to get further than this."

Finian found that odd because nothing outside the cave obstructed the entrance. The water was shallow and the current slow. There was no fear of being swept away in deadly rapids. "What stopped you before?" He asked.

"The cave. No matter how hard I tried to push or trick it, there was a solid barrier between me and the entrance. Sometimes in my frenzy to get inside, I found myself turned around and the cave would be gone." Zarek explained.

"Gone? What do you mean gone? Caves can't move." Finian scoffed.

"This one can." Zarek said with a slight shrug. "Enough, we need to try to go inside. If the cave is open, then there has to be a reason for it."

Agreeing, Finian took one hesitant step forward before something dawned on him. "Wait, I have a question."

"I'm shocked." Zarek said impassively.

Finian ignored him. "It's just that, at the table my father asked you to report your findings, but you didn't mention anything about this cave. Why?"

A slight twitch of his jaw was the only indicator his question struck a nerve. Was he keeping secrets? Had Finian been so reckless in his attempts to leave Olympus he trusted anyone offering a way out?

Zarek fought an internal battle, hesitating slightly before he said, "It is a complicated matter. Your father doesn't have the best history with this cave, and I've never told him I've continued to come back. This does not help his attempts at finding who the new key player on the board is or whether they are behind the Unhallowed. I didn't see it as necessary to mention irrelevant information.

Finian's brow creased. He did not like Zarek withholding information from his father, even if it seemed to be irrelevant. Clearly this place was important somehow. Finian was in no position to lecture the god about honesty when he just snuck out of his father's sanctuary to return to the human realm. Seemed rather hypocritical.

Still, Finian was unsure just how much Zarek conveniently left out. For now, it could wait.

He continued forward until he stood by the mouth of the cave. Zarek quit gawking and closed the distance between the two of them. He stared at the entrance as if seeing a ghost. Raising a brow, Finian asked, "Do you need a minute?"

"What I need is for you to stop talking." Zarek growled, mostly out of annoyance rather than anger. Finian never met an individual so annoyed by everything he did. It was actually entertaining.

"Right. No talking. Got it." Finian saluted, earning another glare from Zarek.

Wordlessly, both men began to walk into the mouth of the cave. Whatever lay inside, Finian hoped against a wild animal, like a bear. He was fairly certain that Zarek would be able to kill it, but he was still unwilling to take the chance.

As they continued to walk, Finian expected resistance after what Zarek told him earlier, but there was none. He no longer felt the ancient power the cave radiated outside. It looked and smelled like a damp cave.

It was rather disappointing.

After five minutes of walking in silence and crouching low so their heads wouldn't hit the top of the cave, they reached a point where the ceiling grew taller, and the side walls expanded. The spacious den made Finian think back to the bear theory from earlier. He did not want to be dinner.

"This can't be all there is." Zarek said after a moment. He strolled past Finian, getting a better look at their surroundings, which were...rocks.

"Are you sure this is the right cave? I'm no expert, but don't all caves kind of look the same?" He asked, kicking a small pebble at his feet.

"Of course this is the right cave!" Zarek shouted, his voice amplified in the hollow interior. "But it doesn't make any sense. There should be something here. I...I don't know what, but I know there must be a reason it didn't allow anyone to come in. I highly doubt it was to protect a family of bears."

"Ah, so you thought of the bears too." Finian commented. "Listen Z, maybe-"

"It's Zarek."

"-this cave protected something once or held something within. But look around," Finian gestured by expanding his arms and doing a half spin. "There's nothing here. Only darkness and-"

A moan.

The hair on the back of Finian's neck stood on end as both men spun towards the sound.

"Fire, kid. Now. I need to be able to see what we are about to walk into." Zarek commanded, voice low. If Finian wasn't so invested in the noise, he would have chastised Zarek for calling him a kid again.

"Right. Fire." He tried to remember his lessons. Usually, his father had him light a candle or start a fire on items he placed out for practice. This was different. Zeus said he didn't need a candle because he was a torch. Except this torch was still going through basic training.

Closing his eyes, he called upon the divinity that always waited just around the corner. Fire blazed through him, demanding release. Demanding to be controlled. The fire would consume him if he let it, but he was the expert of his own divinity. He put out a hand, imagining a candle slowly flickering to light.

When he opened his eyes, the palm of his hand roared with a small, contained fire. Much brighter than anything a candle gives off, because the small amount of flame brightened the entire room. He was fiercely proud of his accomplishment, albeit a small one. Even Zarek gave him a nod of approval, which served as the equivalent of hearty praise.

"Stay behind me." Zarek ordered, pushing past him to take the lead. Finian, for once, didn't complain.

The light illuminated a few large boulders, but nothing else. Finian remembered seeing them and brushing up against one when he walked in, but neither of them thought of looking behind the rocks.

Zarek rounded the boulder and stopped dead in his tracks. His tan face went completely white, and his body tensed up. "What? What is it?" Finian couldn't hide the slight note of panic in his voice when he spoke to the god.

Unable to wait for a response, and Zarek did not appear to have heard him, Finian moved closer and pushed Zarek aside to get a better look. Only a small crevice lay behind the boulders, and he expected to see a creature of nightmares. Something so horrible it left Zarek without a facetious comment. But no, Finian did not see a creature. He saw...

A woman.

She looked young, though still a few years older than him. Her frail body curled in on itself. He would have thought her dead if it had not been for the moan earlier. Upon closer examination, he could make out the slight rise and fall of her chest, but she needed their help.

Finian moved to pick up the woman, but a hand snatched his wrist quickly and pulled him away. "Don't touch her." The voice hissed, trembling with unknown emotion.

Finian rounded on Zarek to see the man still pale, but responsive now. His attention remained fixated on the woman in front of them.

"What the fuck, Z? She's hurt. We can't just leave her here."

"Do you know who that is?" Zarek's voice switched from panicked to deathly calm. It was unnerving.

Finian looked back at the woman. Her long braided hair obscured most of her facial features. Her skin looked soft to the touch and as dark as Finian's, but nothing about the woman was recognizable, so he shook his head no,

"She's just someone who found their way into this cave like we did. Something happened here, so we should take her before the people who harmed her come back and do the same to us. Why are you hesitating?"

"Because this woman should be dead!" Zarek gritted out, stunning Finian into silence.

Earlier mistrust began to creep back into him. Without thinking or acting, the flame in his hand grew taller as Finian became more suspicious of the man before him. He narrowed his eyes at Zarek, taking a step closer. "Why, Zarek? Why should this woman be dead? What have you done?"

"Me?" Zarek actually laughed. "No, you idiot. You don't understand. I didn't kill this woman. She should be dead because I knew her before I became a god."

"You...what?" Finian's earlier bravado faded and the fire in his hand began to dim. "She's one of us? But I don't sense her. How is that possible? Zeus said that all divinity can detect others of our kind. Who is she?"

"I don't know how this is possible. All I know is I'm looking into the face of a princess I knew centuries ago who should not be alive today. How she has gone undetected for so long is beyond me." Zarek shook his head in frustration, muttering something in a language Finian did not understand.

"Zarek!" Finian barked. The man was avoiding his question. *"Who is she?"*

Because she had to be someone important. Maybe she had some answers to the questions they sought.

Finally, Zarek stopped his pacing and looked at Finian. He pointed down at the woman on the ground. "That, Finian, was the princess of Caister. Her name is Metis. Your father was betrothed to her and made her fall in love with him before he betrayed her."

Well shit. Finian thought. The unconscious woman was another person from his father's past. A past he needed to learn more about. Zeus was about to pull him into a war he started years ago. The only question remaining now was which side was Finian fighting for?

Chapter Twenty-Four

The Before

H E ENVISIONED AN EMPTY cottage, last night's half-eaten dinner left forgotten on the table, and the bed rumpled and unmade. Chloe's things would be gone, or at least as much as she could carry in her haste to leave. Malik would have been next to her, gathering up anything Chloe missed. He would have waited until nightfall to lead her out of the castle and take her to safety; far away from Dasos. She would no longer have to worry, only fuss over the kids she would have with Malik. They would grow old and leave this world as one soul.

More than anything, he wanted to walk through the cottage door and see no trace of his mitera. He'd be alone when he faced his father to lie about Ambrosia, which he wished for. Though wishing never got Zeus anywhere, and he would not be so lucky now.

Instead, Chloe remained at home, sitting in her favorite chair. She slept uncomfortably in a slouched position. Not for the first time that night, Zeus cursed Rhea, the cave, and whatever person, entity, or prophecy led him here, forcing him to make an impossible choice. One that ended in death, but not his own.

Zeus quietly closed the door, not ready to wake his sleeping mitera yet. He walked towards her, an invisible string pulling him closer until he stood over her. A stronger man would have done what he needed to do. Death would come easily and peacefully; she would not have ever known. Chloe would have forever lived in her dreams, but only the happy ones. It was the paradise she deserved, but one he was not ready to give her.

Zeus fell to his knees, placing his head in her lap. He did this often as a child when he needed comfort. His mitera would brush his hair out of his face and hold him until he no longer remembered why he had been upset in the first place.

Chloe took a moment to wake herself. She stretched her neck, stiff from her sleeping position. It took her another moment to see Zeus kneeling in front of her. "Thunder!" She cried and instantly pulled him up and crushed him into a tight hug. For a small woman, she was stronger than most gave her credit for. "I thought you were dead. You've been gone for so long and no one knew where you went. Cronus nearly sent an army to Caister. He was certain Vulcan had something to do with your disappearance."

"No, I left willingly. I did not have time to send a message back to father and frankly there was no point. I would either come back victorious or I would not have come back at all." Zeus said, though victorious was far from how he felt.

His mitera knew him better than anyone else, oftentimes better than Zeus knew himself, so she sensed the change in him. "Zeus, what happened? You look as if you've seen a ghost."

He laughed bitterly at how close to the truth she was. "Something like that."

"Thunder, what happened? Did you find Ambrosia? That's why you left Vulcan's kingdom, isn't it? You were going to search for Ambrosia." There was no question in her voice, so Zeus did not bother to confirm it.

Rather, he said, "I saw her."

"Saw who?"

"Rhea."

Chloe sucked in a deep breath and sat back in her chair, staring at him, but not truly seeing him. Her mind was elsewhere. The words seemed to pour out of Zeus, and he told her everything from leaving with Zarek and Hermes, to finding the cave, and then to seeing his mother. Throughout his story, Chloe kept quiet, never once stopping to ask a question. When he finished, they lapsed into a tense silence.

Chloe finally spoke after taking a moment to digest Zeus's tale. "You said she told you where to find Ambrosia? That the elixir has been at Dasos the entire time?"

His throat went dry, and he nodded. He had yet to tell her the sacrifice demanded of him. Saying the words out loud would make them real, and he wanted to live in ignorance for just a little while longer.

"Your mother was a powerful Enchantress, you know." Chloe spoke feebly, this time catching him off guard. He heard many stories of Rhea, but never one of her being able to wield magic. "She was also very secretive. I only know because she needed someone to trust when she got pregnant with you.

"One night I walked in on her weeping. Rhea never cried, so I went to her side. That night she told me she had made a terrible mistake, though she refused to tell me more, no matter how many times I asked. All she told me was she upset someone. Those who loved her would now have to pay the price of her disobedience."

"Rhea was a Queen. She did not have to answer to anyone." Zeus said. "Not even to her husband. He adored her."

"Even Queens and Kings answer to someone in the end. Rhea was scared and people who are afraid make foolish mistakes. She went up against a force she was not prepared for, and no deed goes unpunished. Her death did not erase the chaos she unleashed, she only prolonged it until her last heir came of age." Chloe paused, squeezing Zeus's hands. He felt as if they were coming towards the end of the final act in a play and both figured out how it ended.

"She told me to do something terrible," Zeus said, no longer able to meet the eyes of his mitera. He caught the tear rolling down her cheek before he looked away like a coward. "And if I didn't, something far worse would happen."

Unlike him, her voice did not waiver or break. "Zeus, my son, I already know."

I already know.

The words hit him like a physical blow, stunning him into place. She knew and still chose to stay. "But how?" So many questions and with each answer came more. His entire life was one of servitude and deceit. A personal weapon to Cronus, and by extension Gaia, to be wielded as they saw fit. The dead took advantage of him too, not just the living. Rhea controlled his fate since birth. She had been there, watching it all unfold.

The next time he saw her, Zeus would decimate her ghost until she wandered eternity in black oblivion, unable to hurt anyone again.

"Rhea came to me in a dream last night." Chloe admitted, answering Zeus's question. "She told me about Ambrosia being in Dasos and you would be the one to claim it. I always knew you had a purpose, Zeus. I knew you were going to be far greater than they allow you to be."

"Enough, Chloe!" Zeus snapped, surprising them both. He never raised his voice at her, and he never called her Chloe. Hearing her name had the desired effect though, she stopped talking long enough for him to get a word in. "Do you know what Rhea told me? To get Ambrosia, I must kill the person I love most in this world. If I refuse, the death of millions will be on my hands. Ambrosia needs a host; it cannot remain untethered for much longer. Either scenario, you die."

Zeus had been trained for battle and understood one day he would take a life. It was part of what warriors did, so he spared little thought of when that day may be. The first kill haunted a person the longest, but over time would fade and killing would be second nature.

Those kills were supposed to be faceless and not some-one he loved. What kind of man would he be if he slit the throat of the only mother he ever knew? What kind of man would he be if he let millions die because he was unable to kill one person?

Fuck Ambrosia and fuck Rhea. She started this and did not see it through to the end. Neither Poseidon nor Hades could do what needed to be done because their father corrupted their hearts with greed and power. None of them knew love the way Zeus did, not even Poseidon with his wife Amphitrite; he would not hesitate to lose her to spare his own life.

How ironic love was the one thing he had that his broth-ers didn't.

Chloe smiled, but it was forced. She cupped his face in her gentle hands, callused with years of hard work. "I knew the moment Rhea asked me to raise you that my life would be a short-lived one. I did not expect to have sixteen years with you, but these sixteen years have been the best time of my life. You gave me purpose, Thunder. You've taught me how to love unconditionally and effortlessly. You've made me a mother and I could not be prouder of you. Always."

"I don't want to do this." He pleaded, knowing the out-come would not change. One person to save the lives of many. He read tales about this before and never understood why the hero found this choice so difficult. Why save only one life when you can save many and be a savior? The real world didn't work that way though.

"Of course you don't, I know you don't." Chloe laughed through her tears. "Which is the very reason you must. What waits for you is divinity and godhood. Think of all the people you can help and the differences you can make. I want nothing more than to give you that. All mothers wish for greatness and a long life for their children, and I have the chance of giving that to you."

Chloe pressed a single kiss to his temple, and then released him. She disappeared into Zeus's room and reemerged a few moments later. She held his dagger in her hands, the one he received on his tenth birthday from Sir Ilys, the Sword Master, despite Chloe's many protests.

"Every young man deserves a proper dagger before they enter manhood." Sir Ilys had insisted, and with much sarcasm added, "Let the boy keep it. Considering how popular he is around here, he's certainly going to need protection."

Numbly, he took the dagger from Chloe, his body moving without his consent. He felt like a bystander watching this happen. Zeus could see how hollow and tormented he looked, making him appear much older than his sixteen years. Chloe, on the other hand, looked smaller in comparison. She looked like she wanted to reach out and comfort him, as if she burdened him with the sacrifice. His mitera thought of everyone else but herself.

"I have one request." She said softly, and he vowed to grant anything she requested. "Do it by the fountain. The one outside the south wing."

An odd request, but he was in no position to deny her. "It's where I met your mother for the first time." Chloe explained. "Where she told me I would be...be..." Finally, the moment hit his mitera full force, and she convulsed into a fit of sobs. He reached for her, catching Chloe just in time before she hit the floor. Her entire body shook with violent sobs.

"I'm...so-sorry.," She hiccupped, fighting to regain control of her emotions. "I'm...scared. For you. I know this...will change you." She shook her head and grabbed for his tunic, bunching the fabric up in her fist. "Don't blame yourself. Don't let this change you. Hate and anger are easy emotions to give yourself over to. Love is harder, much harder but so very worth the trouble. Don't lose sight of that Zeus. Don't ever lose sight of that."

"My heart will always be with you, mitera. You are my strength." Zeus no longer recognized his own voice, but Chloe smiled. That was all that mattered now. He picked the woman up, unwilling to let her march to her own death. She sensed the stubbornness in him and did not argue. Instead, she rested her head against his chest, listening to the beating of his heart and knowing that her son would be okay. He would weather this storm and become exactly what he was born to be.

A god.

The man she raised blossomed into the strongest, kindest, and bravest person she ever had the pleasure of knowing. Chloe took comfort knowing she played a part in shaping him. She showed him love and compassion, and in return he learned what it meant to sacrifice and persevere. So naturally she wept, but not for herself, but out of happiness knowing she would leave Zeus with love, memories, and wisdom.

The stretch from the cottage to the fountain seemed both endless and abrupt. Endless because both were in deep thought of the lives they led and the profound impact the other had in shaping who they were. Chloe experienced motherhood, while Zeus learned how love is the only driving force in the world. Abrupt because the life they shared together was ending; a story that had just come to its greatest moment of suspense, only to find the last few pages ripped out.

The sun was setting, marking the end of the day when Zeus delicately placed Chloe down on the stone exterior. She dipped her naked feet into the cool water and let out a sigh. Her tears ran freely, but she smiled still. If she closed her eyes, she could almost sense Rhea next to her.

"It is going to be okay. I'll be with you." Her friend seemed to say. It was only fitting both of his mothers were witnessing Zeus in his final moments as a mortal man. He would carry her blood with him into divinity. Chloe liked the idea of him carrying a piece of her for eternity, that way she'd always be there if he needed her.

"I love you. So damn much. And I'm sorry. I will right the wrongs that led us up to this moment, I swear." Zeus growled through gritted teeth, vision blurred by tears. He would never forget this moment and never forgive those involved. His heart would be black, tainted by years of being used as a pawn in a game he was never meant to win.

Once, he wished to be the hero and devote his life to the greater good. Now, however, he learned how easily the world makes people villains. History would forget the meek boy who only sought acceptance. No, they would remember him for this moment and every horrible deed that came after.

Chloe opened her mouth to remind him not to let hate fuel his heart or let anger lead his decisions, but the words never came. The clean slice of the dagger across her neck came rapidly and unexpectedly.

Her mind did not register the pain. The water around her began to stain red with her blood. She had a single moment of clarity, one where she saw the god Zeus eventually became. He was glorious, as she suspected he would be. Then she saw Rhea, offering her hand and at that moment, Chloe was no longer scared. She reached for Rhea's hand and smiled.

She was home once again

Zeus watched the water turn from a faint pink to a deeper red as Chloe's blood ran down her neck. Had she felt pain? In her last moments did she hate him? He cradled her in the end, but his mitera's eyes were unfocused and distant. A roar of anguish left his body the moment she stopped breathing.

In death, if one could ignore the bloodied cut on her neck, Chloe looked peaceful. He pictured her sleeping and at any moment she would awake and wonder why she was in a fountain. They would laugh, of course, because of the absurdity of that statement, then he would walk her home to start dinner.

None of that would ever happen again. Zeus would be alone in this world. Yet, he did not fear it as he thought he would. A sense of acceptance washed over him. There was a certain sense of comfort in not knowing what came next.

Admittedly, he expected for a momentous cataclysm to occur after killing Chloe. For the ground to shake or the skies to open and claim him. None of which happened. Zeus did exactly what Rhea told him to do: take Chloe to an area of water and offer her blood to Ambrosia. Ambrosia would come once called upon, though she did not mention how long he must wait.

Unable to bear seeing his mitera bloodied and face down in the water, Zeus gently picked her up. He was careful, handling her like a glass doll. Chloe deserved a proper burial, and she would have it once he had Ambrosia.

The water began to change the moment Chloe was out of the fountain. He laid her body down, kissing her forehead as she had done to him many times before. There would be time to avenge her, but he needed to finish what he started first.

Zeus's attention drew back towards the fountain, feeling the familiar alluring pull when in the presence of Ambrosia. Only now, the feelings intensified as the crimson liquid, no longer made of water nor blood, illuminated the small fountain.

He crouched down, sensing movement coming from behind him. The soldiers would spot him soon and alert Cronus to what he did. By then, it would be too late.

The elixir burned when touching his flesh, growing hotter in his cupped hands. He welcomed the sensation, greeting it like an old friend. From his hands he drank, Ambrosia burning down his throat and spreading to the rest of his body. He felt as if he were being scorched alive from within and though he tried to scream, no sound left his mouth.

Zeus heard a cry of absolute despair and someone screaming Chloe's name before fire erupted inside him.

The air was thick with the scent of decay and damp earth. It was unusually quiet, none of the normal noises from castle life emanated through the walls. More so than that, his body hurt. He felt as if he had been trampled by dozens of royal guards on horses. When he tried to move, Zeus let out an audible hiss of pain. He felt a burning sensation on his left side, right above his hips.

He wondered what happened to lead him here...whatever here may be. With great effort, Zeus slowly opened his eyes, blinking away the darkness threatening to consume him again. After they adjusted, Zeus took in his surroundings and realized he was chained to the wall.

In the castle's dungeon.

He couldn't recall how he was brought down here, nor comprehend the pain he was in. He took this moment to look down and saw the deep crimson stains. Blood. He was uncertain if it was all his, but the stab wound near his left hip was definitely covered in his own blood.

Despite seeing all the proof of his wounds, it still did not explain the deep ache within. A loss so heavy it suffocated him.

And then Zeus remembered.

Chloe. His mitera.

Everything came rushing back. Rhea. Ambrosia. Chloe. He killed his mitera. He killed her as an offering, but when he consumed Ambrosia, everything burned. How long had it been? Who brought him here?

"You're awake." A voice spoke, breaking through the silence and slicing through his internal agony. Zeus jerked his head up, too fast, so his vision blurring momentarily until he made out the silhouette on the opposite side of the bars.

The dungeon was not well lit, as per Cronus orders. He liked his "criminals" to remain in the dark, both physically and mentally. Only a single lit torch illuminated a small section around him.

The figure steadily continued their descent forward until half of their body came into the light. Zeus did not trust his own eyes, for his entire sixteen, almost seventeen years of life, he had never seen this man so disheveled. But gazing at Cronus now, the man did not resemble the mighty King of Dasos.

A man with hollowed cheeks and blackened under eyes stared back at him. He favored his right side over his left, and Zeus noticed significant bruising around his father's neck and arms. If it were anyone but his father, he might appear concerned, but all Zeus could muster was grieving anger, laced with a hint of pity.

There was a new look in Cronus's eyes Zeus had never seen before. He had seen anger and sadness, but never desperation.

And fear of him.

"What have you done?" Cronus's chilling voice filled the room.

Zeus would laugh if he had any strength left in him. "Oh father, don't tell me you are harboring any regrets."

"Enough!" Cronus roared, fist striking out to connect to the iron bars. Cronus winced, but nothing else. He was too far gone in his current state to feel pain. He saw haughty anger written across Cronus's formerly handsome face. It was easy to feel superior when the other was locked behind bars.

"You had specific instructions to come to me the moment you learned anything about Ambrosia. Do you understand the damage you have caused? *Do you?*" The last words came out as a shriek, as Cronus gripped the bars like a madman.

Still, Zeus was lost. Nothing in him changed, other than the fact he was a murderer. He grew tired of the King's riddles.

"Either explain to me what is troubling you or get the hell out of here and let me rot in peace." Zeus said.

Zeus never got his way before, so he doubted Cronus would provide him with any answers. He lived to make his unwanted son's life a living hell. Pressing his face into the bars, he began speaking like a madman and surprising Zeus. "No one was supposed to know Ambrosia had been found. By nature, people are greedy and will take whatever they can to become important or relevant in the eyes of others."

The irony of that statement was not lost on Zeus, but Cronus was oblivious to his own hypocrisy.

"When Vulcan heard of your disappearance and the death of one of his own guards, he knew you left in search of Ambrosia. He brought his army to storm my castle in search of you. To my great surprise, I realized my ungrateful son decided to go rogue. I knew it would be a matter of time before you came back for your precious Chloe. I needed her as leverage against you, so I sent Malik to retrieve her. Do you know what he found?"

Excruciatingly slowly, the moment of Chloe's death came back to him. Reliving the loss of his mitera dredged up unbearable raw emotions that threatened to overwhelm him.

Cronus took his silence as confirmation and nodded. "That's right. Poor, beautiful Chloe was already dead. Her neck sliced clean open. We warned her many times that you would be her downfall. She should have let Malik take her away when she had the chance. I will never understand her undying devotion to a son who already killed one mother."

Cronus words stung like a slap. He recoiled back into the wall, chest heaving as if he had run a mile. Cronus was right. Zeus killed two women, both he considered to be mothers. One who birthed him and the other who raised him. This was his curse, and he alone would have to live with his consequences.

He should have never been born in the first place. Death and destruction awaited him at every corner.

"Two days ago you were discovered, and all hell broke loose." Cronus continued oblivious to Zeus's internal agony. "There were no longer my men versus Vulcan's men. Not with Ambrosia at their disposal. Chaos ran rampant and anyone caught between the crossfire was a dead man.

"All except you. Someone thought you were worth saving." Cronus finished, looking at him a moment before delivering the final blow. "Metis was such a pretty girl. You didn't deserve her. She died, because of you."

Metis? His Metis? She came for him and pulled him away from the battle. She kept him safe despite him having left her weeks before. His hatred for himself came back tenfold, but for a completely different reason. He did not deserve Metis's love. She was another casualty in his ongoing war.

Cronus continued to fill the gaps in Zeus's memory. "I had been right in my assumption Ambrosia needs a strong host and not everyone can house the power of a god. Many men and a few women risked their lives for a chance of immortality. The second the elixir hit their throats, they wailed in pain. Ambrosia burned them from the inside out, turning them into little more than dust.

"Even Vulcan attempted to take it, the fat imbecile." Cronus scoffed. "He shit his pants before he died. Have you ever smelled bile, blood, and shit together? It's foul and the smell lingers."

Zeus did not need to know that, but he also wasn't incredibly sad about Vulcan's death. The man loved his granddaughter Metis, but he treated those he considered beneath him poorly. The world could do without another tyrant.

Zeus was struck with a single burning question: why was he here? If he had been incapacitated for two days, why had no one tried to kill him? He outlived Cronus's usefulness, and even though he tasted Ambrosia, nothing felt different. He felt like himself, human and worthless. Only now, he had blood on his hands.

"Where is everyone?" Zeus asked, noticing for the first time Cronus was alone and not flanked by a half dozen guards. .

Cronus's jaw twitched, the anger rolling off him in waves. Zeus grew accustomed to anger, but this was different. This was anger from a man who was scared.

"Gone." Cronus snarled, his voice barely above a whisper. The fear gave way to anger, and his father soon gripped the bars of his cell in a death like grasp.

"Dead or vanished." Cronus raged on. "With your brothers by my side, we fought our way to the fountain with the last loyal guardsmen. They watched over us as we drank Ambrosia, which was rightfully ours. We knew the risks, but that did not stop us. The chance of godhood was too good to pass up.

"I drank first, wanting Hades and Poseidon to wait and make sure it worked before risking their lives. The kingdom still needed to be ruled if I died. When I did not immediately feel the burning sensation from within, your brothers felt it safe enough to drink as well."

Zeus remembered Rhea saying not everyone would be able to handle the power Ambrosia held. In fact, very few people could survive the change.

"Then what happened?" Zeus asked, his curiosity getting the best of him.

Cronus laughed humorlessly. "I woke up. Surrounded by rotting corpses. Your brothers and a few others were nowhere in sight, but much to my disappointment, you were there. Still incapacitated. I dragged you down here myself, locking you in this cell. Killing you would give me no answers. Tell me what you found on your journey and how I can locate my sons."

Zeus laughed bitterly. "Locate Poseidon and Hades? How would I even begin to tell you where they are? Have you considered they left on their own free will? They may have been tired of living under your rule and your sick obsession with power."

"They would never."

"Are you certain about that? Did you raise them to love you, or did you raise them to *be* you?"

With a movement so sudden and impossibly fast, Cronus reached through the bars of the tiny cells, grabbing Zeus around his neck. He yanked him forward, Cronus's grip tightening around him. "Pathetic, disgraceful boy. I should have forced Rhea to end her pregnancy with you. I should have killed you the first chance I got or given you over to Gaia. You've been nothing but a problem for me."

Those words and fears he heard his entire life. Useless. Unwanted. Nothing. They soon became a mantra in his head until he knew nothing but those words. He knew his worth in Cronus's eyes, the King made his feelings apparent.

But to Chloe, he had been everything.

At that moment, her love was what he thought of. The nights she would stay awake and sing him to sleep after a nightmare. When she cooked his favorite meal on his birthdays. The way she loved him unquestioningly and without reservation.

Through her love, he felt power in his veins. Power so unattainable and pure, he had never felt the likes of it before. And it was his, pumping through his veins, waiting for him to command. Zeus let it consume him, to take over his body as lightning cracked from above him. It should have been impossible because they weren't outside. Yet, more lightning cracked around him and a bolt hit Cronus hard, sending him flying back.

Only moments ago, Zeus had been sure Ambrosia hadn't changed him. And now....

Now he was a god, and no mortal chains would ever hinder him again.

The restraints around his wrists seemed laughable now. All it took was a single solid tug before they dropped to the ground and released him. Not even the cell door held Zeus back. His lightning hit, melting enough of the bars for him to walk through.

True terror played across Cronus as he looked up at his son. How many times had he pictured his father trembling before him? Yet, he didn't take joy from his fear. Something broke in Zeus, and he would never go back to being the boy he once been. Perhaps he was always destined to become the villain.

"I will say this once." Zeus spoke, though he hardly recognized his own voice. "This is the last time I will let you live. The next time you, Hades, or Poseidon face me, I will not hesitate to strike you down. Until then, I hope you live out your useless days in miserable isolation until you understand what it means to be insignificant."

With that, Zeus pushed past Cronus. He did not look back but knew Cronus wouldn't chase after him. He felt the man's icy stare on his back as he retreated. Without the title of King to strengthen him, Zeus saw just how weak a man Cronus had been all along.

There were only a few things Zeus knew for certain at this moment.

One: he was a god. He felt his divinity in his bones, the new power yet to be discovered. Chloe's love and sacrifice made it possible, and he would carry her with him until he drew his last breath.

Two: his father possessed power. He sensed the divinity within him but was unsure what that divinity was. He didn't think his father had a single clue either.

Three: his brothers were out there somewhere. Very much alive. Whether it be kin or this newly founded god-hood, Zeus distantly sensed their divinity. Stronger than Cronus, but still not as potent as his own. The two of them together would mean trouble though.

And finally, Zeus would atone for his mistakes. He had a responsibility to the people he loved, and he would fail them no longer. He had not meant for Ambrosia to fall into the hands of so many. He'd spend lifetimes correcting his wrongs, but he wouldn't rest until his mistakes were paid in full.

Zeus continued to walk. Out of the dungeon and through the castle. Death lingered around every corner as piles of bodies lay unmoving. He was seeing the full force of the fallout of his actions with his own eyes.

Zeus did not stop walking until he reached the edge of the grounds and looked up at the small cottage he shared with Chloe. He felt closest to her here. If he pretended hard enough, he could believe she was still inside and not dead by his own blade.

"I will right this wrong, mitera. I will see to it that whatever deal Rhea made doesn't corrupt and plague this world. I will deal with my brothers and make sure they are not causing any more harm. Above all else, I will make you proud of me. I'm so sorry."

With one last glance at his former home, Zeus walked out of Dasos and would not return for centuries to come.

EPILOGUE

THE BEFORE

A NOTHER SHARP TURN SENT her falling hard against the wooden carriage door. She snarled, more so out of annoyance than pain. She thought once again of everything that led her to this moment. How everything went so wrong so quickly when it started out so well.

But then she had to go and fall in love.

When he left her, without warning and in the middle of the night like some common thief, her world shattered. She needed to pick up the pieces he broke, leaving her as easily as the day turns into night.

Maybe she should thank him. Because of him, she saw clearly for the first time in her short, sheltered life. She once called her grandfather a fool, behind his back of course, because he chased make-believe stories, but her beloved grandfather was wiser than she originally gave him credit for.

"We are almost here, princess." Boreas spoke from up front, capturing her attention. He had been the only guard that escaped Dasos alive. In fact, she believed she was one of the few who fled the war-torn kingdom alive.

Clutching the small vial closer to her chest, Metis took a deep breath, inhaling the potent smell of what lay within. Obtaining the small sample nearly cost her life, and to anyone that saw, it most certainly looked like she died. But her fake death served a bigger plan. One that placed her in this carriage, on the way to speak with the Queen.

No more than a few minutes later, the carriage came to an abrupt halt. The crisp air warned of the coming winter and not for the first time, Metis wished she wore more than her simple dress to keep warm. She did not need extra layers in Dasos, but now that they were closer to the northern kingdoms, she was in dire need of more clothing.

The carriage door soon opened, and Boreas offered his hand. Metis took it and allowed him to help her out, only to be surrounded by at least a half dozen guards in silver uniforms. She wondered if they had been made aware of her potential arrival. Judging by their defensive stances, she highly doubted that.

"State your business." A red-headed guard ordered. His silver uniform complemented his flaming hair.

"You will address princess Metis by her proper title, or I will cut your tongue from your mouth." Boreas hissed, reaching for his own sword. Metis appreciated the gesture but rolled her eyes at the blatant display of testosterone.

"I'm here on behalf of the Queen's orders. She will be expecting me, and I guarantee when she finds out you made her wait, she will not take kindly to you." Metis spoke, channeling her confident inner princess when she really felt meek and scared. She couldn't show fear though. Not here.

The red-headed guard who spoke first, looked to his other men. A silent conversation passed between them before he relented, still unsure whether she told the truth. He did not want to risk the Queen's wrath.

"Very well, Your Highness. Follow me." He spoke and turned to lead her inside.

Boreas raised a questioning brow to Metis, but she did not offer him anything in return. Instead, she pushed ahead and followed the guard. She heard soft footfalls behind her signaling he was following.

Being a princess meant Metis visited many palaces. Never though had she stepped foot into this queendom. She was known for her reclusiveness. The castle itself was as cold as the air outside. Beautiful, yes, but chilling as well. A lethal combination.

Metis followed the guard directly into a throne room. Seated atop the only throne in the room, perfectly poised and as deadly as the chill in the air, sat the Queen. Older in years, but her beauty still lingered. Many wondered why she never remarried, but Metis did not think any man stood a chance at courting her. She was far too intimidating for weak men.

Upon seeing Metis, the Queen did not rise or offer her a formal greeting. It would have irritated her if she hadn't been scared for her life. Metis dipped her head slightly, hoping the Queen would view her as an ally and not useless.

"Princess Metis. What an unexpected surprise." The Queen spoke, even though no surprise laced her tone. The Queen knew she would come. Metis did not know how, since she scarcely ever spoke to her, but the Queen was clever.

Since there was no need to prolong introductions, Metis fished the vial out and held it up for the Queen. "I have brought what you asked of me."

This time, the Queen showed emotion. Her eyes widened a fraction and Metis was sure she saw her breath hitch. "Is it so?"

"It is." Metis replied. "I was there when it happened. Dasos was in chaos, and this was the most I could secure."

A few years ago, during one of the many dinner parties her father regularly attended, the Queen found Metis exploring a castle that did not belong to her. She had been a terribly curious child and that often got her into troubling situations. Usually, she was able to smile her way out of them, but that did not work when this Queen found her. The woman made her a bargain instead. One that she could not refuse.

The Queen continued to look on, her face unreadable. Metis tried not to squirm under her penetrating gaze but found that task to be difficult. Then, without warning, the Queen stood and raised a single hand. "Seize her."

Before Metis could so much as blink, two sets of hands were on her, grabbing the vial and holding her in place. Boreas shouted and attempted to reach for her, but the sword aiming for him was faster. It pierced his chest and Metis screamed, watching the only guard she had left die.

Now she was truly alone, and it was all her fault. She had fallen for Zeus's sweet lies; her lovesickness blinding her from the truth. He'd never loved her. He wanted what every other man wanted from her when they found out her grandfather was the King. Ambrosia.

The Queen ignored the chaos and walked forward, stepping over Boreas's lifeless body like he was nothing more than a pile of dirt in her way. The guard who wrestled the vial out of her hands handed Ambrosia over to the Queen.

She inspected the vial before popping the cap. "You've done well, young Metis. I require one more thing from you." She said and directed the next sentence to her guard. "Open her mouth."

What? No! This wasn't how this was supposed to go. Metis struggled, trying to put all her weight into each movement, but she wasn't trained like these guards were. It was a pitiful attempt that only lasted seconds before one of the men pried her jaw apart. Tears rolled freely down Metis's cheeks, as she tried to beg them to let her go.

"Enough, child. If this works, you will be thanking me." The Queen said before pouring half the vial down her throat, leaving only enough for one more person. Presumably, the Queen.

For a second, nothing happened, and the guards let her go. Metis struggled to stay up right, frantically trying to stop the tears. Suddenly, a heat so intense ravaged through her body, causing her to scream loudly. Beads of sweat appeared on her forehead, and she felt as if she were being burned from the inside out.

Metis desperately tried looking around for someone, anyone, to help her. But the Queen and her guards simply stared at her like this evening's entertainment. Metis managed a small step forward before her body gave out completely, and she went crashing to the floor. Instead of the release of death, her body continued to spasm and burn from the inside.

Then, Metis went limp.

The Queen watched a moment longer, before gesturing to the closest guard. "Check her pulse." She ordered.

The man knelt obediently, placing two fingers on the woman's neck. After a few seconds, he nodded. "It's faint, your highness, but it is there."

A small smile played on the Queen's otherwise icy exterior. The Ambrosia worked. At long last her reclusiveness paid off. Many advised her against waiting, but none of them understood how to play the game. She did and it was about time she showed the world exactly what she was capable of. The Queen spent years in search but sat back and let others take the lead. She would not risk her people but would gladly risk theirs.

For the first time in a long time, Queen Gaia had a plan.

Acknowledgments

There are so many of you that have been extremely supportive of The Ambrosia Throne, (some of you have been here since it was called Lilith the Last!) and I can't even began to put into words what you and your support means to me. I'm still going to try.

I couldn't began my thank you page without starting with my Whimsy Queens, Candice and Shelby. You girls already know how much you mean to me, but what you might not know is how much you truly helped me along my journey. Y'all have been here for every road bump, teary text messages about a website that shall not be named, and for all the successes. Shelby - how did I become so lucky to have my best friend (who is a freaking teacher of the year!!!) to become my editor? I will forever be grateful for you! And Candice, you have been my cheerleader and confidant for so long. You've pulled me out of some dark times more than I can count.

Thank you to Brad and Emmaline for being the best author besties (and real life friends!) a girl could ask for! I never realized how important it was to surround yourself with people who believe in the same goal as you, but it has been amazing! I know who I can run past any random idea by or ask for reality checks! I hope you know how much I value our friendship and I can't wait to support you in your publishing endeavors!

A HUGE shout out to my fellow Tour Gals for spreading The Ambrosia Throne love and sharing in my excitement. I couldn't ask for a better group of amazing women to share our book adventures with!

And lastly, thank you to YOU! Yes, you! The person who is still reading despite the book being over (for now) and supporting me on this journey. I never thought Lilith, Finian, or Zeus would see the light of day, but all of you made it possible! I can't wait to continue to grow as a writer and have you along for each part of that journey.

ABOUT AUTHOR
TATI B. ALVAREZ

Tati B. Alvarez is a debut author from Austin, Texas living with her family and two adorable cats: Leila and Stella. When she is able to tear herself away from her laptop or a book, Tati enjoys nerding out over all things Marvel and Disney, hanging out with her in-person and virtual friends, as well as spending all her time playing with her niece.

Growing up, she dreamed of becoming two things: an author and a teacher! Currently she works at a middle school teaching English as a Second Language. Before then, she got to share her love of literature with her 8th grade English students, (yes, you read that right. She teaches middle school.) Writing has been a passion throughout her entire life. As soon as she learned to read, she knew that one day, she'd write her own book.

Aside from fantasy, she also writes romcoms and is not so secretly obsessed with them! There is just something about a fun and spicy happily ever after that she adores.

Printed in Great Britain
by Amazon

86987795R00205